IT TAKES 1 SECOND

BY

MIYA J KEETCH

IT TAKES 1 SECOND

This book is dedicated to my grandma Janiece

who I know is cheering me on

from Heaven.

TRIGGER WARNING:

Violence, abuse, talk of murder, talk of addiction, mild kissing.

Enjoy :)

Contents

Prologue

Disappearance

My hands tremble as I grasp for the handle, continuously missing the tarnished metal. Stray strands of hair fall over my temple, blocking my sight from my tedious mission.

A hiss escapes me as my fingers wrap around the locks and throw them over my shoulders; my heart pounds against my rib cage, hitting my ribs violently, leaving behind a shaking terror within my body.

My fingers finally connect with the drawer's handle—it brings little relief. It slides open, its deafening creak splitting the air. I cringe and crane my neck toward my door. The hair on my arms stand on end, creating goosebumps.

The door remains shut.

I don't have much time though.

I sift through the compartment, shoving junk aside. An item shoots out of it, colliding with my cushioned bed. It rolls off the covers and strikes my carpet. I almost let out a shriek but luckily its sound is stifled by the floor. I let my heart start up again and comb through my items once again.

Okay, it was just a rolling tape. But... where is it? Why isn't it here?

Glass smashes against a wall downstairs. I feel the house shake upon impact and a tingle trickles down to my toes, tickling my skin uncomfortably. As my heartbeat quickens, I watch the door again, my shoulders growing tenser. My muscles ache at the sudden rigidness.

They are going to be coming soon. They can't have already forgotten about me.

As the commotion downstairs continues, so do I. I shake the terror off my bones and move swiftly to the second drawer in my nightstand. Blood rushes in my ears as I seize the wad of tens hidden in the junk.

Tumbling sideways into my bed, I shove the money into a drawstring bag. It joins several items, including my phone charger. My fingers run across my embroidered name on the front, it's lettering a perfect, stark white on top of the harrowing, raven fabric.

Another crash echoes from the kitchen, followed by more screeching. I tighten the strings to my bag and swing it onto my sweaty back. They haven't fought like this before, but I suppose it's my fault.

Although it's not my problem anymore.

The yelling goes quiet downstairs. I attempt to move my feet but they do not respond to my pounding head. *What happened? Why did they stop?*

No longer can their yelling mask my loud actions.

I take one more look at my door and it puts me right over the edge, forcing me from my still spot. I step toward my window as footsteps echo throughout my house. They advance rapidly toward my room. My name is sung on the other side of the wood... like a siren's song that tries to usher me closer to rising danger. I open my window and examine the muddy grass underneath, my heart pounding as the voices come closer. As the knob begins to turn, I hop down the two-story drop, leaving behind no one and everyone.

As I land, I hear my name screamed—I have one thought:

Run.

CARTER

Monday, May 16, 2022, Present.

My pocket isn't weighted by a crumbled-up 'Missing' flier as it should be. That is exactly why my eyes are set directly on City Hall as I walk down main. The street light I pass begins to turn on in response to the arriving night, the rest following quickly behind to warn me to be on my way home instead of pursuing a hopeless mission. I can't go home though. The police are wrong. So *very wrong.*

My nimble fingers wrap around the metal door handle and pull it open. The metal is still warmed by the day's searing sun, meaning summer's coming; even in Bear Lake Valley where it still snows occasionally… even though spring is nearing its end. In fact, the snow-capped mountains won't melt for several months. That's how it has always been around here, and for a summer-loving guy, it really sucks.

"Carter Miller, as I live and breathe!" a voice beckons from within. Blinking my eyes to try and adjust to the bright fluorescent lights, I step into the warm city hall.

"How are you, son?"

I come eye to eye with Sheriff Reggie as he waves around a case colder, his hair a graying brown.

I was looking for a city police officer but a county sheriff works. In fact it works perfectly, better than I could have imagined. The higher the chain of command, the better.

"Sheriff," I greet, flashing a smile as I shake hands with the man.

"How're your grandparents, Carter?"

My grandpa, John, was the previous sheriff. He retired three years ago, a year before my mom, sister and I moved to Montpelier, Idaho. We came to help my grandpa and grandma out because they were getting older. Plus we never got to see my father's parents because we originally lived thirteen hours away on the Oregon Coast.

"He's been good... staying very busy." I shove my calloused hands into my front pocket, their calluses rubbing against the denim. I wish we could subside the small talk. I'm not here to talk about my grandparents. I'm here to talk about someone else I deeply care about.

"Sounds like him," Sheriff Reggie smiles, turning around to hand the secretary the case file in his hands. He turns back around and places a hand on my upper back. My neck twitches in response. "What do you need, son?"

I scan the makeshift city hall briskly. It isn't much of a city hall because it's located in an old bank. They tore down the original one in March. It was an old two-story building that was starting to crumble and was becoming more and more unsafe. So since then, the city hall has been located further down Main Street from the haunting plot of the old one.

I flash my eyes back at the sheriff.

"She isn't a runaway."

Sheriff Reggie's eyes flash with visible confusion. "Pardon?"

"Evie Baker," I snap, examining the carpet below me. "She couldn't have run away. Trust me. We were close, Sheriff."

My throat is dry and a lump has formed in it already, restricting my lungs. This morning I noticed Evie's absence from school and she never misses school. Her grades play too big of a part in her life for her to miss even *one* day. Her parents never let her skip, even when sick.

When I asked Kace Baker, Evie's little brother, he said that the county sheriff's department and the city P.D. had written her sudden disappearance as a runaway per request by her parents. I know for a fact that something is wrong though. Something *has* to be wrong. Evie wouldn't just run away without telling me. She just wouldn't.

"Carter..." the sheriff sighs.

I knew this would happen. I had the biggest hunch.

Sheriff Reggie continues: "I really can't discuss the details with you, but I will tell you one thing... that girl ran away. All the signs are there. Even her parents said she has tried to run away before."

That's not true.

"But how do you *know*? You can't possibly know!"

I don't care that my voice is rising because so is the temperature of my blood.

"A lot of her essentials were missing; money, phone charger, some clothes, maybe some granola bars she had stashed. You can't mistake the facts, Carter."

No, I can't. Sheriff Reggie is right... but so am I. I have to be. I check my watch. It's almost nine and I have school in the morning. I run a hand through my light brown hair and scratch the back of my head. Mom always gets worried when I'm not home by nine.

I take one last helpless crack.

"Sheriff, would you *please* just take another look?"

A buzz vibrates my front pocket. '*It could be Evie,*' is my first thought, but when I pull out my phone I see it's my mom. The hundreds of text messages I've sent to Evie still go unanswered.

Sheriff Reggie places his hand on my shoulder and squeezes momentarily. "Carter, you should be focusing on school. You graduate soon. Go home and get some sleep, son. You don't need to be looking into the runway. There is nothing to worry about."

I find myself stepping away even though I have so much more fight in me. I had a whole rehearsed speech but, I find myself giving up. I am so tired from school and the stress of graduating. For a split second, I hear a voice in my head saying Evie probably ran away like everybody thinks she did.

EVIE

Sunday, October 31st, 2021, Past.

The autumn air teases my baby hairs that are pulled in front of my face, tickling my chilled nose. It would be relatively warm if it wasn't for the glacial breeze.

"Two please."

"What flavor? We have strawberry, blue raspberry, and grape."

The mother before me looks down at her little girl and smiles with all her heart, projecting her love proudly. I feel my stomach drop. "A strawberry and blue raspberry one."

I grasp the two freshly-spun cotton candy bags containing the flavors and hand them to the mother. "Here you go. Enjoy the carnival."

I gaze after the mother-daughter pair as they drift into the carnival's crowds. For a brief moment the child looks back at me, delight plastered on her face. I force a smile as a sigh pushes itself out. Adverting my gaze to the scorching candy floss machine in front of me, I discard purple sugar into it, readying a paper stick. As I spin the stick around, purple cotton sticks to it, forming a perfect ball of floss. Enveloping the stick in warmth… comfort.

Trudy—the adult I'm working with—holds a plastic bag open for me. With care, I set it in and tie it gingerly. I glance up, hearing a familiar jingle of laughter off in the midst of children's gleeful screams. My knees tense up, threatening to buckle. Not *today*. Not *today, please*. It isn't a sense of dread that floods over me, per se… But, it feels like it. I'm kind of happy to see him but—I don't know. It's a love-hate relationship, I suppose.

His coffee eyes glance toward my way. Those creamy, chocolate eyes. My heart skips a beat as I realize we have made eye contact. Too late I angle my head down and hide my tomato-red face behind the large machine. A second too late.

I find myself peeking over the candy floss dome. There fifteen feet away stands the boy I have been obsessing over for at least four months. His melodic laugh echoes through the autumn air as his friend spouts out a joke. At least he isn't looking my way anymore.

"Talk to him," Trudy laughs, luring me to my demise.

My hands find a cup of pink sugar. Casually, I brush off my emotions and dump the sugar into the hot bowl. Some of the sweet flavoring escapes the dome and sticks to my skinny jeans. I take a hand and swipe my pants, the dark fabric sliding against my soft hands.

"I have no idea what you're talking about."

"Evie, I may be fifty but I'm not blind."

I sigh, admitting defeat. I've never been one to fight. "I really couldn't…"

"Nonsense. You can do anything you put your mind to."

I look back at the boy, a lump in my throat as I spin another stick of delicate floss. Trudy smiles. "What's his name?"

"Carter. Carter Miller."

Trudy stops me quickly, landing one of her weathered hands on my shoulder. Its warmth migrates through the fabric of my black long-sleeve. "Evie, go take a twenty-minute break while we wait for the machine to cool down. Make sure to be back."

"But–"

"–No. Go. You have been here with me for three hours and frankly, I'm getting sick of you," my advisor teases.

As much as I'd rather not admit it, I am exhausted. I have been mentally begging for a break since the carnival started. And here it was and I don't want to take it. I know I have nothing to do or nowhere to go. I have no friends to hang out with. What would I even do?

"My time is better spent here," I argue softly, brushing a stray piece of curly hair behind my ear.

"Evie, go," Trudy laughs, her voice unusually stern.

I exhale sharply and slide my plastic gloves off of my hands. I throw them in a trash bag and thank her kindly. Trudy laughs, shaking her head as I grab my small cinch backpack. Swinging it onto my back, I leave the stand, not bothering to fix my naturally-curly hair that sits in a low ponytail. Strings of it fly into my face and get stuck in my mascara-covered eyelashes. I brush them back behind my ear and walk along the crowded sidewalk. As I stride past everyone, I hear bits and pieces of conversation. It's crazy how everyone has a different and unique story. No one else shares the exact same story. Everybody is having different conversations and are leading completely distinctive lives. Maybe that's why I feel so alone... because no one understands me. No one understands me and my story... or my life.

An empty bench inserts itself into my vision. It's alone too and far away from the crowds. *Perfect.* This is shockingly by far the biggest, low-budget carnival the elementary school has had.

I slide onto the wooden bench and pull a book from my bag, quickly appreciating the fall wind circulating the smells of burgers, hot dogs, and pulled pork sandwiches around me. My fingers find the bookmarked page in my book and flip to it. The pages are as crisp as the air and covered in the beautiful writing of an author that has come before me. My eyes scan over the inked words and I get in about a page until suddenly I go stiff again.

Laughter.

Carter's deep, melodic laughter.

Somehow daring enough, I look up from my refuge. There he is again at the edge of a crowd that surrounds the court where a shoot-off is taking place. It's one of those 'carnival games' I wouldn't play. I've never been good at sports—except for cheer I suppose. Although nobody says that counts because 'it's not a sport.' Forgive me, but people are idiots.

Carter's hands are shoved in his front pockets casually, his built body shivering from the cold and his back hunched. His messy brown hair flies like a flag in the wind, twisting every which way. His eyes are set on the game that is happening before him which means–as creepy as it may sound–I can continue to watch him and not get caught. I can watch as his messy, light brown hair flies in the breeze, tickling his ears and neck.

He steps back from the crowd as a ball goes flying toward him. Carter's brawny arms wrap around the ball as it slams into his chest, sending him stumbling backward. His friends exclaim things along the lines of 'Good catch, man!' and 'Yeah, Carter!' Hearing his name would usually cause me to blush a great deal but I am focused on something else.

Those eyes fall upon me like autumn leaves.

Carter Miller is staring at me, a slight grin touching his lips.

As quickly as it happens, he nods in greeting and returns to his friends, throwing the shooter their ball back. I shut my book without putting in a bookmark and shove it into my raven cinch bag. My trembling fingers yank it closed and set the raven straps on my shoulders. I get up from the bench and quickly return to the cotton candy booth, looking back at him as he looks back at me, confusion plastered on his face as I dash away.

Idiot. Idiot, I repeat to myself, swerving around mobs of children and parents. Instinctively, I look around for my parents, praying they saw none of that. Relief floods my body as I realize they are tucked away at home, avoiding the community event.

Fifteen minutes later I am officially back to work at the cotton candy stand with Trudy rambling beside me. I'm happy for her constant talking. It makes me feel less lonely in this dense world. Though I find myself zoning in and out sparsely. It happens quite a lot, especially when I'm around others. Even this much human interaction drains me severely.

"You're going to be making cotton candy in your sleep!" Trudy remarks as yet another eager child and loving mother walks away, pulling me out of my trance.

Scoffing, I grab another paper stick and twirl it in my hands. It's oddly rough against my smooth skin. Sudden nostalgia spreads over me as I'm reminded of an event that happened a long, long time ago. Well, actually it wasn't nearly as long ago as it feels.

The paper stick felt a lot like the lollipop stick I held only three months ago. Around me was a stout man with a serious beer belly, a trash bag of a woman, and my two little sisters and my younger brother. We were under the July sun at city park, sitting on a splinter-ridden picnic table. In the distance rings the sound of a baseball hitting a metal bat in one of the city baseball diamonds. It sits next to the underused tennis courts. No one in Bear Lake knows how to play tennis. Or has the equipment needed.

Mom growls as she stares at her phone, causing my father's aggravated attention—except he isn't aggravated toward her. He never has been angry at my mother.

What is it this time? my father sighs.

I eye my little brother Kace—who is one year younger than me. He gives me a sympathetic side-eye, trying to manage a smile. It's as if he's telling me, *One day. One day you will get out of here.*

I'm still waiting for that day.

Beside me Trudy clears her throat, pulling me from my tender reminder. I meet her hazy blue eyes as she nods her head in the direction of the carnival. I follow her signals and find a pair of caramel eyes examining me closely. In Carter's hand are two weathered one-dollar bills.

"Um, could I get a cotton candy?"

Beside me, Trudy nudges me, a wide grin spread across her wrinkled face. ,

Why now? Huh? Why now?

"Yeah... Yeah, of course," I stammer, trying to keep my face level. I've never been so nervous in my life. "What kind?"

His eye contact is like a suffocating fog that grasps my lungs, squeezing them.

"What do you got?"

I list the flavors one by one, designating each flavor to a finger. My skin itches for me to pick at it the entire time. It's a habit I picked up over the last two and a half months... and not a good one.

Carter's smile melts my insides, setting my heart ablaze. "Grape."

"On a stick or in a bag?" Trudy asks him to my relief. The less words I say to him right now, the better. I could say something stupid and embarrass myself.

"A bag if you don't mind," Carter chirps, turning his attention to Trudy briskly.

Shaking, I somehow step over to the blue railing and grab a grape cotton candy off of its clip. I make the short walk back and hand the purple candy floss to the boy in front of me.

"Thank you, Evie."

I freeze, my entire body going stiff. "You know my name?"

Carter's laugh echoes through my head. It's not mocking but instead warm. "Uh, yeah. We had three classes together last year and four this year," he rang his melodic laughter again. "Don't you remember?"

My heart flutters dangerously. I need to control myself. "Yeah... Uh, yeah. Sorry, I do. It's just we've never talked."

No, no, no. I just giggled! And not the cute giggle... the awkward giggle.

Carter stands there a moment, his beautiful eyes looking into mine, saying nothing for a good thirty seconds. "Doesn't mean I don't know your name, Evie."

I nod, watching nervously as Trudy leaves to greet one of the middle school teachers. I look after her, silently begging her to come back and protect me from self-caused destruction. She doesn't see my longing glances though. I turn back to Carter slowly, trying to manage a smile but it's weak.

Carter sticks out his hand, a goofy smirk plastered across his face. "I'm Carter."

Still frozen in place, I ignore the gesture. "I-I know."

"See, you know my name," he chuckles awkwardly, sticking his disregarded hand into his front jeans pocket.

That's because I have had a huge crush on you since you came to my school a year ago. I also watch you when you're not looking in history, art, mentor, and english. Of course I know the name of the boy that makes me feel less numb when I see him in the crowded halls and in class.

I spill my thoughts into my empty head, filling the void with trembling words. It's the only way I can be safe not to let something slip from my chapped lips. I've done it since I was just tiny–nothing but a mere child.

"Can you believe fall break is already over tomorrow?" Carter questions, breaking the loud silence that has suddenly developed around us.

"Couldn't come sooner," I sigh without even stopping to think. I squint my blue eyes shut and wallow in self-pity, welcoming the voices in my head taunting me. *No, no, no. This is great. You did it again, Evie Janiece. Great job.*

Light chocolate eyes examine me closer than I'd like. This is what happens when I don't think before I speak. Lately I've been good at keeping my mouth shut about my feelings or any topics that could make people look further into me. But, around Carter... that all goes out the window apparently. Every self-preserving mechanism I have taught myself over the years simply diminishes.

"Usually seventeen-year-old high school students don't want to go back to school. At least these days they don't. I mean it's not weird that you want to go back to school. I mean I totally do but like–you know what? I'm going to stop talking."

Carter's eyes twinkle with something so special... and suffocating. All at the same time. Something about the attention I'm receiving is unnatural to me. His attention is new and challenging to my heart.

Luckily, to my relief, another customer comes up behind Carter, causing him to step aside and bid goodbye.

CARTER

Tuesday, May 17, 2022, Present.

My eyes beg to be closed for just an hour. They are so desperate that I would even settle for only a few minutes of sleep. So, I do. I have to take advantage of the moment. It's mentor class—which is basically a homeroom where you only work on homework—and I should be working on my senior project portfolio, but right now all I want to do is shut my eyes for as long as I'm able. My portfolio isn't due until next week anyways. So, today I'm only going to worry about getting some peaceful, much-needed rest.

"Carter looks like *crap*," I overhear my best friend Nixon whisper to Dave, my other friend. They both sit at the same table I sit at and have been my friends since I got to Bear Lake High School a year and a half ago.

Dave agrees with Nixon which leads them both to erupt in laughter.

"I can hear you, you know," I mumble quietly, not bothering to lift my head off of my crossed arms that sit on the desktop.

"Well then do you care to tell us what's got you looking like a zombie from the *Walking Dead*?" Dave questions from my right, glancing in between me and Nixon no doubt.

Groaning, I lift my head up slightly to stare at the whiteboard on the light green wall in the front. It's covered in *Romeo and Juliet* material for the freshman English class.

"I didn't sleep a wink last night."

I turn my head slightly, facing Nixon. He takes off his baseball cap and ruffles his black mullet. Nix places his white and blue hat back on his head despite the dress code. He smiles sheepishly. "What girl is calling and texting you all night this time? Let me guess... you were on facetime all night?"

Shaking my head as I do it, I look over to where Evie would be sitting if she hadn't 'ran away' as her parents suspect. I would be over there right now, talking to her, laughing with her, and joking around with her. We would work on history, english, and art homework together. But, then Evie Baker disappeared Sunday night without a word or warning.

Nix's contagious laugh rings out. "Oh, is this about that Evie girl you hang out with so much running away? I heard Ms. Jones talking about it with another teacher before class today."

Today his laugh isn't contagious though. In fact—instead of laughing—I shoot a glare his way, lifting my head completely off of my arms. "She didn't run away, Nixon. I'm telling you. It isn't like her."

Nixon puts his hands up in defense, "I'm just stating the facts. Chill."

Of course, Dave has to put his two cents in too: "Come on, bro, be real. Evie up and left. She's a loner, bro. I don't blame her for dipping. I don't know why you suspect anything else."

I find myself standing up, my fists clenched and my glaring eyes twitching. "Dave, put a cork in it. You don't know her as I do."

Suddenly, I'm aware of *everyone*'s eyes on me. They are all watching for my next move. *Was I going to punch my best friend? Would I chicken out?* They were all thinking it. *Would he crack? Would he really hurt his best friend?* They were all worthy questions that I didn't know the answer to yet. Dave was being a jerk about a matter he had no information about. He didn't know Evie. He just assumed she ran off because it was the easier and more scandalous explanation.

Nixon stands up behind me, pushing his chair back with so much force that it goes sliding into the pastel green-painted brick wall. A large hand lands on my shoulder and squeezes it tightly.

"Carter, sit down. Don't do something you'll regret," he demands in my ear. I shrug his hand off and spread my fingers out momentarily before clenching them back into a fist.

"Not until Dave apologizes."

This was not how I imagined my morning to go.

"Carter, what is up with you?" Nix interrogates in a whisper, staying put behind me. "You have *never* acted this way."

I scoff sharply. "I'm only defending Evie, Nixon. She isn't here to defend herself so someone has to."

Dave stares up at me from his chair. I crane my neck to eye Nix. He looks at me with empty eyes that remind me of Evie's. I've never realized that before. "I can see that, bro. Just sit down and don't start something. Sit down."

I glance briefly around me. Every single pair of eyes are drilling into me, watching me like this was an episode of *Keeping Up with the Kardashians.* They are all waiting for me to mess up. Everybody wants to see the golden boy mess up right? I leave them unsatisfied and sit back down. My head falls onto my crossed arms once again, waiting for the onlookers to get back to their lives.

It doesn't take Nix long to break the peaceful silence that envelops the room. "Look, Carter, if you want you could come over after school. My truck's got something wrong with it and I could use your help. You're the expert."

Keeping my head down, I decline. "I've got stuff to do."

The bell rings shortly after that, splitting my brain in two. A sudden migraine pounds in my head as I sling my backpack straps over my broad shoulders. I give no mind to Nixon or Dave. I'm done with them for today. Or, I'm done with them for the rest of the week... I can't decide. I've learned over the years that it isn't smart to make big decisions while you're 'worked up.' So, I walk out of the room and down to the office to check myself out for the day, even though I have only gone through my first period out of six.

***

I get home and take some ibuprofen immediately. But, when I lay down to take a nap, I can't do it. I try to take a nap in my room *and* the living room but neither place works. I know that soon Mom will be calling and texting me about skipping school so I power off my phone and leave it on the kitchen counter. I can't deal with her right now, no matter how much I love her.

It's nearly two before I give up on sleeping. But, luckily, my migraine has subsided. So, I take it upon myself to grab my hooded, red and black checkered lumberjack jacket and my powered-off phone. I cross through the front door and onto the porch. The May sun shines brightly, the yard basking with its bright light. The breeze chills me to the bone so I shove my phone in my front pocket and slip my jacket on. I shutter as I walk to my truck that sits alone in the driveway. I get in and drive into town.

I live outside of town toward the North. To be specific, on Pescadero Lane which lies past Bennington. Bennington is a small town in Bear Lake County that is to the North of Montpelier. It is about an eight minute drive.

There are several towns and unincorporated communities surrounding Montpelier. But, despite the several communities, we are one big one that looks out for each other. Or at least I thought we did, which is exactly why I'm headed where I am.

Going into Montpelier—headed South—I am greeted by the fairgrounds, the high school, and several businesses. The farther you go down the highway known as 4th Street, the more charming the town gets. I turn down Washington Street at the stop light intersection—which we usually just call main—and drive down it till I come to another. When it turns green I go through it too and soon enough I am passing City Hall. They aren't going to listen to me there so I have to try something new. I have to try something to get people worried.

Making a right turn down 9th, I tap my fingers on the steering wheels. My teeth gnaw on my bottom lip as I drive further and further down the road. Despite rarely coming to the house, I remember exactly where it is and what it looks like. I park on the shoulder of the road at the white, two-story house.

I'm stiff at first, for this house brings eerie feelings. It doesn't tower high but it seems to cast a long shadow over everything on the block. I'm sure to others, it looks like a perfect, milky white family home… but to me, it seems to resemble what happens inside. It seems neglected and abused, though there is a fresh coat of paint on the exterior. The neatly trimmed yard was a very vibrant green with only a lawnmower on it. If I didn't know better, I would think it was the house from *Monster House*, a 2006 film my family and I would watch. That movie scared me out of my wits when I was younger and apparently still does. I know it is a made-up animated film but I am afraid to step on the lawn. It might eat me up like the one in the movie.

I shake my head and laugh to myself. I'm a *seventeen-year-old senior*. I'm not an eight-year-old child. *I can do this.*

Probably…

I pull the door open and my feet find the asphalt and I shut my door. I amble around the front of my truck, hands in my jacket pockets, ready to face the human eating house.

I stop at the front door and freeze again. *Am I really going to do this? After all they did?* I lift my fist and let it pound on the white door.

It doesn't take long until I am face to face with Mr. Baker—or Paul, whatever you prefer to call him. It also doesn't take long before Paul notices who I am because he slams the chalky, white door in my face. I stumble backward, eyes wide and a little bit afraid. It only took Paul three seconds to shove that door in my face.

"Mr. Baker?" I call, knocking again. I turn my head and scan the neighborhood. "Can I talk to you please?"

Silence. Pure silence and rejection.

Then, the door comes open again and Mr. Baker is before me. I flash a smile and stick out my hand in greeting. "I'm Carter. I am–"

"My daughter's boyfriend," he coughs, looking at my hand in some form of disgust. I retreat it back into my jacket pocket awkwardly.

I think he means it as a joke because Evie and I went to huge lengths to make sure they never found out about... *us*.

"Nah, I barely knew her. I'm just a friend from school, sir." I chuckle, shrugging my shoulders. Something about Paul makes me nervous. I also despise being kind to this monster of a human.

"Look, do you need something? I've got crap to do. Don't waste my time."

Paul's bald head shines in the sunlight as he nods to the lawnmower on the lawn. I gulp as he grimaces at me, waiting for my answer. I freeze for a moment, not knowing how to ask. So, I put it out there simply...

"Do you and your wife really believe Evie ran away, Mr. Baker?"

Mr. Baker's body tenses, including his face. His clutch on the door frame tightens significantly. I take a step back.

"What's your vendetta, boy?"

"I... I just... I don't think she ran away sir. There's no way," my voice squeaks on its own. I've suddenly lost control of it.

Paul scoffs. "And you would know better than her own father? She packed a bag and everything. Just because she didn't tell you, doesn't mean it didn't happen."

I take another step back as another flood of fear drowns me. "Sir, I wasn't... I wasn't suggesting–"

A voice from inside keeps me from saying something I'll regret. "Paul! Who is it?"

A woman in her forties appears beside Paul. She has curly blonde hair much like Evie's and wears a denim jacket, skinny jeans, and a white and pearl striped shirt. Her locks were short compared to Evie's shoulder length hair, reaching just below her ear.

"Oh... who's this?" she plasters a fake smile on, looking directly at me with skeptical eyes.

I introduce myself and shockingly enough, Mrs. Baker recognizes my name too. Evie didn't talk about her parents much with me. It was a sore subject. In fact, all Evie told me was that she never talked to them unless instructed to.

Paul interrupts our small talk. "Carter... I think you should be going. Really."

Once again Paul begins closing the door in my face. I stick my foot in between the door and door frame, preventing it from shutting any further. "Wait!"

Joanne turns to her husband and opens the door back open. "Paul. Let the boy talk." She seems to be conveying some sort of secret message with her eyes that I don't get. It works because Paul nods, getting the message clearly. Joanne turns back to me, a smile painted on again. "Carter, go ahead."

"Once again..." I take a deep breath, "You really don't think she ran away, right?"

This time, Paul's tense shoulders sag deeply, followed by Joanne's. I furrow a brow at his actions. His demeanor has completely changed even though I had already asked him this.

"Look, Carter, my wife and I were *shocked* when Evie ran away... as you are. We—the entire family—are broken up about it, we are. She never even bothered to say goodbye to us, *her parents*. That takes a toll on us, it does. We just wish she would come back, okay? You coming here and asking us about her is a rude thing to do. Look what you did to my wife." His wife embraces him hurriedly as she begins to sob. He rubs her back, staring back at me with sorrowful, blue eyes. Evie's eyes.

I bite my tongue, holding back a retort. *Were you all 'broken' up after you hit and hurt your daughter?*

CARTER

Monday, November 1, 2021, Past.

The bell shrieks in my ear at an astounding volume. It ushers all of the hall hoverers into their classes, warning them of tardiness. I'm usually late to mentor but today my body hates me so I didn't want to walk around any longer. I stayed up until two last night which is proving to be a very bad idea. I can't even tell you what I was doing. Most of the time I was effortlessly carving away at a block of wood with one of my knives, not fully aware of what I was doing. Or what I was making. That happens a lot.

My friends sink into the seats around me. They are always late. I brush a strand of my hair out of my face and pull my school laptop from my backpack that sits below my feet.

"What do you think is for lunch today," Dave—one of my lankiest friends that sits to my right—asks, interrupting my friend, Nixon, as he recalls some funny thing that happened at the carnival.

Nixon hits Dave's oddly built arm, laughing. "It is only our first class. We have three more to go before lunch, you fat lard."

Dave brushes Nixon's words off and shrugs, "So? I like to think about lunch to keep me going."

A laugh escapes my throat and I look at Dave. Dave is always thinking about and eating food, although he is the skinniest boy ever. I'm not sure how he gets that lucky. It really is some kind of superpower or gift. Dave's face turns a slight shade of red in the dispute. It always does this when he gets angry. I have never seen him truly angry before but this is the closest he ever gets.

"Hey! It really does help!" Dave argues, hushing our chuckles.

I pat his back, smiling profusely. "If you say so."

Nixon interrupts the conversation to continue his 'epic' rendition of when I caught the basketball from a shoot-out game. This was after Nixon threw it at me after losing. Nixon is more of a baseball player, not a basketball player, so he really did suck.

Ms. Jones calls Nixon's name from her desk and instructs him to get his work done. Mentor is a class that you have all of high school. I moved here a year ago from a coastal town in Oregon so I obviously haven't. I only had it a little bit of junior year and all of this year. You have the same class every year and you basically just work on all of your classes during it. It was a better—almost knockoff—version of study hall. We usually used it as a class to wake up in though. Although Nixon is always intent on messing around. He somehow gets all of his work done... Well, just enough for him to be able to play sports.

My eyes wander from Ms. Jones to a girl that sits in front of her desk. Coincidentally, I was thinking about her randomly last night. I have rarely talked to her even though we have had countless classes together.

I search her face, knowing who she is... but not *really* knowing. Her headphones are in, the strings running along the fabric of her black hoodie and she sits arched over her computer. She just keeps to herself, alone and not talking. In fact, she never joins the class when we will play card games every Thursday. She sits quiet in her little spot, watching us with lifeless eyes and earbuds in.

I had my first conversation with her yesterday at the carnival, and she seemed nicer than others let on.

Right now, her blue eyes are closed and her curly, dirty blonde ponytail lays upon her slim shoulder. This high school may be small but it is *very* noisy, so it's natural to look at the first unnatural thing around: a quiet girl. Around her are laughing girls that are doing Tik Tok dances and girls chatting with their friends constantly... and then there's her. She's set apart from the rest. Perhaps that's why I am so curious about her. Maybe it's just the mystery of her, but she's pretty in such a natural way too.

"She's trouble, Carter. Don't you think about it."

"What?" I blink, coming back to reality.

Is he talking about her? How did he know I was even looking at her?

"Evie—"

"–I know who you're talking about," I snap, looking Dave in the eyes.

"Well, that doesn't matter. She is bad news."

What is he even trying to tell me? How does he even know what he is talking about? He's not the one who gets to judge whether or not someone is bad news.

Nixon joins in the conversation as he usually does, shutting his laptop aggressively. "Dave's right. She has been since elementary school. She's just *weird*. Seriously, I haven't heard her talk since third grade."

I look at Evie as she is unaware of the words being said about her behind her back. I don't know what Dave and Nix mean about her being weird because she's *quiet*. I mean, come on: in May, we'll all basically be adults. There's no time to be making childish rumors about the girl no one wants to approach.

Dave chimes in again, leaning back so his chair is balancing on only two legs. "It's always the quiet ones that shoot up a school or commit mass murder."

"Yeah, and it's always the hungry psychos like you that commit cannibalism." I snap, laying back into my chair. Beside me, Dave's chair almost comes unbalanced and he seems to have a mini heart attack as he swings his chair back on all fours.

After settling, he eyes her again. "Come on. Am I wrong? I get the vibes from her that she has nothing left to lose," Dave shrugs, his eyes full of uncertainty.

I sneak a glance at Evie, who is completely unaware of the possible danger lingering over her head right at this moment.

I look back to my nosy friends and try to soften their views up a bit, no matter how useless it may be. "Have you ever thought about why she may be so quiet?" I wait for Dave and Nix to argue but their voices don't shred my ears, instead, all I hear is my heavy breathing and the soft music being played by our mentor teacher. No one deserves rumors being spread about them. I know that if it was happening to me, it would not make me feel very good.

I take one last look at Evie Baker and then return to my laptop to do the English homework I didn't finish last night. I can't focus on anything else right now or I may go crazy. My goal this year is to actually graduate. The sooner I get done with school, the sooner I can help Mom out with my little sister Daphne and the house when she's at work. When I graduate, I will be able to be home all day to help out with the animals and I'll be able to get a job without feeling like it's taking away from my highschool grades and sports. I can't have a job now without it taking away from all of those things *and* family time. I try and be with my mom and sister as much as I can.

* * *

The bell rings, forcing us out of mentor and to second period. I shove my laptop into my backpack and swing it across my broad shoulders. I set my eyes on Evie and begin walking toward her. Nixon grabs my arm tightly, trying to hold me back, but I shake him off aggressively.

"Evie... Hey."

She takes one look at me and her eyes widen in surprise. It evens out as quick as it comes though. Her face is back to its blank self. "W-what?"

"Long time no see," I chuckle, grabbing my right backpack strap with my left hand.

She stares at me for a minute—her face unfazed by my words—before returning to packing up her laptop and phone. "I have to get to my next class."

For some reason, something deep in my heart cracks, emitting a small amount of pain. So, I watch as she zips up her backpack, puts it on her shoulders, and walks from the room without another word. For a second I make eye contact with Nixon and Dave who give me 'I told you so' looks. I shake my head at them and follow Evie out. I jog to catch up with her.

"How are you?" I question as I push through traffic. Our school halls definitely don't fit as many people as they should.

Evie keeps her chin in her chest, ignoring me as she rushes to her second period.

"Evie?"

Finally, I get to her and she looks into my eyes: goosebumps rise on my neck. She comes to a stop and so do I, causing traffic to go around us as if it's a normal occurrence.

"What do you want, Carter?" she asks softly, her attempt at a stern voice failing miserably.

"To be friends...? This isn't some kind of trick question right?" I chuckle, trying to lighten the mood in the crowded hallway. Evie must not find it funny because she looks down at her feet and not a single expression except for emptiness crosses her freckled face.

She chokes on nonexistent words and looks around nervously, as if looking for someone. "I have to get to class."

She hides her emotions well. Too well. So, as she walks away I have no idea what she's feeling or thinking. This leads me to watch her until she completely disappears from view, melting into the bustling crowd.

I don't get that uncomfortable feeling that Dave says he gets when talking with her. I don't understand.

CARTER

Tuesday, May 17, 2022, Present.

The front door shuts downstairs, followed by the rustling of what can only be my mom and Daphne. A collection of full grocery bags slam against the island counter.

"Carter Chase Miller! Get your butt down here!"

My fist pounds on my white carpet once as I silently cuss. I push myself off the carpeted floor and onto my feet. Since I got home from the Bakers' house I have been laying here, staring at my white ceiling. Nothing makes sense to me. Nothing has since Sunday.

"Carter!" my mom screams again, this time louder... and angrier.

Inhaling deeply, I open my door and head down the stairs. Mom stands against the island, her arms crossed against her chest, while Daphne puts away groceries behind her.

Just like a bomb, she explodes at the sight of me.

"You *skipped* school?! Then you refused to answer my calls and texts! What is *up* with you, Carter?!"

I bite my cheek, drawing blood. Behind Mom, Daphne snickers, looking directly at me. Shooting a glare at her, I bite my lip.

"Carter! Answer me. I was worried sick," Mom demands in a shrill voice I rarely hear.

"Nothing is up," I whisper, looking down at my feet. "I just didn't feel good."

It was all true. I don't feel good. I haven't slept since the hours between Saturday night and Sunday morning. It didn't help that I always got like this when I didn't sleep. Mom knows that too.

That's why I was prescribed melatonin when I was younger. If something is ever bothering me, I physically can't sleep.

Mom places a hand on my upper arm, squeezing it briefly. It brings memories of bruises–not my bruises though but Evie's. Several times I had done that exact thing to Evie, which led her to wince from the blackening skin. That's why I headed to the Bakers' house today.

"Sweetheart... I know how you get when something is bothering you. You can talk to me."

Could I talk to her? She would call me crazy like the sheriff, the Bakers, and my friends did. I loved Mom and I trusted her but she wouldn't understand. She had only met Evie once.

"It's nothing," The weight on my shoulders gets heavier.

I look up from my feet to find Mom staring at me, her eyebrows upturned and her lips slim. That was how she looked whenever she admitted defeat.

I slink past Mom and help Daphne with the groceries. Daph looks up at me, a smirk plastered across her face. I ram my elbow into her shoulder softly, flashing a quick smile. I watch as Mom's shoulders sag as she walks to the medicine cabinet next to our silver, two-door fridge. She opens it and pulls out a small, yellow cylinder with a white lid. With a tired-like smile, she hands me the melatonin.

* * *

The ceiling above me is basked with the morning's sunny glaze. My semi-opened curtains let in a strip of light that settles on the navy wall to my right. The yellow light illuminates my cedar dresser that sits underneath the slit of sun. My eyes wander to Chev, our family's dog, laying at my feet, watching me with his beady, husky eyes. His gray, white, and black fur covers my ebony blanket.

"Chev!" I yell, kicking him off. "How did you get in here?"

Chev jumps off my bed and slips through a crack in my door that my mom must've left before she left for work this morning. Groaning, I listen carefully as his claws click on the cedar stairs. She came in to tell me I didn't need to go to school—that I needed to rest.

My head doesn't pound nearly as much as yesterday, to my relief. All that is left is a light headache that can easily be dissolved using Ibuprofen. But, I don't want to get up quite yet, even though I have a strong urge to go do something worthwhile. Today was my one day to just sit around and rest.

Nails scratch at the front door, no doubt engraving the wood with Chev's markings. I force myself out of my hairy covers and sit with my legs hanging off the bed, my head in my hands. Adding a whine, Chev scores the door.

Pushing myself onto my feet I head into the well-lit hall. The window at the end of the hall brings in much-needed light, that is reflected by the white walls. The cedar flooring is frigid on my bare feet and sends icy shivers through me. The May sun does a terrible job of warming this hall up for some reason. There is always a draft. Though, I should be grateful. It is always worse in Winter.

As I make my way down the wooden stairs, I find Chev running circles at the door—waiting for me like a puppy. It was always humorous to me when Chev acted like a pup because he has to be eleven years old. Dad and I had rescued him from a shelter in Coos Bay, Oregon where we originally lived. They estimated he was about one or two at the time because they truly didn't know. Chev had been found at Walmart by a couple of the shelter's volunteers. He was in pretty bad shape and clearly hadn't been fed or watered properly since birth. So, when Dad and I adopted him we took it upon ourselves to fully care for Chev. Mom didn't like the idea of it at first because I was only eight at the time, but we quickly convinced her. A year after that, Dad went missing.

I open the door for Chev with intense care and shut it softly behind him despite me being the only one home. Dad used to always yell at me for slamming the doors in the house in Oregon. Since he disappeared, I've always made sure to shut the doors softly. Call it guilt.

Making my way to the snack cupboard, I ruffle my hair with my fingers. It was a ratty mess despite how soundly I slept last night. I didn't toss and turn as much as I usually do—because of the effects of the melatonin. Opening the cupboard, I grab a s'mores granola bar. It opens with a loud crinkling from the foil.

I take a large bite of the granola bar and step out on the front porch where Chev lays. With my free hand I pet him and then sit at one of the rocking chairs that are on opposite sides of a wooden end table. The grass before me is greener than ever due to Mom's extensive watering. She has some obsession with keeping it as green as the emeralds that represent May. On top of that, she keeps the lawn free of pesky dandelions—which I thought made the lawn '*pop*.' I don't know how my mom has the time to do all of this, honestly.

My eyes drift to Chev who still lounges on the cedar porch, admiring the grass like I am. "Hey, Chev? You want to go for a walk?"

I could go to school since I'm feeling better but I really don't feel like it. School is the farthest thing on my mind and frankly, I need some fresh air to clear my mind and set my brain straight. Chev must feel the same way because he jumps up and runs to me, his tongue and tail wagging. A smile spreads across my face and I go inside to get dressed.

***

Montpelier Canyon is—to me—beautiful. There are plenty of trees and places to go on walks. My favorite spots are the reservoir and the Rearing Pond which aren't very far from my house. When I need to clear my mind, that is the place I go to.

No one and nothing could bother me there. It's where fishermen, campers, and outdoorsmen go to be alone with their thoughts or family.

My hand finds the stick and I put Big Red in park at the Rearing Pond. There isn't much of a parking lot–or a pond for that matter–so I park only feet from the water. I get out and cross over to the passenger door. As I let Chev out of the front seat, a rainbow trout jumps from the water. It lands with a loud *splash*, causing barks to echo through the mountains as Chev runs around my legs, nearly knocking me over.

Chuckling, I follow my dog around the one acre pond as he sniffs at various plants and sage brush. The air is humid with the smell of fish and moss which–oddly–feels like home. Before we moved here, we used to go camping all of the time here at the Rearing Pond and at the campground below the reservoir. We took vacations here every summer to visit grandpa and grandma and camped here while doing so.

There is a hill that acts like a wall of a bowl that holds the reservoir water in. Conveniently, the campgrounds are right at the foot of that grassy wall and there is also a tiny dam that lets the reservoir water down into the creek. It isn't much of a dam but it functions enough to get the job done.

When Chev and I are done touring the pond, we leave the truck behind. Holding his collar, we cross the quiet highway's bridge that the creek runs underneath. There's a giant metal tube that the brownish blue water rushes through. It unlocks many memories of when I threw large sticks in to get sucked up and pulled to the opposite side. It kept me busy for hours on end. I would race sticks to see which one would get to the other side of the highway first by dropping them in and then sprinting across the highway. I missed it all. It was almost certain that we weren't going to camp much this summer because of Mom's job. It was a shame because this area really is my favorite and holds so many good memories. It was my escape from all of the craziness in the world and at school.

Chev drags me out of my thoughts... literally. I still have a firm hand around his black collar but that doesn't stop him from towing me up the red, dirt road that leads to the reservoir. I let go and follow him uphill to the body of water. The many campground spots below me get lower the higher we get, becoming as small as the palm of my hand. The public outhouses become as small as my thumbnail.

We get over onto flatter land and the blue water is revealed to us. It stretches out proudly and glistens like a million diamonds in the sun. The shore is covered in sagebrush and diverse amounts of bushes in most places but on the South side of the water–the wall that towers over the campground–is covered in rocks, big and small. That was where Dad and I went fishing on my seventh birthday. I remember sitting on a boulder next to the water with my pole. I didn't catch anything that day but it was still an awesome day. Dad had accidentally tripped on a medium sized rock and biffed it... *right into the water.* Water went everywhere, coating me and the rocks on the shoreline. Dad was *soaked* and I couldn't stop laughing.

Barking pulls me from the memories. The realization that Dad isn't here is enough to make me want to roll up in a ball right here on the dirt-covered road. But I don't. I can't. It's been nine years since he vanished. I've halfway come to terms that this is how life is. Tragic things happen to everyone. My dad being presumed dead is *my* tragedy.

I follow my dog away from the rocky shore and farther down the red road. From here on the bank is dirt, grass, and bushes. Chev and I always stick to the road because it's like an unspoken rule between us that we don't go down without probable cause. Chev knows I get beyond mad when he gets muddy because he's my dog and responsibility... Which means I have to bathe him, which is a pain.

The road is much easier to walk on compared to the rough terrain and I get a much better view of the reservoir from here. The morning sun beats down on the water, which in turn leads me to go blind as it reflects the rays. Blinking away the whiteness, I keep my focus on my feet until my vision comes back. But, when I look back at the road in front of me, Chev is missing.

"Chev!" I scream, examining my surroundings. "Chev!"

Below me, a bark sounds. I sprint to the edge of the road where there's a slight incline of a hill that leads to the bank. Chev barks at a spot of disturbed mud. He looks at me briskly before digging up the mud more, covering him in brown soil.

"What is it?" I ask before immediately feeling stupid. It's not like he can answer me. But, most likely, it's a dead fish or skunk.

I watch as Chev goes crazy over his find. Shaking my head, I follow after him into the bank's sludge. He isn't going to budge as long as he has a hold of his new deceased chew toy. I have to bring him back up myself or he will stay there.

Chev stops digging and barks at me again. Going quicker, I slide down the hill toward him.

“Move, Chev! Let me see!” I growl, waving him away. To my satisfaction, he moves away but doesn’t keep his eyes off of the muddy find.

My eyes find raven fabric that is covered almost completely in the bank’s mud. On the bag is writing that is basically camouflaged. I grab a handful of water and splash it over the sack. My heartbeat quickens significantly as I read the words. Beside me Chev goes as quiet as me, letting the discovery soak in.

The embroidered name burns inside my mind:

Evie Baker.

CARTER

Tuesday, November 2, 2021, Past.

The roaring of the crowds deafen me, but I know to keep my mind on the game. "Hut, hut, hike!" I hear a voice yell. Just like that, all at once, organized chaos begins. In front of me, everybody is getting sacked... but watching my teammates struggle isn't my job. So, I run across the field, the leather ball under my armpit. I listen to the quickness of my breath, aware of the enemy behind me. That is always the most exhilarating part of the entire game, in my opinion.

The stands grow louder the faster I run and the closer I get to the legendary line. *It's right there*, I have to remind myself. It's funny to me how fast the end zone is appearing too. Behind me, I hear the quick steps of the opposing team as they try their hardest to stop me. Funny enough, I listen to their pounding steps as motivation... not the roaring crowds.

Suddenly I'm only a couple of feet from the painted white line, which leads my heart to beat quicker. *Just a few feet!* But, I can hear someone getting closer with their thumping feet that *must* be made of hammers. These hammer feet must be designed to break the Earth because that's exactly how my ears hear it. But, just like that—somehow—I pass the line, dumbfounded, the ball in my hands. *The* line. The line that hasn't been crossed in years.

I look up at the scoreboard in disbelief, my eyes full of what could only be dignity. The crowd's screams and whistles are louder than ever. That is the first touchdown we have gotten in *three years.* The buzzer rings with a chirp, sounding happy about the accomplishment.

"Touchdown: Bears!" The intercom blared. And it's official.

I am immediately surrounded by teammates and the high school cheerleaders, who pat me on the back, high-five me and jump around me. A large weight is lifted off of my heart in response to the splendor, and relief floods through me, Carter Chase Miller, the first person to score a touchdown in three football seasons.

"Touchdown made by number eighty-seven, Carter Miller!" the man announced as everyone cheered.

My grin stretched from ear to ear at that moment. I had done it.

The administration doesn't even care that the players and cheerleaders have flooded the field as the buzzer signifies the ending of the first half and the start of halftime. They bounce around *me*, celebrating *me*. It's refreshing and beautiful and exhilarating.

After what seems like hours of splendor, I find myself on the sidelines, chugging a bottle of water. The liquid dribbles down my chin, escaping my mouth. I swipe the back of my hand across my chin, watching as the cheerleaders bounce to the middle of the field. I haven't paid much attention to the cheerleaders this entire season, especially since usually for halftime the football boys spend the time in the boys' locker room. But it's fine, a few minutes won't hurt the team. It may anger the coaches but it's whatever. Cheerleaders put in just as much work as we do to make the football games full of cheering and spirit.

As the rest of the boys make their way to the locker room inside the school, I stay leaning against the chain link fence that separates the track and field from the crowd and school. I almost drop my water bottle as I miraculously spot *her* in the front row, dead middle. *Evie* looks at the ground, followed by the rest. Her once quiet voice calls a cheer as loudly as it possibly could. That quiet girl can yell *loud.* It seems impossible, but nonetheless, it's true. I furrow my brow again, realizing I do that a lot when she's the topic running through my brain. Only because she keeps becoming more of a mystery.

I examine the cheerleaders as they hop and chant, their bodies tight and their smiles big. Evie looks so different when she cheers. Her hair dances as she moves; her hair is in a low ponytail with a black bow placed tightly in it. Her black, blue, and white uniform fits perfectly over her average form and the word 'Bears' is over the chest of her uniform. The cheer ends briefly before music blasts over a speaker.

In less than a second, cheerleaders begin dancing sharply. I watch with amazement plastered across my face, mainly caused by Evie Baker. I didn't know she could dance or cheer like that. She is *good.*

After a few more seconds the music begins fading into the background. I clap with the crowd, cheering louder than any bystander possibly could. As the cheerleaders jog off the field, waving at their audience, I relentlessly chase after Evie. She walks across the track–where they cheer during games–and I am hopeful to engage in conversation. I feel such a need to talk to her, especially now.

"Evie! Hey!"

She spins around to face me, her eyes such a bright blue that they remind me of Bear Lake. Bear Lake is the lake that our valley is named after. It's what people usually came to Bear Lake Valley for. It is our biggest tourist attraction. In the summer it filled up with Utahans, Californians, Oregonians, Washingtonians, Wyomingites, and lastly Idahoans. But, mainly, Utahans took it over.

Bear Lake is known for its distinct turquoise-blue color that is made by microscopic particles of white-colored calcium carbonate that so happens to reflect the lake's natural color to the surface. Bear Lake is also known as 'the Caribbean of the Rockies.'

"Carter, hi. Wait, why aren't you in the locker room?" she asks, searching the area around us for more football players. When she finds none she looks at me with a confused expression.

"I wanted to watch you guys and support you. But, look. That was *really* great. You were the best one out there. *Seriously*."

Her cheeks flush a scarlet and she begins fidgeting with her fingers. "T-Thanks. You did great as well."

"Thanks. I can't believe that I got a touchdown."

That is true, I really can't believe it. I am still in shock.

She smiles. Her teeth are vividly white and her smile genuine. She seems to have forgotten she is refusing to speak with me... "The first one in three years.

That's pretty awesome."

A fuzzy feeling begins to flutter inside me, warming my cheeks up significantly. I was already hot before but this is different. It is how I felt in middle school when I sat near Jessica Smith. I got that feeling whenever she would flick her hair in my direction. It constantly smelled of lilies.

I shake off the feeling and gesture to her one blue and one white pom poms. "I had no idea you cheered."

Evie shrugs, tugging at the hems of her uniform top. It represented our school colors perfectly. "Ever since seventh grade."

My eyes widen. N*o wonder she is good*. She has been doing cheer since middle school. That is around six years of all-year, all-summer cheer.

"Anyways..." Evie coughs pointing toward the group of cheerleaders gathered on the track, "I've got to get back to my team."

"Wait... Could I get your number?" I call as she begins backing up.

Evie's cheeks flush a bright pink color as she runs to her cheer bag to retrieve her phone. She comes back, her cell in her right hand. I watch eagerly as she goes to her contacts and allows me to put in my number. I hand her the red-cased phone back and survey her as she runs back to her team.

The rest of the game I play with a grin plastered on my face... that is until last quarter.

The clock is moving backwards at an astounding speed as I'm running for yet another touchdown. The line is so close but apparently not close enough. We are—somehow—ahead by twelve but that isn't enough. To be completely honest, I am getting greedy for more and more touchdowns. I mean this has never happened before. Our team sucked last year—and the year before that and before that and before that—and here we were scoring touchdowns left and right on our *second* game.

When I tell you that I'm only *feet* away from the end-zone, I'm not joking. I would have gotten another if it isn't for a player playing for the opposing team. He tackles me to the ground only eight feet away from the line, taking me to the grass with him.

Then, my knee erupts in pain. I yelp and push the hefty guy off of me, letting go of the ball. My hands find my left knee and clutch it. The boy that took me down continuously apologizes, calling for EMTs in between each 'sorry.' I squeeze my eyes shut in pain until I can hear my coaches around me, followed by what sounds like two EMTs. There were always two EMTs that sit at the football games in an ambulance just in case someone iss injured. Usually they never get any action, but tonight I guess I thought I'd give them some.

"Can you let go of your knee, Miller?" Coach Weber questions in my ear.

I nod and bring my discarded hands to my face. Tears begin to well up in my eyes but I hold them back as knives stab at my knees.

"Carter, we need to get you in the ambulance," Coach laughs beside me. Coach is always one to lighten the mood in the worst situations.

I drop my arms to my sides and look up at Weber. "Did I dislocate it, Coach?"

"No," he rings his melodic laugh again, "No you didn't."

I let out a large sigh of relief and let the people around get me up as painlessly as possible. But, as painlessly as possible isn't nearly enough because I end up yelping as they carry me away. Somehow the pain grows as time goes by.

They place me on the floor of the ambulance with my feet dangling to the ground.

"Give us one second," the older of the two EMTs smiles, hopping into the back of the ambulance behind me. I nod, tugging at the hem of my royal blue jersey. Grass stains it in various spots.

"Are you okay, Carter?" a voice urges in front of me. I look up to find—of all people—Evie Baker. She has distanced herself from her poms and stands in her uniform as she did at halftime. Although now she holds her duffel bag and backpack. Her curly ponytail isn't as in check as it was earlier but instead is messy from the night's sudden wind. Dirty blonde baby hairs fly across her freckled skin.

"Yeah, I'm good," I find myself laughing. "I figured I'd make the game interesting."

Evie's desolate facial expression gives way to reveal a no teeth, all dimple, affiliative smile. In my book that is a big win. Though, her smile doesn't reach her dim eyes.

"Yeah... well at least we won right? It was overall a great game," Evie nods, fidgeting with her slim, pale fingers.

I hadn't even realized the game had ended already. They must have made an agreement to end the game instead of continuing on for only a few minutes.

For the first time in a while, I am out of words and I can feel the awkwardness growing between us for every second our eyes shift to random places. I don't want to end this conversation until I absolutely have to. Today had been the day where I had gotten the most words out of her since meeting her officially.

I gulp, itching to say something. *Anything.*

"Well... um... thank you for checking up on me, Evie."

My fingers grab onto the skin of my arm and squeeze. I am stupid.

Evie looks up from the ground with a gentle smile. "Of course. I'll let them take you to the hospital now, I guess."

I bob my head and she begins walking away hurriedly, her duffel crashing into the side of her leg as she half jogs away.

I clench my fists tightly and yell after her before she gets farther up the hill that the football area is surrounded by. "Evie! Wait! Come back!"

Evie spins around, confusion spreading across her face. "What?"

"Come back?"

She *laughs* and tips her head to one side. "Why would I do that?"

Her laugh is crooked and lost and I wonder where her joyful, bright laugh is. Everybody has a light-hearted laugh yet here she is without one.

"Well, I know this is going to sound weird but do you... I don't know... wanna hang out tomorrow?"

I don't know how to describe her face. It is like she is fascinated and happy but horrified and startled all at the same time. Strange and soft. Guarded and delighted. So many different words came to mind but the most prominent one is glee.

"Wow, um, you know what? Sure. I would love to."

Evie's eyes turn a bright sky blue and her lips widen to reveal a white-toothed grin. From just ten yards I can see the blush forming on her freckled cheeks. Though her smile fades as she pulls out her ringing phone. She brings it up to her ear and begins listening intently. Evie barely speaks during the phone call and only nods occasionally. She shuts off her phone and stuffs it back into her duffel.

"Sorry, that is my dad. He's waiting for me. I have to go," She points to a white F-150 sitting in the parking lot past the Crow's Nest, the announcer's building.

"Wait, can you not drive?" I question, craning my head to look up at the vehicle. I can barely make out the figures because of the dark. All that I can make out about this sudden change in situation is Evie's abrupt change in demeanor.

"No, I can. I just don't have a vehicle," Evie keeps looking at the truck, fiddling with her fingers again. She looks once more, clearly uncomfortable "Look, I *really* have to go."

I follow her gaze again and nod. "Yeah, of course. I'll text you later."

Evie bites her lip, turns away, and dashes up the hill in a hurry. As she opens the truck door, the lights inside turn on, revealing what can only be her parents. Her dad's hair is missing and is replaced by a shiny scalp and his eyes are surprisingly friendly. I divert my eyes to the mother. Her blonde hair lays in short curls along her shoulders and her eyes are wrinkly, her eyelashes coated in dried black goop. They seem like kind and down-to-Earth people.

***

Turns out I only minorly sprained my knee which is a blessing. It will take about six weeks to heal which means I can get back to football in seven. The only downsides were that it hurt a *lot* to walk on and I have to wear a brace everywhere. I called Mom on the way to the hospital but she is already waiting for me because she was watching the game on live stream and saw it all go down.

She didn't gone to my football game because Daph didn't want to go and naturally someone had to stay at home with her. Daphne is Mom's favorite unquestionably and usually got what she wanted.

After my 'diagnosis' and signing papers, Mom and I left. I stared out the car's window as we passed the town's welcoming sign. We ventured past fields and rural farms for fifteen miles until we pulled into our driveway. My house is in the middle of nowhere practically and the closest neighbors were a mile away. I look at the brown barn which stands a good way from our small, two-story farmhouse. The chickens were still roaming, which is bad to have because of the coyotes and foxes that hung around. "I'll get the chickens." I grinned, grasping for the door handle.

"Your sister is already getting them," Mom's light brown hair is still pulled back with a claw clip from work. Coincidentally, Mom is a nurse at the Memorial Hospital in town.

"I can though, Mom. I'm not handicapped." She gives me a smile and eyes my right knee and I immediately know what she is about to say. "Do not say what I know you are about to say, Mom." My mother laughs heartily.

"Your sister is okay. You can remind her though. Obviously, she needs reminding."

I carefully get out from the car and begin to head for the lit-up house, which is surrounded by ten acres of land. I listen to the moos and clucks from the cows and chickens carelessly. Most of our land is taken up by cows, horses, and the main house and barn. Most of the animals are owned by neighbors that we rent the area out to.

I walk up the porch steps and swing the screen door open, then open the main door. My sister, Daphne, sits on the couch, binging a movie. I find myself rolling my eyes. "Go lock up the chickens, Daph."

She looks behind her, startled, then she smirks. "How's the knee?"

My eyes squint into a glare. "Go. Mom is going to yell at you."

Daphne groans and swings her legs off the couch. She switches the TV off and tosses the remote onto the cushions. She eyes my knee, giggles, and slips outside barefoot. A chuckle forces itself from my throat and I slowly make it up the stairs. Each step is agonizing pain that causes me to wince. The pain in my knee spread to my leg and almost made my knee feel like it couldn't breathe in some way. Like all it can do is feel pain, nothing else.

I get to the top of the flight of stairs and stop abruptly. Tears sting my eyes but I blink them away. I waddle down the cedar-floored hallway to my room. I lower myself gently onto the foot of my bed. Not long after Mom comes in to set my bags onto my floor. She leans against the door frame, her arms crossed on her chest. She's wearing her usual 'at-home' clothes of a zip up jacket, a plain t-shirt and joggers. Her face is stripped of makeup as it usually is. Ever since she had to be a widowed parent she never had time or energy to dress in anything else really. She is always running around taking care of Daphne, me, and the farm. To add, she also had to deal with working twelve hour shifts at the hospital. In fact, Mom never really went anywhere anymore... not even with her friends.

"Are you good now?" Mom asks, watching me closely. Her eyebrows were upturned as usual and her hazel eyes seem to look into my soul.

"Yeah. Absolutely," I smile. It is the truth. I honestly am not that bad. "I'm just a little bummed about not being able to play football for a while."

She nods, smiling monotone. It rings something in my brain. Her smile is empty like Evie's.

"Are you good, Mom?"

"Just tired," she sighs, looking down at her feet. "I'm going to drop you off at school tomorrow since your truck is still at school, okay?"

"Sounds great," I smile positively and look down at my football pads, jersey, and football tights. "I think I'm going to *try* and change out of these. I love you, Mom."

"I love you too, Carter."

I watch painstakingly as she shuts the door and leaves me alone in my football gear. I strip out of my football pads and jersey and slip on a loose tee. I hate to admit it but while changing out of my tights, a tear or two slips down my cheeks. I leave my brace off, set it on my nightstand, and somehow don't move my knee as I slip on some basketball shorts.

I hop to my backpack on my left leg and grab my phone from the front pouch. I shut off my light and use my phone's flashlight to navigate my way to my black-blanketed bed. The light bounces off the navy blue walls and illuminates the room with a bright glow. I lower myself onto the bed and turn off my flashlight.

Staring out the window at the star splattered sky, I sigh and open my contacts. I click on Evie's name and shoot her a text.

CARTER: HEY EVIE! IT'S CARTER.

EVIE: OH, HEY! WHAT'S THE PLAN FOR TOMORROW?

I haven't even thought about what I am going to do with Evie tomorrow. I haven't put too much thought into it yet.

CARTER: AFTER SCHOOL WE ARE GOING TO HAVE THE BEST EVENING EVER... :)

As soon as I send it, I feel like an absolute moron. I fumble to delete the text but I know it is impossible. I hate how you can't delete texts after sending them. What if you said something you knew you'd regret like I *just* did? Evie for sure would think I am weird. In fact, it takes her a total of two minutes to respond. By the time she responds I have already beat myself up silently.

EVIE: SOUNDS GREAT! CAN'T WAIT!

Relief floods over me and I collapse backwards onto my bedding, leaving my legs dangling off the side. Evie and I continue texting until late in the night and by twelve o' clock, both of us are slowly falling asleep. My eyelids droop dangerously and Evie reports that so are hers. We come to a mutual agreement to go to bed and I fall asleep with a gleeful smile spread across my face. I just hope nothing could ever ruin this.

EVIE

Wednesday, November 3, 2021, Past.

Carter's truck is a red, rusted, 1988 Chevrolet pickup that doesn't ride all that smoothly. In fact, we bump along the highway that leads to the South side of the county and several times I feel as if I'm going to fly out of my seat at the tiniest bumps. But I trust Carter—who is beside me. He thumps his fingers on the steering wheel to the beat of the rock music that bellows over the radio, seeming to be immune to the potholes.

I'm nervous sitting this close to someone, let alone a *boy*. My father would murder me if he found out I am on some sort of 'date.' (If that's what you call this.) I am strictly forbidden to date or be around any boys until I am out of the house. Until now I have distanced myself from acquiring any friends, especially boys. It's too risky for them and me. My family is *not* a typical American family.

From my peripheral vision, I spot the familiar boy looking over at me, a smirk plastered across his perfect face. My breath lodges in my throat, refusing to budge. I feel violated sitting next to him, for I feel I don't belong sitting next to such a perfect figure. His skin is perfect, his hair is perfect, and overall he is perfect. My cheeks begin to warm and I quickly look away. My skin is in terrible condition. My hair is always greasy and ratty. I am the opposite of him. The complete opposite.

In fact, I have no idea why Carter Miller even asked me to hang out with him. I'm not the type the cutest boy in the twelfth grade would even remotely talk to. But, hey, I'm not complaining. Although, I can see this is going to be a treacherous disaster. All happy things end in a disastrous mess. Time has shown that to me clearly.

Carter drives for fifteen minutes along the highway until we come to the 'Now Entering Bloomington' sign on the outskirts of the small town. The hairs on my pale skin begin to rise as I realize *exactly* where we are.

"My grandma used to live here," I reminisce into the music-filled cab. I haven't been this way in years but I still remember exactly where North Bear Rentals and the post office are along the road. It all comes back to me in flashes. This town of only about two hundred people used to be where I spent all of my days.

Carter looks at me with a smile and turns the music down. "Oh really?"

I nod and scoot forward as we turn left onto Bloomington Bottoms Road past the post office. A smile edges itself onto my lips as I point. "Actually she lived right there."

Carter slows in front of the cream-colored house where all of my fondest memories originate. My *only* fond memories actually. The front door which I used to go through thousands of times every weekend is still its original white and is under a triangle roof that breaks off from the rest of the house. Its main roof is square and peaks after a gradual incline that I always wanted to slide down but Grandma always said no. The spacious yard is surrounded by a mahogany picket fence that briefly breaks for a small pergola gate.

"Right there?" he asks, admiring the green lawn and the various flower beds that I used to help Grandma tend to.

Blinking away sudden tears, a laugh forces itself out. "I haven't been this close to her house since she died."

My fingers run over the scar that travels an inch above my eyebrow. Suddenly shivering, I clasp my hands in my lap and try my best not to pay attention to it.

"When... when did she die if you don't mind me asking?"

I have never talked about that day... not with *anyone*. Not with Kace, my younger brother. Not with my younger sisters Allie and Riley. And especially not with my parents. So, why am I about to talk about it with Carter? Why am I allowing myself? He's a boy I only started talking to a few days ago, yet here I am telling him hasty details of the rollover.

"Nine years ago in May, Grandma got into a rollover and was pronounced dead at the scene."

It is a brief description that leaves out *many* elements but it is extremely painful. I don't remotely come near to mentioning the major details that *one hundred percent* should be mentioned.

Long story short, May twelfth was the day my life completely fell apart.

Carter sits quietly as he gapes at his steering wheel, "Oh... I'm so sorry, Evie."

Some contorted version of my laugh echoes throughout the air as I shrug. "It's all in the past now."

A red-bellied robin glides past the windshield and Carter begins driving again. We pass two more houses in complete and utter silence and eventually, we are surrounded by countless fields. Though a half mile after the last house sits a lone home. As a six or seven-year-old, its color reminded me of a robin's blue egg like the one I once found in a nest I made at Grandma's. I had taken a paper bowl, covered it in mud, outlined the inside with twigs and dead grass with more mud, and left it on a tree branch for a bird family. Kace had made me believe that it could never happen and I had lost hope after a week went by. Then suddenly there was a sliver of hope when I spotted three little eggs lounging in my makeshift nest. Unfortunately, two days later, during an unexpected wind storm, they fell and cracked. I remember I bawled my eyes out next to the shells for over an hour until Grandma scooped me up and hugged me tightly.

Carter pulls into the rock-covered driveway behind a green pickup and turns off the ignition.

"What are we doing here?"

He laughs, hops out of his Chevy, and limps to my door before I can get out. His right hand wraps around the handle and rips it open. A giggle escapes from me as I climb out. A *giggle*.

"I know this is lame but this is my grandparents' house," he shuts the passenger door, "and we are here because I need to check up on them. Every other day either my mom or I pop in to say hi and today so happens to be my day of spontaneous love."

Where did this boy come from and how did I come across him? No one—and I mean *no one*—is this perfect or nice. My younger brother Kace wouldn't drive fifteen minutes to check in on my grandparents. Now, I'm not saying Kace is a terrible person because he is in fact the kindest, sweetest boy I know... that is until I met Carter Miller... But, I'm just saying that he wouldn't bother.

"It isn't lame at all."

Carter nods as if he feels accomplished and ushers for me to follow him up the weathered, wooden stairs that lead to a planked deck and the white front door. An American flag is anchored to the log railing and flies freely in the November autumn air. Under the flag, is a red-branched shrub that is planted against the deck's pillars.

I stop briefly and lean up against the railing that points toward the west. From here I can spot my grandma's old house, the two neighboring houses, and as well as a red barn. The mountains in the distance tower over Bloomington and are already snow-capped despite it only being November. Winter always starts coming early this time of year. In fact, the first snow was around the beginning of October. Although recently we have had oddly warm days that have melted most of the snow in the valley already.

The sky is a bright blue that stretches on for miles and is mostly free of cotton candy clouds. A few dot above the West mountain range and hide the tip of Paris Peak, the tallest mountain around. It is significantly taller than all of the snow-capped mountains and is almost completely covered in snow already. The mountains around it are a distinct red, orange, and yellow from the tree's fall colors and as are the trees outlining Carter's grandparent's log fences that run along the perimeter of their land.

"You coming?" Carter pulls me away from further gazing, an unsure smile spread across his face. I nod and comment on the view before stepping into the house. He agrees as I shut the door behind us.

The house is the perfect amount of warm and lit by a ceiling fan that is hanging on one side of the inclined ceiling. The pastel blueish gray ceiling slants up and stops abruptly at a large beam that runs along the ceiling and is painted the same dusty blue color.

To match the ceiling, the living room walls are painted the same and are filled with all sorts of decorations. Most of the decorations I personally wouldn't think would be put in a grandparent's house but here they were. On the other side of the room on the right wall is a wall of clocks—all real except for a giant wooden one made out of what looks like a wooden wheel with roman numerals painted on it in black. Next to it is a picture of a temple.

The majority of Bear Lake's community are members of the Church of Jesus Christ of Latter-day Saints. My grandma was and my mom grew up in the church. Although when my mom moved out she stopped going to sacrament meetings and so me and my siblings never learned the gospel. I've only gone to church once and that was with Grandma when she was alive.

I tear my eyes away from the odd clock wall and shed my feet of shoes as Carter does. Is Carter a member?

"Are you a member of the church?" I quietly ask. *That was probably out of line.*

We step onto the carpet, going around the spiral staircase that's directly in front of the door, and cross the spacious living room. Carter looks at me with a smile. It doesn't *seem* to offend him.

"My mom, my dad, and I were baptized at eight but we stopped going to church after Dad... Daphne, my little sister, was never baptized but my grandparents are active members."

I nod as we go through a doorway into the kitchen. The walls are dark gray and the cupboards and drawers are midnight black with white handles. A woman with gray hair pulled into a low bun stands at the island, wiping down the white countertop with a red rag. Her blue eyes find Carter's and a smile spreads across her wrinkled face.

"Carter! How are—" she makes eye contact with me and I feel my cheeks reddening. Subconsciously I begin picking at the skin on my wrist, "—oh you brought a friend!"

He looks back at me as if forgetting I am here. That usually happens a lot with people. I truly am that easy to forget. "This is Evie."

His grandma sets down her rag and clasps her hands together underneath her chin. Her eyes don't seem to glaze over me like everyone's eyes always do when they meet me or see me. She looks straight at me, with a soft grin.

"Evie," she echoes. "That's a *beautiful* name. It's nice to meet you."

A lump grows in my throat and gradually gets bigger. "Thank–thank you, ma'am. It's very nice to meet you too."

The room goes silent momentarily but Carter breaks the awkward barrier of silence. "Where's grandpa?"

A strained cough echoes through the house as if on cue. It's scratchy and deep and clearly belongs to an older fellow. The woman in front of me softly chuckles and points into the living room at a mini hallway that contains at *least* two doors. I'd imagine there's a third because of the warm yellow light that floods the tiny hallway. "Bathroom. He *thinks* he can fix the leaky pipe. Although I'm sure he's just making it worse."

The sound of plastic against metal fills my ears and is followed soon after by the man's yelps from the bathroom. "*Arghh!*"

Mrs. Miller stomps over to a white-handled drawer and pulls out several dish towels. "I'm sure he has just been soaked. That fool probably broke the pipe in half! He doesn't know anything about fixing things like that! I tried to tell him, I did."

A melodic sound rings softly. It's a gorgeous sound and carries so much happiness. My head looks between Carter and his grandma in search of the maker of the sound but it's neither of them. It's me.

It isn't forced or fake like my laughs usually are… No, it's an actual laugh. It's sudden and shakes my core peacefully. The dark brick wall around my heart chips away slightly. This is a wall I have had since grandma died and now it is splintering at the tiniest chuckle. When I tell you that wall has kept me alive these past nine years–and I mean breathing not actually *living*–I'm telling the truth. Many times the wall blocked out the several heartbreaks I'd suffered over the years... all caused by Dad. Dad broke my heart before any boy could and continues to do so every day with every brui–

Heavy stomps get louder the closer the man comes. He's a familiar gruff man with a soaked blue plaid button-up. "Annie! Where 're the towels? That stupid pipe has burst on me!"

Everything about him sets me in shock and holds my breath in my lungs. His familiarity squeezes my lungs until I am near to gasping for sweet, sweet, privileged air.

John Miller hasn't changed one bit. He's stumpy and short with a belly of a drunk but I know for a fact he's not a drinker. His gray beard looks as scruffy as it was the day we met. I can still remember how the beard pricked the skin on my neck as John Miller carried me. With that memory came the fear I had felt at that moment and the extreme distress I was under. Only minutes before, I had watched as the shattered glass flew around me from the orange Toyota... That *stupid* Toyota that so happened to be the same color as the corgi dog we swerved around that changed my life forever. How symbolic, right?

In my ear, the man whispered that I was safe, but that wasn't relevant to me. I wanted to know if Lena Marlowe was on her way to a casket or not. John continued to pull me away from the wreck and toward a flashing ambulance, refusing to say anything but "I got you. You're safe." He refused to tell me anything about the fate of my grandmother. At the time I hated him for not giving me the answers eight-year-old me demanded but now I'm relieved someone shielded me from that insufferable pain.

"Evie Baker..." John gasps, running his shaking fingers through his graying beard.

I hold back the tears somehow. But honestly? I'm holding on by a thread. John Miller even remembers who I am.

"I haven't seen you since..." he continues but trails off, eyeing the island's countertop. "You've gotten so big, Evie."

I gulp, not being able to take my eyes off Carter's grandpa. Here this man is in plain sight... a reminder of how it only takes one second to ruin a life. Grandma looked away from the wheel for *one* second. That started a chain reaction of dreadful things that will be following me around until the day I die.

CARTER

Wednesday, May 18, 2022, Present.

"I told you, I don't know anything else, officer."

A rookie officer sits diagonally from me on our sofa, a pen and notepad in his lap. He watches me carefully with curious eyes. I wish he'd leave. I'm done with this crap. I'm done. I have been sitting here with rookies for two hours and they refuse to leave. I've told them a million times I know nothing else besides that I found the bag there but they *won't leave it alone*.

"Yeah, Carter, you've said that. I'm just trying to be as thorough as possible," the older officer insists. His hair is graying and he's got to be at least fifty which isn't odd for police officers around here. These days only older people work. The generations are becoming less prone to want to do hard work. Although, his partner has got to be in his early thirties for he has bright green eyes and youthful skin. His brown beard is only stubble while the older gentleman's is much longer.

"We understand this, Officer Garrett," Mom sighs, squeezing my hand softly. "Carter will answer any other questions of course, but truly he seems to have told you everything."

Mom has been at my side ever since I was escorted home by the police and won't leave it. This entire time she has had my right hand in both of hers and has been intent on letting the officers ask over and over "are you sure that's what you saw."

The older gentleman, Officer Garrett, nods slightly and makes eye contact with me. "Carter, you said your... dog... found the bag?"

"Yes! With all due respect, sir, you've asked me this twice already."

I want to storm out but Mom keeps me anchored to the leather cushions.

"Carter," she scolds, her voice high-pitched and shocked. "You will not disrespect these *nice* men. They are only trying to help your friend."

Tears threaten to spill but I keep them back. I'm nearly a grown man. Grown men don't cry. I'm the man of the family now and I can't break down, I really can't. I gulp and turn to Mom, my voice quiet.

"She wasn't just my friend, Mom... She was my girlfriend."

Mom barely seems surprised by the news: "Well, I should have known. You were constantly hanging out."

I had never told anyone that before. It isn't because I am embarrassed. No, not at all. I am proud I have a girlfriend as gorgeous and perfect as Evie Baker. Never in a million years did I think I would, *really*. It's just Evie and I decided together that no one really *needed* to know. There were her parents who would *kill* her if they found out. They made it clear last November when I gave her my hoodie that if she continued to hang out with me they'd—well she didn't share that detail with me. No doubt they threatened to hurt her... more. But, we took the risk and for her well-being we didn't tell anyone. I didn't even tell Nixon and Dave.

Officer Garrett scribbles something down on his notepad with intense volume. "So you two were *dating*. I didn't expect that and I'm fifty-four years old."

Well, there goes that secret.

Nothing stays a secret very long in a small town.

The younger officer's radio sings static noise before breaking out in a clear voice. "Hey, do you still got the boy?"

Both officers glance at me before getting up and walking away to the front door. "Yeah."

The officers continue moving into the kitchen, trying to get away from earshot clearly. But before they can I go stiff with the other end's words: "Good, because we've got an arrest warrant for one Carter Chase Miller."

They leave me in a dimly lit room with a two-way window. There are no other windows but instead white fluorescent lights that hang from the ceiling. They sat me at a wooden kitchen table in the middle of the room ten minutes ago and haven't bothered me since. The metal chair I sit at is incredibly uncomfortable to the point where I'm constantly shifting. I've got to look guilty but I can't help it. If they wanted me to sweat by making me wait, they succeeded.

Ten more minutes pass before the wooden door creaks open. In comes Sheriff Reggie, a beige file clutched in his hand.

Immediately I stand up, my hands shoved in my front pocket. "Sheriff. Finally... Can you please tell me why I'm here?"

"Sit down, Carter," he demands sternly.

I lower myself back into my seat, setting my hands on the wooden slab. I clasp them together as I watch Sheriff Reggie take his own seat across from me in a similar chair. He sets the file in the middle and leans back in his chair, arms crossed against his chest.

"Do you believe me that she's missing now?" I challenge quietly, staring him right in the eyes.

Reggie chuckles lightly and nods, leaning forward onto his elbows. "Yes, and I have an inkling you had something to do with it, Carter Miller."

What is this? What is going on? I'm the one trying to find her and they think I had something to do with her disappearance? This is all so backward and terribly wrong.

But, before I can speak, the sheriff continues. "You came in here on Monday and asked questions and insisted she wasn't a runaway. You are the *only* one that has come in, Carter. Now, tell me why is that? Are you trying to nudge us in the 'right' direction? Do you think that when we find her... deceased... it will cause countywide terror? Is that your plan? You *did* find the bag which is fairly ironic, don't you think?"

A scoff forces its way out of my throat before I can stop it. "This is absurd, Sheriff. With all due respect, you should listen to yourself. I wouldn't hurt Evie, and to add, we don't even know if she's... if she's..." *dead.* By some chance she could be alive. I'm not going to allow myself to think otherwise. I can't. I won't.

I wait for him to speak but he stays silent, glaring at me harshly.

"If someone did something to her it would have been her parents, sir."

His eyes flutter with curiosity, watching me more intently. He furrows his brow and sits back again. "What makes you say that?"

"Well, th–they give her bruises. They hit her. They do."

Sheriff Reggie laughs very loudly for this being our topic. Anger runs through my veins as I watch him think this is a *joke.* This isn't some sick joke I am making up. My clasped hands go white from how clenched my fists are.

"Carter, you honestly crack me up," he begins laughing again. "Paul Baker is a very well-respected man. I have known him since *childhood*, you hear me? He would never hit his children. Paul is a very good man."

That's what everyone says and it always turns out to be wrong.

"Seriously?" I growl, running a hand through my brown hair. It's rattier than usual and my hand doesn't go through smoothly. Instead, it gets caught on rats. "Why would I joke about a parent hitting their child?"

He goes silent for a few solid seconds, staring at me earnestly with his dull gray eyes. I watch him closely as he opens the file, refusing to show me the contents. Reggie pretends to look it over but I know these tricks. The amount of cop shows I watch is outrageous.

"Now, Carter," he starts, placing a large photograph in front of me. "Can you tell me why we found this in Evie's sack?"

The photograph is of a piece of ripped notebook paper, the ink bleeding significantly. The ink has turned blue from the black marker. The blue lines lining the paper bleed as well, creating blue water stains. Some mud is covering the bottom left corner too. But that's not what I notice at first. In messy writing in the middle is two words: Noah Miller.

Why in the world *would Evie have a paper that says my* dead *father's name?*

CARTER

Wednesday, November 3, 2021, Past.

I grasp the steering wheel tightly in my fists. My hands cause the wheel to become slippery with sweat. Next to me, Evie slumps quietly as we remain parked still in my grandparents' driveway. This is how we have sat for the last ten minutes. Not speaking... just sitting. And I've kind of had enough of it...

"So when I asked you to hang out I didn't expect..." I circle my pointer finger toward the house, "...*that* to happen, if I'm being honest."

Evie looks up at me with large, cerulean eyes that reflect the setting sun's light in such a beautiful way. The warm orb of sun sits in the whites of her eyes.

"When I accepted, I didn't think your grandpa is the man that basically loved me because the only person that did was dead beside me in that car," she croaks, burying her face into her hands. I can't help but notice that she looks so tiny next to me. "Also I can't believe your grandparents were close *knit* with my grandma. Like they were best friends."

This is true. Grandma and Grandpa sat us down at the kitchen table and we all talked about Lena Marlowe. Now, they want Evie over for dinner next weekend.

"It's crazy..." I sigh, running my hands down the wheel and into my lap. My head turns to find Evie in a distressed position, basically curled up in an upright fetal position. "This has got to be a lot to be going through in one night, Evie... Is there anything I can do like give you a hug or something?"

Evie lifts her head and tugs at her shirt's long sleeves, adjusting them carefully and perfectly. "I've never really talked about my grandma, Carter. I think I should probably tell you that. Please don't expect me to talk about it all... It's just–oh, I don't know."

I don't know what possesses me but I reach my hand over to her and grasp her arm softly, shaking it slightly in sympathy. Evie yelps and shakes my hand off her upper arm and begins rubbing the area.

"Oh... I'm sorry, did I do something? Did I hurt you? I didn't mean–"

She shakes her head while still rubbing her arm, and takes a deep breath. "No, you didn't, Carter. It's okay. I'm okay. It wasn't you."

My eyes strain as I look at the blonde haired mystery. Well, she isn't as much of a mystery to me anymore... She is more than a mystery. She is a person that has gone through a tragedy–one at least. She isn't some mystery to figure out like it's a YA thriller novel in the school's library collection. Evie Baker is a person that needs comforting.

She is also shivering with her arms crossed on her chest. I had to admit Big Red is cold and getting colder every second the sun goes down.

"Are you cold?"

Idiot. Of course she is.

Evie looks at me with those blue eyes and only nods. Chuckling, I stick my arm into the empty space behind our seats and take out a brown Fox Racing hoodie. It's a little torn at the neckline and has a few burnt in holes around the chest area. Out of all of my hidden hoodies in Big Red, this one is the cleanest. I hand it to her and watch as she stares at it in shock as it sits on her knees that are brought to her chest.

"It's okay. I never wear it anyways. Well, only camping but I haven't gone camping since..." *...Dad disappeared.* "I keep it around even though it doesn't fit me. I wash it too, don't worry. But I think it'll fit you."

Her blonde head bops lightly and she pulls on the singed coffee-colored hoodie. It fits as perfectly as it did on me when I was nine.

"Thanks," she laughs. It's a half laugh that seems forced that's not like the one I heard when she was talking with Grandma. That laugh was one of the most beautiful things I'd ever heard. "I left mine in my gym locker after P.E. class."

Nodding quietly I turn the key in the ignition and back out of the rocky driveway. Evie sits up appropriately and fastens her seatbelt on. It clicks into the part of the seat belt connected to the webbing of the car. We drive past Evie's grandma's old house in a new kind of silence. It isn't until we've passed the post office that my heart stops pounding and my lungs stop clenching. I can't imagine how Evie feels.

My first 'date' with Evie Baker is nothing short of a disaster. Honestly, there goes my chances—if there was any to begin with—or there being... well... an us. At this point I'd be lucky to be her friend.

After fifteen minutes of driving to the silent hum of the radio's music, Evie begins directing me to her house in Montpelier. We go over the concrete overpass that is a sort of bridge over the railroad tracks onto Main. She instructs me in a soft voice to take a right onto ninth street. We drive almost all the way to the end of the street where a mini tree forest sits. Evie has me pull in front of a two story, white house that is surrounded by several quiet homes. I've personally never been this way and the only way to truly describe it is that the neighborhood is inhabited by grandparents and the occasional outcast family. The house's lawn next to hers is cluttered with junk and random broken bicycles while hers is neatly mowed and perfectly manicured.

Evie clears her throat and unbuckles her belt. "Thanks, Carter. I guess I'll... um... see you tomorrow."

My eyes follow as she makes her way into her home. It seemed like a nice place to grow up... fit for her, her kind siblings, and her loving parents.

***

Lockers open and slam around me loudly as the bustling highschoolers get ready for first hour. I pull my backpack from mine and slide it onto my shoulder. It's heavier today since Mrs. Carlsen, my math teacher, assigned several assignments that all so happen to be in a textbook. I don't think Mrs. Carlsen has accepted the "no paper, use computers only" policy the school districts board members put in place last year. They decided to buy every single student a school laptop to do work on. Mrs. Carlsen is one of those teachers that didn't *fully* believe in the power of electronics and it shows with the weight on my back.

I slam my locker shut with my palm and begin wobbling toward mentor. Before I can actually get two feet on my sprained knee, a hand lands on my broad shoulder. My body goes tense briefly until I turn my head to find a dirty blonde haired girl, her blue eyes duller than usual. A smile spreads across my face instantly but Evie doesn't return the favor, though she is *still* wearing my hoodie.

"Thanks for last night but..." She begins taking off the hoodie right in front of me "... here's your hoodie back. I–I don't deserve it."

I swear–I *swear* something inside my heart cracked. A very loud *pop* sounds in my ears and causes me to feel almost sick. I watch her in horror, searching in dreadful confusion. I move my eyes from her emotionless face and to her arm. As she takes off my hoodie it lifts her shirt's loose long sleeves. Immediately I feel like running to the principal or the police but I stay rooted in place.

"Oh my gosh, Evie," I gasp, reaching for her arms that are covered in big and small spots that vary from green, to purple, and to black. "Who did that to you?!"

She steps back like my touch has burned her severely, gasping herself. Evie's shaking fingers grab her black sleeve and pull it back down to her wrist. "No one. It's nothing. It's really nothing. Just... just... I have to listen."

"You have to listen to who?" Anger boils inside me rapidly. Who hurt her? Who knows how many bruises she has spread on her arms. I only saw her lower arm which is already hard to bruise... so, what does her upper arm look like?

She shoves my hoodie into my arms and she storms off into the distance. I yearn to follow her but my feet don't move. Too many questions flood my brain at once. I feel as if I'm in overload.

"Oh, Evie... You are much more complicated than you seem," I croak underneath my breath, my voice cracking in anger and emotion.

CARTER

Wednesday, November 10, 2021, Past.

It has been a week since Evie has talked to me. I pass her in the halls and she doesn't even acknowledge me. For the first few days I tried to talk to her but to be honest, she made it very clear that she did not want to talk to me. Now, I've essentially given up. I feel bad about it but I don't know how to get her to talk.

Although, I can't get her out of my head. Those bruises... They were some old and some new. Evie wouldn't tell me who did it but I have a pretty good idea. When I first saw her parents they seemed like nice people... from far away. Close up they must be monsters to hit their child or children. Evie has siblings. Are they hitting her siblings too?

But, right now I don't want to think about this mess.

Wearing a white shirt, my jeans, sneakers, and my knee brace I limp through the basement hallway and out into the autumn air. School was sucky today and now I am just hoping watching the guys play football will help me out. So, with my chin on my chest, I walk across the track and onto the football field in the middle. Very few people are here already so I collapse next to a junior, being extra careful with my knee. It had gotten better since I sprained it but not by much. It is likely I won't be able to play for a while, which is a huge bummer. Playing football is what helps distract me from my problems.

The junior is stretching his right leg with his messy dirty blond hair that flies in the chilly breeze. His bright blue eyes catch sight of me quickly, causing him to nod in greeting.

"What's up, Carter," he asks, running his fingers through his sandy-colored locks.

"Nothing much," I shrug, picking at an old grass stain in my blue jeans that refused to wash out. I think I had gotten it when Chev dragged me across the lawn once. Despite his age, he had dragged me for a good twenty feet. "I'm just thinking."

"Penny for your thoughts?"

Half-heartedly I laugh, picking harder at the green stain. When I look up at him the eyes and hair finally click.

"Hey, Kace? You're Evie's brother, right?"

Kace and Evie were practically identical. So much so that they could be twins, honestly. I'm an idiot for not remembering. Kace nods and shifts around to stretch his other leg.

"She's been avoiding me for about a week. It's like she's isolating herself... Did I do something, do you know?"

Kace's bright blue eyes downcast in a sorrowful manner. I don't miss how he tenses at the mention of his older sister. He glances around us as if checking no one is listening before he leans in ever so slightly.

"You can't tell her I told you."

I kind of chuckle and shrug. "It's not like she's talking to me anyway."

Kace watches me sternly before speaking, his eyes still dejected. "She's not allowed to see you. After she came home with your hoodie, my parents flipped and forced her to give it back the next day. She's basically on house arrest now. She goes to school and has to immediately come home."

So her punishment is all my fault. *I'm* the reason she isn't talking to me. If I hadn't given her that *stupid* hoodie all would have been okay.

The junior continues. "But, of course, it's not your doing. It's our parents. To be honest, they are especially hard on her. They... discipline... her more than our other sisters and I combined."

Discipline as in hit her? I think it but don't say it.

"*Why*? Evie is the sweetest girl I've ever met. She's never done anything wrong. Why is she disciplined more?"

"I personally think it's because she survived that accident with our grandma but Grandma didn't."

I stare at the lit up rectangle in my palm. It hurts my eyes in the darkness of my navy room as my thumb hovers over her contact picture. There is something so comforting about sitting in the pitch dark alone.

At the top of the screen I have a good amount of notifications but I have no motivation to actually check any of them. Most of them are texts from my friends anyways. Why should I talk to my friends if Evie doesn't have the luxury to do so?

A large sigh escapes my throat as I collapse backwards onto my black comforter. I lift my phone into the air above my face, my eyes staring at the large "E" that is placed within the blank, yellow contact picture. I haven't gotten a picture of her yet, but that is the case for mostly everyone on my phone.

Hesitantly, my thumb begins to hover over the fluorescent green call button. I haul myself back up to a sitting position and click the button underneath her name. I bring it up to my ear and listen to it ring several times.

My shoulders begin to droop slowly as the ring continues. I don't know why I thought it'd go through honestly.

Then the ringing stops and the call goes answered.

"Hello," the raspy voice of Evie greets. Something in my heart begins to ignite in sorrowful pain. Her nose sounds stuffed and she sounds as if she had been crying only moments before. Millions of question fill my mind profusely.

"It's... um... been awhile," I manage to croak into the device. If silence had an emotion, hers is sad.

"Sorry."

"No, don't be sorry, Evie," I rush to say, sitting up straighter. "Honestly, don't be sorry."

The voice on the other side of the call goes mute. I take the phone away from my ear to check if she hung up but she didn't. I bring it back to my ear and with my other hand I pick at the seams in my black bedding.

"Hey, so guess what. We are housing a border collie and you'd love her. You really would. She's the cutest dog ever," I cough, looking out the darkened window.

Evie clears her voice. "A border collie? What do you mean by housing her?"

Outside on the front lawn's grass, Chev–my husky–wanders around. Luckily, Chev had been getting along with the three year old border collie, making the transition all the much nicer. We were nervous at first but he proved to us he was mature enough not to attack her. Which makes sense because of his age. Chev is getting old. He is an old man.

"We are fostering her until she gets a more permanent home. Maybe sometime you can come over and see her?"

There it is. I had asked her to hang out *again*. But, this time I'm not so sure she can seeing how she's punished for the last time.

Evie sigh rings through my ear. "I can't. I'm... not allowed."

Yeah. I know.

"Oh, that's okay," I say instead. I promised Kace I wouldn't tell her that he told me what happened.

I am running out of things to say and I *really* don't want to end the call. This is the first time she had talked to me in forever. I am not about to end it.

"Why can't a nose be twelve inches long?"

Really, Carter? Really? You are an idiot.

Evie laughs but it's not like the one I heard at Grandma and Grandpa's. "*What?*"

"Why can't a nose be twelve inches long," I repeat slower with a smile. I suck in my lips to attempt at hiding it... I don't know why I try and hide the smile. It's not like she can see me.

"Are you telling me *jokes* over the *phone*?"

"*Why can't a nose be twelve inches long*?"

Evie goes quiet for a while, leaving me to smile to myself in the pitch black of my room.

She finally returns, her voice high pitched with what I hope is glee. "I don't know, Carter Miller. Tell me why a nose can't be twelve inches long."

"Or it'd be a foot..."

Holy crap, she laughs. It's still the sweetest, prettiest sound I've ever heard to this day. It reminds me of the birds' songs on a summer morning. It oozes with the happiness I've wished upon her since I met her.

"That shouldn't have made me laugh!" she exclaims, giggling abundantly.

I laugh along with her with an elated heart and mood. When she is happy... I am happy.

Then the sound of a door coming open on her side of the call echoes. Evie's laughing stops and immediately after so does mine. I listen intently even though I know I shouldn't.

"Mom..."

A woman's angry voice booms in my ear. "Evie Janiece Baker, who is that? *Who is that*?"

Evie gulps and must lower her phone onto her bed because her voice gets quiet. "Just a friend."

Something in her voice causes fright in me. I go still, my entire body seizing up. It is a different kind of fear. It is a kind of fear I haven't heard in several years. Eight years in fact. I haven't heard it since my dad went missing. Mom spoke with that type of fear that day. We had no idea where he went, all we knew is that he went missing here in Bear Lake. No foul play was suspected because, well, this is Bear Lake. Nothing like that really happens. Even I knew that and I wasn't even living here at the time. We were still in Coos Bay, Oregon—the West-coast town I lived in until about last year.

"Tell her you need to go! We told you aren't allowed to speak to people. You lost that right!"

"Mom! He is just trying to be nice and talk to me!"

I can tell Evie knows she's messed up. She didn't need to include I am a boy, her mom already thought I was a girl.

Her mom has a field day with that. To be honest, I've stopped breathing, leaving my lungs begging for air. They burn as I listen to Mrs. Baker scream at Evie. The thing that saddens me more is that she doesn't fight back anymore. She sounds like she is used to it all. It sounded like she is used to getting punished. Kace had said they were rougher with her than her other siblings—which makes more sense now.

The door opens again and another person enters the room. Based on the heavy footsteps, it seems to be her dad.

"What did she do this time," an older man groans, his voice tired and filled with angst.

"Your *daughter* disobeyed us and continued to talk to boys," she hisses. I imagine she's standing at the foot of Evie's bed, her arms crossed on her chest.

I should hang up but I can't bring myself to move. I feel like I'm violating Evie by listening to this.

"I... He... He called me. I haven't talked to him until now." I can tell she's holding back tears because she chokes and her voice is once again hoarse and throaty. The phone moves again, this time farther away from her. I think it's in an attempt so I don't hear her but I hear her every word and it *breaks* my heart. "Mom... Dad... He's my only friend... Please."

With that I finally start moving and slam my finger on the red 'end call' button. The line goes silent. I can't listen to them *attack* and *demean* her every word.

My breath is shallow and shaking and I'm not one to cry on a daily basis, but tears sting my eyes. They begin to run erratically down my cheeks in warm, itchy streams. I feel so bad for her. Her whole life is falling apart in front of her and she can't piece it back together. Evie has been neglected by her family. She has been alone in life for a while now and I can tell it is killing her. I can't imagine being alone and having my family hate me.

I swipe my palms under my eyes as the tears spill, not being able to take my eyes off the 'call ended' screen that flashes on my phone. I have no idea what to do now. I don't know how to help Evie and that is killing me. I want her to be happy but with her parents, how can she?

The doorknob jiggles and I hurriedly wipe away my last tear. The light from the hallway floods in and illuminates Daphne's figure. I must have been too slow because she looks at me with worry. "You okay, bro?"

I nod quickly and turn off my phone. "What do you need?"

Her hazel eyes watch me warily as she stands there, a hand still on my doorknob. "Mom made dinner."

Despite my mom's drowsiness after long shifts at work, she still makes dinner most nights.

"Yeah, okay. I'll be down in a minute. Thanks, Daph."

But she doesn't leave. "Are you sure you're okay, Carter?"

"Yeah, I swear."

With that, she walks backwards and shuts the door, leaving me in darkness again. My eyes once again adjust to the shadowy walls. I stand up carefully and shove my phone in my front pocket. I wipe my eyes with the hem of my black shirt for good measure and open my door. I step into the brightly lit hallway and wobble down the stairs. The smell of savory spaghetti fills my nostrils and the scent of garlic bread causes my nose hairs to dance despite my mood. Mom's food did that.

I get to the bottom of the stairs and shuffle across the wooden floor into the kitchen. Mom is rushing around grabbing a stack of three plates and forks to go with them. She hands me one of each with a smile and Daphne as well, who is examining drink options in the fridge. I thank her quietly and scoop noodles that sit in a strainer in the clean, empty sink onto my white, porcelain plate. I then move to the stove and shovel meaty sauce onto the noodles. Beside me, Mom opens the toaster oven and hands me two pieces of garlic bread.

"How's the knee," she asks, filling her own plate with food. Her light brown hair is pulled back in a messy, loose, medium ponytail and she still wears her mint green scrubs even though she's been home for about four hours.

"Sore." Walking on it isn't nearly as painful as it was but it still hurt to the point where I unconsciously wince everytime I walk on it too long. The walk from my bedroom to the kitchen is even straining it too much.

"I still think you're faking," Daphne smiles, filling her plate up with noodles. My head begins to shake in disbelief and I find a seat at our kitchen table.

"I don't know why. You literally watched it on live, Daph," I groan, shoving a fork full of spaghetti into my mouth.

Daphne shakes her head and sets her food down across from me, an empty cup clutched in her hand. Mom sits in the seat next to her as Daph walks back into the open concept kitchen. The living room, dining room, and the kitchen is all in the same room. She sets it on the island's granite top and opens the kitchen.

"Mom, is the milk good?"

Mom sets down her fork and looks over her shoulder into the kitchen.

"Check the date."

Daphne goes silent as she grabs the jug from the fridge and sets it down next to her cup. "Well, what's today?"

"November tenth," I answer, scooping spaghetti onto my garlic bread. It is my favorite thing to do with spaghetti. I set down my fork and take a huge bite of the spaghetti covered bread.

It must not be bad because I watch as she pours it carefully into the cup with two hands. My eight year old sister twists the red cap back on and sticks it back into the silver double door fridge. Watching the liquid intently, she leisurely walks back to the silent table. When she sits down Mom finally takes a bite of her spaghetti.

Daphne takes a large sip of milk, leaving behind a white mustache of dairy. She leaves it there and begins to twist her fork in the saucy noodles. Before she takes a bite, she finally swipes the back of her hand across her upper lip. Her hazel eyes look up from her plate to find mine watching her and she sticks out her tongue.

"Stop staring at me, nerd," she growls before eating a forkful of spaghetti. Then with her mouth full she still talks. "What is up with you tonight?"

"Nothing."

I watch as she glares at me and then returns to chewing her food. I shift my eyes to Mom who is eating her food slowly, staring off into the distance beside me. Her eyes are dropping from lack of sleep but she continues on. That's how my mom is. She is the strongest lady I know. My mother is exhausted but she still made dinner for us. My mother works long shifts but still comes home and cares for us. Not only is she strong but she is deeply caring and loving. Even when Dad vanished she was there for *us*. She never broke down—at least not in front of us.

A singular tear sheds from my eyes and runs down my cheek and onto the table. I don't know what's up with me. I don't typically cry... like *ever*.

Before I can wipe away the residue of the tear, Mom's tired eyes find mine. Her eyebrows furrow in worry and she sets down her fork.

"Carter? What is it?" she urges, reaching her hand across the table to grab mine. "Are you okay, honey?"

I nod slowly, looking between her and Daph. "Yeah, I am. I was just thinking."

Mom's brown eyes squint gently as she watches me further. Her hand squeezes mine tenderly. "What about?"

A lump grows in my throat, causing my breathing to shallow steadily. I gulp in an attempt to rid myself of the brick but it stays strong.

"I'm just so glad to have such a great, loving mother and sister."

CARTER

Wednesday, November 11, 2021, Past.

My eyes droop dangerously. I continued to toss and turn all night. I'll admit... It wasn't an ideal sleep. My mind couldn't stop buzzing at one hundred miles per hour for several hours. At around three I had enough of it and took melatonin. Even with that it took me an unnaturally long time to actually pass out.

I've barely been able to stay awake in my classes so it being lunch is a blessing. I hike up the stairs leading straight into the commons area, my legs beginning to burn. The stairs are bustling with chattering highschoolers slowly moving outside or into the cafeteria. I, as usual, start to make my way outside but I am stopped when I spot Evie's familiar dirty blonde hair. She is several feet in front of me, pushing one of the four front doors open.

"Evie!" I call, reaching my hand out for her. She looks over her shoulder, her blue eyes peering at me in confusion until she recognizes me. "Wait up."

"Oh, hey, Carter..."

I catch up with her and we begin to walk through the second set of front doors shoulder to shoulder. We stop in front of the school on the concrete as other high schoolers make their way to the East parking lot.

"What's up...?" Evie brushes a hair flyaway behind her ear as the autumn air tussles her low ponytail.

An itch suddenly builds on the back of my neck. I take my hand and scratch it softly, watching her closely. I really don't want to bring up last night with her. "I was just about to go to Arctic Circle for some lunch but maybe... maybe you'd want to go with me?"

Her fingers begin to pick at the skin on her wrist and hand and her eyes graze our surroundings quickly. Evie finally meets mine again, takes a deep breath, and nods gently. "Yeah, that'd be nice. I was just going to sit out here for while so that sounds much better."

A weight lifts off my shoulders and I strain to hide my smile but I have a feeling I'm not doing too well. "Come on."

Evie walks beside me as we make our way down the concrete sidewalk that leads to the parking lot. The sidewalk is relatively narrow and we walk with our shoulders touching, which sends a soothing warmth through me.

I clear my throat, hoping to degrade the awkwardness that fuels between us. "I haven't been able to stay awake in any of my classes. How 'bout you?"

She giggles softly, eyeing me with a smug smile. "Yeah, I'd say. You were basically asleep in both Mentor and English. I also have a good hunch you were asleep in whatever third period class you were just in."

We walk through the parking lot as I laugh. "I didn't think anyone would notice, to be honest. But, surprisingly I was too scared to even slightly doze off in Mr. Henderson's math class. Last time I fell asleep, he threw a marker at my head and then dropped a textbook onto the table next to my desk. It was the *worst* wake up call ever."

The joyous sound that is Evie's laugh fills the air alongside the sound of roaring and starting engines. Her cheeks are extra rosy from the cold and her eyes are that beautiful bright blue I love seeing. It's one hundred percent my favorite color.

"That's..." she giggles, stumbling as we walk up to Big Red, "That's literally the best thing I've heard in awhile."

"Glad you think so," I grin, opening the passenger door for her. She climbs in and sits alone in the truck's cab, trying to catch her breath. I walk around the front and climb into the driver's seat, my smile the biggest it has been all day. Suddenly the fatigue is gone.

I turn the key in the ignition and put the truck in reverse. I cautiously back out of the spot, put it into drive, and slowly make my way through the maze that is the large parking lot. We pull onto Boise Street– the street the school sits on – drive the short amount to the highway, and pull out onto it. Our laughing fit has dissipated, leaving behind a suffocating silence. I open my mouth to say something... anything... but nothing comes out. I'm deliberately avoiding the conversation about last night's phone incident so I'm not sure what else to talk about.

"Is this going to be one of those awkward car rides where no one talks so we just sit in silence?"

Evie coughs and begins laughing again. "Now that you said that it will."

A smirk finds its way onto my lips. "Well I think it is going to be regardless."

"It doesn't have to be," she giggles. "Well, I haven't been to Arctic Circle in a while, to be honest. My family don't really go out and eat much."

"My family is the complete opposite," I laugh, pulling off the highway and into the Arctic Circle parking lot. "My mom's a nurse so she works a lot and really doesn't have energy to cook so we eat out a lot. I mean, I'm slowly trying to learn to cook but I'm not that good yet. I really can only make macaroni, spaghetti, and Ramen."

I park in a free spot next to the door and turn off the truck.

"How about your Dad? Does he ever cook or does he work a lot too?"

Oh.

"Um, no," I choke. I know I can trust her but something deep inside me holds me back. But, I push past that. "My dad disappeared when I was nine."

The fear in Evie's eyes is unmistakable. "Oh my gosh, I didn't know!"

"No, no I know you didn't. It was so long ago and he was presumed dead so I've kind of moved on," I shrug. "I mean moving here was a little weird and heartbreaking but we did it anyway."

Her brows furrow abundantly as she stares at me with her lifeless blue eyes. “What do you mean it was weird?”

“He disappeared here in Bear Lake.” I really haven’t talked to anyone about his disappearance except for the therapist my mom made me see after it happened. But, I stopped seeing that therapist three years later. “Should we go in?”

She nods but seems to be off in another world. Evie stares at the handle quietly for about a minute before actually opening it. I follow her lead and step out. We walk side by side until I stop to open the glass door. My fingers wrap around the chilly metal and pull it open for her. She gives me a half smile and walks in.

Despite it being November, the fast food place is frigid with a strong icy breeze from the air conditioner. It brings me chills and one glance at Evie lets me know that she has them too. We step into the short line and I really don’t look at the menu. I get the same thing every single time. Chicken rings, fries, and a lime rickey. Chicken rings sound exactly as it is—breaded chicken in the shape of holed donuts.

When I look at Evie she seems to not be looking at the menu either, she just stands there looking at her feet.

“Already know what you want?” I ask, running my hand through my hair—which I do so much you’d be surprised my hair doesn’t get greasy easily.

“Yeah. I get the same thing every time. How ‘bout you?” Evie smiles, looking up at me. I have at least a full foot on her.

“Me too. I always get chicken rings, fries, and a lime rickey.” The line shortens more as another high schooler orders and goes to sit down.

Evie's eyes brighten and a smile builds on her pale freckled face. "That is my exact order."

"Really?"

What were the odds? Is it weird that I feel more attracted to her? More connected?

The junior in front of us has ordered and walks off. He flashes a smile toward me and allows Evie and I to step forward. I order for both of us and despite Evie's demands, I pay as well. She looks at me with a face of disappointment but I can tell she's hiding a smile. My heart flips upside down and I stick my wallet back into my front pocket.

The floor is tiled and is recently wet, causing our shoes to squeak as we make our way to a booth in the corner. It's right next to the room where the jungle gym is, which is silent from children. I settle in with my back to the room and she sits across from me. I glance out the window, watching cars pass as they drive on the highway, then back at the girl in front of me. She is doing the same.

Say something, I urge myself silently. *Don't be a wuss.*

"So... um... how'd you sleep last night?"

Yep, that was creepy. Way to go, Carter.

Evie coughs, laughs, and looks at me with her bright eyes. "Clearly better than you."

A smirk finds its way onto my lips. "I could see that."

I watch intently as Evie looks down at her clasped hands that sit on the booth's table. Her mouth opens briskly before being replaced with pursed lips. She seems to want to say something but must keep rethinking her words.

"I'm sorry about your dad," she gulps, keeping her eyes off of me.

I don't know what inhabits me to do it but I reach out and grasp her clasped hands with my right hand. She looks up at me with those beautiful pearls, shocked. "And I'm sorry about yours."

Evie nods, forcing a smile. I retreat my hand back into my lap. "It's whatever."

The thing about people who answer to their misfortunes with 'it is what it is,' is that you can't hurt them more than they already are. They are so used to being hurt or disappointed that they don't care anymore. They know that more bad luck will come their way. That's the most dangerous type of person.

Now what scares me most is I'm that way too. I haven't been hurt to the point where I'm used to it per se. I just have one of those attitudes where I know this is all supposed to happen. Every bad thing that happens to me is meant to happen.

"How's that new puppy of yours," Evie questions, pulling me from my thoughts.

I clear my throat and pull my phone from my front pocket. "She's great. I've got a picture."

I scroll through my photo gallery but don't have to go far. I click on a picture I took of her the day we received her. The three-year-old border collie was playing with Chev in the front yard when I snapped the picture. Well, I say playing but it was more like Chev was laying down while the puppy messed with him. Chev happily obliged by letting her too.

Evie examines the picture closely when I hand her the phone. She squints her cerulean eyes and a smile spreads across her face. "I'm a sucker for puppies."

"Yeah, same," I laugh. Evie zooms in on something, stares at it, and hands me back my phone.

I take it back and pocket it into my front pocket.

"What's the story of Chev? I mean that's a pretty unique name."

A chuckle escapes my throat and I angle my chin down to where I'm looking at my lap. "Dad and I named him after Chevrolet. Like the truck brand."

I look up to find Evie smiling. My breath escapes me and I'm left with no words. This girl.

"He's pretty old. When did you get him? When he was a puppy, or older?"

I glance outside again, to gather my thoughts... and air. "In Coos Bay, the town I lived in before moving, Dad and I adopted him without my mom's permission. When we came home with him after we were supposed to go get groceries, Mom was *furious*. But, I was already attached. I think Mom was more angry that we hadn't grabbed groceries at all."

Evie giggles and I continue telling her the rest. I tell her about how filthy he was and how you could tell he'd been living on the streets since birth. I tell her about how the shelter just guessed he was two so that's what we've gone by.

"He sounds like he's your best friend," Evie beams, her teeth white and oddly straight.

"Yeah," I sigh, looking back at my lap. "After Dad was presumed dead, I lost my best friend. Chev kind of took over the best friend position… He's been here with me ever since. I don't know what I would do if I lost him too."

The sound of Evie gulping echoes loud enough I can hear it. "Does it ever bother you that your Dad was never found?"

Oh yeah, I think. *Even though I've basically come to terms with it all, it still sometimes keeps me up at night.*

When we moved here some part of me just hoped he'd walk through our front door, perfectly alive and well. I hoped he would embrace me and apologize for not getting home sooner. Then, he would pet Chev and take my mom and Daphne in his arms. Mom would finally be able to stop working so hard to keep us afloat.

It is silly of me, I know. There is no way it is going to happen. The thing my Dad loved most in the entire world was family. He wouldn't willingly leave us.

"Everybody has a tragedy. My dad's disappearance is mine. Me not knowing what happened is mine."

That's what I tell myself every time I want to roll up into a ball and cry for Dad.

A server interrupts us and place a tray with our food in front of us. The server frightens us both to the point where we almost jump out of our seats. She gives us a ginger smile, her brown locks in two low buns. Evie and I quietly thank her in unison and then watch as she walks back into the kitchen, occasionally dodging a highschooler or elderly couple.

I look back to Evie, smile, and we both dig in as fast as we can. We don't say another word about each other's trials.

CARTER

Wednesday, May 18, 2022, Present.

Dad was one of those likable guys. He was the kind that had no enemies just friends and more friends. It's one of my favorite things about him. Hands down. Growing up he was my role model... well, he still is.

Coos Bay has a very large homeless community. Dad *always* helped folks he ran into that were struggling to find income or food. Or just struggling in general. I remember once we were eating at this *amazing* burger place called Vinnie's and an older lady who was probably in her fifties was sitting on the curb. Dad and I were eating outside and we could hear soft sobs coming from her. Her head was buried in her hands and her matted brown hair laid on her shoulders.

Without a word, Dad got up from the outdoor table and crossed the parking lot to the busy curb. I watched in wonder as he sat next to her, his blond hair standing out next to hers. He looked into traffic as the lady mumbled something. Still sitting a good fifty yards, I can hear nothing but unintelligible murmurs.

Dad nods and gets up. The lady gets up along with him and nervously follows him to our table, keeping her eyes down in what seems to be embarrassment.

"Here, sit here, Gladice," he had urged, ushering toward the seat across from me and next to his. The woman looked up at me with her dreary, empty, wettened brown eyes and then back at the seat. "Go on. It's okay."

With that, she takes a deep breath, then a seat, and looks back at me. The eye contact makes me fiddle around in my chair.

"Gladice, this is my son Carter." He turns his attention to me. "Carter, this is Gladice."

I stick out my hand in greeting, giving her a gentle smile. "Nice to meet you."

The pale-faced woman gulps sharply and takes my hand in hers. I shake her hand and return my hand back to my lap. A little hint of a smile spreads its way onto her face, causing glee in me. I flash her another smile and look for my dad but he has abandoned us. Gladice must realize this too because she begins to get out of her seat, glancing frantically around the parking lot.

I reach out for her. "No, Gladice, please stay. Please."

Her wrinkly face stares back at me and she immediately calms. The woman looks back around the parking lot and sits again.

"How old are you," she wondered in a scratchy, quiet voice, tugging at her long sleeved shirt.

I look down at my burger and fries and close the styrofoam box. I push it aside and set my hands on the table. "I'm seven. *Almost...*"

The wearisome lady smiles and runs her fingers through her shoulder length hair. "That is an amazing age. My son is six too."

That had confused me. I don't know why but something rung out in my ear 'she's homeless and has no child with her. She has got to be lying.' I was only six. I didn't understand.

"Your son? Where is he?"

Gladice looks up at me, shocked, and begins tugging at her shirt more hectically. Those brown eyes grew saddened and her wrinkles deeper with sorrow as she turns her attention to the blue sky. "Well he's up with his maker."

Oh.

The silence between us is deafening to the point where I think I can hear the ocean. I'm clearly mistaken because the ocean is still miles away. Even if it was possible, we wouldn't hear it, the bustling traffic would drown it out. I later depicted it as the ringing in my ear.

To my relief, dad came back five minutes later, a styrofoam box like ours in his right hand. Gladice tenses at the sight of Dad but when he hands her the food she softens drastically. Gladice looks down at the box placed in front of her then to my dad who is beginning to sit down. I watch carefully as tears touch her eyes.

All three of us ate together in the outdoor seating area, bathing underneath the sun's hot warmth for the next hour. Dad made small talk with the woman while I just observed.

An hour and a half ago he had seen this woman crying on the curb and his first thought was 'I've got to help this woman.' He bought her a smoked burger with fries and made sure she was okay on his *own* time. His smile lit her heart much like he lit mine everyday until he was declared missing. Sometimes to this day his smile still warms me and his kindness inspires me everytime I see a picture of him in our home or on my phone.

Now I'm sitting in a police station, staring at a picture of a piece of paper with his name written on it. What makes it all the more bizarre is it was found in my missing girlfriend's drawstring bag.

“Son, I'm going to ask you again... do you know why it was in Evie Baker's bag,” Sheriff Reggie repeats for what feels like the hundredth time this interview.

No. *I really don't*, I repeat in my head for what also feels like the hundredth time. I have been here for over two hours and have said the very minimum. Finally all of those true crime and police shows are paying off.

I don't meet Reggie's eyes but instead keep them in front of me. Two days ago, on Monday, I went to the station to convince them to investigate Evie's case, and now today—Wednesday—I'm here in the station not as a concerned citizen but as a suspect. A suspect for what very well may be Evie's mur... Evie's disappearance. I don't want to think about how she may not be alive at this moment. I'm just hoping she made it out of Idaho and maybe into Wyoming.

Sheriff Reggie doesn't give up, I'll give him that. “Carter, why do you think Evie would write down your Dad's name? He disappeared here in Bear Lake about eight years ago, correct? That must have been hard. Especially when he was presumed dead, am I right?”

What is your tactic here? It doesn't make any sense.

This man is all over the place. The only thing he is consistent about is thinking I had something to do with Evie's disappearance.

I look up to find he is staring deeply into my eyes, as if searching them for the answer he is so sure he will find. His gray eyes are almost calm for the amount of loaded questions he has asked. Although the wrinkles invading his face are deep with worry. He has got to be in his thirties at least.

"I have an alibi, Sheriff," I try and tell him again. I made sure to tell him earlier but he didn't care. He is dead set on getting me locked up in juvenile detention. I think most of it is a stereotype of me. Back in Oregon there are a *lot* of drug users and criminals where we lived. I'm sure he is unfairly stereotyping me.

"Oh yeah?"

Did he forget that I told him this already or was he not listening?

I look to the door, looking out the mini window on it. Mom still stands there, watching from a distance. I insisted I was fine and she could watch from the door's window.

"I was with my little sister Daphne and my mom on Sunday."

Reggie looks over to my mom and shakes his head. "We already depicted that she willingly left her house that night. It's our most highly possible theory."

Theory. It is all theories.

"Monday morning I was at school. Check the security cameras. Immediately after school I picked up my little sister and we went home. Then, I drove to the station around 8:30 and spoke with you. I have an alibi for all of Monday too."

I cross my arms over my chest and lean forward, putting all my upper body weight on my crossed arms. Sheriff Reggie has a defeated look to him but only for a split second. He wipes it away and sits back in his chair, crossing his arms too.

"I'll have to bring in your mom and sister then."

I hold back the urge to roll my eyes by shutting them. "You do that."

The room goes silent for a good two minutes and all I can hear is the ragged breathing of the sheriff. He doesn't say a word and only stares at me for the entire two minutes. I don't think he is even blinking.

"You want to know our theory of what happened, Carter Miller?"

Unconsciously I begin shaking my head back and forth, groaning deeply. "Go right ahead, Sheriff. You are going to tell me even if I say no."

He chuckles half heartedly and sits back up in his chair, pretending to look at the case file that has been sitting on the table the entire time. "Maybe Evie had your Dad's name in her bag because she knew the cops would see it. So, if she went missing or died we would find it and know exactly who he was because of his cold case from eight years ago. Then, in turn, we would be interrogating you because you are his son and you murdered Evie Baker."

"*What*? How does *any* of that make sense?"

Sheriff Reggie gets up from his chair, the file in hand. "Admit it, son. You murdered her."

Murder? We didn't even know if she has been murdered or hurt. For all we know she could have hitchhiked or walked to Wyoming. She could be in Cokeville for all we know. It'd be easy if she hitched a ride with someone. It's only like a thirty-five minute drive. *Murder* isn't a sure answer to this. Even if it is, I am the *least* likely candidate for *murdering* her.

There are so many faults to the theory. It would *never* hold up in court.

"Why would I call in that I found the bag? Why wouldn't she just write down my name? Why not save you guys the trouble if she was afraid I was going to... *murder* her? Admit it this is *insane*. I'm *seventeen* and her *boyfriend*."

"You could be lying that you two are dating to give you more rapport. Plus, we've been talking to some of your friends and *none* of them knew you two were dating. You can be a murderer at any age, even seventeen, Carter."

I scoff and bury my head into my hands. "We didn't want anyone to know."

"Why? Were you ashamed of her?" he presses on, placing the folder back onto the table.

I snap my head out of my hands. "No!"

I can't believe something so innocent like secretly dating her would get me accused of murder. No body has been found and I'm already getting accused of her murder. Oh gosh, *I need a lawyer*.

"Then *why would you hide your guy's relationship*?" he urges, pressing his palms on the wooden table. He leans his body weight on them.

"Because her parents would hurt her more if they found out," I blurt, my voice cracking severely. A familiar lump forms in my throat, causing a feeling of borderline suffocation.

The sheriff rolls his eyes and cocks his head back. "*This again*? I'm beginning to get annoyed by your accusations against her parents."

"I wouldn't lie about something that serious! I'm not kidding," I growl, rubbing a sudden itch beside my right eye.

Sheriff Reggie walks over to the two way window and helplessly stares through. "Paul Baker is a very respectful man. He is very respected around here. Now, I know you are somewhat new to the area and may not know that–"

"I've met him," I interrupt, feeling useless as I sit here. No one is going to believe me. No one is going to look past what they *think* they know to look at what makes sense. "I went to their house and talked to both him and his wife."

"You did *what*?!" He turns around, anger screaming in his eyes. "Their daughter just went missing so you decided to go over and accuse them? What were you thinking, son? You are *nothing* like your grandpa!"

Growing up I was always told that I was exactly like my grandpa. We had the same big heart and also shared that heart with my dad. Hearing I'm nothing like him *hurts*. It really does hurt.

"It was when she was declared a runaway. I wanted to change their mind since you wouldn't."

I'm getting sick of this and I'm hungry and tired. I just want to go home, eat a burger, lay down, and watch a movie. These past two days I have had are the most stressful days I've had in a *really* long time. I just need to unwind and not think about this situation for one night. Is a break too much to ask for?

The wooden door opens. I strain my neck to see and find my mother, her arms crossed on her chest. She looks almost as tired as I feel but that doesn't hide *her* vexed expression.

"Sheriff Reggie? Do you have any concrete evidence that my son is involved," she demands, walking over to me. Mom stops and stands at my side, a hand placed on my shoulder.

The sheriff stares at my mom in disbelief and shakes his head. "Not yet but –"

"Carter will be going home then. He has alibis and you have no evidence to prove he has something to do with that girl's disappearance."

Thank you. Thank you. Thank you.

Sheriff Reggie looks like he's about to fight but back down. His hand clutches the file so violently that before he can change his mind I get up out of the metal chair. He watches as we make our way out of the dimly lit room. I stop at the door and look back at him. "Have a good rest of your day, Sheriff."

***

I collapse on the couch, a Ranch Hand burger in a styrofoam box. Ranch Hand has been my favorite place to eat since we moved here. It sits beside the highway in between Bennington and Montpelier and is mainly a truck stop for semis. It has a cafe inside and a gas station as well.

I grab my bacon cheeseburger and take a large bite out of it, feeling fry sauce drip down my chin. I'm almost too exhausted to wipe it off. Diagonal from me, Daphne scoffs in disgust.

"Aren't you going to wipe that off? You are disgusting."

I shake my head and slowly chew my bite. I swallow and set down my burger. "I'm suspected for a murder they aren't even sure happened. I think a little fry sauce on my chin is the least of my worries."

It's supposed to be my version of a joke but Daph does not laugh, neither does my mom who sits in the recliner with her eyes closed. She opens them momentarily to stare at me and almost looks disappointed. I put my palms in the air in defense.

"I'm only trying not to mope around, Mom. Sometimes my way to cope is by making jokes."

Mom shakes her head and closes her eyes again. She brings her hands to her head temples and begins massaging them. A strong pang of sudden guilt invades my heart. *Oh. I'm sorry, Mom.*

I swallow my culpability and quietly eat the rest of my bacon cheeseburger and fries, listening to the ear-splitting stillness. After years of taking care of me, I'm doing harm to my mom...and none of it she deserves.

EVIE

Monday, May 16, 2022, Past

Chilled rain runs down my neck and into my back, causing an icy bite to spread throughout my body. My trembling fingers wrap around the hood of my state cheer hoodie and pull it over my already wet hair. I look down at my soaked-through white hoodie. It probably wasn't the best choice of clothing.

I look back toward my house. It's nowhere in view which comes as a blessing but I hurry my footsteps anyways. I'm still on ninth street which takes away my sigh of relief. The farther I am away from that house, the better. I'm not quite sure what I'm going to do but I'm sure I'll figure it out. As long as I don't have to go back to that house. If you met my family, you would understand.

Ford Motors is to my right with the dance studio to my left. Main Street is deserted without a soul or car in sight. Courtesy of living in a small town. I don't even glance to see if any cars could potentially hit me before dashing across the street. I make it to the other side with my converse soaked through from the puddles gathering on the road. Something drips down my cheek. I can't tell if it's sweat or a raindrop. Or a tear. What can I say… tragedy runs in my blood. I expected tonights events to go down sooner or later.

My legs stop abruptly as my eyes land on the darkened police station. I could go in. I should go in. I should tell them what's going on, I should. My legs become mobilized again and I step forward toward the door, reaching out with my trembling hands. It quickly comes apparent that no one is there. Not a single light is turned on and it's got to be close to midnight.

I force my legs to keep walking. They want to collapse from underneath me but I keep on walking. I have to keep on walking. The storm's frigid wind is immobilizing and feels like ice on my skin. My hoodie doesn't help with the chill and neither does the water dripping all over me.

I stop again, this time underneath the theater's awning, or a marquee as it's commonly called. It's lit up with lightbulbs and presents the times for some new Marvel movie. The best part of the marquee is it keeps the rain off of me. I can finally do what I've been meaning to since I found it out.

I take my drawstring bag off of my back and pull it open. I reach in and grab my phone. It glows as I press the 'on' button, illuminating a picture of Kace and me after a football game. I remember he forced one of his friends to take the picture. I move my eyes to the time. It's eleven forty-eight. My eyes wander again but to a fresh notification. Usually a smile would cross my lips but none comes. Carter sent me a good night text a few minutes ago accompanied with a yellow heart emoji, my favorite color.

Carefully I shove it back into my bag and get down to business. I grab a piece of notebook paper I ripped off from a notebook page as I was making my escape. Along with the piece of paper I grab a fat sharpie I snatched as well.

I take one more glance around the deserted street before scribbling down 'Noah Miller.'

Just in case, I repeat to myself. *Worse case scenario.*

I thrust the sharpie and paper back in my bag and swing it back around my shoulders. The rain drips off the awning and gathers in puddles. I *really* don't want to brave the rain. It's cold and *wet*. I've only been out in it for twenty minutes and I'm already sick of the constant soggy feeling.

I dig my chin into my chest and walk past the pizza place, Studebakers. It's deserted too. My feet travel across eighth street and onto the sidewalk again. The rain drenches me to the bone once again but I'm slowly getting used to it. Maybe by the time I know what I'm freaking doing I'll be fully used to it. I silently chuckle to myself.

My ears prick up, causing me to look over my shoulder. I *wasn't fast enough. I didn't make it far enough fast enough.*

I'm greatly mistaken though. The car that slows beside me is nothing like my family's van. It's a white 2017 Hyundai Elantra that rides low to the ground. It is *certainly* not my family. A sigh of relief escapes me.

The tinted drivers window rolls down, revealing an elderly face. She smiles at me warmly but her eyebrows are upturned in worry.

"Do you need a ride, sweetheart?"

I want to say yes. I really do. But, I don't know her. Just because she's elderly and has a warm, kind face doesn't mean she can't kill me or sell me off.

I remember she's staring at me with her kind, emerald eyes and snap back to reality. I shrug and look around again. Mom and Dad could be on their way for me right now. They know I know something I shouldn't.

"You're soaked through, dear," the lady observes. Her platinum white hair is cut in a pixie cut and she wears dangling copper earrings. I'd bet money she's a grandma.

"Where are you headed," I gulp. It *is* cold and wet and I may not be able to stand it anymore. Plus I can see her heater is on full blast. I can feel it from here. It tickles my face, causing a torn feeling.

"Geneva," she answers, watching the rain drips down my soggy hoodie.

Geneva's a good bet. From there it's a good three hour walk to the Wyoming border junction. That may sound like a lot but it's better than having to walk to Wyoming from here. That would take *at least* eight hours.

So, I guess I'm going to Wyoming.

"Can I... Can I hitch a ride, if possible?"

She nods toward the passenger seat, a gentle smile on her wrinkled face. I return the smile, walk to her lane, and walk around the front of the car. My quivering fingers wrap around the metal handle. It's like a glacier to my skin. I pull it open and sit in the warmed black leather seat.

"I'm sorry, I'm getting water everywhere." My voice is croaky and ragged. She probably thinks I'm crazy.

The lady chuckles quietly and presses the gas gradually. The car gets to the speed limit–twenty five. This car is nice and kept very well. The interior is a clean black and the heat is like a blessing. Only now do I realize I'm shivering.

"Why are you out in the rain so late? Look at you, you are quivering, sweetheart," she questions, glancing at me every other word. Other than that she keeps her eyes firmly on the darkened street. Everytime we pass under a streetlight, her pale hair and face light up with a warm orange glow.

I just shrug again. I need a story. I need an excuse... an answer. She would *never* help me run away from home. I may be seventeen but I look younger.

"Are you in trouble? Do you need some help?" She looks at me again, her milky eyebrows upturned again. "I can help you, honey."

"No, I don't need help," I lie, concluding it by biting my lip. "I'm not in trouble."

Another sideways glance. We go silent until the intersection of Main and Fourth where we have to wait at a stop light. *Could this go any worse?*

"I'm Olivia. You are?"

Should I use a fake name? No, I'll be fine, right? "Evie."

She nods and doesn't press for a last name. I silently thank her and watch as the car spins slightly as we take a left. I clutch tightly onto my knee and my eyes fly shut. I *hate* turns. Olivia doesn't bat an eye.

"Where am I dropping you off, sweetheart?"

Sweetheart. Honey. Dear. She's more motherly than my Mom ever has been. Well, I guess my mom did love me once. Before the accident.

Wait? Where *is* she dropping me off? I should have thought about it. I could have her drop me off in Geneva but that's suspicious. She may call me into the police or something. Then I'm thrown back into that house with dangerous people. I'll be right back where I started.

A light bulb. Growing up we used to camp at this one campsite. It was Kace and I's favorite as little kids. We always treated it as a vacation and it was such a big deal because grandma would come camp too. It was also so convenient to camp there because, well, there is a creek, a reservoir, and a pond.

"The reservoir just up Montpelier Canyon. It's on your way," I answer, trying to cough away my husky vocal chords. My throat is sore and hurts every time I speak.

"Yes, I know the one," she laughs. Her laugh is like a light from above. "Why the reservoir and why this late, honey?"

Think fast, Evie. Have mercy, Evie. You are an idiot just like everyone says.

"I-I was at a friend's house and stayed late. My family are camping at the reservoir and I couldn't get a ride back to the campsite."

Smooth. I guess growing up with the family I did, acquired me some serious lying skills. They must be good because Olivia seems to be believing me. She nods along with my lie and turns right onto Canyon Road. I almost feel bad.

* * *

I know we are here when I see the sliced hill. When the road was built through the canyon, they cleanly sliced through the mountain, leaving behind a unique landmark. In the daytime it is usually mutely reddened, but here in the pitch dark with no light, our headlights don't make out the color.

There are no streetlights out here which was always my favorite part as a kid. The only visible light is the campfires still lit in the tree ridden campground underneath the reservoir. Despite the time, families still gather around their fires.

"You can just drop me off right here. Beside the road. I can walk down to save you the trouble," I insist, already unbuckling my seat belt and dreading the outside's cold. The only good thing is it isn't raining out here. Olivia looks concerned with my plan and doesn't come to a complete stop yet, she just slowly cruises toward the entrance road to the campsite.

"Are you sure, Evie? It's no problem to me. Really, it isn't."

I cough a little and shake my head almost too aggressively. Olivia doesn't seem to become suspicious and nods quietly. The car comes to a complete stop and Olivia's fingers press the unlock button on her door. I take a deep breath and push open the door, triggering the overhead light in the cab. Making sure my bag is on my back, I step out.

"Thank you, Olivia."

She nods a 'you're welcome' and flashes me a smile. It warms my heart, her kindness. There needs to be more people like her in this corrupted world.

As soon as I step out I am welcomed by a frigid slap to the face. The rain left the canyon's air crisp and the ground severely sticky with mud. It's *going to be a rough night*. It's often warm during the summer but spring has bled into the May month. You can barely call it summer. No one in the valley is complaining though, we need the rain. But, tonight is a sucky night for it to have rained. Of all nights.

After I softly shut the door Olivia drives off toward Geneva. I watch quietly–hugging myself–as she drives past the sliced mountain and then around a bend where she disappears forever.

My shoulders are heavy with grief I haven't moved past quite yet, or addressed. I'll pass that bridge when I get there. Although I don't want to at all. I don't want to think about tonight's events.

Pushing back my shoulders, I travel down the gravel road leading to the campsites. I take a sharp right and sneak into the brown public restroom. I shut the door and cover my mouth. It's likely this restroom hasn't been cleaned in a *really* long time. It's smell is putrid and seems to singe my nose hairs.

I quickly use the toilet and take off my hoodie. Bumps form on my skin as my skin comes in contact with the chilly air. I shove it underneath the air dryer and it shoots to action. I'm so glad they put this in a few years ago. It's slow though and doesn't do much. After ten minutes of my jacket being underneath the dryer it is still soggy... but warm.

I slip my arms in and chills go up my spine. Once it is fully back on I almost have the urge to smile. Nothing comes. I think my smile is broken. Shaking my head, I pull my black drawstring bag back on and step back out of the restroom. Another wave of frigid air hits me.

I keep my head down and head across the gravel road and to the creek. Almost immediately I can hear the singing water as it rushes around rocks and boulders. It's music to my ears. Moving water is generally drinkable. In dire situations...

I'd call this an emergency, I think to myself, crouching on the grassy bank.

I take my bag off of my back and open it up. I have to dig for a minute before I find an empty plastic water bottle I dug out of my trash before I fled my home. The water is freezing as I fill the bottle up. My fingers tremble more than usual and start to go fully numb. My shaking hand brings the bottle to my lips and I take a long sip. I quickly swallow before I can throw up. After twisting the lid back onto my water bottle I stick it back into my bag. It hits a granola bar and makes a sound that is flushed out by the creek's tune.

The night's darkness makes it extremely hard to see but as my eyes adjust it becomes easier. I spot a grassy spot underneath one of the tree bush things. Its leaves are a mixture of red and brown and it towers me by a foot or two. I stick my bag underneath the bush and curl up. Laying my head on it, I close my eyes, shivering severely. Let's hope I don't get frostbite or something. Or freeze to death.

I have no idea what I'm doing and I fear I'm not safe. Not until I get out of this county.

CARTER

Saturday, November 20, 2021, Past.

I pull into the Broulims parking lot as the sun is high in the cerulean sky. The lot is full despite it being Saturday and not tourist season. I have to drive around the lot for five minutes before a spot opens up in the back.

My fingers wrap around my key and twist it then pull it out. I take a minute to sit and agonize walking before actually pulling open Big Red's door. It opens with an ear splitting *creak* but to me it's a beautiful sound. It's a sound that oddly gives me comfort.

A breeze ruffles my faded red 'Dr. Pepper' shirt, giving me chills. I probably should have worn a hoodie. Fall is approaching fast—which is very normal around here. By October it will already be snowing. It makes for a cold Halloween, which is a thousand percent my favorite holiday. Last year, when I moved here, I was super bummed it was snowing on Halloween... and that we couldn't hand out candy because we are in the middle of nowhere basically. I would have liked to go trick or treating but I'm seventeen and my friends aren't into doing that kind of thing. It worked out though because I stole some of Daph's candy.

I'm thankful for my thoughts because not once have I thought about my knee, which is throbbing now. The automatic doors slide open and another burst of cold air hits me. I take a sharp right in the small hallway type thing to where they keep the carts. There's a good thirty in here that sit in an unordered fashion. I pass the bulletin board that is overfilling with flyers and posters and grab my own cart. On the child seat flap there's a sticker that goes into great detail about how a child should never hang off the front or sides, but come on we all did that. If you didn't as a kid you didn't have a childhood.

The main grocery store doesn't seem as crowded as the parking lot but that's probably because it's a fairly big building. I mean it isn't as big as the average Walmart but that's also because this is a small valley. Although, this building is even chillier than outside. I shiver again and push my cart to the produce section. Mom is stuck at work for the night shift and sent me for groceries for some dinner she's planning. It's weird that she's planning a dinner because she doesn't seem to have friends... not since Dad's disappearance. She's been so caught up in taking care of Daphne and me that she doesn't go out and make friends. I feel guilty about that. Having no one to vent to or talk to takes a huge toll on a person. Mom needs girlfriends to complain to when Daph and I are acting up. Maybe she finally did find some.

Wheeling my cart toward the meat aisle, I double check the list Mom texted me. It's a fairly short list which is also odd because we *always* need a bunch of stuff. It's never shorter than five things like this one is.

I snatch a plate of pork chops and place them into my empty cart. We have pork chops quite often... well when Mom cooks. You really can't mess them up.. I'm not saying Mom is a bad cook, she's amazing, but sometimes the flavor isn't there.

"Carter, hey," a voice exclaims from behind me. I turn around to find bright blue eyes and messy dirty blond hair.

"Kace," I greet, shoving my left hand in my front pocket and setting the other one on the shopping cart's handle. "Fancy seeing you here."

I haven't talked to him since that one practice that I asked about Evie at. Except now his hair isn't drenched in sweat. I swear he is the only guy I've met that is already sweating before football practice even starts.

"Here alone?" The junior shoves his own hands in his pockets and comfortably glances around me. After he finishes his short inspection of the large produce section of the store his eyes land on me and almost take my breath away. They honestly are identical to Evie's and it's slightly unsettling.

"Yeah. My mom's working the graveyard shift at the hospital so I was sent for groceries. You?"

Judging by the lack of a shopping cart for Kace, he is definitely with someone. Maybe it's Evie. I would *kill* to talk to her right now. I'd kill to see her. That girl has got me wrapped around her finger and she doesn't even know it.

"Oh, I had no idea your mom is a healthcare worker. That's cool," Kace grins, his teeth showing. Then, it drops, causing him to hide his face as he stares at his dirty sneakers. "I'm with my mom, actually."

The mom? As in the mom who verbally and emotionally abuses Evie... his sister? The mom who may even be abusing her physically. My grasp on the shopping cart tightens profusely, initiating my knuckles to grow inhumanly white. My teeth clench down on my bottom lip and I feel my lungs shut down slightly. Why couldn't it have been Evie?

"Oh."

Kace nods, seeming oblivious to my sudden rising anger, and runs his fingers through his messy mop of hair. His part sits to the left on his head and he has somewhat of a Tom Holland haircut. You can tell he tried to use gel to smooth the messy hair but it has been brushed out of his hair by his fingers. The traditional scissor cut matches him and his clear skin perfectly.

My eyes wander behind him as a lady sneaks next to us hesitantly, wheeling a silver cart in front of her. She can't be more than forty but her wrinkles tell a different story. Her dyed blonde hair is worn in tight curls and she's dressed in a black, unzipped runners jacket, light wash skinny jeans, and a purple and white striped shirt. The lady dresses young but that doesn't help cure her wrinkles.

"Oh, Mom, hi," Kace greets, forcing a smile as she settles next to him. "This is my friend."

His mom's smile doesn't reach her dark blue eyes as she meets mine but I return the smile anyways. Well, the best smile I can force. Evie's eyes are *nothing* like her mother's and maybe that's a good thing because they remind me of the bottomless ocean in a storm. I watch with disgust as the lady offers her hand. I don't want to shake her hand. Not now with what I know. It would imply that I respect her or that I'm happy to meet her. This mother doesn't deserve that. I saw those bruises on Evie.

The woman retreats her hand back to the gray handle of her half-full cart awkwardly and nods simply. I just can't stop watching her and I want to say something but I'm completely silent. My jaw freezes and my brain races. I should say something. I should ask what drives a parent to hit their child. Or children. Although Kace wears short sleeves constantly and there isn't a single sign of bruises. Maybe it is just Evie. But, unfortunately I can't say a word.

A thought protrudes my brain. There could be a chance that Evie isn't being hit by her mom and only her dad. The dad could be hitting her mom as well and she's too scared to leave. The thought brings puke to my mouth. I swallow it back and force another smile.

"How are you ma'am?" I muscle, trying to relax.

Kace's mom glances at him before looking back at me with confusion. "Joanne. Please call me Joanne."

Gulping, I nod with a smile. "Joanne. Okay."

I look to Kace for him to dig me out of this hole but he's unaware of how awkward and anxious I feel. He just smiles as he looks between us, bubbly as ever. Like a plan has come into motion or something.

"And what's your name?" Joanne quizzes, examining the different bags of cereal and milk in her cart briskly.

"Carter."

She smiles but once again it doesn't reach her stormy eyes. "Handsome name for a handsome boy."

Kace chokes on air and I can't help but hold back a chuckle. *What*? The junior boy and I make eye contact and begin laughing together.

He clutches his stomach, peeking at his mother with his squinted eyes. "*Mom*! That's not–Mom..."

"Well I'm sorry, Kay! He is a very handsome boy. Am I not supposed to compliment your bigshot friends?" Her voice is high and hysterical but lined with laughter.

With that, his laughter dies down and I follow his lead.

Kace leans in and keeps his voice to a whisper. "*Mom*, he's a senior!"

I don't think he wanted me to hear that but I snicker anyways. Seniority rocks.

Joanne looks at me warily and uses one hand to shove her son away. "What's your last name, Carter?"

"Miller. My full name's Carter Miller."

"Who are your parents?"

That is such a parent question. Whenever Mom ever meets my friends she *always* asks who their parents are. I don't quite understand why.

"Brinley and Noah Miller."

I will never forget the fear shown on her face in this moment. It invades her face starting in her eyes. It then spreads to her eyebrows, then her mouth, and then her jawline. It's like a plague that I don't know the cause of.

Joanne was all smiley but now she's been infected by a nameless plague.

Joanne grabs ahold of Kace's arm and begins pulling him away. "Come on, Kace, we need to get home. We can't stand here all day. We have important stuff to do." Kace looks as shocked as I do as his mother drags him away. With his free hand he waves at me. "Talk to you later, Carter!"

"Yeah," I cough underneath my breath.

What just happened?

EVIE

Monday, November 22, 2021, Past.

My fingernails dig at the skin on my wrist, causing a pain to rise in my arm. Anything to keep my mind off of the anxiety that crawls around in my brain and body.

He's coming, I repeatedly think to myself. *He's going to come.*

But is he?

I want to think that he's coming and I should know he's coming. He could be late. It happens. People are late all the time. He's probably running late. Carter is the sweetest boy ever. He's not abandoning me.

Have mercy, I'm speaking like he's leaving me at the altar. I am pathetic. He's only running late to the movies.

Shaking my head, I look up at the awning thing above me that displays the times. From this angle I'm unable to see the movie but I know it's some new movie Carter invited me to see. All I see are lights emitting bright gleams despite it being only sunset, and the wooden boards lining the awning.

I direct my eyes to the poster that sits between the theater and the pizza place that shows the movie. I stifle a giggle in my throat and shake my head again. *Clifford The Big Red Dog*. It's not even the cute cartoon I used to watch with Grandma when I was little. It's a creepy live action version. Of all movies, of course Carter chose this one to watch.

The familiar rhythm of a truck's engine causes my ears to prick up. I turn around to spot a rusty red pickup pull into the parking lot beside the building. I lose sight of him quickly because the parking lot is out of my view. I face the city hall and watch the sidewalk carefully, suddenly aware of how much I have pinched away at my arm. I lift my hoodie sleeve and examine the red that lives among the purple and green. As Carter rounds the corner and begins walking on the sidewalk, I quickly slide my sleeve back down. He greets me with a warm smile and a wave.

"Sorry I'm late! I had to drop my sister off at a sleepover and Google Maps was no help."

A small smile spreads across my face. *He's here.* "You're okay. I was perfectly well underneath this awning thingy."

He seems satisfied and nods, a happier smile on his face as he stands perfectly in front of me. "It's actually called a marquee. That's it's official name."

I finally begin smiling fully and almost start laughing.This boy just keeps surprising me. *No one* knows that. At least I don't. "Why do you know that?"

Carter shrugs and looks up at the wooden board lining the bottom with his creamy caramel eyes. "My dad told me about it once when we were visiting my grandparents."

Sympathy stabs my heart and I feel like I want to throw up. I feel regret every time I bring up his dad even though he has no unresolved pain in his facial expression. Carter has come to terms with it all. I don't understand how though. He has no idea what happened to his dad or even if his dad is dead. But he's just moved on from it all. It honestly makes *me* feel pathetic. I wish I could move on from Grandma's death. I'd do anything to move on. Anything.

Carter snaps me out of my head and points to the doors with his thumb. "We should probably go in."

His smile just melts away my problems.

Together we walk to the paying booth that sits outside the theater and next to the current movie poster. An older man sits in it and I recognize him but I never remember his name or why I know him.

Carter pays for me—which I didn't tolerate but he did it anyways—and we go in through the glass doors. *Which he held for me.* It makes me go all dizzy and red and I have to pinch myself back to reality. I thank him and join a ton of children in the small lobby.

The smell of buttered popcorn causes my nose hairs to dance and my cravings to start. Centre Theatre—the name of the movie theater—has the best popcorn around. No one can beat it. It is, and will always be, my favorite. Although, there's a long line to get some so my cravings will have to wait.

"So... *Clifford The Big Red Dog*, huh?" I look up at him and giggle. I become suddenly jittery as he smiles and chuckles heartily.

"Yep. It's a classic."

I can't help but stare at him in silence. I know I've already said this but THIS BOY. I mean it, where did he come from? No one has ever been this good and *cute*. No one I've met.

Carter doesn't wait for me to talk and continues, running his tan fingers through his chocolatey locks. "The truth is I can't wait for another movie—preferably not meant for kids—to come out. I wanted to take you out on a date now. I can't wait. So, I guess we get to watch good old Cifford."

I think you know what I'm going to say. *This boy* came out of nowhere and I guess I'm shocked. I thought Grandma was the last good person and maybe that's because ever since... Well, ever since she passed, everything has gone downhill and all of the people I've come into contact with were terrible people. There was never a person who didn't use me to yell at or release steam. There was never a person who didn't tease me or bully me. Now, suddenly, there is someone who doesn't yell at me or hit me. There's finally someone who doesn't tease me or bully me.

It's hard to swallow back the tears but I somehow still do. Carter must notice too because his eyebrows arch into U's and his mouth opens slightly. He closes it quickly and doesn't say a word. I am grateful for that. Crying or anything like that gets me punished in my house.

"You could've waited a few more days," I smile, forcing it considering what I'm trying to hold. "*Encanto* is being shown soon and it's supposed to be *really* good."

He just laughs and shrugs. I've noticed he does that often.

"So, what's your favorite color, Eve?"

"Eve," I question, rolling it around my tongue. "Eve?"

Carter seems more worried and scratches the back of his neck nervously.

He seems to do that when he's skittish. "Is it okay that I call you that?"

I nod because it is. I've never had a nice nickname before. Plus, it makes Carter smile which is always a good thing to see.

"So, what is it? What's your favorite color?" he repeats, shoving his hands in his front pockets. He does that often too. So does my brother. Maybe it's a guy thing.

I examine the beige walls just so I don't have to make eye contact. That's probably one of my worst qualities. "Yellow. What's yours?"

The line gets significantly shorter as a big family of five make their way carefully past some curtains that lead to the theater itself.

"I like blue. Why do you like yellow? Any specific reason?"

I shrug but I know exactly why. It's a happy color and I'll do anything for a little happiness. Yellow reminds me of the sun. The sun reminds me of sunsets. And sunsets are the promise of a new dawn. A new tomorrow. But I can't tell Carter that. He'll just think I'm some depressed girl. Or he'll laugh.

Another family gets their popcorn, candy, and drinks and leaves the tiny lobby. This means we are next after the family of three in front of us who are ordering. Carter and I step forward and once again I'm examining the walls. From the floor to a little over a quarter of the wall there is dark red carpet with a very old pattern of what looks like light red leaves topped with a grayish green. It's the same kind of carpet that covers the floor. It probably is the same carpet they put in when they first built the theater in 1923. Ew. And cool.

Finally it's our turn. We get a large popcorn tub, two Dr. Pepper's, and no candy. I insist on paying at least for this one but Carter turns me down again, insisting 'we are technically on a date and the guy always pays on the date.' It doesn't really change my mind because we are literally in the twenty-first century. But, I let him do it just this time. I'll pay next time.

'*Next time.*' If there's a next time. Oh, I hope there's a next time.

After Carter pays, we grab our stuff and make our way to the entrance of the theater. There are two ways into the theater and each entrance has a red curtain draped beside them. When the movie starts they close them to block out the lobby light. We take the left door and are immediately greeted by dim light. The lights are turned on slightly, just enough to where we can see in front of us. The large screen at the bottom of the theater is playing ads and trailers for different upcoming movies and blares the sound. Most of the seats are filled with large families so we make our way down the carpeted aisle to the left section of padded seats. There are three sections, the left, the right, and the middle.

We settle near the front.

We have an entire three rows of seats to ourselves, which is a blessing. I don't think I can deal with kids kicking the back of my seat the entire time. I take a seat first, the fifth seat from the wall, and Carter takes the seat next to me.

"Excited for Clifford?" Carter laughs, popping a singular piece of popcorn into his mouth.

I follow his lead, finally giving in to my popcorn temptations. "Oh yeah, I hear it's a rager. Lots of violence and gore."

Carter smiles smugly and chuckles quietly. "Yeah, I heard that too."

The final ad ends and the lights slowly turn off. There's a reminder to not be on cellular devices, then it begins.

"Here we go," Carter whispers into my ear, his breath warm.

I stifle a giggle and reach my hand into the popcorn tub for a handful. Carter must have the same idea because soon our hands are touching and an electrical current runs up my spine. Our eyes meet and time freezes, but I begin freaking out internally.

Is this happening? Am I going crazy?

This always happens in the movies but never to me. *Never* to me.

Carter grins ear to ear, shrugs, and takes my hand into his. I'm lucky it's pitch black in here or he would see how red my entire face is. I don't have to see it to know I'm blushing uncontrollably.

The movie screen flashes white and my strawberry-colored face is displayed for Carter to see. I can't help as giggle when I see Carter… *Carter*… is blushing too. It's just how they describe in the books. The sparks and all of it. With the amount of electricity running through me, my hair should be sticking straight up. Maybe it is, but all I'm focused on is Carter's eyes.

He squeezes my hand and leans in to whisper. "I meant to reach in at the same time. I totally meant to do that."

Carter Miller even winks before turning his attention to *Clifford The Big Red Dog.*

***

When I say I couldn't focus the entire movie, I'm not kidding. I don't even know what happened in that movie. I just know that the live action version of Clifford is terrifying. No cartoon animal should be put into a live action movie. It's just plain scary. It's nightmare fuel.

Carter and I emerge from the doors along with some children. We both haven't stopped laughing since the movie ended. The ending wasn't funny or anything, we are just laughing uncontrollably. I don't know why he's laughing but I'm laughing because of how frightening Clifford looked next to normal human beings.

It's chilly outside but lively. Children are running around laughing and playing as they wait for the theater to open up for the next showing of the movie. The lights above us embedded in the bottom of the marquee are warm but the frigid air bites my face. Carter and I stop right under the awning in the middle, facing each other, still giggling and smiling.

"Please tell me that you thought that Clifford is creepy too," I ask, out of breath.

Carter meets my eyes and nods enthusiastically. "Oh yeah. Big time."

We begin laughing again and I think I might get abs. My stomach hurts with a good kind of pain. A happy pain. Infact, I'm crying. Tears of joy and happiness streak down my cheeks and drip off of my jaw. I peek at Carter to see if he's doing the same thing but he's only smiling, watching me. My laughter dies down dramatically and leaves behind a toothed grin as I examine his gentle features. He has such a perfectly sharp jaw and rosy cheeks. His skin is a warm tan that doesn't begin to match his cozy eyes. Those calm, caramel eyes.

Carter takes both of my hands and it should feel familiar from the entire time we held hands during the movie. But, it doesn't. It's unfamiliar in a way that I want to get used to. It creates warm tickles in my body and a bigger smile to my face.

The bustling kids around us melt away and then the world. It's all cliche but all true. There is no one but us in this moment. No one but two seventeen-year-old teenagers standing in a warm, yellow void.

Then my heart stops as he begins to lean in. Ever so slowly. Ever so gently. No hesitation. He wants to kiss me and I want him to. I don't care that it's our first date.

His lips are only inches from mine. Carter is so close I can feel his warm, butter popcorn breath. So close.

Then a kid slams into both of us and pulls us from the moment. Carter pulls away and steps back. He begins scratching at the back of his neck and I begin digging at the skin on my wrist. The kid isn't more than eight but his mother scolds him anyways. She was probably watching us, cheering us on, but her little boy interrupted us.

Man, I could have had my first kiss. My first kiss at seventeen. But, that little kid ruined it.

I look at Carter. Carter and I make eye contact. Then we switch it to the kid. Then to the mom. Then back at each other. As if on cue, we both double over in laughter.

I guess we will have to try again next week at Disney's new *Encanto*.

EVIE

Tuesday, November 23, 2021, Past.

"How come you didn't tell us you got a C- on your math test?"

I've never been very good at math: not in elementary school, not in middle school, definitely not in high school. I know that if I keep it up I have no possibility of getting out of this place. Essentially, my life depends on it.

I keep my eyes on my half-eaten dinner. I'm not really hungry tonight. I never really am anymore. "That was two weeks ago, Mom."

"Well, you should've told us sooner. It's been two weeks. We had to hear it from your math teacher. Do you know how embarrassing that is for us?"

"I'm sorry," is all I can spit out. I know it means nothing to them but with some childish hope maybe it'll work this time. "I'll do better."

My father joins the argument. "That isn't good enough. You are going to go to that teacher tomorrow and request to retake it."

"I will."

The sound of metal against glass echoes across the dining room. My body tenses as I meet mom's eyes. Her furious eyes. Her fork is no longer in her hand but on her glass plate. Holding back my tears, I meet my brother's sympathetic gaze. This isn't the only time my parents have blown up on me. I'm the disappointment of the family. I'm used to it all.

"Evie, you do realize we want you to do better but you go around all 'I don't care about anything. I'm better than everyone else,'" Mom glares, her fists clenched on the table top.

"That isn't fair," I growl underneath my breath.

As soon as I say it I know I've messed up. These slip ups are dangerous.

"What did you just say to me, young lady?"

"I said that isn't fair."

Jeez, Evie. You could have left it there but no, you had to go the whole ten miles, huh?

Afraid to meet their eyes, I eyeball my cooling food. I have never done anything like that. I have to be careful, yet here I am running my mouth with the free will I don't have.

"Young lady, you better go up to your room before you say something you'll regret," Dad steams, pushing his chair out so he can stand up. "Now."

My stomach sinks dramatically as I sit here, unable to move an inch.

"Evie Janiece Baker, I said get to your room!"

Evie, move! Move! Stand up! Evie, seriously!

It doesn't take long before he's charging around the table, headed straight for my chair. It all seems to happen in fast forward. Dad's hand clutches my chair and upheaves it, taking it out from underneath me. I land hard on the dining room floor, slamming against the wood harder than I have ever. A crack echoes in the dining room/kitchen.

"Dad!" Kace screams somewhere in the near distance.

Strong fingers grab my upper forearm, dragging me up with so much force that it can only be my father. Everything is a dramatic blur of the colors of the dining room walls. A yelp escapes my throat as I am put back on my feet. Stinging pain rings across my cheek that quickly shuts my screams up. Another sting demands to be noticed. My wrist.

Somewhere in the hassle, I make eye contact with my two sisters, Allie and Riley. Their eyes are wide with fear. They are huddled together by Mom—who doesn't give a hoot about what's happening to me. Nonetheless, Allie and Riley shouldn't see this. They don't need to see their oldest sister hurt by their father. They don't need to see their father break their older sister's wrist.

"You do what I say, Evie Janiece! You hear me?!" my father's voice explodes in my face. His eyes are wild with the rage I'm so used to seeing.

"Yes-Yes sir," I croak, praying silently that he lets me off the hook. Also praying silently that my throbbing wrist will quit. It needs to stop.

"Paul, I think she's learned her lesson," my mom sighs, urging my siblings back into their seats at the table. "Evie, go to your room. Kace, Allie, Riley... sit down and finish your dinner."

Dad stares into my eyes longer, his grasp on my arm tight. Will he ever let go? I doubt it. Dad has never stepped down from a fight.

"Mom. Dad," Kace's voice rings out, soft and quiet. "I think her wrist is broken. She needs to go to the E.R."

I clutch my eyes shut, still being handled by my father.

Please, I silently beg. *Please take me away from here. I'll settle on anything else. The* E.R. *The mountains. A ditch.*

Mom sighs and to my surprise—and relief—Dad pushes me away. I stumble backwards, eager to flee to the safety of my room before I begin crying like I know I will. My eyes have already begun to blur. But, I can't flee to my room.

"I'll take her," Kace offers, still refusing to sit down. His eyes are dead set on me but he's clearly talking to his parents. *His* parents.

"No," Mom snaps, her voice echoing dangerously. It's so high pitched it may shatter the dinner plates.

We all flinch, even Allie and Riley. Dad, though stays still, his fists clenched at his sides. He watches me with his teeth clenched and his eyes full of fury. A shiver runs up my spine, causing goosebumps to form on my skin.

"I will take her. I will. You understand? I am her mother," Mom growls, stomping to the kitchen counter to grab her keys.

Yeah, right. What a mother you are.

"Go get your shoes on," she demands, causing me to snap into action.

I dash to the door and slip on my converse with my free hand. I keep my broken wrist level in front of me—every single movement causing a twinge of unbearable pain. It's nothing like any pain I have suffered through.

I leave me shoelaces untied because it takes two hands and I go out the door without my mom. She groans in the kitchen and kisses my father before following me. She *kisses* him.

Opening the truck's white door, I keep my hand on my swelling left wrist. I'm lucky it wasn't my right. *Lucky*. Isn't that funny?

Mom trudges across the lawn to the driveway that sits in front of a separated white garage, her face sour with rage. She throws the truck door open and slams it. The truck starts and Mom floors it out of the driveway and onto ninth street.

She's furious like this is all *my* fault.

***

After the hospital I stagger into my room, not wasting time.

My legs give out within seconds of stepping foot into my refuge. Unfortunately, I miss my bed and melt to the ground despite my fractured wrist. Why am I even crying? I need to get my act together. I can't fall apart now. Or ever. That's the last thing I need and want. Nonetheless, my sobs ring out into the quiet, echoing against the wall. My hand flies to my mouth, clutching it closed. If Dad hears my cries, he would surely hurt me more than a slap to my face or a push to the ground.

I breathe in and out in careful motions, steadying my trembling breath. I shut my eyelids, listening to the eerie sound of silence.

"Grandma? How—How are you?"

Silence. That is typical.

"Why is my education more important than my mental health?" My cheeks are itchy from my sultry tears as I hope she can hear me. "Why must I endure eight hours of torture and suffering each day in what seems like a prison. They say they care about us students but when they fail us they don't help us improve. It's all corrupted. But hey… at least it is better than being at home where I'm not loved, cared for, and not welcomed. Where I'm constantly being yelled at and falsely accused. My mental health is slowly getting worse each day but at least I haven't murdered myself…

"The only attention I receive is negative. I'm never noticed by anyone unless they need someone to take their anger out on. I'm never noticed because of my achievements and good qualities but because of my mistakes and wrongs. Life keeps getting tougher, and I… I keep getting weaker.

"One of these days I won't be able to deal with life's torture and challenges. Which is exactly what everyone wants, right? Not even me crushing on a guy makes me happy for long periods of time. It only lasts an hour before it is crushed by the heels of life's heavy boots. Every day more of me dies, taking my ability to be happy to its grave... I don't know how I'll make it through this."

Only one year more until you're out of this, I tell myself she's saying.

The ceiling is nice to look at. It's platinum white, dyed with the night's darkness. It takes my mind and nurtures it. The ceiling changes every few hours depending on the position of the moon and sun, or the light fixtures that are inserted into the painted drywall. Just like me. Except my mom and dad represent the darkness while the sun and moon's light are nonexistent. Grandma was my sun, moon, and light. But now she's gone, leaving me behind to suffer.

"How is heaven, Grandma?" I croak into the stillness.

It had been nine years and my grandma had never answered me, but I—for some odd reason—never gave up. It is my one last sliver of hope in this dire world.

CARTER

Wednesday, November 24, 2021, Past.

Nixon and Dave insist that I sit next to them. In fact, they are quite literally begging. But, I have my eyes on Evie. We almost *kissed* Monday night at the movies. I almost *kissed* her. Then that stupid kid got in the way. Usually, I'm not spiteful about kids but this particular one... I really am mad. I was so close. I felt her warm breath. It smelled like the buttered popcorn served at the theater. She told me it was her favorite even though she's never had any other movie theater popcorn. Although, I have and it was definitely the best. It was the perfect amount of salt and butter and it had something else in it. Oddly, it made her breath smell pretty good. It wasn't going to be my first kiss but it was definitely going to top it. *Definitely.*

"Dude. I don't even know why you're going over there. I mean look at her," Dave argues, ushering toward Evie with his head. She sits alone like usual but she looks like a mess from here... and that's saying something because she's beautiful.

Evie's wearing a black hoodie with a singular, white outlined sunflower where her heart is.

"Shut up," Nixon snaps at Dave, burying his head in his hands. "If he wants to go over. Let him. Stop fighting. I'm glad that girl is getting friends, even if it is Carter."

That comes as a surprise. Usually Nixon is annoyed but today he isn't fighting with me. I shift my eyesight from Nixon to Dave. Nixon looks perfectly fine. No eyebags or anything like that. He's clearly not struggling with anything that I can see.

"Nix, you good?"

He nods his head and smiles his 'clueless' smile. Nixon's smile always looks to be like he's clueless. "Yeah. I just think that no one should be alone like that."

Dave coughs and shakes his head. "Whatever."

"Look, Dave," I begin, glancing over at Evie and then at him. "I don't need your approval. You've got Nix. Evie needs me."

Nixon ruffles his mullet and Dave glares at the ground. "Well then go, Carter. Just go."

I give Nixon the 'look' before walking away. He seems weird. The other day we were fighting all over the place but now... now he's supporting me. I wonder if he's going through something. If he is, I hope he talks to Dave about it. Nixon doesn't talk much about feelings and stuff like that but maybe he knows it'll eat him alive.

I take a seat next to Evie but she doesn't notice me immediately. Her music must be too loud. I tap her shoulder, causing her to jump. When she sees me she looks suddenly calm... but not *fully* calm. I watch as she pulls her earbuds from her ears and give me a half smile. It's nothing like the smiles I've witnessed. I guess everyone is going through something today.

"Hey," she greets quietly. Her voice is soft but strained. Something happened.

I gulp. This is always a loaded question but here we go. "What is it? What's wrong?"

That's when I notice it: the white cast hidden underneath her black sleeve. She tried to hide it but I can see it where it wraps between her thumb and index finger.

"Evie! What happened?!"

She shushes me as others look, looking for the cause to the commotion. I take a deep breath and reset the volume of my vocal cords.

"Evie... What happened?" I repeat in a low whisper.

Her eyes are puffy and she wears no mascara today. She always does but today the only sign of it is a little residue she missed underneath her chin. Like she had been crying and it streaked down. No, I bet that's exactly what happened.

"I fell and broke my wrist, no biggy," she answers in a raspy voice. She stops typing some kind of essay and closes her dead blue eyes. I thought I had cured that dead look in her eyes. Apparently not. I also know she's lying. Yes, she broke her wrist, but she couldn't have fallen.

"Eve," I warn, setting my hand on her arm to avoid the cast.

She stays silent as she stares at the back of her pale eyelids. But, I can't stand the silence. Not with the question throbbing at the back of my head.

My fingers squeeze her arm. "Evie. Who did this to you?"

Her eyes snap open and find mine. She has some fight in her but not enough to *convince* me she fell.

"I fell," she repeats, sounding out of breath. It sounds like she's been holding her breath for hours. Maybe she has. Evie's probably been holding whatever happened for hours.

"Evie, if they did that to you, you should tell me. I can help. I can. I promise."

A tear rolls down her left cheek, causing her pale, acne-ridden skin to glisten a sickly glow. "No. No, you can't help, Carter. There's no way to help."

"No, I can. We can go to the police. Together. Your parents will be charged and all will be fine. All will be okay."

Deep down, I know I can't talk her down from this ledge. She's broken and fractured with no place to go. School is agony. Home is torment. At this given moment, I'm all she has left. She lost her grandma and everything went downhill, now I understand that. I've got to do *something* to fix this though. I've got to fix this problem of hers. I have to. This girl can't survive much longer. Even I know that.

"I can't–" her voice breaks, "–put my siblings in that situation. If I turned my parents in we will all go to some abusive foster home or juvenile detention. That's where they send the kids like me. But, I can't do that to Allie, Riley, and Kace. My parents love them and actually care for them. If they get taken away–"

More tears roll down her cheeks so she sets her forehead on her computer keyboard, oblivious to the several letters being put down on her document. I leave my hand on her left arm. I don't think I can do this.

"Evie..."

"No, Carter. You hear me? No."

I let out the breath I've been holding and let my eyes wander. Nixon and Dave are watching me like hawks. Dave looks very smug while Nixon looks genuinely worried. I give Dave a very nasty finger. He deserves it.

Taking a deep breath, I squeeze her arm again.

"I'm afraid that if you don't tell *someone*, something bad... *really* bad will happen to you."

Evie lifts her head and looks me square in my eyes. Her eyes set off a bone chilling sensation in me.

"It's just a broken wrist, Carter. Get over it."

CARTER

Friday, May 20, 2022, Present.

I haven't come out of my room except to go the bathroom. I'm too antsy to eat or talk to anyone. So, I just pace back and forth across my bedroom in front of my window. It's got to be around nine in the morning but I don't really know. To be honest, I didn't even get a wink of sleep last night. I was either sitting at the edge of my bed, bouncing my leg up and down, or wandering around my room aimlessly. I even took melatonin last night but it did nothing because I couldn't settle.

Since I got home from the police station, my mind has been running a million miles per hour. I'm still in shock about the whole 'Evie writing down my Dad's name' thing. Sometime as she was running away, she felt the immediate need to write down the name of my missing, presumed dead father. It doesn't make sense. I see no reason to why she did it. There is no apparent reason.

Did it have something to do with what happened that night that led her to run away? Or maybe the sheriff is right and she was scared I was going to hurt her. Though it's an outrageous thought and very unlikely. The chances are slim. I was the only one there for her. I was likely the only person ever nice to her. *Right*?

Suddenly I'm aware of my door opening. I spin around away from the window and make eye contact with my mom. Her light brown hair is down around her shoulders in perfect curls. That isn't entirely normal. I haven't seen her wear curls in her hair for ages.

"Breakfast," she informs me with a small smile, smoothing a wrinkle in her white shirt.

I find myself shaking my head immediately. I'm not in the mood to eat. I can't eat.

"Not hungry."

Mom steps deeper into my bedroom and tries to smile bigger. It looks very fake. "Carter, you need to eat."

Turning back toward my open window I shake my head 'no.' I watch as Chev wanders the lawn. Behind me, I hear Mom step closer.

"I know you're worried for your friend but if you don't eat you won't be able to help find her. Okay, sweetie? You are no help if you don't take care of yourself. So, come on. I made blueberry waffles. Your favorite."

I try to hide my upturned eyebrows as I give into my mom's demands, but I can't. The aching worry plasters my face. The gnawing confusion. The throbbing anger. It's not much anger, but just enough.

As soon as I step out into the hallway I am hit with the smell of baked pancake batter. Normally it makes me insanely hungry but my stomach doesn't jump for food this time. I make my way downstairs at my mom's heels, trying to drive away my intrusive thoughts. I can't think about it all. It's making me crazy.

"About time you came down here," Daph laughs from the sofa. She's curled up with a plate of waffles watching the news. She's a nerd like that. Every single morning she does it.

I stop behind her and watch it as well. It's just going over some roof that blew off of a house somewhere in Utah.

Mom nudges my arm with something cold and I jump. I turn around to find a white glass plate with a singular, plain blueberry waffle. "Just how you like it. I figured you should try eating one first and then if you are hungry you can have another one."

I take the plate and thank her quietly, looking at the food with hidden disgust. Unlike Daphne, I sit at the wooden kitchen table. I don't want to watch the news right now. Or anything. Plus, I don't want to be around anybody right now.

I pick at my waffle for about thirty minutes, only eating chunks of blueberries in the batter. It seems to be the only part of it I'm interested in. But, now I'm over it. I scoot my wooden chair back and walk into the kitchen where Mom is doing the dishes. She must be off today. She sets a plate into the dishwasher and watches me warily as I throw away the torn-apart waffle.

"Well, if you wanted just blueberries I could have gotten you some instead of a waffle, sweetie," Mom jokes, wiping a light brown curl out of her face with a wet hand. Some water drips off of her hand and the shirt absorbs it, making that spot off-white.

She's trying but all I can do is shrug. I lean back against the island and cross my arms over my chest. I look out the sink window—which faces the barn—and watch the grass beside it dancing in the wind. Out of my side vision, I can see Mom watching me with her hazel eyes but I don't mind. Let her see. Let her see how messed up her son is.

"Carter—" she begins but becomes interrupted.

"—CARTER!"

Both Mom and I are so shocked we don't move.

"CARTER! CARTER!"

I spin on my heel to face the living room where Daphne is shrieking. She's frantically pointing at the television, her face ghost white.

"What is it?" Mom asks before I can, quickly wiping her hands on a dish towel.

Daphne points with her other finger.

I cautiously make my way to the living room, my eyes deadset on her. When I'm leaning against the back of the couch, I shift my eyesight to the TV.

I wish I didn't.

I really wish I didn't.

It's helicopter footage of a body of water and its shore. Its shore is rocky and covered in police officers, EMTs, and even firemen. The camera zooms in on a tarp that lays on top of something. Someone.

That's when I realize that that body of water is the reservoir up Montpelier Canyon. It's also when I remember that's where Evie was last seen. My Evie. *My Evie.*

There's a caption underneath the footage that states in bold red letters:

'Girl's Body Washes Up In Montpelier Canyon, Idaho.'

The denial comes first.

"That can't..." I gasp, my hand covering my mouth. A tear rolls down my cheek and then underneath my hand. "It isn't her. It's got to be someone else. It's not..."

Mom and Daphne are as motionless as I am as we watch the news program. I'm the only one that dares to speak.

Then the denial fades away as wind catches the tarp and lifts it just enough to reveal the right shoe. People dash to cover the body back up but they are too late. I saw the shoes. I saw those shoes. White, low-top converse. I saw her shoes.

"Carter... were those...?" Daph begins to ask, her voice quiet and hesitant.

I only nod, my eyes set on the blue tarp in the rocks. Those rocks are the same rocks I fished with Dad on all those years ago. The ones that dad tripped on, which led him to fall into the fishy water. Once those rocks were the keeper of a good memory. Now they are the keeper of a bad one.

Mom's hand finds my arm but it gives me no comfort. I *really* didn't want her to be dead. I prayed and wished she was just in Wyoming. That she just lost her bag and that's why it was at the reservoir. There was no way I was going to think she was dead. Wishing that she was going to call and say she is okay and safe was exhausting, but it kept me grounded. Now, I feel my soul lifting out of my body as hers already has.

Oh.

She's gone.

I don't even stop the tears as they stream from my face. I'm not as good at keeping them hidden as Evie is. *Was.* As Evie *was.* I hate that word. That *stupid* word. Was, was, was. Was. Evie *was* a great person underneath her cracked mask. Evie *was* strong and a fighter. Evie *was* missing. Evie *was* alive.

And I'm sure none of this was an accident. And I know exactly who committed the heinous crime.

We were going to graduate with each other and maybe we could have gone to college together. She would have gotten away from her parents by buying an apartment with me somewhere by campus. I would help her heal her bruises, internal and external. Maybe after a while I could've seen her arms without purple, green, and black bruises covering them. I could take in her pale skin without being worried about how she got a bruise and what she didn't do to deserve it.

But that's not going to happen. She's gone for sure.

My phone starts buzzing in my front pocket uncontrollably. I almost don't pick it up but it might be Evie trying to confirm with me that she's not dead. That's someone else's body. It's messed up... I even think that. I saw her shoes. What more confirmation do I need?

But, no it's not Evie. It's *Nixon.*

I wipe off my tears, clear my throat, and answer his call.

"Carter?" he calls. He's worried. Nixon is the most chill, laid-back dude I know.

"Yeah."

"You've seen the news?" he asks, his voice seeping with concern. He even sounds out of breath.

"Watching it right now," is all I can answer. Since I started hanging out with Evie, Nixon, Dave and I had a mini falling out. We rarely talk to each other.

Nixon is quiet on the other side of the phone for a painful amount of time, like he doesn't know what to say. I can just imagine him tugging at his black hair nervously with his phone up to his ear.

"Do you think...? Do you think it's her?" Nixon questions quietly.

This entire time I haven't moved my eyes away from the TV. I'm afraid I'll miss something.

"I know it's her. I saw her shoes," I snap as the helicopter footage fades, revealing a lady and a man in a newsroom.

Nixon's voice stays level despite me snapping at him. He kind of deserves it though. "Well my Dad is the coroner so if he comes home and tells me anything, I'll call you, okay?"

"Nixon?"

"Yeah?"

"*Why?*"

It's a question that has been on repeat in my head since I saw his name pop up on my phone. Nixon has been ignoring me since I started hanging out with Evie last year. He's been nothing but cold toward me during classes and stopped inviting me over to help him with his truck and stuff like that. Nixon has been nothing short of a jerk. I mean, yes, I made

Evie my priority but he could have at least been nice and understood.

"Because I miss my best friend," he simply replies.

Then he hangs up.

***

Nixon calls me around six in the evening. I've been waiting for his call since he hung up on me hours earlier. I've been antsy and haven't been able to sit still. I went for a walk with Chev down our dirt road and back twelve times before going back into my house. My house makes me feel so claustrophobic despite its size. I can't catch my breath in it.

Mom finally made me come back into the house around four for a snack. She seems to notice I haven't really eaten. I heard her on the phone with Grandpa about me in the living room while I paced my room. I stopped just in time to hear her saying how she's worried about me. Mom has got nothing to worry about. I'm fine. I mean I could be better but I'm *fine.*

"I've got news," Nixon says immediately when I pick up.

For the first time in a while, I sit down on the edge of my bed, eager to hear what he's learned. "It's her, isn't it?"

When Nixon tells me yes, I expect my brain to explode but I'm oddly calm. I knew this. I knew it was her. Yet I'm glad for the confirmation. But I don't know what to do about it... What *can* I do?

"There's more," he coughs, clearing his throat. "I heard Dad on the phone with a consultant from Pocatello that's going to help the Sheriff's Department with this case. He said she was shot–"

"–Shot?!"

So it was murder. Or suicide, I guess. Evie may have been depressed but she wouldn't have committed suicide, though. I know her...

...Or maybe I don't know her as well as I'd like to think I do.

"Evie was shot execution style. To the back of the head, Carter."

What? I've watched enough true crimes with Mom to know what that means. Luckily the police will know too. Typically when someone is... *shot* like that it means the murderer is someone close to them. They had too much guilt to be able to shoot them point-blank in the face. So, because of this guilt, they shot Evie in the back of the head.

This could either be very bad for me or very good. It could be pinned on me and the real murderer would never be found. On another note, Sheriff Reggie hasn't once believed Evie's parents abused her, but with her body found they will be able to depict that. If parents can abuse their child, they might even be able to kill them.

Puke rises in me but I swallow it back. I can't even imagine. If I'm righ and her parents *did* do this. I feel like there's no hope for this world if parents are killing their children.

"Are you still under investigation?"

I'm almost glad for the subject change but I know as soon as Nixon and I end this call, my mind with go right back to thinking about it.

"I think so," I cough, laying on my back. I never made my bed this morning so it's fairly uncomfortable.

"Do you have any guns in your house or anything like that? Anything registered in one of your family members names?" His voice is still so calm and I'm not sure how. I can barely keep mine level.

"No, nothing like that. We don't hunt."

Downstairs I can hear Mom yelling at Daphne. I don't know about what but I can tell Mom is fed up about something.

"Well, then you'll be fine. I'm sure the heat will be taken off of you."

I *hope*. I just want the real murderer to be arrested.

Neither of us talk for probably about two minutes, but we stay on the line anyways. Plus there's something so comforting about knowing he's there but not having to talk. I've only known Nix for a few years but I guess he is my best friend. Under all that cowboy is a good friend. He acts tough, but he really is kind.

Someone slowly makes their way up the creaky stairs and down the hall. They stop at my door and knock quietly.

"Come in."

Daphne appears at the door, her dark brown hair spilling over her shoulders. She blinks her hazel eyes and nods toward the hall. "Mom needs you."

"About?"

"I think Sheriff Reggie called."

Well, I guess that means I need to go down to the station. That could mean one of two things: I'm still under investigation or I'm not anymore. I guess we will find out.

EVIE

Monday, May 16, 2022, Past.

The sound of chatting campers wakes me from a cold sleep under the bush. My body seizes more than it already is from the chilly night. I know they can't see me but the worry still hangs in the air. The campers open the bathroom door and slam it shut, waking me up significantly.

I sit up and wipe the rest of the sleep from my eyes, not caring that there's dried mud stuck to my palms. When I wipe my right eye, pain rises around it. I wince and retreat my hands to my hoodie pocket. Sometime in the night I must have put on my second hoodie because now I wear my gray 'Bear Lake' hoodie.

The sun is just barely coming up so it must be around six thirty. Shadows cover me, keeping me from thawing out from the cold night. Of all of my ideas, sleeping in the cold has got to be the worst. But, the good thing is all of the mud froze in the night.

Birds chirp from across the rushing creek as I crawl to the water. I'm slightly glad I slept only a few feet from the creek because it definitely drowned out my snores. The creek water is clear and shows my reflection well. I bite my cheek as I examine my matted, muddy hair. Chunks of mud smear my face but what I really focus on is the swollen bruise around my right eye. Last night it wasn't there so I was really hoping it wouldn't come at all but there it is.

I tear my eyes away from my new battle wound, trying not to think about how I got it, and clean my hands off in the creek water. The water sends a shock through me that causes me to gasp. It's colder than I am, which I didn't think was possible. I suffer through the pain though and wash my face off next. I even contemplate washing my hair but I think that heightens my chance of pneumonia or something.

I'm fully awake after washing my face off with the freezing water. Now I can think about what I'm *really* going to do. My biggest thing is I have nowhere to go. I have no family I'm close to and I can't stay with Carter. Mom and Dad would find me there. I *really* can't stay with Carter. If that was even an option to consider I wouldn't have come all the way out here.

No, really my only option is to hitchhike into Wyoming. That's what I thought last night. That's what I think now. I shake my head and turn my attention to my growling stomach even though I really should figure out what the heck I'm going to do. I find my drawstring bag right where I slept and pull out two granola bars. I unwrap both of them and shove one in my mouth at a time. I barely make a dent in my hunger but it's better than nothing.

A trout swims by me, circling another. They swim right through my reflection, obscuring it. When my reflection settles once more, it reveals my black eye again. I shut my eyes, letting a tear roll out of it.

Then—against my will—I'm back there again.

Mom's angry but Dad... Dad's angrier. He's smashing dishes on the carpeted kitchen floor, screaming things at the top of his lungs. I hide in the corner, trying to get myself out of his vision. If he sees me I'm a goner. He might kill me this time.

Dad throws a plate toward the corner I'm hiding in, the one next to the table. He didn't know I was here but now he does. I don't waste another second. If he's seen me, that means I can run. But, even for his age, Dad's faster.

He grabs my arm, sending throbbing agony up through my arms. Dad spins me toward him and grabs my other arm, making it hard to weasel out and escape. His eyes are red from anger and veins pop out of his neck. I've never seen him this mad. The worst thing is it is all my fault.

"You weren't supposed to find that, little rat!" he screams in my face, his breath putrid and leaking alcohol.

All I can think is that *no, no I was not.*

Then, to my surprise, Dad lets go. But it isn't for long. He takes his right fist and connects it with my right eye. I lose all of my breath and sink to the carpeted floor, agony erupting throughout my head. Everything is crimson red out of my eyes but the pain is the worst part. I've never been punched before and I one hundred percent *don't* recommend it.

I've been handled roughly. I've been pushed. I've been kicked. But *never* punched. Dad has never got *this* rough with me.

I should be used to being hurt but this is a different kind of wound. It hurts more knowing that my assailant is my father.

Luckily, I'm far away from him. I'm in the canyon with my phone's location off. He doesn't know I'm here and never will. No one does, and I'd like to keep it that way. I'm done with being a punching bag. Plus, when I make it to wherever I decide to go, I'm going to tell everyone what I figured out last night. I'll tell the world what I did to deserve this black eye. Finally, I deserved a beating I got. That never happens.

I take my trembling fingers and wet them with more creek water. It's not getting any warmer... shocker. I brush my wet fingers through my *extra* dirty blonde locks. My fingers yank at a piece of mud stuck in my hair and manage to pull out a few strands. I shed them into the creek and watch as they float out of view. To be honest, getting the mud out with wet fingers may be impossible. So, I flip my hood over my hair and get up out of the grass and dried up mud. The sun is slowly coming up and as I stand up it takes the chill off of my shoulders. It's too much heat at one moment which causes a chill to run up my spine.

Sunshine gradually fills up the area as the sun rises above the sagebrush-covered mountains. It makes the environment feel less eerie. I felt like something would jump out of the shadows at me all night. Something probably still could but with the sun, it's less likely to be surprised.

I gather my drawstring bag and place it on my shoulders. If I'm going to get anywhere closer to Wyoming today, I should start sooner rather than later. Squaring my shoulders, I make my way out of the trees and bushes that surround the creek. My hair snags on something, causing me to yelp in shock.

When I spin on my heels I expect Dad or Mom holding my hair, but I only find it's snagged on a branch of a bush. I don't even try to untangle it. My mind is racing and my blood is pumping so I just rip it out, leaving behind a chunk of my hair.

In the clearing next to the road leading to the campsites, I gather my wits. Mom and Dad don't know I'm out here. They can't possibly. I'm okay. I'm fine.

I look to the highway which is surprisingly not busy at all for this time of day. Then, I look to the dam to my left that lets out reservoir water into the creek. It's pouring water down it now, which is probably because of the potentially low water level.

Now that I think of the water, I'd like to see it for the last time. I don't plan on coming back after leaving. Plus, I haven't seen the water since I was little. I want to know if it's as blue as I remember. I mean it probably isn't as blue as Bear Lake but I'd still like to take one last gander. So, I trudge onto the highway, over the bridge, then I exit the highway to the right onto the dirt road that leads to the reservoir.

A little pit stop won't kill me.

CARTER

Sunday, May 22, 2022, Present.

I shift Big Red into park in front of Evie's white house. It looks the exact same, except for the grass height. It's getting a bit long. I take a deep breath and unbuckle. Big Red's door creaks open and I step out onto the hot asphalt. I can feel the heat through my sneakers.

I've been meaning to speak with Kace for a while. I'm still suspected for what happened to Evie but I'm not an official suspect, if that makes sense. Still, Sheriff Reggie won't return my calls. I just want to know where they are in the investigation. Which is why I'm going to talk to Kace. I *need* to know.

My fist collides with the door quietly and I think it may be too quiet, but someone opens the door. A middle school girl stands there, her long blonde hair in a curly low ponytail. She watches me with dark blue eyes that threaten to let out tears.

"Hi, I'm so sorry to bother you," I begin, trying my hardest to continue looking at her. This little girl just lost her sister in the worst way imaginable. "Is Kace here, by any chance?"

Evie's little sister nods and slips out of the doorway, giving me entry into her house. It's weird being in Evie's house. I step into a foyer with a rough-looking piano and hooks for coats. Shoes scatter the tiled floor in an unorganized matter. The foyer then leads into what looks like a living room straight ahead and then there's a doorway leading into what could be a carpeted kitchen.

I follow the girl straight into the living room. Upon entry, there's a woodburning stove surrounded by bricks. At the top of the bricks are stone shelves that house all kinds of knick-knacks. No family pictures. The walls are cream-colored but are very unique. Halfway up every single wall is wallpaper about a foot tall that runs parallel to the ground. The wallpaper is a nature scene of elk and deer in a meadow surrounded by trees.

"Kace is upstairs. I'll go get him," the girl informs me before going into an extremely tiny hallway at the back left corner of the living room. She goes up stairs I'm unable to see, but can hear, and leaves me alone in the room. There are two brown couches, one with its back against the front window, and the love seat directly diagonal to it against the left wall. I look out the window that overlooks the front lawn and sidewalk.

I then shift my eyes to the TV that is bolted to the wall above a black desk. It almost looks like they haven't lived here long because of the lack of furniture but Evie once told me she's lived in the same house her entire life.

The sad part is that there are no family pictures on the walls. The only pictures are framed photos of deer and elk.

"Hey, what are you doing here?" a voice questions. My eyes meet Kace as he comes out of the tiny hallway.

"I just wanted to talk to you, I guess," I answer, running my hands through my hair. I don't know why I always do that when I have nothing else to do. It's like shoving my hands in my pockets.

Kace kind of shrugs and ushers toward the couches. "Well, then I guess you can have a seat."

I sit on the bigger couch, leaving the loveseat for Kace. I glance toward the hallway where another girl, older than the other one, peaks around the corner at me. Chills spread over me. The girl retreats but once I shift my eyes to Kace, she peeks back around.

"How has your family been with... everything?"

That is the worst question to ask someone whose sister's murdered body was just found. The worst *by far*.

Kace shrugs and sits back, his pale arms crossed on his chest. His once bright blue eyes now watch me like they have no purpose. They almost remind me of mine... or Evie's. All I can think is that this poor guy's parents may have killed his older sister. This poor family.

"Is it okay if I ask about..."

"About what the police have now that they have Evie's body? I'd say no to anyone who asks me that, but you're not anyone so I'll let you."

I hold back a sigh of relief and go through the thousands of questions invading my head. Now that I've got permission, I don't know which question to ask first. So, I sit here racking my brain in the hope one will jump out. Oddly, it works. But, I start simple.

"Who do you think killed her?"

Never mind, that is NOT simple. That is a very loaded question. A *very loaded* question. But, I'm curious what the brother of the victim thinks.

I said victim. She's *Evie. Evie*, not the 'victim.'

Kace must have an idea because he starts shifting and leans forward. This is no longer a laid-back conversation. Although I don't think it ever was.

His calm expression turns flawed with emotion or maybe even fear.

From the corner of my eye, the girl watches Kace so carefully. I can read more emotion on her face than Kace's but oddly no fear. But she definitely knows something.

But, so does Kace.

"No," Kace sighs through clenched teeth. I notice as he massages the skin between his right index finger and thumb. Everybody's got a way to try to relieve anxiety... That must be his.

"Where are you parents?" I shoot. If I'm going to even remotely mention them, I don't want them near.

"Not here. They are at the station."

Kace continues massaging his hand. I take a long, deep breath.

"A really long time ago–like right around when I dislocated my knee–you said your parents punished Evie unfairly. Look, I'm not going to sugarcoat it, but I saw the bruises. She was constantly covered in them. Eve refused to talk about them but it's clear who gave them to her. I guess what I'm trying to ask is, do you think your parents may have..."

I don't want to finish the sentence. It's still sickening to me.

But, Kace's face now lets me know I'm either on the money or close.

His anxious face hardens into something like determination. His blue eyes turn hard with a chill that causes me to shudder.

"Yeah."

That's when I see it. At first it doesn't register, but when it does, I'm sure I know what it means. It could only mean one thing.

I was trying not to look at Kace. It was almost frightening to. So, I found comfort in looking at the floor. But, what I find on the floor gives me absolutely no comfort. Exactly the opposite of comfort.

Its iconic red case is the exact one I constantly teased her about. In Evie's case is a slender black phone; It's an extremely cheap Samsung because that's all she could afford and it has a very distinct look because of this. That's how I know it's her phone under the couch. It's barely sticking out but I know it's hers. It's muddy too.

I *knew* it was weird that the phone wasn't in her drawstring bag. No *one* brings a charger and not a phone when you're running away. Or so I would assume. Not that I know anything on that subject. But I *knew* it! I knew it! And everyone called me stupid.

But there it is and it's *muddy*. It's most likely *reservoir* mud. Whoever killed her took her phone off her and now it's under the couch in the Bakers' house. It's right there.

Abruptly, I stand up off of the brown sofa, sweat rolling down my back despite the air-conditioned air circulating around the living room. "Uh, I've got to go. I've got–I've..."

Smooth.

Kace looks just as shocked as I feel overwhelmed. But, I start heading for the front door anyway. I can't be here. I should be gone before his parents are even anywhere close to me and this house. I can't come face-to-face with them. Not now. Not with the evidence my brain holds. I have crucial evidence that I *need* to share with the sheriff.

"Carter?" Kace calls after me as I swing open the white front door. I ignore his confused shouts and shut the door behind me, rushing as quickly as I can

But I come face-to-face with another problem–quite literally.

"Carter," Paul Baker's cold voice snarls. His icy blue eyes freeze me immediately in my spot. I attempt to move my feet but they seem to be glued to the heated concrete, unable to perform any of my requests. And the longer Paul Baker glares at me the more frantic I am with my demands.

Now that I'm in real trouble, I can't move from my spot.

How pathetic.

What could only be my girlfriend's *killer* is one foot from me with his accomplice, Joanne, behind him. This was a stupid, *stupid* idea. I knew coming over here was risky and now I'm potentially in deep danger. Would they kill me like they probably killed their daughter?

A drop of salty sweat rolls down my forehead and follows my hairline all the way to my jaw. My legs shake and threaten to give out underneath me. They quiver relentlessly, that being their only indication of movement.

I've got to get out of here. I've got to get out of here. I've got to get out of here. *I've got to get out of here.*

My eyes watch Paul's, who stares deeply into my soul. Does he know that I know somehow? He seems too firm to *not know* I know something. He's got to know. And if he doesn't, he *will* know by how frozen and terrified I am. No one looks this frightened for no reason.

But, for some reason, my feet won't allow me to run or even take a step. The *one* time I *crucially* need them to do something, they fail. Because of that, I may be dead soon. Shot in the back of the head. Dumped somewhere. Forgotten. Never found.

Oh, I want to puke. Maybe if I do it'll distract them and I'll be able to flee.

No, I'm getting ahead of myself. They don't know I found her phone. They don't know. They can't know. I'm just getting ahead of myself. Yeah. *Yeah.* I'm *fine.*

"What are you doing here?" Paul demands, crossing his fat arms.

Paul Baker is not a muscular man but he's got me outweighed by a LOT. He's got a major beer belly underneath his black shirt but that is only one tiny piece of the puzzle. His face is what alarms me. It takes a dangerous spin on Evie's hollowed face. Plus, it's pointed at me, which can't be safe. This man is vicious and not looking for peace.

He glares his icy eyes. "I'm going to ask you again. *What are you doing here, Carter?*"

I open my mouth but nothing but a squeak comes out.

Paul turns to his wife behind him, his voice stern. "Joanne, call the police."

That sets me free of my frozen state. I swerve around him and Joanne, slipping from the hands he reaches at me with. I mad-dash to my truck, hop in it, and start it. Paul goes to open the passenger side door but I lock it with my trembling fingers. Without another glance toward Mr. Baker, I speed a few feet before dangerously turning onto Adam's Street. I don't follow the speed limit as I hustle down the street, trying to put as much distance from Paul Baker as I can. I pass Adam's park and then come to a halt at the stop sign that briefly permits me from getting onto the highway. It's all a blur but I'm alive.

But for how long?

NIXON

Sunday, May 22, 2022, Present.

I know Carter's in real trouble when he calls me in a huge panic. I've been his best friend since he moved here his junior year and not once have I heard him as freaked out as he did on the phone. He was out of breath and frantically muttering.

But, I'm a good friend so I got into my truck and made my way to Montpelier's city park as he instructed. Plus, I am *very* interested in what has got Carter this way. He's usually a pretty chill guy. My guess is Evie Baker.

As I pull into the parking lot, I spot Carter's rusty truck parked in front of the metal pavilion. The parking lot is insanely busy since summer break is here. It's mainly tourists visiting the National Oregon/California Trail Center literally sitting in the park. I've only gone once, which was with my grandpa when I was like ten. It's actually pretty cool. The real Oregon trail is in it, preserved. Basically, they take you in a wagon and then it shakes in place. When it stops shaking, you step out of the other entrance and onto the real trail. They make it look the way it actually did back then. Like there's wagons and pioneer stuff and everything. It's pretty cool.

I park my truck next to Carter's after trying to swerve through the pesky tourists and turn it off. I look out my passenger window at his driver's window. Carter sits in his truck, hands glued on the wheel. His eyes are fixed straight ahead and are plagued by an unknown fear. They are incredibly wide like he's seen a ghost. His normally tan skin is now pale, so much so that I think he might be sick.

My fingers find the handle of my nineteen-eighty-nine, royal blue Dakota Dodge. Shelby's my baby that I bought when I was a sophomore. The great thing about Idaho is that you start driver's education at fourteen and a half and get your license a little after fifteen. My cousins in Utah were always jealous when they visited.

I walk around the back of Shelby and stand at Carter's window. He's sweating erratically, causing his hair to be damp. His brown hair is messier than usual and spikes in all kinds of directions. Something really bad must have happened.

I bring my knuckles to his window and knock with them. It sends Carter into an unplanned terror. He jumps higher than I have ever seen someone do in a vehicle, hitting his head on the roof. His hands come off the wheel and clutch the top of his head. Carter's frantic eyes find mine and they immediately calm. I watch carefully as he lets out a *very* deep sigh and sinks into his chair.

Something *really, really* bad must have happened. Or maybe this is about Evie being found, even though that was so many days ago.

So, *what's got him so spooked?*

Not waiting for him, I open his door and lean on it.

"What is up with you, man?" I question, listening to his ragged deep breaths. "What happened?"

But, he doesn't answer. Instead, he gets up and out, pushing past me. I call for him, watching as he heads for the playground. Shaking my head, I step over the metal rope that separates the park from the parking lot. I walk on the pavement sidewalk and past a metal anchor decoration. Carter swerves around the playset as I'm just barely stepping on the grass. He's quick. Or maybe that's the fear.

I walk the short distance of grass between the pavement the pavilion sits on and onto the sandy pit that is the jungle gym area. The playground is decent-sized since they updated it. I remember how mad I was that they tore down the old one. The old one had a fire pole. This one does not. But, that's not what I need to be thinking about now.

Carter finally stops at an old, wickering picnic table on the other side of the sand pit. I'm relieved because I really don't want to hunt him down any longer. Sundays are my one day off from work. I don't want to do any physical activities I don't have to do.

"Carter? Seriously, man? What is it?" I ask again, settling onto the picnic table. I sit on the table itself with Carter and the playground in front of me. Some kids that are playing stop and look at us briefly.

I'm getting annoyed. I know I'm Carter's best friend, but if he doesn't talk to me I can't help him. He just paces back and forth in front of me. I yell his name, snapping out of his trance.

"I think I know for sure who killed Evie Baker and I have evidence," he blurts, stopping cold in his tracks.

At first, I don't think I hear him right. No one knows who killed that poor girl. Not even my dad, the coroner. I mean he has somewhat of an idea. I've heard him talking with a consultant from Pocatello about it. He doesn't say names and every time he says *anything* about who may have done it, he whispers so quietly I can't eavesdrop.

"*What*? Are you sure?"

Carter nods frantically and begins pacing again. "I'm sure. I'm sure. I'm sure. *I'm sure. I'm sure...*"

I've never seen Carter Miller have a mental breakdown but I'm sure this is it. And it's scary. A little heartbreaking.

"Who?"

That question has been ringing in my head since he first started talking. Who? Who did it? No one in this county knows. No *one*. And it's scaring everyone. My stepmom is terrified I'll be next or something. This murder has plagued our tiny county.

"I saw it. I saw it," he pants vaguely. That could mean a lot of things.

"*You saw her murder?*"

Wait, did Carter do it? It'd be the perfect murder. The loving boyfriend kills his depressed girlfriend. I mean, I still can't believe they were dating and I had no clue. Yes, he hung out with her, but he never once even hinted that he was dating her. That only means one thing: he didn't want anyone to know.

"No!" he snaps. "Her phone. I saw her phone at her house."

Now I'm confused. "What does her phone being at her house have to do with anything?"

He stops and glares at me like I'm the biggest idiot on the planet. Maybe I am, who knows? My teachers think I am.

"She took her phone charger with her when she left. You don't bring a charger and not a phone," Carter erupts, drawing the attention of the kids making a racket on the jungle gym. They go quiet and begin watching us again, wanting to know what's going down. I shoot a scowl at them and watch as they scramble down the slide out of view. I know they're kids but I've never been a fan of kids. They are full of germs, they're annoying, and they're always in everybody's business. That's why I'm glad I'm an only child.

I turn my attention back to Carter who begins pacing again. Does he *ever* get tired? I mean I can tell why he's pacing uncontrollably... I would be too. I can't imagine being in this situation. I can't imagine knowing who killed my girlfriend and not knowing what to do.

"Wait. *Who killed her? Who killed Evie?*" I forgot entirely that he knew and that's why he's in crisis. I'm a terrible friend.

That seems to almost calm him, well he's calmer than he has been for the past ten minutes. He stops moving completely and turns back toward me, his face whiter than it was before—and that's saying something. But, he stops shaking.

"Her dad. Her parents."

I'm not even surprised, just disgusted. Paul and Joanne Baker are nothing short of crazy. They *would* murder their child. But why? *Why*? What is the point? What do they get out of it except a bigger chance of landing themselves in prison for murder? It's revolting. If it was them—which is actually pretty likely—then that proves how *messed* up this world is. If parents are killing their children, is anyone safe?

I overheard dad talking to that one consult and he did say Evie Baker was *covered* in bruises. Her legs, her arms, even her face.

Oh. I feel bad for teasing her in middle school and elementary. She was being abused this *entire* time and I'm sure I didn't brighten the situation. I slightly feel better that I left her alone in high school, for the most part. I feel terrible. *She was being abused this entire time and I made it worse.*

In elementary, she was such a bright kid and I think I hated her for it and *that*'s why I messed with her. But, it was never any fun because she took it like a pro. She just smiled and moved on. One time she even told me—and I remember this very distinctly because it made me extremely *pissed*—that she forgave me because she knew I was just taking out my rage because I secretly had a terrible life. Evie wasn't wrong. In first grade, my Mom left. Just up and left my dad and me. I haven't seen her since and as a seven-year-old, it made me angry and sad. So, in third grade, I took it out on the happiest girl in my grade because I was jealous.

It irritated me that she never revolted against me and it began to be no fun. Then, a few months later, while we were eight, she stopped smiling. Evie Baker, the happiest girl in my grade, stopped smiling. I didn't understand why but I didn't question it for long. Teasing her was fun again.

Oh, I feel so bad.

It makes sense why she always wore a hoodie or a long-sleeved shirt even on the hottest days. She never wore anything that revealed her arms or legs and it suddenly makes so much sense. I can't tell her I'm sorry anymore. I can't apologize or explain.

"*Why...?*" I question Carter, my voice squeaky and rough. I can't swallow back the growing lump in my throat.

For the first time, Carter comes over and sits next to me. He buries his head in his hands and shrugs his broad, shaking shoulders. He then wipes a singular tear using his big hands. His hands form into fists and support his head up from underneath his chin. Carter stares forward intensely, his eyes set on one of the many pine trees surrounding the park. I watch as he blinks himself out of his thoughts and stares at the Oregon trail center to our left diagonally.

"Kace Baker once mentioned to me that their parents have treated her like crap since her grandma died when she was eight. Something about how they wished Evie had died in that car wreck instead of her grandma." His voice shakes drastically.

That piece of information makes me feel even worse. Her grandma died when she was eight too *and* she probably watched it happen. I have a sudden urge to puke but I hold it back. I could have been nicer to Evie. Maybe her life wouldn't have been so terrible. Maybe I could have been that one light at the end of the tunnel.

"You need to tell the police, Carter."

Carter's helpless eyes meet mine. It pulls something in my heart. This poor guy lost his girlfriend to murder. He probably moved to Bear Lake for a fresh start but what he got is nothing even close. I bet he didn't expect that when he moved here his girlfriend would get murdered by her parents.

"I will. I just need to calm down first, Nix."

He's right. It's possible that if he calls them in a panic they will continue to think he did something. I doubt it, but the police is full of people that don't know anything about solving a case of this magnitude.

I'm frightened for this town and I'm especially frightened for what might happen to Carter.

CARTER

Monday, May 23, 2022, Present.

School was painful but I was able to get Kace to come over. I need to talk to him more without the threat of his murderous parents. I haven't called Sheriff Reggie yet about the phone but I will. I just think I need to collect more evidence before I call anything in. What if they don't believe me about the phone? Plus, you probably can't get a search warrant over just one muddy phone. So, I've started a makeshift detective team. I sound like a child but I don't care. It's what everyone does in the books and movies.

Now Kace is my biggest asset and that's why I invited him over. I invited Nixon too. The more the merrier.

So, now I'm waiting for them in the living room. Daphne sits next to me paying attention to the TV unlike me. I keep my attention on the windows, waiting rather impatiently. *Both* of them are late. Well, one minute late.

As if on cue, Nixon pulls into the driveway and shuts off his truck. He calls it Shelby, and I'm not one to judge, but it doesn't quite fit it. But I'm not going to tell him that. I abruptly stand up and move over to the door as Nix makes his way over. Before he has the chance to knock, I pull open the door.

"Well, that was quick. Can you see into the future or something?" Nixon laughs, stepping past me into my kitchen/living room/ dining room. Daph looks over her shoulder and scowls when she notices Nixon. She doesn't take a liking to him. I'm not sure why though. I'm not sure she knows either.

I don't tell him I have been waiting for him for the hour I've been home. Instead, I offer him a drink. Before even waiting for his answer I open the double fridge and grab a Mountain Dew. I toss it to him and watch as he catches it and laughs.

"Okay, then..."

Not laughing with him, I look out the window above the sink. You can get a tiny glimpse of the road and there's still no sign of Kace.

"Look, Kace is coming over too. I hope you're not mad," I gulp, opening the fridge back up. I grab my own Mtn Dew and open it. I don't care for Mtn Dew, in fact, I think it's too syrupy, but I drank the last Dr. Pepper last night. I need the caffeine to stay awake. I'm dragging despite my awakening anxiety.

I look to Nix who leans against the island. He shrugs. "He's a good advantage if we are going to get enough evidence to prove the parents are who killed Evie. Although I'm not sure how we are going to keep it from him that we know it's his parents."

Yeah, I was worried about that all day. If Kace knows that we are trying to gather evidence to put his parents behind bars, he may not help us. I mean he must suspect his parents but that doesn't necessarily mean he wants them in prison. I mean they *are* his parents. Even if they killed his sister.

"We've just got to be careful. None of us can mention the phone, either," I demand as I take a sip of my soda.

Nix stares at me in awe then takes off his Bear Lake baseball hat to ruffle his black hair. In my opinion, nobody looks good with a mullet, but Nixon is an exception. He makes it work, unlike half the boys in school. To me, that's a gift.

Nixon puts his hat back on as Daphne calls from the living room. "Another one of your loser friends is here!"

I force a chuckle and walk to the door. I get there right as Kace knocks. I open it to find him in different clothes than he was in at school. He wears the classic #webelong shirt that every student at Bear Lake High has. It's a lighter version of royal blue with the bear logo in white on his torso. On the back is the hashtag and I *think* the 'Bear Lake Strong' slogan.

"Come on in."

I move to the side to let him in, watching as he slowly surveys the interior of my house. His eyes fall on the family picture we have hanging up on the wall in between my Mom's room and the staircase. It's a semi-old one. It's of the entire family, including Dad. I was nine and it was a few months before Dad disappeared. Daph was only one so Mom held her. I stand to the left of Dad while Mom and Daphne are to his right. It was a nice picture taken somewhere in the trees of Oregon.

"Cool house," he smiles anxiously. I think I may have broken him. He used to be happy and bright then I knocked on his door demanding answers. Or maybe it was the fact that he knows his parents did something to his older sister.

Not everything's about you, Carter.

I'm about to thank him but Daphne immediately butts in. "I'm Daphne!"

She extends her hand and Evie's brother shakes it. "Kace."

Daph giggles like Kace just said the *funniest* thing. She even *twirls* her dark brown hair. My sister begins to open her mouth to say something—probably something to embarrass me more—but I slide in and push Kace up the stairs and up to my room.

"*Bye*, Daphne," I growl from the middle of the stairs. I watch with amusement as she stalks away and into the kitchen, her tan arms folded in anger.

When we are safe in my room Kace begins to laugh. It's a really beautiful laugh that brings joy. "I think your sister likes me."

"I'd say," Nix giggles, collapsing onto my bed. He takes off his hat and tosses it onto my pillow. I shake my head and slap his gut. He groans, clutching his stomach.

I go to my desk at the foot of my bed that's against the wall. It's a cedar desk that matches the hardwood floors in the house. I open the top drawer and bring out half of a white poster board that's been rolled up. It's sat in there since junior year when I used the other side. My fingers grab a few tacks rolling around at the bottom of the drawer and carefully handle them. I smooth out the poster above my desk on the wall and tack it up. On the bed, Nix laughs but I ignore it. This is what all the good detectives do. They always have a detective board so they can put down their clues and anything else they need.

With a permanent marker, I write at the top 'Murder Board' in hollow letters. I grab some packs of yellow Post-its from my second drawer and set them on the desktop.

"Where do we start?" I ask the boys in my room who are watching me like hawks. They all gawk for a moment, not answering.

Nixon sits up. "Well, you need an evidence section to start with. Then a timeline. Then suspects."

I nod and follow his instructions, dividing the board into three sections with my black marker, each section given a name beneath the general title of "Murder Boar." Sticking the lid back on the marker, I set it down and replace it with sticky notes. I place about six of them under evidence.

Kace is the first to blurt out evidence. "Evie's bag at the reservoir."

I write that down and Kace helps me fill in another: her body at the reservoir. This suggests that the murderer knew she was there. That's not the last of the clues Kace fills in. Kace even does all the hardcore ones I refuse to say. I write down 'bruises,' 'shot execution style which suggested the murderer knew her.' I purposely keep off a sticky note about Evie's phone.

My door squeaks open and hits Kace lightly. He scooches away from the door—still sitting on my floor—and lets my little sister in. Daphne surveys each of us, her eyes on Kace too long for comfort. She then shifts her hazel eyes to our detective board and scoffs.

"What are you guys? Twelve?"

"What are you? Eight?" I shoot back, taking a seat in my padded office chair. After I set down my marker, I run my fingers through my brown hair. I can feel it spike up in its messy, fluffy way.

She rolls her eyes and sits on where my pillow would be if she hadn't moved it and Nix's hat just then.

"Excuse you? What are you doing, Daph?"

She shrugs quickly and begins braiding tiny strands in her dark hair. My sister looks at her hair like she's very disinterested but I know she has another objective. "I'm helping."

Um, no. She isn't. Over my dead body. She doesn't need to get wrapped in all of this. She's only eight. Daphne doesn't need to be introduced to murder or any violence this young. I shouldn't even be involved. The last thing I need is for my innocent sister to get involved in any way, even if she's just trying to help me solve my girlfriend's murder.

"Absolutely not, Daph."

Nix stands up straighter and glares at me. "Just let your sister help, dude. She just wants to help," he offers Daphne a fist bump but she only glares at him. "Plus, your sister is cool."

With that Daphne's fist comes into contact with Nix's.

I shake my head but I know I've already lost. Daphne may be eight but she is *insanely* stubborn. So is Nixon. "*Fine*. But don't tell mom."

Daphne tries to hide her crooked-toothed smile but fails dramatically. Her smile makes me feel good. She never smiles at me anymore. She's just always full of insults and sarcastic remarks these days. I swear, she thinks she's a teenager already. She acts more like a teenager than I do.

My sister drops her half-braided strands and leans forward, moving her feet into a crisscross underneath her. She squints at our poster and shakes her head, her smile extremely small.

"It takes a very twisted, broken, lost soul to do what you do," she sighs, making eye contact with me.

I lean back in my chair comfortably and chuckle. "Thanks for noticing. You're too kind."

She shoots me a sarcastic smile and begins braiding her hair again, seeming disinterested. I shake my head for like the hundredth time this hour and grab the marker again. I grabbed it for no reason except to simply have it in my hands. I need *something* to fiddle with. I settle my eyes back on our makeshift detective board and then to Kace who sits on the ground still. His face is soft and kind but you can tell there's tragedy hidden behind his features. His eyes are very fearful despite the lack of danger here.

"Kace? I hate to ask this, but what happened the night Evie ran away? You must know *something* that can help us." I feel bad for pressing him with questions. So bad that I may not invite him to our next 'get together.' But, we need his answers badly.

Kace looks up at me and then closes his panicky blue eyes. "I heard a lot of glass being shattered."

Nixon seems as interested in that as I do. Even Daphne leans forward and stops focusing on her hair. "Is that *all* you heard?" Nix questions, tugging his black hair at his neck.

Kace opens his eyes and they begin to be plagued by a *calmer* fear. I don't know how that's possible, but it is. "Mom and Dad were yelling at each other. Then they were yelling at Evie. And there was a lot of glass being shattered as I told you. All the rest of the sounds fused together."

That's a start. Yelling. There was yelling. A fight must have been going on. You typically don't throw glass items for fun. We just don't know what they were yelling about. It could be anything but it had to be big enough that Evie got scared and ran.

"So, you don't know what they were screeching about?" Daphne asks, giving me a skeptical side glance.

"I don't know, it's all a blur. But I think they hit her. I think they hit Evie. I heard her yelp. I'm not sure though."

If he's lying, he's a dang good liar. In fact, I think he's telling us the truth about the fighting, the glass, and Evie's yelping.

Nixon perks up on my bed and turns toward me, a look of recognition on his face. "I heard my dad—" he turns to Kace "—the coroner—" then back at me "—say that she had a black eye while he was on the phone with a consultant."

So, Kace probably isn't lying. Evie was punched by her father, or at least that's who I guess. Every time I see her mom, I'm just reminded how much she looks like she couldn't hurt a kid. Every time I see her dad I'm reminded of the complete opposite. He looks like a child beater and a mean drunk.

I get out of my chair and write on one of the post-its 'black eye the night she ran away.' I feel the others watching me but I brush it off. I'm going to have to get used to it. Sitting back down, I throw back my head and close my eyes. A sudden headache afflicts my thought-ridden skull.

"Are you still being investigated, Carter?" my best friend's voice probes from the direction of my bed.

I don't shake my head or say anything for fear it will hurt my unforeseen headache. Luckily, Daphne answers for me. Unluckily, she's the worst person to answer that question.

Her voice is cheery, too cheery. "Yep, they're still on him like when two sides of duct tape touch each other." She laughs at her response. So does Nixon. Kace stays silent in his spot on the floor.

"No," I groan. "I'm not a suspect anymore. I'm just being investigated."

Nixon holds back a laugh. "Isn't that what being a suspect means?"

Daphne laughs and I assume they fist bump again. I don't want to open my eyes to watch their stupidity. That's a waste of eyesight.

My bed squeaks as one of them move. I open my eyes to find Daphne on her feet, standing on my bed. "Do you think they called the FBI on you, Carter? I hope you drew the attention of the FBI!"

I shoot her a glare. "Why in the world would you want that? *Are you insane*?"

She smiles her very crooked smile and karate kicks the air, nearly falling off. "What? I've never seen anyone kick down a door before! It would be so exciting!"

Nixon stands up on my bed too and does a crappy version of a karate kick. He doesn't even get two feet above my bed. "I like this girl!"

CARTER

Tuesday, May 24, 2022, Present.

I collapse onto my bed after school, throwing my backpack at the foot of my bed next to my desk chair. All day I avoided everyone and oddly it was a bunch of work. But, I *really* don't want to talk to anyone in my grade or in my school right now. I'm sick of having to pretend I'm okay when I know I'm not.

I let my head hang off my bed. It doesn't take long before the blood is rushing to my head and I begin to feel faint. But, I push my limits and stay with my head upside down for as long as I can take it.

My phone begins to ring in my front pocket. I lay slightly upside down until it has rung twice. Slowly, I sit up using my core and fish it out of my pocket. It's Kace. It takes me off guard, so much so that I almost forget I have to *answer* the call.

I press the answer button and bring it to my ear. "Yeah?"

His voice is shaky but calm—if that makes sense. Shaky seems like his voice's new normal. "Hey, I figured I'd let you know that someone called in a tip today. About my sister. About Evie."

That wakes me up, shunning away my drowsiness. I stop slouching and sit up straight. "Tell me more."

I hear Kace take a deep breath on the other line. "Well, apparently this older lady named Olivia Ward saw Evie's picture in the newspaper and recognized her. She recognized her as the girl she gave a ride to Sunday night in the rain. Olivia apparently gave my sister a ride to the reservoir around midnight because she said her family was camping there."

Holy crap. This Olivia Ward was most likely the last person that saw her alive. I'm sure that piece of information has been keeping Olivia up each night. That must be a terrible feeling—knowing you were the last person to see a teenage girl alive. It makes me sick. What if I had been the last one to see Eve?

This tip also proves that Evie actually ran away. I mean I practically knew but this is the confirmation I needed. She received a ride from a stranger out to the reservoir. Her murderer or murderers didn't take her out there to kill her. But, it makes everything so much more complicated. Somehow her murderer(s) knew she was out at the reservoir. How could anyone had known that? Or, maybe this Olivia lady had something to do with her murder. Maybe she's lying and recognized her as soon as she sat in her car. Then, she called Evie's parents to tell them how careless it was to make her walk in the rain all the way to the campsite. In turn, her parents would know where she was.

But that's just one of the thousands of possible theories.

"Can you come over here again, Kace? I know we met yesterday, but I'd like to tell Nixon and Daphne about the tip." I question, already getting to my feet to go grab Daphne from her room.

"No, I can't. I'll sit out for this one. I've got to go. Bye, Carter."

Kace hangs up before I can even say goodbye, or thank you. He is in a rush.

So, I phone Nixon and ask him to come over. Nix lives in Montpelier so it'll take him just ten minutes to drive here.

I glance at the board and grab my marker. In the middle section of the poster, I begin to write a timeline. I start with when she ran away on Sunday, May 15, 2022, and end it on the tip called in on today's date, Tuesday, May 24, 2022. It takes a lot of brain power to figure out all of the dates, but I eventually get it in eight minutes' time.

I set down the marker on my desk and leave my room. Making my way to Daphne's door—the door the closest to the stairs with mine being the farthest—I whistle because for the first time in a while things are looking up since that one Sunday Evie disappeared. I mean the tip is a small piece of the puzzle to figuring this all out, but it's still an important piece. Plus, if I can contact Olivia Ward I can ask her a bunch of questions. I want to make sure her story is true and stays the same.

I knock on Daphne's door but don't wait for an answer before barging in. She's sitting on her black bedding, much like mine, doing her homework. I didn't even think third graders had homework. I don't come into Daph's room much but it seems to change frequently. It's the same furniture and decorations, just always in a different spot. I like her room actually. The walls are lilac and she has lots of black and white pictures of Paris, France on her walls. She also has lots of art crafts and random items like fedoras hanging on tacks. It's very chaotic but it works well together, no matter how she decorates it. There are definitely a *lot* of colors, which is a good thing.

"Nixon is coming over. There's a 'meeting' happening when he gets here if you want to join," I inform her, leaning against her door frame.

Her face lights up immediately. "So you're letting me join your little cult?"

"First of all, it's not a *cult*. Second of all, yes, I'm letting you join our 'group' permanently. Oh, and Kace isn't coming today, so if that alters your decision to stay, that's okay. I'll forgive you."

Daphne jumps off her bed, leaving her sheets of homework on her bed. She walks across her room and slugs me right in my shoulder. It doesn't hurt at all, in fact it feels like I've been hit by a moth or something.

We walk back to my room side by side, not speaking until we are actually in my room. Mom's at work until pretty late tonight so the house is eerily quiet. It's not a rare occurrence. With Mom at work a lot, it's always quiet. It can be super calming, except when you hear a random, out-of-context noise somewhere in the house. That's always terrifying. Especially when Daph forces me to investigate.

"So why again today?" Daphne questions, sitting where Nix sat yesterday on my bed.

I sink into my chair and take out my phone. I shoot Nixon a quick text to just let himself in and come upstairs. "The police got a tip from someone. Kace called me about it."

She nods her head awkwardly and begins looking around my navy-colored room.

"Did you know that your room reflects your personality?" Daph says, her smile hiding behind her lips, waiting to be unleashed.

"Oh yeah?"

She nods and lets her smile loose. "Your room is extremely bland and boring."

Despite her insult, I laugh and search my room. She's right. I barely have any personalized things in my room. I mean my nightstand has a framed picture of Dad and me during one of our family photoshoots on the beach at the ocean. My desk is pretty personalized too. Personalized with junk and some dead flowers that have sat in a vase on top of it since Valentines day. They were from Mom.

I like my room plain, though. I don't want it to be chaotic. I'm afraid my mind won't be able to sleep in it or something.

Downstairs the front door creaks open and then shut. It's followed by the sound of boots making their way upstairs. We listen as the boots echo through the hallway and then watch as Nix pushes open the door. He's holding a gas station bag full of stuff.

He lifts it up for us to see and takes a seat on the floor where Kace sat yesterday. Nixon looks to Daphne who is eagerly wanting to know what's in that bag. "Hey, little fry. You stole my seat."

She shrugs and keeps her eyes on the prize. Nixon notices and chuckles, opening it up. He pulls out four Dr. Peppers and a bag of Hostess powdered donuts. It's even the good kind: the mini ones a little smaller than the palm of your hand.

"I thought Kace was going to be here. That's why I grabbed four sodas," he explains, handing one to each of us. "I guess you can have the extra one, Carter."

"Score!"

I take the extra one and set it next to my other one on my desk.

"So, what's this tip you mentioned?" Daphne asks after taking a long swig of her pop. I can hear it fizzing and popping from the carbonation from where I am.

***

I spend the next five minutes telling them about Olivia Ward and what the tip was. They listen intently, occasionally popping a white donut into their mouths and taking sips of Dr. Pepper. By the end, half the bag of donuts is finished. In *five minutes*, Daphne and Nixon together ate half a bag.

Nixon is the first to speak. He quickly chews his donut and wipes the white sugar onto his jeans, leaving behind finger and hand marks. "I mean, it's good that we know that her murderer didn't take her out there themselves to kill her."

It's weird how we are talking about murder like it's a normal occurrence. It's not. Things like murder don't happen in our small county. Nothing interesting happens here. The most talk-about-worthy things that ever happen are car wrecks. *Maybe* a drowning at the lake or the occasional dislocated shoulder. Nothing like this happens.

"But, it's also bad, Nix. We don't know how they found her out there. Either we are wrong and it *wasn't* Paul and Joanne Baker and just a driver passing through, or we are right and they have got some tricks up their sleeves. Something is off. Something doesn't fit, but I'm not sure what yet," I groan, looking at the white ceiling. "It makes sense for it to be Paul and Joanne. I mean, we have to think about Evie's cell phone I spotted. It was supposed to be on her body, but it was at their house, under their couch."

Daphne shoots straight up and screws the lid on her soda. "*What*?! Is that evidence—the phone—on the board? I don't see it up there."

I forgot I never told her about Evie's phone or my maybe, possibly near-death experience. I'm still surprised Sheriff Reggie hasn't called. I bet Paul Baker called the cops on me.

I tell Daph about the phone and why we can't tell Kace. I also mention how we are trying to prove that Evie's parents killed her for sure. Daphne thinks it's cruel to use Kace like this but I really don't care what she thinks. We need to if we are going to get cold, hard evidence on his parents. We got to do what we got to do to solve this.

But, Daphne will not let it go. Maybe it has to do with her little crush on Kace. "I'm just saying! You are literally using him! That's mean and careless."

I've had *enough*. "Daphne, are you clinically insane or incredibly annoying? I can't tell."

She rolls her eyes and jumps off my bed, folding her arms in fury. She always does that. It's part of her attitude. "Probably both."

Nixon laughs, still on the floor, but when she kicks him he quiets *very* quickly.

She gets to my door and turns around, targeting me with her dangerous glare. "You know, I had a very good theory but now that you're being a jerk, so I'm not going to tell you."

Really what would she come up with that I haven't already come up with? I've gone over everything. I've come up with every theory possible.

Nixon perks up but I sit back, waiting for her to leave. It was a terrible idea working with my sassy, attitude-prone little sister. It is nothing short of a mistake. She's just going to be a little brat.

"Tell us," Nix practically begs. Daphne shakes her head 'no.' Then the guy offers her the *rest* of the donuts. He's good, but he's also giving away the donuts, which I haven't had much of.

"Fine," Daphne smiles, picking up the donuts as she walks back to my bed. She plops down her butt and eats one. Nixon and I wait in silence as we wait for her '*amazing*' theory. It never comes.

"*You scammer!*" Nixon and I exclaim at the same time. We both get up and charge her, looking for blood... or donuts. Donuts would satisfy our needs. I grab the donuts and tear them out of her surprisingly strong arms. I throw them onto the desk and begin tickling her on her sides. She begins laughing and screaming, wiggling around uncontrollably. I tickle her until she is near tears. I should feel bad, but I'm her older brother, it's literally my job to mess with her.

After we all settle down back in our seats after several laughing fits, the room goes eerily silent. We all suddenly look at each other, waiting for someone to say something. It's awkward but also slightly scary. I shift my eyesight to our makeshift board. I know something's missing.

"What was she doing all the way out at the reservoir? Like of all places why there?" I question underneath my breath.

Fizz escapes Nixon's Dr. Pepper from behind me, interrupting my thought process. He takes a large sip and gulps louder than I've ever heard anyone. That was Evie's pet peeve. She told me once while on a 'date' at Ranch Hand, the local cafe outside Montpelier. Ever since then, I've tried not to gulp or anything like that.

Daphne sighs deeply. "Maybe she wanted to hitchhike to Wyoming."

I've considered this countless times and it never made sense with anything. Not until now, I guess. She willingly went out to the reservoir. She willingly went toward Wyoming. "But what's out in Wyoming?"

I look to Nixon who collapses on the ground, beginning to stare at the ceiling. He inhales then exhales. "It's not what's out in Wyoming. It's what *isn't*. Her parents weren't out in Wyoming."

Nixon, Daphne, and I spend the next hour trying to find a contact for Olivia Ward. We find at least five Olivia Wards on Facebook and so we have to comb through each of their pages. It doesn't help that *all* of them are elderly and live near here.

"I think it's Olivia number five," Nix exclaims softly. We are all getting tired of this. We thought there would be only one Olivia Ward in Bear Lake.

I gave Daphne my computer to search through Facebook so she doesn't feel left out. My sister throws back her head and shifts from sitting up to laying down on her stomach. "I still think it's number three."

This is a nightmare. I had a hard day and I just want to sleep, but *no*, I decided we needed to call Mrs. Ward. I'm making it hard on myself, I know, but I can't stop trying to help Evie. Even after death.

"Well, do any of them have a phone number listed?" I interrogate, massaging my temples. I, personally, am not stupid enough to list my phone number on my Facebook account, but maybe Olivia Ward is. No offense to her, of course, *if* she does.

Nixon's head pops up after staring more intently at his iPhone. "Mine does."

Things are looking up. Hopefully.

"Awesome, I'll call," I inform him, going to the fifth Olivia's account on my own phone. "Let's just hope and pray it's the one."

I copy her number and paste it into my keypad. I take a deep breath and press the call button. I put it on speakerphone and shush Daph and Nix as they quietly fight over the last powdered donut. The phone rings five times before Olivia Ward picks up.

"Hello?" she asks, her voice seasoned with age and honey.

"Hi! Is this Olivia Ward?"

She hesitates for a moment. I don't blame her. "Yeah, this is she. Can I help you, young man?"

A smile spreads across my face and I nod even though she can't see me. "Yes, I was hoping so. You see, I was just wondering if you were the Olivia Ward that called a tip to the police. I'm actually Evie Baker's boyfriend and I really want some more information, if it was you."

The elderly woman goes silent for at least ten seconds. I check to see if she hung up, but the call continues on, the second count increasing. Daphne and Nixon look at me warily and I shrug.

When she speaks again, it almost frightens me. "Yes, that was me."

Relief spreads throughout me and I audibly sigh. Things are *actually* looking up. The universe doesn't hate me after all.

"You have no idea how pleased I am to hear that it's you," I tell her, my shoulders lifting from the sagging position they've been sentenced to since Evie disappeared. "The police aren't really doing anything to solve this, I believe. So, I'm trying to solve it myself. I know it's crazy, but I want justice for Evie."

Olivia sighs on the other line. I look up at Daphne who seems skeptical, and then at Nix who is just staring at the ceiling. "It's not crazy. I don't blame you for wanting justice."

I swallow as she continues. "She was such a sweet girl. I could tell that just from the small car ride. I found her walking down Main Street in front of Napa Auto Parts, soaked through. I just had this inkling to stop, so I did. The girl didn't want to accept the car ride, but it was cold."

It sounds like Evie to refuse a ride offered to her. She never wanted to take anything offered to her. I think she felt she didn't deserve it. I blame that on her good-for-nothing parents.

It's my turn to talk. "And she wanted you to take her out to the reservoir?"

"Yes. She said she was at a friend's house and couldn't get a ride to her family's campsite out there. I was suspicious, though. I shouldn't have taken her out to the reservoir. I should have offered her a bed at my house. I had an inkling the girl was lying to me. But, I thought 'what girl would want to go out to the reservoir for no reason.' So, I dropped her off at the campsite. I feel terrible."

Evie has always been a great liar, so really it isn't Olivia's fault and I'm not mad or anything. She couldn't have known Evie was going to be murdered afterward. My question is, was it that night or the next day?

"You couldn't have known, Olivia," I reassure her, scratching a sudden itch on the back of my neck. "Now, can you tell me how she was acting? It's really important."

Olivia and I spend twenty more minutes talking about how Evie was acting and looked. It's eye-opening and contributes to my main theory that whatever happened that night led to her death. She tells me how Evie was antsy—which is fairly normal—and seemed like she had been crying. Her voice was shaky and she was constantly tense. Eve never calmed down, even when she was finally warm. Also, apparently, Olivia noticed she had a black eye forming when she let her out on the side of the highway at the road leading to the campsite. So, that proves she got it before she ran away.

I'm even more confused with all of this information. It just raises more questions in my mind regarding what happened that night that caused her to think she had to run away. I mean clearly, she made the better decision and left her house. She was clearly in life-threatening danger.

But what happened that night that led her parents to potentially kill her?

CARTER

Wednesday, May 25, 2022, Present.

I pull into the pick up loop in front of the elementary school in Montpelier, A.J. Winters. Daphne stands near the door talking to one of her friends. I think her name is Ashley, but I'm not sure. I just know she has come over before and has a major crush on me. It's cute and really boosts my confidence. And it's also creepy that she has a crush on someone nine years older than her.

Daph spots me and tells her blonde-haired friend goodbye, her hand moving in a fluid wave. She then jogs over to me, her dark brown hair bouncing around. Today she's not wearing her staple outfit: a skirt, leggings, and a colorful shirt, but instead a short-sleeved white shirt covered in different colored butterflies. It ruffles at the bottom and she wears black skinny jeans. Daph wears her bouncy hair in two braids that end in pigtails.

She opens Big Red's door and hops into the passenger seat because of the lack of backseat. She buckles herself in and I pull out of the pick up loop.

"So, I'm just going to drop you off at home, is that good?" I ask her, stopping at the four-way stop sign on Clay Street. I have the right-of-way so I continue down Clay toward the highway, or Fourth Street, whatever you want to call it.

"Where are you going?" She turns the radio to another station that doesn't play rock. "Your music sucks."

I shoot her a glare and pull right onto the highway at the corner of Arctic Circle and Subway. "The reservoir. I want to test another theory of mine."

I have high hopes for this new theory. She had to have slept somewhere that night. I want to find out where because maybe it will tell me if she died the night of the fifteenth or sometime on the sixteenth because the police sure aren't going to tell me.

"I don't want to go home. I'm coming with you," she insists, settling on a station that's playing pop.

"You're coming?"

I didn't think she'd want to come out to the bug infested reservoir with me. She's typically scared of bugs. Plus, she always hated going camping there. I mean I guess she was only ever a baby, but she did cry the entire time.

Daphne shrugs and sets her backpack on the ground of my truck. "It's not like I have much going on in my life right now."

I laugh and pull into the city park parking lot to turn around because the canyon road was a straight shot from Clay Street. The parking lot is full of tourists and tourist buses. It's hard to turn around, but I do it. I then pull back onto the highway and turn left onto the canyon road that runs alongside the park and the Oregon/ California Trail Center.

We drive for fifteen minutes before seeing the iconic split-in-half mountain that tells you you're in the right area. I pull into the deserted rearing pond like I did last time, and park. Daphne and I get out and then walk across the highway to the campsite area. It's full of campers even though it's a weekday. I'm surprised they are all here after a body was found in the reservoir literally right above them. Evie was found right by where the water goes down the dam. I'm hoping there are metal bars in front of the dam that make sure nothing like fish could go down the dam. If not, these campers were close to getting a traumatizing scare. I don't even want to imagine it. Chills run up my back when I do. It's a *horrible* thought.

Daphne follows the dirt road until we are right next to the camp's restroom.

"Okay, let's split up," I sigh, examining the area. I can hear campers laughing at their campsites. It's unsettling to me and I'm not sure why. It just rubs me the wrong way.

Daphne giggles. "That's what everyone says in horror movies and it *always* goes wrong."

"You've never even *seen* a horror movie. You are literally eight, Daphne," I laugh. "Here, you take by the creek and I'll do the restroom side of the road."

Daphne nods, not protesting. *That* weirds me out. I watch in shock as she willingly goes over to the creek, scanning the ground for any clues. I silently chuckle and cover around the restroom. I see no sign that *anybody* slept here. But, I know Evie is smart, so she would sleep somewhere not out in the open. So, I trudge over to a few bushes that tower me. I check the mud for a body shape and maybe any garbage, preferably granola bar wrappers. Reggie did mention she brought along with her granola bars.

A scream splits the air and my heart stops. I spin around on my heel and bolt toward the creek. Daphne could have fallen in. She doesn't know how to swim or fight a powerful current. The creek is five feet long from one shore to the other and can't be any deeper than three feet but the current is strong. It's strong enough to pull her under. It's strong enough to drown her. I can't lose another person I love, especially not in the span of a month.

But, I find her perfectly fine, standing a few feet from the creek.

"Daphne Ann! Why would you scream?! I thought you fell in!" I lecture at the top of my lungs, grabbing her by her arms. I shake her once, looking into her fearful hazel eyes.

"There... There was a snake."

I give her a good thug in the shoulder. I really thought something had happened to her. I'm relieved she's fine, but I'm pissed she let out a blood-curdling scream over a *snake*. It was probably a tiny water snake too. They are more scared of Daphne than she is of them.

I let my heart start back up again and double over to breathe. I close my eyes briefly, silently telling myself my baby sister is fine. I open my eyes and spot a granola bar wrapper stuck in the muddy grass. I push Daphne to the side and crouch next to it. The wrapper is only one or two feet from a body imprint in the mud and grass. My shaky breath gets caught in my throat and I have to stabilize myself using the bush's branch.

"Is this what we were looking for...?" Daphne asks, stepping around me to see for herself.

My head—on autopilot—nods. Then, something begins to tickle my hand in the hot breeze. My eyes stare at where my hand is and spots a chunk of hair stuck in the branch. I slowly get up and examine it. It's dirty blonde and it is proof Evie was here. But, this discovery makes it all the more harder. Her murderer didn't follow her out here Sunday night. Instead, they—somehow—knew she was out here. No one could've known.

No one *should've* known she was out here. There's no way anyone could have known. That's what is going to keep my brain awake every night until I figure it all out. That's a fact. I wish it wasn't.

Daphne lands a hand on my shoulder, pulling me back to reality. "We got to get back into service to call this into the police. Come on."

I nod because I know she's right. *This* is something I need to tell Sheriff Reggie immediately. Even if he'll just get mad at me for finding where Evie slept the night before she died. I mean I did go looking but it's not my fault we found something. But, still, I can't help but think that this discovery will make me more of a suspect and I can't put Mom through it anymore. But, it's also the right thing to do. Dad taught me to *always* do the right thing. So, I scrape myself up, square my shoulders, and get off my knees because it's what Dad taught me to do.

A county sheriff's vehicle accompanied by two city cop cars come speeding toward the Rearing Pond. Daphne and I drove just enough out of the canyon so we had service and then called the station. They strictly instructed us to drive back and park at the Rearing Pond to wait for them. We have done exactly that, so we have a great view of the authorities barreling into the pond parking lot. They all park around us and slowly get out. I meet eyes with Sheriff Reggie as he steps out of his sheriff's vehicle and he does *not* look pleased. He clutches his gray bulletproof vest, his face stern as he frowns at Daphne and me. My eyes slowly wander to the many weapons and gadgets fastened into his belt on his black pants and his vest on top of his shirt, which is the same color. Under his button up shirt I spot a milky white undershirt. Sheriff Reggie snaps his fingers, bringing my attention back to him fully.

I snap my eyes to his and try my hardest not to reflect his glare right at him. That would make me just as bad as him, and I don't need to stoop to his level. Not today.

"Carter," he scornfully greets, his graying brown hair fluttering in the eighty-five degree breeze.

I feel like I need to immediately start defending myself. He already thinks I had something to do with Evie's murder. This may just heighten his beliefs.

"Sheriff."

The sheriff is trying to read me, I can tell. He's squinting his eyes at me and looking me up and down, looking for some kind of tell probably. He isn't going to find anything. I'm sure I didn't hurt Evie Baker. This guy is relentless though.

"You said you found something of interest, Miller?" he asks, clearing his throat.

I nod and he commands me to take him to the spot. So, I do. With Daph attached to my hip, I cross the highway, the many authority figures following me closely. Then, I take them to the spot Daphne and I found only forty-five minutes ago.

"Step back, Miller. Get out of the way," Sheriff demands, shoving himself through the two city cops and me to get his own read. All four of us—the cops, Daphne, and myself—watch him closely as he looks around the area. He makes sure not to touch anything with his bare hands or disrupt anything more than the wildlife has. Then, finally, after five minutes, he turns around and stares me down.

He doesn't look away from me the entire time he's instructing the city cops on what to do. Sheriff Reggie doesn't even speak to Daphne or me until they come back, he just stares. Stares into our souls. *Who even does that*?

"Are you going to say something or make us stand here in silence all *freaking* day?" Daphne erupts, shattering the eerie silence with her sass-filled, high-pitched voice.

I take my hand and cover her mouth. I can't believe she just said that. Daphne licks me, causing me to bring my hand off of her mouth in disgust. I wipe my hand frantically on my jeans and glare at her. "*Daphne...*"

Sheriff Reggie looks as if he's about to laugh, but doesn't. He stays impossibly stern. I watch with some relief as he takes his eyes off of Daphne and moves them to me.

"Carter, I hope you know how this looks."

I do, so I bob my head to say so. I really don't want to talk to this man. Is it bad that I'm happy when he seems angry about my silence? It probably is.

Shifting my eyes to the two city cops, I carefully watch as they take pictures of everything from the mud to the granola wrapper to the hair. It still makes me feel overwhelmed when I look at that spot. Ten days ago Evie slept in that spot. I wonder if she was scared that night before she fell asleep. I can't imagine...

Sheriff Reggie snaps his fingers, bringing me back to him again. He raises one brown eyebrow as he looks at me.

"I'm going to have to bring you two in."

"Yeah, I was aware of that when I called the station." I try to chuckle but it sounds so strained that it sounds like I'm being choked. It does little to brighten the situation, which I really want to happen. Something about Reggie makes me uneasy and angry.

The sheriff brings his hand to his temple and shakes his head leisurely. "Carter, you need to let *me* solve this case. Leave it up to the experts."

I laugh before I can hold it back. '*Experts*?' Yeah, because Sheriff Reggie and his goon squad are experts. They haven't ONCE been around a murder investigation, let alone solved one, I can assure you that. Of all people in the world, they would be least likely to solve this case. I just wish he would just believe me and arrest Paul and Joanne Baker. All of the signs point to them. Now I understand that they need concrete evidence that it was them, but still you'd think the hundreds of bruises covering Evie would be a clear sign that they had something to do with it. And if they can't charge them with her murder, they can at least charge them with abuse of a minor. I've never liked politics and since I moved here I remember why.

"What about that was funny, Miller?" Sheriff Reggie scoffs, stepping forward toward me to where he's only two feet from my face. I can see from his eyes that he hasn't slept for a while. There are major bags underneath them and the rims of his eyelids are a vibrant red. From here I can smell his putrid breath, the odor of which is black coffee and a hint of garlic. I try my hardest not to cringe or break eye contact.

I say nothing else but Daph doesn't have the same amount of self-control as me. She pipes up from beside me and pushes her way in between us.

"Excuse me mister, sir, sheriff, dude, person? My brother and I did nothing wrong here. In fact, we have gotten farther in this case than you have and we aren't even in law enforcement. We haven't even had prior training. Don't you think that's *pathetic* of you guys? A seventeen and eight-year-old are closer to solving this case than you guys are. I think it's pathetic. I mean you should hear our theories. They have real potential. I mean one of them led us to know she hadn't been murdered the night of the fifteenth because she slept *somewhere*. And we found that somewhere.

"So, really, you should stop harassing my brother and start working with him. He knew that girl better than *anyone*... and he didn't hurt her *ever*.

"Three weeks ago, Carter stepped on a ladybug and then fell to his knees, cradled it, and kept apologizing. I thought the freak was going to cry. I didn't even have the heart to tell him it was a red M&M I dropped and was too lazy to pick up. So, really do you think this–" she reaches up and pinches my left cheek "–*baby*... hurt her?"

One of the police officers stifle a laugh behind Sheriff Reggie but not enough to where he doesn't hear. The sheriff spins around and must shoot them the deadliest of glares because the laughing police officer stops in his tracks and turns ghost white. He nods and returns to bagging up the granola wrapper in a plastic baggie.

"Go home you two. Just go home and stop 'investigating' this."

I don't waste another second to get out of the sheriff's presence. I don't even take a few seconds to fully process what Daphne told him. In fact, I grab her wrist and begin walking to the dirt road that leads to the highway.

Something causes me to stop and look back. Well, not just something–a question that intrudes my mind does. Sheriff is watching us leave. He looks confused at my legs stalling.

"Hey, Sheriff? Does this mean I'm not a suspect anymore?"

The man laughs. "No, you're still a suspect."

I nod, disappointed, and we make our way to Big Red. When we get in, we sit in silence for a few minutes. What Daphne finally said floods my mind.

I look to her in dejection, my eyebrows arched into 'U's.' "It was a red M&M?"

CARTER

Friday, May 27, 2022, Present.

I awake to the rapid, shrill ring of my phone. I groan but the person on the other end doesn't give up and hang up. Blindly, I continuously slap my nightstand—knocking several items off—until I grasp my quaking phone. I squint my eyes at the screen. Nixon is the one calling over and over again. I'd say he really shouldn't be calling this early in the morning but it's two o' clock in the afternoon. Technically I woke up at like nine this morning but I forced myself to go back to sleep. I had a sickening feeling that something would happen today. So, because I didn't want to deal with it, I forced myself back asleep.

Now I know I can't avoid the day forever.

Pressing the call button, I bring the phone to my ear and shield my eyes from the little bit of sun that escapes through my blackout curtains.

"Carter?" Nixon asks.

"Yeah, who else would it be?" I groan, pulling my comforter over my face. "This better be really important because I was in the middle of a pretty weird dream that there were these cloud formations in the sky of racoons and bears. Then, their mouths opened up to reveal hundreds of black holes that were beginning to eat Earth."

Nixon doesn't laugh. "Look, dude. You are going to want to get into Montpelier immediately."

"Why...?"

"I drove past Kace's house and there were a *bunch* of squad vehicles there. I think they are searching it."

My heart leaps out of my ribcage and I kick off my blanket. "*What*?!"

"Yeah. No joke. All of the Bakers are on the front lawn being questioned and a bunch of police officers are crawling all over the inside of the house. This is not a drill. Get over here *now*."

I am not going to waste time. Maybe I'll be able to see Paul and Joanne get arrested. I have been waiting for this day for what feel like forever. I pull off my basketball shorts and replace them with jeans. Then I pull a white shirt over my bare chest. Hopping to my bedroom door with my phone stuck in between my ear and shoulder, I force my socks on.

"I will be there in like... well as soon as I can," I gasp, out of breath, as I bolt down the wooden stairs.

"Oh, and hey... Evie's funeral is going to be June seventeenth."

I only have one question.

"Why so far into the future?"

Nixon sighs. "Dad says it's because they still need her body as evidence and to close this case. Or something like that."

I give him a thanks before he hangs up and pass Daphne, who is sitting on the sofa watching three guys review Amazon items on YouTube. She looks over her left shoulder, judging me as I try to shove my sneakers on. Not daring to look at her, I get my right shoe on. Then my left. I reach for the door.

"Wait, where are you going in a hurry?" She questions me, pausing the YouTube video.

"Somewhere important. Now can I go? Or will you be too scared to stay here by yourself?" Mom left super early this morning for day shift at the hospital.

Daphne scoffs and turns around fully, leaning her upper body on the coach's back. "Let me come then."

No, absolutely not. This time she can't come. Mom got *livid* Wednesday when Sheriff Reggie called to tell her to keep us in check after we got home. She said I can't get involved and if I did for whatever reason, I can't bring my sister into it. It's fair. She's eight. She's supposed to be playing with dolls, not trying to solve murder cases.

"No, Daph. You can't. You heard what mom said Wednesday," I reach for the door handle again.

Daphne does her classic eye roll and rockets herself back around toward the TV. "Fine! Don't expect me to tell you anything ever again! Leave then! Leave your only sister behind!"

My hands twist the door handle and I step out onto the porch. The outside has sort of an empty feeling. It's extremely cloudy but bright. Plus, it's *hot*. When I look around at the sky I just feel emptiness. A hollowing emptiness. It makes me stop for a moment.

Nothing good can come out of this day, especially with the threatening rain.

Rain has always been my favorite weather but something has changed. I don't know what changed exactly but suddenly I do not enjoy the rain.

SHERIFF REGGIE

Friday, May 27, 2022, Present.

An anonymous tip was called in last night that they saw something suspicious in the Bakers' house when dropping off a casserole. I personally didn't believe it, I mean, *come on*. It was *clearly* Carter Miller trying to throw us off his scent again. But, the 911 operator who took the call said it was a girlish voice. It was still a guy's voice, but it was sweeter. Carter has a very distinct deep voice so it couldn't be him. My first thought was that it was his little sister he had with him Wednesday afternoon, but it was, once again, a gentleman's voice. So, we took action and got a search warrant from the judge.

To be honest, I was shocked Judge Carson allowed the search warrant because the gentleman didn't specify what he saw, just that it was suspicious. I guess the judge has given us warrants on less evidence before.

Now, I'm standing next to Paul Baker in his front yard, waiting as the deputies comb through the house. Paul and I used to play football together in high school. He was the quarterback and I was the wide receiver. Back then we were inseparable. Now, we only talk occasionally.

He grumbles next to me as a newbie cop looks inside his mailbox beside the door. It's a red barn mailbox on a log. "There's nothing in there, Reagan."

I hate when people call me by my real name but Paul is an exception.

"I know. It's just the paninis from the big shot FBI office in Pocatello thought we should take action when that tip came in. I ain't about to turn them down," I growl, snapping my fingers at the newbie. He stops immediately and shuts the mailbox's lid. "Look, I know you didn't do squat, Paul. Between me and you."

I try to ignore the thought intruding my brain.

Well then who put those bruises all over his daughter?

My solution to that thought is that Carter Miller hit her. *Easy*. On the surface he looks like a sweet boy–his track record says the same thing–but he's a boy that grew up without a father. Who knows what he could be capable of. People with tragedies are always people to look into first.

Beside Paul stands Joanne who is dressed in black leggings and a plain pink shirt. She's an awfully pretty woman, in fact, I had a crush on her in high school. But, she fell for Paul and they had four kids. I remember how bummed I was the night I heard Evie was born. I knew because she was born, Joanne would *never* leave Paul to come be mine. I feel bad about it now. Plus I'm over Joanne. Kind of.

We stand on the patch of grass that sits in between the road and the sidewalk. About forty feet from us the Baker kids sit, their backs against the paint-chipped garage. The boy, Kace I think, sits there stone faced, facing us with an empty expression. His sisters sit a foot away from him, whispering. What I want to know is what's going through the boy's mind. It seems full of thoughts. Maybe he can tell me a little more about Carter Miller. They were on the football team together this year and Paul says Carter has come over to talk to him. Paul's son could be a very good asset to us.

Joanne pulls me from my thoughts. "How long is this going to take, Reggie?"

Clearing my throat, I take my eyes off the boy. "Well, it'll be over soon. I'm sure they won't find anything."

"They won't," Paul insists.

I nod because I believe him and then watch an officer passes by the living room window in the interior of the house. I really hope this doesn't take long either. I've got a Ranch Hand cheeseburger calling my name in my fridge at home. I haven't eaten this afternoon or this morning. It'd make the perfect early dinner.

"We... we... um... Yeah, we need you in the house. Right now," he stammers, tugging at the blond hair on his head. He is one of the newer ones in the sheriff's department, but he wears the same outfit as I do: gray vest, black pants, and a black belt and button up shirt. He's a tiny guy and proof the sheriff's department is scraping the bottom of the barrel to gather deputies.

"Yeah, whatever." I tell Paul I'll be back and then follow the newbie into the house. He brings me to a tiny square hallway that leads to a master bedroom and the stairs. He leads me straight, into the bedroom. Surrounding the bed are three deputies, all examining something on it. I shove past the blond guy and the others part.

I don't believe my eyes. There on the bed is an ebony-colored, semi-automatic pistol. It knocks the air from my lungs long enough that I have to take a second to catch my breath again.

"Where did you find this?!" I demand, scanning the four deputies' faces. One that looks eerily close to Chris Hemsworth but with black hair points at the closet.

It's a basic closet that has sliding wood doors and a pole for clothes. Above the pole is shelving. "Where in here?"

The Chris Hemsworth lookalike stands beside me and reveals a hidden cubby at the back of the closet wall. It looks as if someone cut out the drywall, stuck the gun in, and put the drywall back. Not someone. Most likely Paul. Even if Carter had been here long he wouldn't have been left alone for a long enough time to cut a hole in the wall. I don't want to believe it but it was someone in this household. Paul and Joanne.

Oh heavens, I want to puke.

I close my eyes for a moment and try to breathe through what this means. That gun on the bed is the same make of the gun that killed Evie Baker—based on the bullets. I never expected to find it. I figured it was thrown in the reservoir along with Evie. *Oh heavens.*

"Finely comb through the ENTIRE house. Do not leave a single chair overturned or box unsearched. You hear me?"

Behind me, the four cops nod enthusiastically and file out of the bedroom. I turn around fully and grab an evidence bag from my pants pocket. It's still there from Wednesday when Carter called us out to the reservoir campground. I turn it inside out, stick my hand in, and grab the gun. I pick it up and carefully put the bag right side out and close it.

I carry it by the seal at the top of the Ziploc bag as I make my way through the house. I don't know what I'm going to say. I don't have a single idea what to say first. I'm about one minute from rightfully accusing my high school best friend of murdering his eldest daughter. They didn't teach us this in training.

I walk through the ajar front door and immediately make eye contact with Paul Baker's haunting blue eyes. His eyes wander to the bag in my right hand and then to his wife's eyes, which are set on the bag as well. He opens his mouth as I come closer but nothing finds its way out.

"Paul..." I begin with. "Tell me why we just found the same make and model of gun that your daughter was killed with."

He looks between me and the gun frantically. "That can't be. I didn't do crap to that girl. It's reckless of you to be accusing something like that without getting the ballistics checked first. Just because I own a semi-automatic doesn't mean it's the one that killed her."

'*That girl.*' What father calls their firstborn daughter that? It suggests he had no personal relation to her. The guy probably was hitting her too.

"I'm not accusing you and Joanne of anything, Paul," I inform him, looking between him and Jo. "I'm going to send this to the station and we will know in about twenty-four to forty-eight hours."

Paul looks outraged while Joanne looks purely overwhelmed. "Seriously, Reagan? Do you really think I did it? That I killed my own daughter?"

I don't know what to think, I silently answer.

"I have my men going over your house with an *extra* fine comb, Paul. They will find everything you are hiding if you did it."

The man scoffs and brings his hand to his forehead. He wipes some sweat off of it and rubs his hand on his torn jeans. His gray shirt is completely soaked through at his neckline and under his armpits. "You can't be suggesting it was me. You said it yourself, it was that Miller boy, Reagan. You said it was him."

I look behind him across the street where an older red truck is parked. It wasn't here when I arrived, so it must've parked while I was inside the house. The truck looks insanely familiar and when I spot the driver in the front seat it's none other than Carter Miller—who's watching like his life depends on it, and I guess it does. This kid is relentless. I'm not even sure how he knows about the search. He has got sources, I know that for sure.

I know in Carter's story I am the villain. I'm the man who has never once believed him that Evie's parents are as cold blooded as they might be, as Paul reminds me. I've even spent the entire investigation suspecting him and only him. He has plenty of good reasons why I'm the villain. But still, there's that logical voice in the back of my head that insists not to let the boy off the hook quite yet.

Someone taps my shoulder, causing me to spin around on my heels. In front of me is the blond guy again. This can mean one of two things. One is that they can potentially prove Paul and Joanne could be Evie's murderers, while the other is that they can potentially prove the opposite.

"Found something else?"

To my relief, but to Paul's displeasure, the deputy bobs his head up and down. I exhale sharply and follow him back into the house after instructing an older deputy to watch the Bakers.

The deputy takes me through the carpeted kitchen instead of the bare living room. Unlike last time, three deputies don't surround the evidence. They must all be searching other parts of the house because none of them are in the vicinity of the kitchen area. Blond guy brings me into a laundry room with a washer and dryer to the right of the entrance and a meat freezer and shelves to the left. My first thought is that he's about to show me Evie's dead body in the freezer but I laugh that off. Her body was already found. I'm letting the stress and fear of 'what's next' get to me.

Instead, blond guy grabs a cereal box that sits on top of the horizontal freezer. He angles it just enough to show me what's rattling inside it. A mud-covered cellphone gleams back at me, its blocky case a vibrant red.

"We didn't find her cell phone on her when we recovered her body and we didn't find it in the bag either, sir," he reminds me.

The entire department just figured her phone was somewhere at the bottom of the reservoir, like the gun. None of us even stretched the possibility that her phone had been taken off of her dead body.

"We don't know for sure if it's her phone but bag it up anyways," I demand of him, running my hand from my nonexistent mustache down to my invisible beard.

The deputy does as I say and looks up at me, his eyes big and blue. "What's the plan now, Sheriff?"

I inhale deeply and look to the Fruity Pebbles cereal box the phone was in. "I'm going to go talk to her siblings to find out if it *really* is her phone." I grab the bag from the blond deputy and make my way back outside for the second time.

Paul looks at the bag in shock and looks even more shocked when I slowly walk over to his three remaining children. All three of them look at me and then the bag. I hold it up and try to put on a kind face. "Is this your sister's phone?"

The boy, Kace, meets my eyes and nods quickly. "Yeah, that's my sister's phone."

The youngest girl, who can't be older than thirteen, perks up her calm dark blue eyes at me. "Does this mean Dad and Mom are going away for a long time?"

Something inside my stomach twists, making me want to puke, or weep—which I don't do often. She looks undisturbed by the phone. As if it isn't news. As if all of this isn't news. She either knew her parents killed her sister or had a *strong* inkling.

The now oldest girl hits her little sister in the arm. She's probably about fifteen. "Riley! Shut up."

Riley does shut up. She clamps her mouth shut and looks at her feet.

"Allie, she is just saying what all of us are thinking," Kace growls numbly, looking straight ahead at his parents. His frozen eyes look back to mine and he begins picking at the skin on his wrist. "Please tell me you are going to take them far away from us, Sheriff. You have to. I can't live under the same roof as my sister's murderers. I can't do it anymore. She had an entire life ahead of her and now that's taken away from her. They stole her happiness, then her freedom, and then her life. Take away *their* freedom, see how they like it, sir. Take away *their* wills to live. It's what they deserve after taking away everything she was entitled to. It's what Dad gets for treating her like his own punching bag."

Without listening to another word I turn around and head for Paul and Joanne Baker. If you told me in high school that in twenty-five years I would be arresting my high school crush and best friend, I would have laughed in your face and then thrown you into a locker. But, here I am now. I hand the baggy to the deputy that had been watching them and then I demand Paul to turn around. I grab my handcuffs from my belt.

"Paul Baker, you are hereby arrested for the murder of your daughter, Evie Baker, and abuse of a minor." I clip the handcuffs around his wrists. "Anything you say can and will be used against you in a court of law. You have the right to an attorney. If you cannot afford an attorney, one will be provided for you. Do you understand the rights I have just read to you?"

The older deputy begins arresting Joanne next to me, repeating almost the same exact speech as I.

Paul grumbles something under his breath and curses several times. I clutch his wrists tighter and lean in. "*Do you understand the rights I have just read to you?*"

He yelps and answers yes. "That's all you had to say, Paul."

My eyes shift to Carter's red truck across the street as he makes his way around the back of his vehicle. He leans his back against the tailgate and watches me with his hands on his head.

I feel bad for the kid. He dated that girl and then she was murdered by her parents. He tried to tell me that her parents did it and I shut him down every time. I just couldn't think the good-natured guy I was best friends with in high school could have done it. I couldn't believe the girl I thought I loved in high school could have done it. Maybe if I had trusted Carter Miller, this case would have been closed days ago. I feel like I should apologize to him. But, I'm one of the villains in his story, right? Last time I checked, apologizing is not what villains do in storybooks. I guess I'm okay with being the bad guy though. The longer I wait to apologize to Carter Miller, the longer I can pretend that my childhood best friends didn't kill their innocent, teenage daughter.

CARTER

Friday, May 27, 2022, Present.

I'm sitting alone in Big Red at city park with my ignition off, racking through my brain. Ten minutes ago Paul and Joanne Baker were arrested right before my eyes. It has been what I've been wishing for since Evie was found dead. Now with them arrested, I don't know what to do. Justice has been served. Everything has been resolved. Nothing can go wrong now.

Relief is what floods over me… and a little bit of pride. And sadness. I feel prideful that I was right all of this time and sad that I was right this entire time. But, it's over. The tragedies are over in this town. They have got to be. I can finally be a normal teenager. I can finally 'chill.' I can finally think about school. I'm going to graduate soon. The last day of my entire high school career is next week on the thirtieth. I made it this far. Grad' is on the thirty-first. The rest of my life starts on that day. I have to focus on that.

What drove her parents to snap and kill their eldest daughter?

I want to scream and cry. The pressuring questions will never leave me alone. I just want to be at peace. I think I deserve that at least. But, the questions deserve to be answered too. They need to be answered. They can't be left alone to stir or they will make me go crazy. Although, I may go crazy trying to answer them all.

How did they track her down that night? How did they possibly know she was at the reservoir?

That part is unanswered too. Maybe, just maybe, Paul and Joanne will tell Sheriff Reggie the answer. If they don't I *will* go crazy coming up with theories. The theories will be the main cause of my insanity.

What happened that night that made her run away?

It must have been bad enough for them to track her down and kill her. It had to be some dangerous huge secret. I can't imagine it being a little one. I certainly wouldn't kill someone over a tiny secret I can afford to get out.

And how did this all involve my Dad?

She carried a piece of paper with my Dad's name on it. The bag she had the night she ran away held that paper. It clearly wasn't because she wanted the police to look into me if something ever happened to her. I could run crazy going through the millions of possibilities. One that comes up is that she was pointing fingers at the Bakers. They could have been responsible for Dad's disappearance. It's crazy, and insane, I know. My dad loved going hiking. He could have fallen in a ravine somewhere and never been found. He had no enemies. That's just a fact.

A sob escapes me. It's followed by a thundering silence that does little to put my mind at ease. Then, another sob finds its way out of my mouth. A single tear rolls down my left cheek. I've known all this time that Evie Baker is dead. *My Evie Baker*. But now it sinks in.

Several more tears roll down my cheeks as it settles inside my trembling body. The palms of my hands find my steering wheel and begin smashing it uncontrollably. She's *dead*. Her parents took her away not only from me but from the world that was just waiting to be blessed by her bright presence. I'm angry. I'm *pissed*. I should have mentioned to someone that her dad was physically abusive. I should have mentioned to someone that her mom was emotionally and verbally abusive. It could have made the difference between Eve being dead or alive. This is all my fault and I don't think I can forgive myself.

I stop hitting the steering wheel and settle my hands on it. They are tense as they clutch the wheel and the knuckles are snowy white. The tears begin to get out of control. Everything is blurry. All I can see is the clouds darkening in the sky, threatening a storm. They threaten a storm like the one I'm producing.

I look up at the ceiling of Big Red, holding back my urge to scream. Holding it back doesn't do much for me except make me feel worse.

"This was my biggest fear and I didn't even know," I whisper to myself, doubling over in phantom pain. "My one gaping fear."

Rain begins hitting the metal exterior of Big Red, creating giant *thuds*. With every thud I release more steam. Evie and I could have been so great. We both would have graduated and I would get her out of this town as quickly as possible.

I thought we had more time.

"Evie," I choke. Something inside tells me she can't hear me. I push it down to my toes. "I hope I will find you again. In another life. In another world. In another body and time. We will meet again, I do promise that. I swear I will see you in another life."

Saturday, May fourteenth, we hung out in St Charles out by the lake. We went to the little North Beach shops next to Bear Cave, a drive-in food place, and got ice cream from that cute little shop called Float On. Neither of us had been there before. She ordered a vanilla waffle cone while I got a mama bear float inside a pineapple. I didn't expect it to be big, but my gosh when I got it, I nearly fell over. It was the top half of a pineapple carved out with strawberry ice cream and some kind of soda. On top of the ice cream was the pineapple churned into a freezie. There was even an umbrella and fresh pineapple slices. Evie laughed so hard at me.

Together we finished the huge pineapple ice cream float. I also learned a valuable lesson on not asking how big something is before getting it.

Then, I took her home. I hugged her before she jumped out of my truck.

I didn't know it was the last time I'd see her. If I had, I would have held her tight and never let go.

I look out my window and wipe my eyes just enough to be able to see the leaking clouds. Somehow I convince myself that it's the heavens crying for me. For Evie. I briefly convince myself the rain is Evie crying from above. She can hear me. She can see me. She can feel me.

CARTER

Saturday, December 25, 2022, Past.

I pull onto the side of the corner of Adam's and Ninth street, right next to the stop sign. The sun is setting over the West mountains as Evie bolts across her lawn from her backyard. She doesn't look both ways before crossing the abandoned street and then hops into the passenger seat of Big Red. She's severely out of breath, but laughing.

"Sneaking out is harder than I thought it would be," she giggles as she buckles her seat belt.

I shift into drive and pull right onto Ninth Street fully. "How'd you get out? Your backdoor?"

"In a sense..."

After driving for a minute, I turn right onto Main. My eyebrows furrow as I register her answer. "What? What does that even mean, Eve?"

She laughs and shrugs her shoulders. "I couldn't make it out the *first floor* back door because my mom was in the kitchen. But, luckily there is a second floor back door that I was able to go out of. Although I scraped my palms on the roofing." She holds up her palms for me to see. Sure enough, they are scratched just enough to where they aren't bleeding.

"There's no stairs or a ladder?!"

I peek at her as long as I can before having to return my eyes back to the road before us.

"No. It's just a random door on the second floor. It worked. I think I snuck out without detection."

I can't help but laugh. This girl is something else. I have never met anyone like her. Once you get through her outer shell and she trusts you, you find a little goofball that isn't afraid to make jokes about anything and everything.

I turn left onto the highway once I get to the corner of Main and Highway thirty, heading toward my house where we are having Christmas dinner with my family. Evie isn't my girlfriend or anything but I figured she'd want a good Christmas memory. Her family doesn't necessarily do anything at Christmas time.

It may sound creepy but I really want my family to meet her. My family from Oregon are down, as well as my dad's brother who lives in Montana. I don't want to jinx anything but I think Evie and I could be the real thing. Every time I go to ask her if she wants to be my girlfriend, I choke and then chicken out.

"Tell me about your family members that came down for your Christmas dinner," Evie demands, going through the stations on the radio. "You really need to get an AUX cord so you can listen to the music you want from your phone."

"I like the radio!" I exclaim. We pass the city park.

"Old timer," Evie giggles underneath her breath. "So, go ahead, tell me about your family."

A laugh finds its way out of my mouth. We pass the high school near the outskirts of town. "My grandma Aiden is my mom's mom. She's a widow but she doesn't let it put her down. I never knew my Grandpa Aiden 'cause he died when I was only a baby.

"Then, there's my aunt Crystal—she's my mom's younger sister. She's twenty-eight. My mom and her are nine years apart. My grandma and grandpa adopted her when she was only a toddler. Crystal is like that fun, wine-drinking aunt.

"Then, there is my uncle Jeremy. He's my dad's older brother. They were always inseparable. Uncle Jeremy lives in Montana and rarely comes to see us since Dad disappeared. He only ever comes for Christmas and then stays till New Years. Same with the rest of my family.

"And, of course, Grandma and Grandpa Miller will be there. I don't think anyone else is coming other than those five." I turn my head and wink at her. "And you."

Evie smiles brightly and blushes the colors of the sunset. The butterflies in my stomach flutter, giving me a happy, queasy feeling as I drive down the highway. I drive the rest of the way with a grin spread ear to ear as I listen to Evie switch between each radio station. She lands it on Christmas carols and begins singing the lyrics to "Grandma Got Ran Over By A Reindeer."

We get to my house as the song ends.

I put Big Red in park and turn off the truck. Along with the engine the radio turns off abruptly. Beside me I hear Evie gulp sharply. Subconsciously my hand finds hers which is placed on her lap. Her worried eyes meet mine and almost immediately calm. It gives me warm shivers that shock me.

"They'll love you. You have nothing to worry about, Eve."

She nods but I can tell she's still battling herself. "Seriously, Evie. My family doesn't judge anyone. Except for me."

It's meant as a joke but she doesn't give me her beautiful laughter, just a half-hearted kind. I squeeze her hand and give her another smile.

She finally speaks, her voice uneasy. "If we're going to do this then we need–"

I interrupt her, glancing at the window. I can see Aunt Crystal in the kitchen, her hair ginger. "–A plan?"

A small smirk slowly spreads across her face as she shakes her head. "No! Code names! Really cool code names!"

"*What*? Evie, it's a Christmas dinner," I chuckle, gesturing toward my front door.

"Carter! I'm trying to calm myself down... roll with it."

I stifle a laugh and slink back into my seat. I examine the sun visor above my head. Underneath it are my vehicle's registration papers. A picture of Dad, Chev, and me on a camping trip is paperclipped to the exterior of the visor.

"I'll be Cyclone," I smile, giving in. I can't say no to her. It's just impossible. Plus, her smile gives me butterflies. I'll do anything to see it. I'd do anything to be the reason she brightened.

And she does brighten. The only thing that's even remotely close to her beauty and shine is the summer sun.

Her beautiful blue eyes remind more of the lake on a summer day more than ever. "And I'll be Twister."

Cyclone and Twister. It has a pleasant ring.

"Are you ready to go in now?"

Her smile grows bigger as she bobs her head up and down. We both step out of my truck and shut the doors. We trudge through the thick snow on the lawn, compacting it with every footstep. With me in the front and Evie in the back, we step onto the ice-prone deck and Evie begins to slip. She squeals and grabs onto my right arm to steady herself before I know what's going on. I spin around on my heels to catch her without even realizing I'm doing it. I stabilize her with both of my hands on her waist.

She giggles and stands straight up in front of me, her eyes bright and daring. "Thanks."

My teeth latch onto my bottom lip and I don't feel the dark chill the icy weather brings. Instead, I feel a tingling warmth spread throughout me. "I... Yeah... My pleasure, Twister."

I want to kiss her. I should kiss her. We aren't dating but I want so *badly* to kiss her. I want this to blow my first kiss out of proportion. I mean, we almost kissed once after the Clifford movie all those months ago. It was interrupted. So maybe I *should* kiss her. It would make up for the almost, maybe movie kiss.

From inside, Grandpa Miller's iconic laugh erupts, interrupting us once again. My hands fly off of Evie's soft waist and go to the back of my neck. An itch suddenly arises there, which seems to always happen in awkward situations where I'm nervous.

Evie giggles and points toward the door silently. I'm on the same wavelength so I nod and open the front door. We are immediately greeted with the warmth being emitted from the oven and stove. Chev runs to me as I let Evie in behind me, sniffing me aggressively. I pet behind his ear and slip off my wet, snowy sneakers.

Grandma Aiden and Grandma Miller come sneaking up on us instantly. Grandma Aiden pushes me out of the way and ambushes Evie as she takes off her classic white, low-top converse.

"You must be Evie!" she exclaims, setting a wrinkly hand on her arm. I watch painstakingly as Eve tries her hardest not to wince in pain. Bless my grandma's soul... It's not her fault. She doesn't know how many bruises cover Evie's arms. I've noticed that they have grown in number based on how many usually intrude her skin. It might be the stress of the holidays on her parents. It still makes me sick. So, I've been trying my best to cheer her up lately.

"I am," Evie smiles, her grin charmed.

Grandma Aiden slowly guides Eve away from the door and toward Grandma Miller who stands next to me. My dad's mom, my grandma Miller, gives Evie a smile and latches herself onto Evie's other arm.

"It's very nice to see you again, dear," she smirks, helping guide her to the kitchen.

Grandma Aiden takes it a tad bit farther. "Now, tell me, hun... Are you my dear Carter's girlfriend?"

Evie is as shocked at the question as I feel. As they lead her away, she looks back at me, her eyes twinkling with admiration. Her smile beams from ear to ear, making me feel warmer than I already am once again.

Good luck, I mouth, a huge smile spread across my face.

She glares at me and turns her head around, sending her dirty blonde, low ponytail whipping. I laugh and make my way to the couches where Uncle Jeremy and Grandpa Miller sit. Their eyes flicker at me as I sit next to Jeremy. He looks eerily close to my Dad just with a full beard, not stubble like Dad had. They have always shared the same cocoa eyes, snub tan nose, and sharp jaw bones. The Miller men—my father and Jeremy—were and *are* very easy on the eyes. Every time I look at him, I'm struck with a sense of resolved grief.

"You're not going to be able to talk to her for the rest of the night," Uncle Jeremy chuckles, his voice deep and ragged. His voice never used to be so ragged. I think he took up smoking in the last few years.

"Yeah... I know," I laugh, watching as Aunt Crystal helps her with a yellow apron. It brings out her sunny personality surprisingly well. I've never seen Evie in yellow. Actually, I've rarely seen her in anything other than neutrals.

Jeremy slaps my shoulder when I turn my head back fully around so it's facing the turned-off TV. "She seems special, Tart."

Tart. Uncle J has called me that since I was little. No one really knows why but I think it had something to do with me being a small child. It doesn't fit now because I'm a good five foot eleven inches.

Uncle J squeezes my shoulder gently and lets them fall to his sides. "I never did *that* good with the ladies when I was your age."

Grandpa chuckles warmly and nods, watching Mom, Crystal, Daph, and Eve trying to prepare the remainder of Christmas dinner. "She looks exactly like Lena."

Lena Marlowe, also known as Evie's grandma. She was the grandma that was in the car accident with Eve when she was eight. She's the one that died right next to little Evie as they were trapped in the smashed car. It was the accident that gave her that scar above her eyebrow.

"Did you know I had the biggest crush on Lena in high school, Carter?"

I did not. How is it that so many years ago *my* grandpa had a *crush* on *my* crush's grandma? What are the odds of that? Like what is this? How does that even happen? I find it very coincidental.

Jeremy slaps his knee and doubles over in laughter. "You mean to tell me that you had a huge crush on your grandson's girlfriend's grandma?? *That* is *hilarious*. Were you in love with her? Did you go anywhere with that 'crush'?"

Those are questions that are floating around in my brain as I gawk at Grandpa.

Grandpa chuckles and closes his eyes. He relaxes substantially. "In love was an understatement. I thought I was going to marry her after school. Life was so much simpler back then. But, it never went further than a relationship. We both just drifted. Then, I met Annie and we got married. That was that."

I remember when Evie and I first hung out after I dislocated my knee. I took her to my grandparents' house. It was a boring idea but I really needed to say hello to them. We found out then that my grandpa, John, was the man who pulled her out of the car after the accident. We also found out that he and my grandma were best friends with Lena Marlowe. I can't imagine having been Grandpa on the day of the accident. He probably knew Lena was dead when he pulled Eve out of that vehicle and he didn't break down, he kept strong and took care of the girl that's in the kitchen right now.

"Well, if Evie is exactly like her grandma was, then I understand you fully, Grandpa."

* * *

Evie sits directly across from me, sandwiched between Mom and Daphne. I sit between ginger-haired Crystal and white-haired Grandma Aiden. I'm essentially in for an entire dinner of Grandma and Crystal teasing me about Evie and cooing over her. They are right to coo. Evie is a special girl, just like Uncle J said.

It took the girls about half an hour to finish dinner, which is good because the rising food aromas were making me hungry. But, it was also bad because I still had to wait.

Grandma leans in and my immediate thought is *here we go*. Her breath is hot on my ear and smells of peppermint and potatoes, a very odd combination.

"Never let go of that girl," she twinkles, her voice laced with love. "She's a unique individual, Carter. You may never meet a young lady like that ever again so don't you lose her."

I'm not planning on losing her. Grandma is right. She is so right. There may never be another Evie ever again. If I mess up my chance with her… I can't think about that. I can't. I won't lose her. We may not be dating, but I will not lose her. But, really, how do you lose something you never had? I find myself staring at her. Her bright eyes glisten in the warm lights in the room and her skin glows radiantly. A piece of her curly, dark blonde hair falls in front of her face, getting stuck in her mascara-covered eyelashes as she laughs at something Daphne says. She attempts to blow it out of her face but it doesn't budge. Her nimble fingers wipe it out of her freckled face and behind her ear.

Aunt Crystal leans in like grandma, bringing me back to reality. "If you hurt her I will hunt you down and hurt you, Carter. I will hunt you down and bash your head in, you hear me? Don't take me lightly. We both know I am good at keeping promises."

She pats my hand, smiles her white-toothed grin, and returns to eating her mashed potatoes and gravy like she didn't just threaten her nephew. She brushes her long, ginger hair from her face and pulls it into a low bun.

I never want to hurt Evie. She doesn't deserve to be hurt anymore–verbally, emotionally, or physically. She has had enough of that unfair crap in her life. I don't want to be the reason *ever* that she has more crappy stuff happen to her. I don't want to be the reason that she feels like she doesn't belong or doesn't feel beautiful. She does belong. She is beautiful. She's absolutely gorgeous and dazzling and adorably fetching. She deserves all the love that the world can provide.

The inside of my truck is *freezing*. As soon as we hop into Big Red we both gasp. Somehow it's colder than out there in the snow. I don't know how that's possible because it's like twenty degrees Fahrenheit outside.

"Good thing we brought a blanket," I laugh, spreading the thick blanket over both of our laps. Evie giggles and thanks me gingerly.

I turn on Big Red and let it run for a few minutes, hoping the heat will begin working. We sit here in awkward silence, staring at my house and barn.

This is my window, I quickly realize.

An itch begins to form at the back of my neck, causing me to scratch at it. I hate that that's what I do when I'm nervous. I turn my head and look at Evie who is picking at the material of the blanket. Another piece of her naturally curly hair falls in front of her face like it did during dinner. This time I don't have as much self-control and I brush it behind her ear. We are a good two or three feet from each other so I have to reach.

She seems surprised at first but softens quickly.

"Your hands are cold," She giggles, watching me in the dark as my hand lingers near her face.

I slowly bring it back to my lap and turn more toward her. "You know how my grandma Aiden asked if you were my girlfriend when we first got here?"

Evie nods gradually, blush forming on her cheeks. I'm not sure if it's from the cold or not.

How do I even ask this? I guess it's not supposed to be easy. No gain without pain, am I right? I don't even know. I've never done this sort of thing before. I may be seventeen but that doesn't mean anything.

"I...uh," I stammer.

Get ahold of yourself, Carter, the voice in my head scolds.

I close my eyes and take a deep breath, aware of Evie's cerulean eyes on me.

"I guess what I'm trying to say is... Well."

SPIT IT OUT, CARTER!

"I... Well..."

I open my eyes and make eye contact with her. She gives me an encouraging nod, her smile making me forget about the bitter cold. My heart beats unnaturally quicker, making my hands clammy. I take another deep breath and nod.

I've got this. I'm freaking Carter Miller. I've got this.

"You see, Evie, I'd like you to be my...um... my girlfriend. If you'd like?"

A bigger smile creeps across her freckled face. It reaches her eyes, making them twinkle like the stars above. It reaches her cheeks which are dyed a soft cherry color. She's beautiful. She's freaking gorgeous.

"What do you think?" she grins, smoothing her ponytail so it sits over her right shoulder. "Of course I would. We'd just have to keep it secret until I move out. My parents would be furious. You know how they are by now."

I totally understand her wishes and respect them. Her parents are control freaks who also don't have control. I don't even know how to describe them. Based on everything she has told me about them, I understand it all perfectly. Though, she still hasn't admitted they hit her. Not verbally. But, I understand it's hard on her. I wouldn't want to tell anyone either. Or talk about it. It's normal... I think.

"Yeah, okay. No problem. As long as you're my girlfriend, Eve."

Her smile grows bigger and she scoots in. "Well I guess since we are dating I can sit closer to you."

I laugh hysterically, doubling over, clutching my stomach. "Yeah, I guess that's what that means. I think it also means I can finally kiss you for real."

We both go quiet as I lean in, smirks plastered on both of our faces. When our lips connect it's like the stars have fallen and surrounded us. The moon and stars shine on us in the dark, illuminating this moment, driving away the harsh, biting winter air. Warm sparks run through me and tickle each of my limbs and organs. My heart even does a three-sixty and pounds against my chest in a way that I could get used to. I wonder if Evie can hear it beat as much as I can. I can hear her heart beating.

BRINLEY

Monday, May 30, 2022, Present.

Since Paul and Joanne Baker were arrested Carter hasn't stepped foot out of his room for any reason except to use the bathroom. I'm worried. I'm glad he's finally grieving, as I've recently noticed he has an unhealthy grieving system where he just pushes down the pain and hides it, refusing to believe it's there. He did it when Noah disappeared. He did it when Evie disappeared. Now that all that hidden grievance has caught up to him he's constantly sleeping or sitting in the dark, staring at the wall.

I feel so incredibly bad that I never realized how much Evie meant to him. I mean he never really brought her around so I never thought anything of it. I was sad he never brought her to the house after that one Christmas dinner. I really liked her.

I see so much of myself in my son now that this tragedy has struck. I can't help but think his entire grieving system is jacked because of me. If I'm being completely honest I never really accepted Noah's disappearance. I shoved it down like

Carter is doing now and I refused to accept it when he was declared legally dead. Recently it has kept me up at night. I don't even remember my last conversation with him. I don't remember when I last told him that I loved him. That takes a toll on a person. What hurts me the most is I have no idea what happened to him or if he's dead or alive. There's nights where I pray he just skipped out on this family and didn't die. For me personally it's easier to accept than knowing he's gone forever. Call me crazy.

But now I'm just deeply worried about Carter, my sweet boy. He refuses to eat or drink *anything*. By now he has got to be dehydrated and starving. The problem is that I don't know how to help him. I can't force feed him. I don't have it in me.

But I guess the fifteenth try is the charm, or however that saying goes.

I make my way up the stairs, dreading this. I can feel Daphne's eyes on me as I attempt once again. We both know I'll fail but neither of us will admit it. I get to the top and stop abruptly. At the end of the hall to the right stands Carter's closed door. I should be used to seeing it shut but I get a dreaded feeling for some reason everytime I see it.

I force myself to walk again and slowly make my way to his door. My fingers wrap around the handle and my wrists turn it, causing the door to begin to creak open. I push it open a little more and lean against the doorway.

My son sits at the edge of his bed, staring at his curtained window—saying nothing, doing nothing. Something squeezes my heart and lungs as a lump grows in my throat. He sits with his back and shoulders slumped in dejection.

"Do you want those open, hun?" I ask even though I know I won't get a reply. I never do.

Maybe I should have forced him to get out of bed and go to school. Today was his last day as a senior. Tonight was supposed to be the night of his graduation, but they postponed it. Maybe it would have worked, who knows. But, I guess this is Carter's way of grieving… so really I shouldn't try to stop the process. Maybe leaving him like this is best?

Though I try again. "Would you like something to drink? Juice? Milk? Water?"

Silence. His limbs stay still.

"How 'bout something to eat? I can cook you up some soup or make you a sandwich. We've even got leftover spaghetti you can eat. Or maybe I can get you a bacon cheeseburger from Ranch Hand?" *They are his favorite.*

My heart is squeezed tighter. I think I feel something crack or give way. Nothing is working. He is like a boulder. An empty, hollow boulder. He barely moves. He doesn't talk. He doesn't eat or drink. Something is seriously wrong with him and I don't know how to fix it.

I hate to see my boy like this. I raised him into the boy he is today and I don't want to see my creation cracked and broken.

"Carter? Is there *anything*—absolutely *anything*—I can do?"

Nope.

I shut his door before I can cry. He doesn't need to hear his mom cry. Children aren't supposed to see their parental figure break down.

I stand beside his door, my hand on my beating heart. I try to relieve the squeezing but it doesn't let up. The lump in my throat grows bigger, beginning to restrict my breathing. I try my hardest to breathe but it simply doesn't work.

Slowly I sink to the cedar-planked floor. My other hand finds my mouth and tries to muffle any sounds that may come out of it. When I lost Noah, I thought it was all over. He was the love of my life. We had two kids together. I always thought both of us would live to see our grandchildren have children. When we got married I knew we'd be together until the end of our days. Maybe that's why it broke me so much when he disappeared. It broke me even more when the police stopped looking and presumed him dead.

But, I was a mom of two children: a one-year-old and a nine-year-old. I couldn't just stop functioning. I had to take care of my little loves. I had no time to be broken and cracked. Honestly, I don't think I ever grieved over Noah... *at all.* I'm frightened that that's where Carter learned how to grieve. It would make me feel awful to know that I'm the reason he won't eat or drink.

When you have a kid, you hope life's hardships never go near them. You want to keep them safe and cocooned forever. You don't want a single thing to harm them. I never wanted Carter to know how it was to lose someone you're in love with. I never wanted him to feel it like I did... but he did. It's almost frightening how similar it all is. Noah disappeared. Evie disappeared. Evie's dead and let's face it, so is Noah.

My eyes find an old family picture hanging up on the wall in front of me. It's of Noah, newborn Daphne, Carter, and I on the ocean's beach in Oregon. Noah holds Daph in his firm arms, dressed in a white dress shirt. I'm in a flowy, white, tank top dress that now resides in my closet on a plastic hanger. Carter stands to the left of Noah in an identical dress shirt and I stand to Noah's right. Our smiles are bright, especially Noah's. He loved this family so deeply. You can tell in every single family picture we have starting from when Carter was just a newborn too. We did them almost every year. Noah insisted.

A sob escapes from me and I clutch my mouth harder. Downstairs, the television continues to play at a loud volume. No one stirs in Carter's room.

Sultry, itchy tears run down my cheeks, neck, and into my shirt. I wipe them away frantically but I've bitten off more than I can chew. They come faster than I can wipe.

My hands fall from my face and settle on the planked floor. The tears wetten my lower face and upper chest. It's not worth the time. I just wait for them to slow.

When they do, I rest my head back on the wall and look up at the light fixture on the ceiling. My face is itchy in a way I can't relieve and it bugs me more than the fact that I shove my emotions down again.

"Noah?"

I feel like an idiot. He won't answer. But, still, there's always that tingling hope in my head that suggests it might happen one day.

"What do I do?"

Carter was always his dad's son. They were always together and laughing. The two of them were always making things and doing things like camping and fishing. They went on a lot of father and son camping trips. I never felt left out though. I felt proud and lucky to have such a great man as my husband. He was always able to get to Carter in a way that I never could. I've never reached him like Noah did. I've still never been able to.

"How do I help him, Noah? Come on, you'd know." My voice shakes dramatically, so much so that I can barely make out the individual words.

I wait for Noah to give me a sign, anything, but he doesn't. After minutes pass, it's clear he isn't going to talk with me. It's impossible, I know that, but there's always that hope and dream that you're an exception.

I shake my head and take one last look at the family photo. I give a half-hearted smile and push myself back on my feet. My hands smooth out the wrinkles in my shirt and in my pants. I then square my shoulders, wipe my face one last time, then put my chin up. Life isn't going to drag me down this time. No way.

NIXON

Tuesday, May 31, 2022, Present.

I find myself on Carter's doorstep. He missed the last day yesterday. He also won't answer a single one of my calls since Evie's case was closed. I'm worried, I guess. I've never seen him this way—which isn't saying much because we've only been best friends for a little over a year.

My fist collides with the door softly. I don't think it's loud enough but it must be because the door opens. I'll be honest, I knew Carter wouldn't open the door. In the doorway stands who must be his mom. She's a stunning lady but looks extremely exhausted. Her eyes are hollow with exhaustion and her smile is sluggish. But, despite this, she is still a very pretty woman.

"Hi, Mrs. Miller," I greet, keeping my hands at the side of my jeans. "I'm Nixon Hodge. Is Carter home?"

Mrs. Miller's face abruptly becomes lighter. "*Nixon.* Daphne has told me about you."

Behind her, Daphne sits on the couch like usual. She makes eye contact with me and gives me a thumbs-up. I hold back a chuckle and look back to her mom.

Mrs. Miller rushes past small talk. “Carter is up in his room. He hasn’t left. I was actually hoping you’d come by and try to get him to eat literally *anything*. I’ve tried everything.” Her face drops and becomes darker. I can tell it’s a tough time for her as much as it is for Carter.

Daphne gets off the couch and comes to her mom’s side. She’s dressed in her usual outfit: a sunny yellow skirt, black leggings, and a white shirt with an embroidered sun. Her long, dark brown hair is pulled into a side braid that goes over her left shoulder. “I even ran in there saying there was a fire. He didn’t even budge.”

I nod and laugh, ignoring Mrs. Miller as she scolds Daphne. “Yeah, I can give it a try.”

Mrs. Miller never does finish scolding her daughter but instead takes me to the kitchen. She begins heating up alfredo leftovers from the fridge, looking everywhere where I’m not.

I’ve never met Mrs. Miller before this day but I can already tell she’s a great mother. She is so worried for her son and what he’s going through. She cares for both of her children deeply with all of her heart. I can see that instantly.

I feel jealous of Daphne and Carter. My mom walked out when I was little, leaving me behind with my dad. Dad never told me why, just that we were going to get better because of it. I suppose we were. My stepmom is a really great lady so that’s good. Dad and her got married when I was eleven. I guess in a way Ellie, my step mom, is my mom now but it will never be the same.

The microwave beeps, waking me from my thoughts. Mrs. Miller takes the alfredo out and fills up a plastic cup with tap water. She attempts to give me a smile as she hands me both the glass bowl and the cup. Her shoulders sag as she trudges around me, leading me to Carter's room.

I know the way almost like it's my own room but I let her lead me anyways. I have an inkling that she needs to see her son again to make sure he is still whole. Well, as whole as you can be after what has happened in the past two weeks.

Carter's mom opens the door and peeks in quickly, her eyebrows upturned. "Honey? Nixon is here."

I don't hear Carter's deep, kind voice, instead silence rings in my ears. Mrs. Millers looks back at me with hollow eyes. I give her a reassuring nod and slip into the blackened room. My eyes take a while to adjust but when they do I spot Carter sitting at the foot of his bed, staring at the evidence board still hanging up above his desk. He sits unmoving, just staring at the board. Carter doesn't even look at me as I shut the door.

His brown hair is greasy and lays every which way. With the lighting, I can't see the true extent of his eye bags... but I know they are there. I feel bad thinking about it, but he looks like he just crawled through Hell. There's something so creepy about his posture. He doesn't have terrible posture like most people, but instead his back is straight like a metal pole is running through him.

"Your mom says you haven't eaten."

He doesn't even look at me, he just stays there, fixated on the wall. I walk in front of him and set his food and his water on his desk in front of him. I wave my hand in front of his face and get no reaction.

"I didn't realize how hot your mom is," I prod, hoping that will get a reaction. Carter breaks his gaze and begins glaring at me. His glare gives me shivers, the kind that invades my body just right, leaving me chilled to the bone.

"Go away, Nixon."

I take a seat in Carter's office chair and set my feet next to him on his bed. "No can do."

"Seriously, Nixon. Leave. I want to be alone."

Carter finally moves, laying on his back. He brings his hands to his face and covers his eyes like the sun is hitting them. But, there is no sun, just empty, dreary darkness.

"Dave and I missed you on the last day of school."

More silence.

"They postponed graduation until after her funeral."

They haven't set a time for graduation but they've set a day for Evie's funeral: June 19th. They were going to have it earlier but they still need her body for the investigation, even though it's closed. They need it as evidence for the Bakers' court trial on June 10th apparently. I feel it is unjust to keep her body above ground that long. The poor girl needs to be put to rest already.

"I wonder what led Evie to run away THAT night..."

It had been bugging me since we started our own investigation. I'm one of those people that needs to know how things work to be satisfied. Dad also said that the sheriff can't get the Bakers' to tell him what happened that night. That's suspicious.

It's like Carter *wakes up*. He sits up out of nowhere and looks at me with these *frightening* eyes that drill into my body with a dull saw. They aren't the same chocolatey brown anymore but now full of shock and determination. He runs his hands through his hair and smooths it back, staring at me with those ghoulish iris's. His hands slip down his face, wiping invisible stuff off of it. One of them falls to his side while the other stays just below his bottom lip on his chin.

He breaks his eye contact with me and glances toward the investigation board. He leans forward and grabs the bowl of alfredo and begins shoveling it in his mouth like he's never eaten anything ever. He then sets down the fork and takes a large gulp of the water, guzzling all of the contents. I watch in shocked horror as he continues devouring his food, stopping occasionally to mouth words.

I should be glad I broke him from his trance but I'm honestly kind of terrified. And guilty. I think I broke him with that one question. I broke him.

DAPHNE

Wednesday, June 1, 2022, Present.

What do I think? Well, I miss my brother to be frank with you. I don't think I've seen him in like four days. I miss his stupid face, okay?

This is all taking a giant toll on Mom too. When she's home she's constantly hovering around Carter's room, waiting for that one moment when he steps out of it for something other than the bathroom. I feel bad. Maybe a little neglected. It's no secret that I'm the one carrying the heavy weight of being the favorite child in the family on my shoulders. So, I can't help but feel neglected during all of this.

So, I stay on the couch, watching tirelessly as Mom goes up and down the stairs and paces the length of the kitchen. I think she is in more pain than Carter must be in, if that's even possible. Over the length of hanging out with Carter I really got a feel for how much he liked her. Loved her even. I may be eight but I know what love is. I loved Timmy in the other second grade class once. Then he gave Jessica a flower. He cheated.

That's why I'm never going to fall in love ever again. I mean can you blame me? Carter's girlfriend got killed by her own parents. Dad disappeared. Love eventually ends in disaster.

I don't remember what Mom was like when my dad was presumed dead because I was only like one. But, I see Carter's pain and how affected he is by it. I don't want to feel that way. Ever.

But, I will admit, Evie's death had something good come out of it. Investigating it brought my brother and I closer. No doubt about it. We were never that close. We just kind of stayed out of each other's ways. Then, we were finally hanging around each other. We investigated Evie's case together. We are one hundred percent closer because of it.

I mean, I wish it wasn't his girlfriend's death that brought us closer. It's awfully sad.

The sound of a shower starting upstairs gets my attention. Mom isn't home. A sly smile finds its way on my lips. Carter must be out of his spell. It must've been Nixon yesterday. He did mention to me on his way out that he seemed better. I didn't quite believe him though. Carter is really messed up.

Maybe the shower is a sign that he's done grieving or something. If so, he barely grieved or anything. I expected this to go on for weeks, not four days. Since I was little and didn't remember anything about Dad's disappearance I had to rely on what Carter told me. He said Mom picked herself up and just put all of her energy into caring for us. That gives me the impression that she never grieved for Dad. Now, the same thing is happening to Carter. It can't be healthy for the Miller family. I just hope I never end up that way. I hope that if the day comes and I do have to grieve over someone, I will do it properly. I'll heal properly. I won't bury it like Mom and Carter.

Upstairs, the shower stops. I take the remote and turn down my TV show just enough to where I can hear Carter mumbling to himself. It's incoherent but he *is* talking to himself. Carter has always talked to himself but this time it's creepier somehow, like he's talking to someone else. He could be on the phone with Nixon but it's odd to call someone seconds after you get out of the shower.

But, hey. I ain't judging. I've always known Carter was weird.

The bathroom door opens and I watch carefully as Carter comes down the stairs, no phone in either of his hands. He comes down in a red short-sleeved shirt and jeans. I half expected him to be wearing sweats. But no, he's clean shaven and his wet hair is brushed through with a comb.

Warrily, I survey my brother as he makes his way to the fridge. He searches it for a solid two minutes, mouthing words. So, he was definitely talking to himself earlier.

He takes out tupperware full of alfredo and then another tupperware full of hashbrowns.

"Hungry?" I giggle hesitantly. He looks at me and nods.

"Do you think Mom would pick up some hashbrowns for dinner? Or no?"

I hold back a laugh and pause my show. "Just hashbrowns? You want only hashbrowns for dinner?"

He looks at me like I'm the crazy one. "Yeah. For dinner I want a pile of hash browns. That's it."

I can't tell if this is how he normally acts. There's definitely a screw missing in his brain. I blame Nixon for messing him up. He woke him from his grieving way too soon. I mean who wants just a pile of hashbrowns for dinner and nothing else? A crazy person that's who. At least he's eating, I guess.

I should be relieved.

CARTER

Thursday, June 2, 2022, Present.

I pull onto Ninth Street, sweat trickling down my back. My air conditioner stopped working while I was in despair. It doesn't help that it's in the nineties outside. So, I drive with both of my windows down, advancing quickly on Evie's two-story white house. Within a minute, I pull in front of the chilling house in my usual spot on the road. It towers but seems to give off more of an eerie gleam since I was last here, a.k.a. the day the Bakers were arrested. I still can't get the image out of my head. I can still see Joanna and Paul being guided into the squad cars, incarcerated with silver handcuffs. The sun gleamed on the cuffs, blinding me in a pleasant way. It was everything I had been hoping for and it was glorious.

Inside, the living room curtain ruffles as someone either peeks out of it or walks by it. I open my door and step out onto the pavement, the heat of the road rising up through the soles of my shoes. When I step onto the grass the heat slowly disintegrates. But, it soon comes back when I step onto the sidewalk leading to the front door. When I stop in front of the door I can feel sweat building in my socks.

The door opens before I can bring my fist up to knock. Kace stands in front of me, one hand on the door frame and one hand on the inside door knob. His eyes smile and gleam with happiness I don't expect for someone whose sister just died at the hands of his parents.

"Carter, I didn't expect to see you," Kace coughs, his dimples flaring.

I shrug and take a peek inside, only seeing the old piano because of the placement of the door. "Are you guys staying alone? Is anyone watching over you?"

Kace nods and leans against the door frame fully. "My Aunt Jeanne—my mom's sister. We are moving in with her in a little over two weeks. She lives out in Ogden, Utah."

I should have known the remaining Bakers would be moving away. I'm just glad they have family to stay with and won't have to be foster kids; the one thing Evie never wanted was for her siblings to end up in foster care or juvie. It was the main reason why she never told on her parents when they broke her wrist all those months ago. I know she'd be happy they are ending up in a family member's home. I just hope their aunt is a decent person that will care for them like they should have been cared for in the first place.

"Why are you here, Carter?" Kace finally asks, confusion coating his light-colored facial features. In the warm summer breeze ruffles his dirty blond hair. I still am in awe to this day how similar he looks to Evie. They have the same eyes, same hair, same skin, same dimples when they are happy. Really the only difference is that Kace doesn't have freckles and has no acne.

"Oh, yeah. The real reason I'm here is I need to ask you some questions about the night Evie ran away. Frankly, I don't believe that you don't know what happened that night. I need to know. I don't know why I need to, but I do. Please be honest with me, Kace. *What happened that night that led Eve to run away?*"

The happiness drains from his face and he becomes instantly tense. His jaw clenches and his bright blue eyes ignite. He stops leaning on the door and tightens his grips on the door knob and the frame. Shivers run up my back and for the first time I think I may be frightened. The quiet, talkative, kind boy was erased with one simple question.

His knuckles are white and his cheeks red. "It is all over now, Carter Miller. Give it up. My parents were arrested for her murder. It's all over. *Okay*? Don't worry about it anymore. Evie's dead, okay–" his voice cracks, showing a chip in his armor. "–as much as I hate it, she's gone."

I can't even get in another word before he slams the door in my face. The air from the door hits me and flings my hair backwards. I feel it vibrate the sidewalk and the house. The living room window shakes, causing the curtains to replicate it as well. With my eyes closed I listen to Kace stomp around the house. I can even hear him stalk upstairs with heavy feet. Someone calls after him but he refuses to answer.

Kace has reason to blow up on me. I know deep down that I should leave it alone. He's right. His parents were arrested. Justice has been served. But, something about it is bugging me. Of all nights she chose to flee, why did she choose that one? She could have fled the night when her parents broke her wrist. She could have fled numerous amount of times after they hit her. She had so many options and she chose May 15th, 2022. I need to know why. Something tells me that it has a strong significance to why she was killed.

Suddenly the door opens and a younger girl steps out. Her hair is blonde like her mom's. I remember her from the day I came over and saw Evie's phone under the couch. Now she has eye bags underneath her dark blue eyes. She's about Daphne's height but clearly is older. She looks up at me helplessly and I step back to give her more room. Her cold hands grab my arm and she pulls me to the front of the house, away from the door and windows. I face the house with the sidewalk on my left. The girl stands with her back to the house.

She keeps her voice as hushed as possible. "I'm Riley, Evie and Kace's youngest sister."

"Um, nice to meet you, Riley... I'm–"

"–Carter. I know who you are. You're not exactly a strange name in our house."

For some reason that weirds me out. Either they talk bad about me or the opposite. I'm leaning toward the first option. Just a hunch.

Riley's blonde hair is pulled into a low ponytail and she wears denim shorts and a Bear Lake Middle School cheer team shirt.

"You must be a cheerleader like Evie was," I smile, whispering just in case someone inside hears. She clearly doesn't want them to hear us or know she's out here talking to me.

Riley smiles softly and I feel relief. Her smile is true and not worn down like Evie's was. She isn't as defeated as Evie was. Riley Baker still has hope to turn out a happy girl. I just hope the same goes for Evie's other sister. If this one is Riley, the other one is Allie. I hope Allie turns out untroubled and cheery.

"This is actually Evie's shirt from her middle school cheer. Technically I made the team for seventh grade, but since we are moving I can't be on the team. It's all good though. I'll try out at my new school for my eighth-grade year." Her cheeks are as pale as Evie's always were and lack freckles. I wonder if Evie is the only child with freckles.

I give Riley a sympathetic smile. I can't possibly know what she's going through, but if I lost Daphne I would be a wreck. I don't think I'd recover. Ever. This poor family.

Suddenly, I think Riley remembers why she pulled me out of view because she suddenly turns nervous. The sweet girl is replaced with a nervous wreck. She begins brushing her fingers through her long ponytail and glancing around the street. She knows something of use to me.

The middle school girl stops glancing around and sets her dark blue irises on me. Riley bites her lip nervously and takes a deep breath. "I wasn't supposed to be awake because they have my bedtime at nine. But, the shattering glass woke me up."

If Kace can't help me, Riley can.

"Did you hear anything else?"

Riley nods and closes her eyes as if trying to put herself back to that night. "I mean it was hard to hear because my bedroom was upstairs but I did hear some things..." She takes another breath and continues to run her fingers through her hair. "Evie found something. It led to her figuring out some dangerous secret. Then, Mom and Dad started fighting with each other about whatever my sister found out. There was a *lot* of smashing glass and overturning dining room chairs. I knew that Evie was in huge trouble if she didn't sneak out of the kitchen and dining room and get to her room."

She abruptly opens her dreary, blue eyes. They are frightened and tearing a hole right through me. It tickles something in my spine, leaving it briefly chilled. "Dad hit her. Punched her. She didn't get out of the kitchen fast enough. Then, she got up and I heard her run up the stairs and to her bedroom. I peeked out my bedroom door as she shut hers as softly as possible. We made eye contact and I could tell she was really in trouble this time. I could see it in her eyes, Carter."

A lump has formed in my throat and my jaw stands open. The warm weather quickly parches me but I pay no attention to it. It's comforting in a way knowing what Riley heard that night. But, unfortunately, it is *not* comforting to hear what Riley heard that night. Eight words flood my mind. *The deeper you dig, the darker it gets*. I don't know how I'll ever stop digging at this point. Every shovel full of dirt I collect, the closer I get to figuring this all out.

"Carter, I'm glad my parents are going to go away. I just hope they are put away for forever. No parents that abuse their child—whether it's verbally or physically—should ever be free or *alive*."

That's when I truly feel humanity is lost. When a child wishes for their parents' death or incarceration, you know the world has gone to crap. Will this be the world I raise my future family in? Will I have to raise a family in a world where parents abuse their children? Where parents kill their children? How? I'm not even sure I want to bring children into this corrupted world if it ever comes down to it. It's not worth it. It will never be worth it until this world is cured. This world is full of broken people. Honestly, I don't think it can be cured until the good outweighs the bad and currently, I'm not seeing a whole lot of good.

None of the Baker children will *ever* be kids again. Like Evie, they are all being forced to grow up. They all met evil at too young an age. How do they even continue their childhood? Is it even possible at this point? I pray it is.

CARTER

Thursday, June 2, 2022, Present.

Nixon's visits have become a regular thing these past two days. He comes after each work shift no matter how tired he may be. He works at the local Ace hardware store and rarely gets time off. He's working extra hard to collect money for an apartment or small house. Nix has also been mentioning to me about going and working out at the mines, which is about a forty-five minute drive. With the drive, I personally feel like he shouldn't because of how expensive gas is these days, but he insists he'll make more money. He's probably right, to be completely honest.

Now, Nixon sits on my office chair, staring at the spot where the investigation board used to be. I took it down this morning. I was getting sick of looking at it as I try to fall asleep each night.

"Now tell me again what Evie and Kace's sister told you," Nixon repeats for like the third time since I told him about my experience at the Bakers' house this afternoon. He can't seem to wrap his head around it. Neither can I though.

I pick at the seams in my bedding as I recite the details of what Riley told me when she pulled me aside. I can't get over how terrified Evie must have been that night. I can imagine the fear in her beautiful blue eyes if I close my own brown ones. I can see the tears and her worsening black eye from being hit. Her tense, pale body as it trembled. Riley also told me as I was getting into my truck that she watched as Evie jumped down the two-story drop from her window, just as someone was stomping their way upstairs.

I can't imagine. It's a miracle she didn't break anything from the jump. But, I guess if she did, that would be the last of her problems. I wish she would have called me that night. I would have dropped everything and came to pick her up. Mom would let her stay at our house, I'm sure of it. We could have turned her parents in for abuse and neglect. She would still be alive. We could have gone to a college together and lived through life side-by-side, either as friends or something more.

Where would we be if we were free? That's the question that is constantly disrupting me and rattling my brain, demanding to be thought out... heard. It'll drive me crazy. It will all drive me crazy. All the 'what ifs' my mind is screeching... I know I will go nowhere in life if I get stuck on the 'what ifs.' So, why do I chase the answers to those questions constantly all day, all night? Why do I do it when I know it will always be a dead end? None of the roads will ever happen. There is no chance any of it will happen one day, not with Evie gone and dead.

I didn't think it was possible to fall in love with a girl in the span of eight months.

Nixon snaps his fingers, forcing me back to the real world where Evie isn't.

"Sorry, what?" I ask. Obviously, he's been talking and I just haven't been listening.

Nix isn't mad at me, for he gives me a smile. A sympathetic one. It hits me in the gut. I'm not sure why it affects me in the way it does. Maybe I just don't want anyone feeling sympathetic for me.

"Riley said that Evie found out some huge secret her parents were keeping. Did Riley have any idea what it was?"

I shake my head, fiddling with my fingers. An image of Evie doing the same thing one of the millions of times pops into my head. I take my hands and sit on them.

"I have no idea either," I sigh, glancing out the window. I think I hear Mom's car pull into the driveway which means it's around seven in the evening. "It was definitely big."

Nixon scoffs and leans forward onto his elbow. "I'd say. It was so big that they killed their daughter over it. They did *not* want it known."

I want to puke every time Nixon or anyone else mentions Evie's death. I have to swallow it back every single time. Even when I think about it on my own.

Downstairs I hear the front door open as mom comes in. Chev's claws thunder across the hardwood floor as he swarms Mom. She orders him to get down in a worn-out voice. I get off the bed and cross over to my door. I open it and call for Chev to come up to my room, hoping that will get him to leave Mom alone. She must have had a bad day at work, I can hear it in her voice.

Almost immediately, Chev is running up the stairs. Despite his worsening age, he is quick. He barrels past me and into my room, ready to attack Nix with licks for the third time since Nixon arrived here an hour ago.

"Chev get down," I demand as Chev hops onto my bed, covering it with his husky hair. Chev gets down and settles on the floor at Nixon's feet, sprawling out on his side. Instantly he falls asleep and begins snoring. I wish I had that skill.

I take a seat back down on my bed, crossing my legs Indian style like they taught me to do in elementary school all those years ago. I lean over and grab my Dr. Pepper from the nightstand and unscrew it, taking a large gulp. I tighten the lid back on and prop it against my pillow.

"It's going to drive me crazy that I don't know the secret," Nixon sighs, leaning back into his chair to look at the ceiling. "I mean it's got to be the entire reason they killed her."

I nod, keeping quiet. He's right, once again. It's the answer to the entire thing. Everybody wants to know why those two parents killed their daughter. Since they got arrested the story has gone viral. This morning I woke up to six different texts from my old buddies in Oregon asking about it. Of course I told every single one of them to mind their own business. I know I shouldn't have been harsh with them because it's not like they knew I was in a relationship with her. None of them knew that I was dating the murdered girl. They couldn't have possibly known. Maybe I should apologize. I'll add that to my large list of 'to-dos.'

"I also can't wrap my head around the fact that she was abused. Like how did that start? How do parents just start abusing their child out of nowhere?" Nixon just keeps on going, asking questions we don't know the answers to.

For once I know some of the answers. I was the only person Evie ever told about her grandma's death and what happened afterward. "After her grandma died, her parents went off the deep end. They blamed Evie for surviving. It's a childish reason. They should have never become parents if that is what it took to hate their first daughter. If anything you should blame the dog that jumped out into the road that caused Lena Marlowe to swerve. Not the survivor."

It was all corrupted and disgusting. Paul and Joanne Baker are childish parents who should have never had kids. They doomed their kids as soon as they had each and every one of them. No one like them should ever conceive kids. No kid deserves parents like that.

Nixon scoffs and shakes his head, his eyes full of calm fury. "That's messed up. No wonder Evie was the way she was."

And what is that supposed to mean, I want to yell. But I know he means well. He didn't know her, he just saw how secluded and lonely she was on the outside.

We stay silent for two minutes, each of us staring at random places in the room. For a while, the only sound is Chev's snoring, which sounds like a train passing the house. It used to make me so annoyed when I was little but now it's comforting to me. As he's gotten older I've gotten even more frightened that he would die in his sleep. He's a living reminder of my dad and I can't lose him. If I lose Chev, it'd be like losing dad all over again. I'd lose both Dad and Chev at the same time.

Nixon clears his throat, causing me to pull my eyes away from my aging husky. I meet his gray gaze and wait for him to say whatever's on his mind.

"What if it wasn't Paul and Joanne that killed Evie?"

My first thought is that Nixon Hodge is an idiot. But, I have considered this. It's kept me awake sometimes just thinking about how Evie's actual killer could just be roaming around and I would never know. But, it's absurd and a stupid theory. I'd bet everything I have that it was her parents. All the evidence is there.

I sit up straighter and grab my soda pop. "Shut up. Don't be a moron."

I wonder how many times Evie's own parents told her that exact thing. It strikes something in my heart.

Nixon looks shocked, his gray eyes bathed in confusion. "I'm sorry."

I take a deep breath and apologize for my words, gripping my plastic bottle with so much force that my knuckles are whitened. Nixon only nods and moves his eyes back to the wall where the investigation board was. He then takes a deep breath, runs his fingers through his black hair, and eyes me. I can see just by his eyes how many questions are swarming his brain.

He tries to smile but lets off a nervous, awkward smirk. "So, is it time to bring out the detective board again?"

CARTER

Friday, December 31, 2021, Past.

"Pay up, Carter!" Daphne demands, her eyes drunk on power. Her palm is extended toward the ceiling, awaiting my paper money impatiently.

I eye Evie—who sits next to me on the couch—as she giggles, glancing at my whittling pile of cash. Keeping my hand on it, I stare at the Monopoly board on the coffee table in disbelief. Of all properties to land on, it *had* to be Daphne's most expensive property rent-wise. Park Place was the one property I did *not* want to land on. I don't think I even have enough to pay the stupid rent. She's even got a hotel on it *and* she owns the entire color group. That makes the rent three thousand Monopoly dollars.

"This game is stupid," I insist, slowly sliding my small pile of four one-hundred dollar bills away from my sister. "Let's play a different game, okay?"

Eve laughs and nudges my shoulder with hers. "Don't be a sore loser, Carter."

I scoff and shake my head, dodging Daph as she tries to reach for my cash. "I am *not* a sore loser!"

Evie gives me a smug look and shrugs, sitting back with her arms across her chest. "I can't be friends with a sore loser."

We haven't told Daphne that we are dating. I haven't even told Mom. For Evie's sake, I've got to keep it a secret. Speaking of Mom, she isn't here–which of course isn't rare–but she isn't at work, she's at a friend's house celebrating New Years with them. Daph and I chose to be left at home and I obviously invited Evie too.

I look at my girlfriend and smile.

I love saying that. 'My girlfriend.' I've had a girlfriend before but none like her. When I look at Evie I don't even remember my ex's name. Why should I?

Daphne takes this precious time and grabs all of my Monopoly money, bankrupting me fully. I don't even protest, I just let it happen. I throw myself back against the back of the couch, crossing my arms across my chest as Evie does. She giggles and leans forward, ready to keep playing with my little sister.

She doesn't seem nervous in the slightest. When she first arrived I could tell she was *very* nervous and anxious. But, as the three hours she has been here for has passed, she has become comfortable with Daph. They laugh and joke like they are siblings.

Slowly as the game progresses Evie somehow dodges all of Daphne's properties. Daphne isn't as lucky and constantly lands on Evie's properties, her money beginning to run dry.

"This is impossible," Daphne growls as Evie dodges another one of Daph's properties, her hazel eyes full of deep confusion. Evie laughs and hands the die to my sister, a smug smile across her pink lips.

"What, did you finally realize that you are most likely going to lose?" I prod, watching as my sister sits completely still on the rug around the coffee table.

She looks up at me, glares, and drops the die on the board. She gets a six, putting her on one of Evie's most expensive properties. I watch carefully as Daphne dies inside, staring at her small stack of cash in defeat. Her shoulders sag and she closes her eyes, contemplating her options. Newsflash: Daph has none.

Then, as if she's finally cracked, Daphne begins shoving the game pieces into the box laying on the ground. She folds the board, nearly ripping it, and shoves it in with the pieces. With tense hands, she grabs Evie's stack of money and shoves it in the game box, not bothering to put it into the money holder. She doesn't put in all the items correctly so the lid doesn't fit, making her all the angrier.

Evie laughs as Daphne stomps into the kitchen, fuming as she repeats 'I never lose.'

"Wow, you guys are just a family of sore losers, aren't you?" Eve giggles, looking at the TV—which is playing music. I haven't even been listening to the music, to be completely honest. I forgot I put it on when Evie got here.

I shrug my shoulders and chuckle as she leans back, taking my hand in hers. I don't even try to hide my smile. "Don't worry about her. She'll get over it."

Evie smiles, her teeth white and surprisingly straight. Her blue eyes glisten in the warm living room light, capsizing me.

"I could stare into your eyes for days on end," I whisper, giving her a harmless wink. Evie's cheeks flush scarlet and she awkwardly giggles, brushing her hair out of her face. Today her dark blonde hair is put into two dutch braids. Several baby hairs have escaped her braids, causing her to constantly brush them behind her ears. I've had to resist the urge to do it myself since we have been around Daphne.

"We really shouldn't be holding hands with Daphne here. We've been doing such a great job at hiding this from everyone," I sigh, nervously looking into the kitchen. Evie tightens her hold on my hand and shrugs.

"She's in there," she insists, her voice a low whisper. "We'll be fine for a moment."

Keeping our relationship a secret has been *killing* me. But, I don't want Evie to get hurt by her parents if they find out. The guilt would eat me alive. I could never live with myself again. So, I have to push past my eagerness for her safety. I *really* like her, man. I do. Maybe more than like. I don't know. I've never felt this kind of love before, but I'm sure it's real.

I look at the time on my phone, turn it off, and throw it across the couch away from me. 11:09. Fifty-one minutes until the New Year. I'm just glad I get to spend it with her of all people. I wouldn't want it any other way.

"What do you want to do until midnight?" I ask her. "I have Uno. We can watch some of a movie. It's fully up to you, Eve."

She looks at me and gives me a smile. Her breath smells of mint. "Movie."

We spend the next thirty to forty-five minutes trying to find a movie, failing miserably. By the time we decide on a movie, it's ten till midnight. We tried to go for a rom-com but none stuck out to us. Then we tried for an Adam Sandler movie or a Kevin Hart and Dwayne Johnson movie but Daphne was in the kitchen and she's not old enough. We were so desperate to find a movie that we almost picked one of the stupid Barbie movies. None of the Barbie ones were even the good, old ones that Mom would make Dad and I watch for no reason. Like Barbie and the Diamond Castle. I'm talking about the ones made in the early 2000s.

Evie and I give up on picking a movie and flick the TV to the annual New York City countdown that everybody watches. I'm always amazed at how many people are able to fill Times Square. It's huge and filled with so many billboards that flash different events and businesses. Normally the lights would be overbearing anywhere else, but they aren't there. New York City's Times Square makes it work. It doesn't make me want to have a seizure... I just want to sit and gawk.

"It'd be nice to be in Times Square for the celebration. In person, you know?" Evie sighs, watching the camera pan over Times Square.

I nod and run my fingers through my messy hair, waiting for her to continue. I love listening to her talk. Her dovelike voice soothes me, making me forget about any problems I may have.

To my glee, she does continue. "I want to tour NYC one day. I would love to look over it from the top of the Empire State building, with all of the clouds below me. I'd be on top of the world, the farthest I can get from my parents.

"Ooo, and I'd like to make it to the top of Lady Liberty and look out over the Atlantic Ocean. Did you know that Paris, France has a mini Statue of Liberty facing ours? We gave it to them to commemorate the French Revolution and our alliance. I want to see that too.

"I also want to visit Ellis Island's National Museum of Immigration. I had some ancestors that went through Ellis Island's immigrant inspection and processing station before it shut down. I feel like it'd be a cool place to visit.

"I want to visit everything. I want to visit the Twin Towers Memorial and ride ferry boats. I want to read in Central Park. There's something so magical about it, at least from my point of view. Don't you think, Carter?"

Just by the way her smile widens when she talks about the places she wants to visit, I know how special Evie Baker is. The way her eyes twinkle and her dimples deepen. The way she holds her dainty shoulders back and her chin up confidently, not a worry in the world. The way she uses her hands to talk, making big gestures. Just by the way her eyebrows are raised and how her crows feet are wrinkled in glee. I could get used to it. Oh yeah, I could never get enough of her. Ever.

"Carter?" Evie questions, waving her small hands in front of my face. "Earth to Carter. Hellllooooo?"

I snap to attention and bring my right hand to the back of my neck, smoothing down the hairs that have pricked up. "We'll have to go to the Big Apple together one day."

Evie's freckled cheeks shine scarlet again and she smiles wider. "I like the sound of together."

Daphne comes barreling in from the kitchen, causing us to quickly move away from each other. Immediately I yearn to be next to her but I know now our time is up. It pains me, squeezing my heart as I see her so near yet so far. I can't wait for after graduation when she gets to finally move out legally. Only one hundred and fifty days to go. Not that I'm counting or anything.

"We've got two minutes, guys!" Daphne exclaims, turning up the TV even more. She's right and I didn't even notice. "Do you think they'll set off fireworks in Times Square?"

"I'm not sure about there but I'm sure if we go outside we'll be able to see some over Montpelier," I answer, watching the timer tick down as it gets closer to midnight. Upbeat electric music plays over the timer, a old video of fireworks playing behind it.

Daphne seems appeased to my answer and nods enthusiastically, taking a large sip of her sparkling cider that I got for all three of us at Broulims. I stand up from the couch and make my way to the kitchen to pour myself a glass.

I open the cupboard to grab a mason jar for me and turn back toward the living room. "Hey, Eve? Do you want some sparkling cider?"

She perks up, standing up from the couch and nods, a huge smile on her face. A piece of her hair is stuck in her face again and she has to brush it back again. She seems annoyed by it but I'm certainly not annoyed. I'm not sure why.

Instead of staying where she is, Evie skips into the kitchen, leaving Daphne alone in the living room watching the broadcast. Eve leans against the counter, her hands clasped on top of the island, as I grab two mason jars carefully.

"I could have brought it to you, you know."

Evie shrugs and hands me the sparkling cider next to her. It's in a green bottle and honestly looks like champagne. But I swear it isn't champagne. I mumble a thanks and pour each of us a glass quickly. I hand her hers and we walk back to the living room in a warm silence.

Daph shoves confetti poppers in both of our hands and places party hats on both our heads. They are silver and we use the hats every year. We are kind of cheap.

Then, the countdown begins. We chant to the countdown, counting down from ten. Daphne has mor energy than I think I have ever seen her have. She jumps up and down each time we count lower, anticipation killing her. I look over to Evie as we hit one, not bothering to watch it hit zero. Her blue eyes are bright and happy and her smile is wider than it has been all night. I didn't think it was possible but here we are.

Her dimples are enhanced and her cheeks plump with a glee I've rarely seen on her. I wish I could stare forever. I wish she could be this happy forever. I just want to freeze time and gawk at my gorgeous girlfriend, my stunning best friend, my exquisitely lovely soulmate.

But, I can't.

"Happy New Year!" Evie and Daphne scream, pulling the strings on their confetti poppers, sending pieces of colored paper everywhere around us. They float down from the ceiling, getting stuck in Evie's heavenly hair, catching me completely off guard. She turns to me, her smile lines deep with exhilaration and true joy.

"Happy New Year," I find myself quietly whispering, not being able to take my eyes off of her.

She reminds me of the fireworks. The feeling inside me feels like the fireworks, setting me ablaze and lighting my heart up. I've never particularly enjoyed fireworks, but now... Now I have a reason to.

CARTER

Sunday, June 5, 2022, Present.

I get the call as I'm just stepping out of the bathroom after a much-needed shower. I don't expect it, especially since I'm the one that calls Sheriff Reggie, not the other way around.

Something has got to have happened. Evie's parents escaped from the jail in Caribou County is my first thought. It's the closest jail to us so they could easily find me. Hurt me. Kill me as they did to Evie. They are childish fears, but valid ones.

I pause my music and press answer, still drying my shaggy hair with a tan towel.

"Is this Carter?" Sheriff's rough voice asks, slightly out of breath.

Yep, they escaped. They are on their way to kill me. I'm going to get beaten to a pulp.

"Yeah," I gulp, momentarily going frozen, my hand and towel still on my head. I'm getting ready for him to tell me that the police are on their way to protect me. That my family and I are safe.

On the other end, Sheriff takes a deep breath, contemplating his words carefully. My heart continues to race and I feel out of breath after running through so many frightening theories. I should slow down. Why would Joanne and Paul Baker be on their way to kill me? I'd be their last target. Personally, I would go after Sheriff Reggie. He's the one that put them away, that arrested him. They have no reason to hurt me.

"Carter, are you sitting down?"

"Yeah," I lie.

You probably shouldn't lie to an officer but I don't have time to walk somewhere and sit down.

"I wanted to call you personally before I called your mother," he begins. In the background, I can hear lots of talking. He's either at city hall or the sheriff's department at the courthouse in Paris. "Carter, we think we might have found your dad."

Blood rushes in my ears, the pounding rhythmic with my heart's. My body tenses, a chilling, metal pole running through it. My hand cramps and my towel slowly runs down my body, hitting the floor softly. Even the tiny sound it makes is too thunderous and deafening for my sensitive brain and ears.

Tunnel vision settles over me and I begin stumbling to my room, my hands trying to grab ahold of the walls. I'm able to get a few steps toward my room, but my next step sends me crashing to the cedar-planked floor. My head hits the wood, causing my eyesight to blur and become red. Somehow I hear

Sheriff Reggie's voice as he calls for me, even though I'm pretty sure it is not in my hand anymore. I don't care where it is. It's the least of my problems.

Of all things I expected that call to be about, that wasn't even in the top ten. No, I never imagined. Ever since Dad disappeared, I have been waiting for the news that he was found. I didn't even mind if he was dead, just as long as he was found and brought back to us. Of course, I always wished he would come back to us in one piece. But, as the days, weeks, months, and years went on, the possibility whittled. But, in the back of my mind, the question arises.

Dead or alive?

For him to be alive would be a miracle. But, it would also be a miracle if he was found dead. I spent my life wishing and praying that he would just be found. We needed closure and answers. Now here is that closure I have been waiting for since I was nine.

Slowly I rise off of the floor and sit on my ankles, searching for my phone. My head pounds a fiery red, causing my eyes to go in and out of focus. But, regardless of this, I am able to spot a black rectangle laying near the bathroom door frame. I crawl to it, wanting to cry because of my pain.

It takes me several tries just to grab my phone with my trembling hands.

"*Carter?!*" Reggie's voice shouts, laced with some form of concern and fear.

I bring it closer to my ear and allow myself to collapse to the ground again, trying to catch my diminished breath. I hit my head again but this time I welcome the pain with open arms. It is a reminder that this is real.

"Carter?"

"Dead or alive?"

"Are you okay, son?"

"*Dead or alive?*"

A deafening silence from the sheriff ensues. All I'm able to hear is the blood still rushing in my ear and my heart striking my rib cage. I repeat my question again, ignoring Daphne's voice from downstairs as she calls for me, asking if I'm okay.

Sheriff Reggie takes a long deep breath, his own voice shaking. "Dead, Carter."

I don't know why I ever expected him to be alive. For him to be alive he would have had to walk out on us. Family was the single most important thing to my dad. He would *never* leave us behind.

But, it's soothing knowing he's been found. It's confirmation that he didn't leave us. It's confirmation that we can get closure.

Sheriff continues, not waiting for me to say anything. "Some campers were up Emigration Canyon and found human remains. Some animal had dug up the shallow grave, allowing the body to be found. Our coroner was able to identify that they've been dead for eight years."

The same amount of time that Dad's been gone.

"Now, Carter, we aren't completely sure if it is him yet. But he was the—"

"–he was the only missing person reported that year," I interrupt, hoping my head pain will rise. I need a distraction.

"Yes," he confirms. All of the voices in the background have been quieter, I realize. They all are probably trying to eavesdrop, desperate to hear the moment my life ended again. "We called back the coroner consultant from Pocatello to fully identify if it's your dad or not. We sent the dental work of the body into the labs...but it will take weeks. We are hoping the consultant can identify the age of the skeleton so we can get a better idea if it's–" his voice breaks "–Noah. You know, before the dental results come back."

"The same consultant that took Evie's case...?" My voice is squeaky and drowned in acid. It breaks constantly as the lump in my throat grows, cutting off my breathing just enough.

Sheriff Reggie confirms again.

We don't talk for at least a minute, giving us both time to gather ourselves.

"Carter, I'm going to call your mother to let her know. This new case is my top priority, I assure you."

Mom's at work. He can't tell her there. I check the time on my phone

"Sheriff, do me a favor, okay? Don't call my mom right now. She's at work, but she gets off in fifteen minutes. Don't call her for another thirty minutes. I want to be here when you call her."

"Of course."

And that's it. I hang up, refraining from the pity goodbye. I close my eyes and focus on strengthening my breathing. I don't know how I feel. I don't know how I'm supposed to feel.

What have I done that was so bad in life that caused all of these things to happen to me? I lost Dad. I lost Evie. I mean, what sin did I commit to deserve this? I've been a good kid. I have *never* done *anything* wrong. I can't have deserved any of this, right?

I have been righteous. I have been kind. I have never judged another. Dad taught me well, so what could I have done wrong?

I make myself dizzy with the questions. Or maybe that's my head that's making me dizzy. To add to all of my problems, I may have a concussion. But, I don't have time to worry about a stupid, *possible* concussion.

The minute I move, my head begins to pulse dangerously. I push through the pain and force myself back on my feet, using the wall as support. My legs are wobbly at first but after a few steps they are bearable. I leave the towel on the hallway floor and slowly and carefully make my way down the stairs. Daphne sits on the couch, staring up at me. She looks ready to sprint.

I don't even get to the bottom of the stairs before she forces questions in my face. "Did you fall? Why does the sheriff have to call Mom in thirty minutes? What was that call about? Carter, should I be scared?"

Her hazel eyes are fearful and swimming with all kinds of emotion. No girl her age should have to be concerned or burdened with those kinds of emotions. It isn't playful fear, but true fear.

Daphne wasn't old enough to remember Dad, but I made sure to tell her all about him in an attempt to help her grow up like him. I made sure his memory not only lived on in Mom and me, but her as well. But, she doesn't have the attachment to Dad that my mom and I have.

I was a year older than she is now when I lost Dad and I didn't quite understand what was happening and what it all meant. So, honestly, I don't know if I should even tell her now. Her brain might not be developed enough. But, maybe that's a good thing.

I forget Daphne is only eight.

"No, Daph. You don't have to be scared. You just need to hug Mom and be there for her, okay? She's gonna need us," I insist, petting Chev who comes to my side as I reach the bottom of the stairs.

Daphne looks at me, confusion taking over her soft facial features. She glances out the window and then back at me.

"I'm going to go on a drive with Chev, okay? I'll be back before Mom gets home, I promise."

Daphne's small beady eyes look at me closer. "Carter?"

I make my way to the door, grabbing my truck keys from the dining table. I motion for Chev to follow me and he does gladly. "It'll be okay, Daph. I'll be back."

I leave her behind, sitting on the living room couch. I probably should explain to her what's going on and settle her fears. But, I need to breathe fresh air. The house feels stuffy and my head feels like it will explode.

It's stuffy outside too though. The heat grabs at me, parching me and closing my airways. It's heavy, causing me not to want to move. I almost immediately feel sweat building on my body, some of it trickling down.

Welcome to Bear Lake.

For some reason it digs up a memory that I do not remember having. Maybe because I blacked it out, erasing it from my main memory.

Little nine year old me was sitting on the couch, much like Daphne was just now. I was much like her, just more anxious not for Mom to come home but for Dad to come home. While he was visiting Grandma and Grandpa Miller, I whittled my first complex piece of wood on my own. It was a sitting dog and about a quarter of a foot long. Dad had always helped me carve my projects but I wanted to surprise him and do it on my own. So, I sat in our tiny living room, my sculpture bouncing around in my hands impatiently.

As I stared at the front door I could hear Mom on the phone with someone in the kitchen. The kitchen was in a complete other room, the entrance a small door frame. It sounded urgent, causing me to sneak to the frame, intent on eavesdropping. I was a pretty nosy kid. Probably where Daphne got it from.

"John, are you sure he left? He should have been here by now."

The phone is on speakerphone. I peek in. It's laying on the kitchen counter as Mom does the dishes, her light brown hair curled. It's cut at her chin and she wears a yellow, short sleeved blouse and dark blue skinny jeans.

Grandpa Miller's voice booms, echoing throughout the kitchen, "I'm quite sure he left, Brinley. He even came to say goodbye to Annie and me. Don't worry, I'm sure his flight was delayed or something."

Dad would've drove up from Bear Lake into Salt Lake City, Utah—which is a good two hour drive—and then got onto a two hour flight to Eugene, Oregon. After that he would have had to drive another two hours back home to Coos Bay. It was a long journey. But, it was better than the fifteen hour drive.

"He hasn't texted or called since yesterday afternoon, John. Plus, I checked his flight. It wasn't delayed. I even checked to see if there were any car crashes on any of his routes." She stops washing the dishes briefly to wipe her face with a rag.

At the time, it was nine in the evening on August eighteenth, two thousand thirteen. I didn't know at the time but August seventeenth was the day my dad disappeared in Bear Lake County, Idaho. I had no idea that my dad was nowhere to be seen.

"Brinley? Have you checked to see if he even got on his flight?" my grandpa asks. In the background I can hear my grandma, Annie, asking what's going on. "Check that, okay sweetheart? Then you or I can report Noah missing, okay?"

Grandpa was sheriff in those days.

Mom nods, wiping away a tear with the back of her hand. I watch as she grabs her phone and frantically taps different buttons. I can still remember the way her face dropped when she pulled up the public record of who boarded the flight. When she realized Dad never boarded his flight to Eugene. In a second all of her beautiful youth was sucked from her, causing her to age ten years at least. I saw the moment her hands started trembling and the moment she forgot to breathe. It was a terrible sight watching as she realized her love hadn't been seen since he left his parents' house. What a sight that was...

Chev nudges my leg, awaking me from the memory. I shake my head, immediately regretting it as the pain comes, making me feel light headed. I bring my hands to my temple and massage as I make my way to Big Red. His red doors open with an ear splitting creak as usual, giving me some routine in my bustling mind.

I slide in and roll down the windows in an attempt to air out the ablaze truck. Chev jumps in onto my lap and struts to the passenger seat, his sharp claws digging into my thighs. Letting air out of my clenched teeth, I start Big Red and crank the A/C as high as it can go.

My head pulses furiously in the heat, making me even more light headed. I push away the feeling and put Big Red into reverse. I turn left, away from the highway and toward the backroads.

I did not think my day was going this way. I was going to do some light investigating and talk to Grandpa to see if he knows anything about why Joanne and Paul did it. I just want that question answered already. It'll kill me. It *has* been killing me.

To be honest, when I got out of bed I had no idea that I would receive news that after eight years my dad could have been found. Dead. Could have been found *dead.*

I suddenly want to puke but I hold it back, barreling down the dirt road. I can't imagine what Mom will do when she hears. Will she cry and scream? Probably not. Will she collapse? Maybe. Will she freeze and pretend everything will be okay? Probably. Mom's like that, I've realized. It's her coping mechanism, I get it. It's not healthy... but at least she's coping?

I don't want to be there when Mom finds out, but I have to. Is it bad that I hope she doesn't fall apart? Is that selfish? I'm terrible, but at least I'm aware of how cruel I am... right?

***

I get home minutes before Mom arrives. To my surprise, Sheriff Reggie shows up too. He tells me he decided to tell her in person. I respect that. Maybe I should have never judged the sheriff. He seems to be a decent man after all—once he gets past his ego.

Sheriff Reggie gets there only five minutes before my mom and as soon as I pull into my driveway. We shake hands and I walk him into my home where Daphne awaits, sitting in the same spot.

We sit awkwardly in the living room, trading glances at different objects, waiting for my mother to come home. No one speaks. I don't even tell Daph what is going on... I don't tell her what the sheriff will tell our mom.

When Mom steps through the door, her keys jingling in her left hand, I forget how to breathe.

When Sheriff Reggie tells my mom the news, she doesn't collapse, she doesn't scream, she doesn't cry. She lowers herself onto the couch and stares into the distance at a family photo. No tears invade her eyes. Her jaw is clamped shut.

She doesn't collapse. She doesn't scream. She doesn't cry.

CARTER

Monday, June 6, 2022, Present.

Dad could have been found. Not alive though. If that skeleton belongs to my father, that means he's gone forever. My mom can finally grieve. I really don't think she ever truly grieved for my father. She didn't have time. At least, I don't think she did. I don't remember because I blacked out that part of my life.

It'll come as a relief if it's him. But it'll come as damage and pain as well.

Is he found? Is he still gone?

I don't know which answer I prefer to hear when Sheriff Reggie calls me. If he calls me. I still don't completely trust him. I should but something deep inside me tells me not to.

I want the relief but I don't want the pain.

I don't know if I can handle the pain right now, not with what's happened to Evie.

But, I need some relief in my life right now *because* of what's happened to Evie.

I feel as if I'm on a cliff, ready to plummet into some deep, deep ravine. One little tiny wind stroke can push me over the edge.

I fear the wind is churning around me.

Teasing me.

Threatening me.

Will I tip? Will I stand my ground?

I don't even know.

A hand clutches my shoulder, thrusting me to reality. Suddenly I'm back in my living room, aware I have been staring at the black TV for the past hour or so. I tear my drooping eyes from the screen and to Daphne, who stands behind the couch. Her dark brown hair is pulled into two pigtail braids. She's dressed in a sunny yellow, tanked sundress. Daph looks very put together.

"Hey," she smiles. "You okay, Carter?"

I force a smile because it feels right. I shove the darkness stirring inside me.

"Yeah. What do you need?"

My sister runs her fingers over the freckles on her arms, making constellations. "I know I don't remember Dad... but can you tell me more stories about him like you used to?"

I don't really want to. The thought of telling stories about Dad makes my heart heavy with grief. But, Daphne looks at me with eyes that sparkle with want and need. I can't say no to my sister. Not to something like this.

I pat my hand on the couch cushion next to me. She smiles and hops over the back of the couch, landing in the spot successfully. Her smile is big as she waits for me to continue. Something squeezes my heart as I take a deep breath.

There are millions of stories, all worthy of being heard.

“Back home in Oregon, Dad and I went crabbing once.”

Daphne cringes. She’s never been the type to fish, camp, or go crabbing.

“It was on this one dock in Charleston, I believe. You remember Charleston? It was only like a fifteen minute drive from home. It’s right there next to the ocean,” I explain. I don’t know how much she remembers from Oregon. “Well it was on a tiny dock right off the highway, right near the bridge that crosses over the river. The river was made up of a bunch of sloughs, coves, and inlets and was very wide. The water was dark blue and hid so many kinds of sea creatures.

“The dock was very slim but nonetheless worked for crabbing. There were a bunch of fishing boats along the shore. Sometimes if you looked at the right time you could see jellyfish and crabs riding the current. A spotted seal even popped its head from under the water, watching Dad and me as we lowered the crab cages down below the dock. It did tricks for us, dancing around the water. Then another seal like it joined. Dad and I decided to call them Bert and Ernie.

“After like an hour of watching the seals as they did tricks, we pulled up the crab cages. We didn’t catch much. In fact we only caught like ten. I remember Dad stuck his finger into the cage to grab some seaweed out and a crab latched onto Dad’s finger. I kid you not, Daphne… The seals *laughed* at Dad as he cried out, using his other hand to pry the crab off him. They actually *laughed*. It was *hilarious*.”

Daphne giggles beside me, her eyes wide and her smile bigger than I've probably ever seen it when I recalled memories with Dad. Her brown eyes glisten and glow and her smile lines are deep.

"I like that one," she exclaims, giggling lightly.

"Me too, Daphne. Me too."

The memory brings a small smile to my face. A true smile. It's not forced. It's a nice distraction from the suffocating feeling as I await the call. In fact I practically forget about the call all together.

"Tell me another," Daphne pleads. "Please, Carter. Please."

So, I do. This time I tell her about the time when Mom, Dad, and I went to Sunset Beach. It's a popular attraction where–you guessed it–you can watch the sunset. It's breathtaking. It was one of my favorite places to go. One time I even took my old girlfriend there on a date. Right before I moved.

Well, on this particular day, I was seven and we were there to watch the sunset together. Mom, Dad, and I got there at low tide and had one mission in mind: to get to the rocks that are usually stranded in the beach's water. Because it was low tide we could get to them. Dad was ahead of Mom and me on a completely different boulder, trying to race us to the rock that's the farthest out. Our goal was to watch the sunset from that rock. I realize now that it was a stupid idea. At sunset the tide comes in.

Dad began to be trapped as the water slowly came in, the beautifully orange sunset behind him as he scrambled toward us. But, he was laughing the entire time on his way back to shore.

Dad was that kind of person. He was constantly laughing. He was constantly smiling. He was constantly a role model to me and he was constantly an upstanding citizen. Nothing could bring him down because he was always lifting people up. Always helping people out and donating. It sounds fake and too good to be true but I swear it's all the truth.

Why is it always the good people that disappear or die?

The people who don't deserve it.

Suddenly all of the air escapes my lungs as a familiar ring fills my ears. It paralyzes me, its source buzzing in my front pocket.

Daphne pokes my shoulder. "Carter, your phone is ringing."

I slide my trembling hands into my pocket and pull my phone out. It's the call. The call Sheriff Reggie promised me yesterday. The call to confirm or deny if the body is my dad's.

Never in a million years would I ever think I'd say that.

I press answer seconds before I miss the call.

"Hello?" I gulp.

The sheriff clears his throat on the other end. He's got to be at city hall due to the voices flooding the background. "Carter. How are you?"

I have no patience for small talk or niceties. "Is it my dad? Does that body belong to my dad?"

The man goes silent.

Tell me, I want to yell. *Just give it to me straight. Tell me. Tell me now.*

He keeps me waiting. I'm not sure if it's intentional or not.

My heart pounds in my chest. I can hear the blood rushing in my ears. Even if Sheriff Reggie did answer me, I'm not quite sure I'd be able to hear him over the sounds thundering inside me.

I do. I'm glad for it too.

"No."

A mixture of dread, relief, and confusing emotions flood my senses. I am unable to depict between the different feelings. There is none that I feel more than the other. There isn't one that stands out.

Daphne grips my arm tightly, demanding to be heard. Without meaning to, I drown her out. I drown Sheriff Reggie out. I drown out Chev as he barks at something outside.

Dad hasn't been found.

Mom cannot grieve.

Dad hasn't been found.

I cannot breathe.

There is little relief, for Mom and me.

There is little grief. Can you blame me?

I didn't want him found because maybe, just maybe, he could be somewhere out there. But, now that he hasn't been found all I want is for that body to be his. Even if that means he's dead and never coming back.

Somehow the sheriff's voice slips past my noise blockade. "The man we found was younger than your father. A good ten years younger. I'm sorry, Carter."

I cough, trying to remember how to speak. At least I don't have to grieve.

"We sent in his dental so we can possibly get the name of the victim."

"My dad was the only missing person that year around here," I remind him, glancing toward Daphne. She still sits next to me, still gripping my arm. The subtle pain it gives me is a nice reminder to stay in reality. It's a nice reminder to not live in my thoughts, making myself deaf to surrounding sounds.

"Yes," Sheriff Reggie confirms. "But he could be from somewhere else. We are going to–sorry I shouldn't be speaking the details with you, son."

I wish you would stop calling me son.

I don't blame him for not speaking about the details of the case with me. He knows I'm prone to trying to figure out things myself.

"Carter. I need you to promise me something."

I wait, not speaking.

"Do *not* investigate this. I know you were right about the Bakers but we do not need your help. Carter you could be endangered. Hurt. It isn't safe. So please, *please* leave the investigating to the authorities. You got that? I don't want you investigating foul play or anything like that until you yourself are the police. Understand?"

I gulp. I don't want to promise. I want to help. But, I have no choice. I could get arrested with obstruction of justice. So, I agree. I don't want to, but I do.

Sheriff Reggie thanks me and I tell him I will inform my Mom the news myself. It'll be better coming from me. Plus, she's only in her bedroom. Her employer forced her to take a day off from work and so she shut herself behind her door, nestled in her covers.

I hang up, quickly tell Daphne what I've learned, and make my way to Mom's door. It's not far away from the couch. It's not much of a walk.

I open her door.

She's hidden under her blankets.

I wake her up.

She's confused.

When I tell her it wasn't Dad, she only blinks. She then nods. Mom doesn't cry or scream. She stays together and only nods her head.

* * *

The seals in Oregon had an average life expectancy of thirty five years. *Thirty five years*. My dad was thirty one when he disappeared and was presumed dead. That means an average *seal* outlived my dad.

That may not mean much to you but it paralyzes me.

The average male seal begins to mate at six years of age. Its pup basically grows besides its father. It's usually not supposed to lose its father until it's twenty-nine years old.

I lost my dad when I was barely nine.

My dad was not the average seal.

I am not the average pup.

There are three hundred and thirty thousand seals in Oregon on average. Most of those seals outlived my dad.

Seals are in some of my very happiest memories. I used to love seals and they used to remind me of happiness and childhood... until I learned they have a life expectancy of thirty five years.

Now the very things that made me happy, make me want to drop to my knees and curl up in a ball. They make me feel like I'm drowning.

An average seal can hold their breath for thirty minutes and not drown.

I am not the average seal. This is because I have been holding my breath for nine years. Although finally I am beginning to drown.

CARTER

Tuesday, June 7, 2022, Present.

Mom went back to work today. When she came out of her room fully dressed, showered, and smiling, I felt my heart be squeezed.

We are a presentable family according to my grandparents. We are '*perfect.*' They don't see that no one grieves. We push things down and 'flip the frown upside down.' We are not perfect. At all. We are not normal.

Daphne went to a friend's house, leaving me alone in the empty house. It's too quiet. I am used to the clink of dishes in the sink or the television playing some random show or video. I can't stay here alone. The silence is heavy.

Nixon is working for at least another hour. So, I have to be alone. Gas prices are pretty high these days so I can't just go for a drive and waste gas. Because of this I sit at the kitchen table, thumping my fingertips on the glossy wood. It creates a sound. It makes it a little less dense.

The silence brings questions I often refuse to ask myself. It also brings thoughts—and events—I try my hardest to push down.

What's wrong with me? Is this what falling apart feels like? I can't fall apart. I can't be falling apart, okay. I'm seventeen. I turn eighteen on June 17th. I'm basically graduated from high school. I go to college in two years, AKA two thousand twenty four. I applied to Idaho State University in Pocatello, Boise State University, and Utah State University in Logan. ISU and USU are both around an hour and a half away while BSU is five hours away. I think all three are doable. The acceptance and/or rejection letters should be coming soon. Within days.

I've just gotta keep going. That's how it works, right?

A familiar buzz paralyzes me. Never in my life have I ever been so terrified of phone calls or my phone going off. It's a weird fear, but to me a rational one. Every phone call I have had in the past three days is bad or conflicting news.

Maybe I should take my phone off of vibrate and change the ringtone to something funny and stupid. Like the *Barbie and The Dreamhouse* theme song. Or the *SpongeBob SquarePants* theme. *Anything* but the monotone buzzing. I will take anything but that.

I almost miss the call but I quickly take it out of my pocket in time. Though, I don't see the caller ID in my dash to answer the call. In the background I can hear the faint sounds of people shouting orders and machinery beeping.

I greet the caller hesitantly, waiting for them to begin talking.

"Hey, Carter!" the voice is yelling over the sounds that thunder around him. "I've got some news. I overheard my dad talking on the phone again about this new body. It's not life changing or whatever, but it's something."

So it's Nixon. I should have guessed that. I must *really* be out of it. There's a voice that begins discussing something with Nix but gets cut off. He must have pointed at his phone or something.

He keeps talking, not waiting for me to answer—not that I have anything important to tell him.

I've kept him fully in the loop about my dad and everything and so has Nixon's dad. Mr. Hodge went to high school with my dad and played on the same football team all throughout their high school years. It was a pretty good team. Once my dad and all the other seniors graduated, the team went downhill, creating a massive losing streak. I beat that losing streak. Dad would be proud I know that for sure. Although his team definitely could have beat my football team easily, no trouble. Our team really sucks compared to them.

"Anyways, I will be over after work. Be warned, I'm not going to take a shower."

I realize I heard nothing he said before.

"Yeah, okay," I squeak, my voice cracking.

Nixon pauses, hesitating. He coughs and then sighs. "Okay, well bye dude. Love you. See you later."

"Love you, bye."

And that's it. He hangs up and I go back to fiddling my fingers on the kitchen countertop, waiting for Nixon to get off work. It'll feel like a lifetime in this hushed home.

In one hour, I tidied up my room, did the dishes, and even organized the fridge, throwing out spoiled leftovers. I couldn't sit there in the silence for another hour so I put my music on full blast, playing over the living room's surround system, and did chores and even more chores. I had to be careful with my playlist. I knew for a fact there were some songs that would knock me down to my knees. With my luck, one of them even came on.

Right now

I thought we'd be

Driving 'round

Living wild

Loving happily

Somehow, you're not next to me

I tried, and I lied, and now you've gone away

Softly by Thomas Day is just one of those songs. I've never been one to listen to sadder music but I added this in my time of despair after Paul and Joanne were charged with Evie's murder.

I would die for you

I would lie for you

I'd give my life to you

If you love me

Hold me softly

I tell you this

So you believe me

I'm still in love with you

Yeah, I'm still in love with you

My trembling fingers grip the countertop, steadying me as I stand at the base of the sink, looking into the empty, clean kitchen sink. A lump grows in my throat and I have the sudden urge to puke. My brain seems to be beating, slamming against my skull dangerously. My eyes trail to the ibuprofen bottle hanging out to my left, waiting to be used. I take the chance and let go of the counter with one of my hands and reach for the bottle.

My fingers itch to open it. They itch to feel the dusty coating on the hundreds of painkillers. My head aches for the resolved numb feeling everybody always says happens. My tongue and throat tingle.

The bottle is chilled against my heated fingers, cooling the humid feel to my hands.

It doesn't take much effort to push the lid and twist.

It doesn't take much to pour pills onto my shaky palms.

Just this once, I assure myself. *It will only be this once.*

That's what everybody *says, Carter*, that voice in my head rings. I had forgotten the sound of the soothing voice over the years. But, plain as day with no question, it's my father's.

Dad had an uncle once that said that. He yearned for those dusty coated pills. He eventually ended up overdosing.

Dad told me once the odds of getting addicted. I was eight. I didn't know what it was about at the time but he made me roll a six sided die. He told me if I rolled an odd then he wouldn't let my mom serve me dessert for a month. If I rolled an even then I could have extra dessert.

I had quite the sweet tooth as a kid so I did not want to take the chance and roll the die in fear I'd get an odd. I asked:

"Do I have a choice?"

He said yes. If I didn't roll the die then I would still get extra dessert. I passed. I was confused. Why would I take the chance and roll for an even when I get the same reward if I pass? It didn't make sense. Not at all.

Then, Dad upped the prize if I rolled an even. He changed it to letting me buy the Lego set I had always wanted. It was from one of my favorite Star Wars scenes. It was expensive though.

He asked again if I wanted to roll, saying the reward for passing and the punishment for getting an odd was the same. Something inside me told me to roll and I did.

The die rolled around, teetering from side to side as I rolled it on the carpet in the living room. I watched intently as it rolled to even number than an odd than an even number, then an odd... It stopped.

I almost cried when my dad told me I couldn't have dessert for a month. I was very dramatic.

After the month passed Dad came to me again. He asked me how it felt when the pies, cakes, cookies, brownies, and sweets were restricted. To be completely honest, I cried the first few nights, begging for it to be changed. But, as the days went by I slowly got used to it.

Because I chose to roll the die I theoretically did drugs. Because I rolled an odd, I got addicted. If I had passed I would have been fine. If I rolled an even that means I did the drugs and didn't get addicted. I had a fifty-fifty chance of getting addicted. Fifty-fifty is just too high of a percentage.

I blink myself out of the memory and pour the pills into the fat, white bottle. All except two. I pop them into my mouth and swallow them without the aid of water, letting myself feel how uncomfortable it is when the pills run down my throat. They seem to get caught but I do nothing about it except stare at the white dust on my left palm.

"Carter?" a voice calls.

I turn around to find Nixon standing near my kitchen table, watching me.

"I didn't hear you come through the door," I cough, twisting the bulky lid back on the painkillers. I set them on the counter and wipe my white hands on the kitchen towel hanging on the handle of the oven. It leaves a streaked handprint.

I face my body toward Nix, forcing a smile. It can't look real. There is no way Nix wouldn't be able to see the fakeness of the grin. It feels unnatural as my teeth are pressed together and my lips are curled up around them, revealing my brushed pearls.

Nixon seems to be looking me up and down, looking for something I suppose. "I knocked but you didn't answer so I just let myself in. Was that not okay?"

Nixon still wears his Ace Hardware work shirt, the red fabric vibrant. His hair puffs out underneath his black cap and looks to be in need of a washing.

"Yeah, totally," I assure him, hoping he didn't see my moment of weakness. I pray he hadn't been standing there long.

I realize my music is still playing so I take out my phone and pause it. It's on a song by 3 Doors Down. "Kryptonite" I think. I stick my phone in my pocket and make my way past Nixon into the living room. I sit down on the couch facing the staircase. Nix stands where he is for a moment before following me into the living room. He sits on the other couch, the one facing the television.

"How was work?"

Nixon shrugs and pulls off his hat. He brushes through his hair and sets his hat down on the cushion next to him. "It was work."

I almost forget why he's here. My brain has been fogged up lately, causing me to have some memory loss.

I lean forward, eyes set directly on my best friend. "What was the thing you needed to tell me?"

Nixon seems to have forgotten why he was here too because he looks surprised. Then his expression softens and he begins messing with his hat, picking it back up.

"The mystery guy's cause of death was blunt force. I heard my dad say it while on the phone, as usual." He doesn't seem done with his thought so I just watch him, waiting surprisingly patiently. Nixon fidgets almost as bad as Evie did, his eyes bouncing from the different family portraits we have hanging up. “There’s something else. I really shouldn’t tell you but you’re my best friend and it’s about your—”

My ears prick up and I grow tense. “—my dad? I’m guessing it's about my dad, right?”

Luckily Nix doesn’t keep me waiting long. He closes his eyes. He’s not as comfortable with this whole murder talk as I am. I can tell it’s getting to him.

“Obviously the guy's clothes were still on him...” he pauses briefly as if that sentence pained him. I feel bad for my best friend. “In his pants pocket they found a piece of paper with your dad's full name on it. It had another name on it too but the ink was all smeared from water or something. The other name was unintelligible but your dad’s was plain as day.”

My best friend watches me like a hawk, waiting for me to break down, I suppose. I think he knows me better than that though. I think he knows that that piece of information will keep me up for days on end. He knows I won’t break down. I’m past that point. He knows I will just want answers.

This mystery guy is the second person to end up dead with a piece of paper with my dad’s name on it. The *second.* The piece of paper Evie had was clearly written for a purpose. It was consequential. Clearly this second piece of paper is too. No one writes names on a paper for no reason and has it on them when they are found dead. There is a reason behind every single thing we do as humans: nothing occurs without a reason. So, what’s the reason for this one? I still haven’t fully figured out why *Evie* wrote down my dad’s name so how am I going to figure out why this John Doe did the same thing?

Perhaps I don’t need to figure it out. I can let the police do it.

No, *absolutely not*. They will accuse my dad of something ludicrous.

But what if he did do something ludicrous? That tiny voice in my head questions, giving me a sudden headache. Despite the ibuprofen I took only minutes ago, the headache rages.

I look up at Nix. He seems to have the same facial expression as me. But, when he sees me looking at him, he hides it.

I wonder if he's thinking the same thing as me. The impossible thing.

My hands are suddenly clammy so I wipe the sweat onto my jeans. It doesn't help. If anything it makes it worse. No matter how many times I wipe my damp palms on my pants, I can't shake the possibility that my dad may have killed this man. I can't escape the possibility that my dad could have killed this man and ran.

Is it so bad that I wish that's what happened? Because maybe–maybe that meant that he was out there alive.

CARTER

Wednesday, June 8, 2022, Present.

I'm not the only one with the theory that my dad—my kind, loving, selfless dad—killed the John Doe and ran. When Mom got home last night she received a call asking if she would come in today to answer some questions regarding my dad. She left around one this afternoon. It's four now.

I didn't tell Mom what I figured they'd ask her. In fact I just simply refused to tell her anything about the piece of paper. Of course I felt bad for not telling her but it was for our own good as a family. If my mom went into that interrogation already knowing about the paper then they would take it as they were right that my dad killed that man and that she knew about it. My mom could potentially be charged with aiding and abetting. I can't let that happen.

This whole situation is insane. I know it sounds cliche but my dad would never hurt a fly. *Never*. I mean while growing up Dad taught me that violence was never the answer. He helped homeless folks, struggling citizens, and despair-ridden people. That's who he was. My dad is not a murderer.

But still there's that voice in the back of my head that insists otherwise.

I sit next to Daph on the couch, watching some kind of weird Nickelodeon tv show. I haven't ever seen it but she seems to enjoy it. It's definitely not like the Nickelodeon shows I grew up with.

"Can I watch something now? You've had the TV for probably like a few months," I ask my sister, eyeing the remote in her hand. Surprisingly she hands it to me without so much as a protest—very uncharacteristic of her.

I switch off of the show she insisted on watching and switch to one I grew up with: *The Fairly OddParents.* I start where I left off so many months ago.

"What *is* this?" Daphne questions, looking at the TV with confusion and maybe some disgust as the theme song plays. "Can we just go back to *Henry Danger*? I don't want to watch this."

I try my best not to roll my eyes. These next couple of days are going to be hard so I've been trying my best to be the good brother I'm supposed to be. But, it's so hard with Daphne. She pushes and pushes until she can't push you anymore.

"Don't you have to be stupid somewhere else?"

Without hesitation, Daph looks up at me and glares. "Not until six."

This time I roll my eyes, not holding it back. But, I hand her the remote. As I do that Mom comes through the front door, her hair brushed back into a low messy bun. She makes her way to the kitchen table and collapses in one of the chairs.

I watch as she brings her head into her hands and begins massaging her temples.

In a beat I am off the couch and at her side. I sit across from her and grasp her upper arm gingerly.

"It's okay, Mom," I repeat over and over.

She looks up at me and tries to manage a smile. She fails.

I can tell by the way she squints and looks at me that she has a headache. I let go of her arm and make my way through the kitchen to where I last left the ibuprofen. It's still in the same spot next to the sink. I retrieve two of the circular pills and a glass of water before returning back to my mother. Mom nods a thank you as she swallows the pills down.

A million questions go through my brain as I watch the pills slowly take effect against her raging headache.

What did they ask her?

What did they show her?

What did they tell her?

What happened overall?

I can't ask her any of them... it wouldn't be right. So, I just sit here and let my mom know I'm here. Not through my words but through my presence.

My mom doesn't deserve any of this. She doesn't deserve to be questioned on a matter the police know nothing about. Mom doesn't deserve the life she's been given. In fact she has done absolutely everything right. I mean she provides for Daphne and me and is the best mother she can be... and then some. I've never seen or heard her judge a single person or do anything that was considered bad. Next to my dad, she is one of the most selfless people I've met.

I don't understand how this world works.

Mom shatters my thoughts and brings me back. "Carter?"

"Yeah, sorry. What do you need, Mom?"

Her hazel eyes look empty as she stares at me. They bring cold chills that invade my spine.

"I love you," she simply says, placing her hand over top of mine—which still rests on her arm. My mom pats it and closes her eyes.

"Mom?"

"Yes, Carter?"

I promised myself I wouldn't.

"What happened at the station?"

I'm weak with temptation.

She slips her hand out from underneath mine and buries her face, groaning softly into her palms. Mom then drags her hands up and runs them through her scalp. Her haunting eyes stare me down.

"They think it was your dad who... hurt that man."

I nod and look behind her at Daphne. She sits on the couch, paying more attention to the TV than us. Which is good. She doesn't need to be listening. "I figured they would, Mom."

She looks at me warily with hazel eyes then bobs her light brown-haired head. Each of her eyebrows are creased into

'U's' and her wrinkles have deepened significantly. Her skin is weathered and her eyes dark and burdened. Mom's fingers tremble and her leg bounces up and down.

My mother is only thirty nine.

"Noah couldn't have, Carter. You know that don't you?"

I nod my head even though I have my doubts. Anything is possible. Especially in Bear Lake. At least *lately* anything is possible. Nothing ever happened in Oregon.

Mom continues defending my dad. "I mean your dad was the most selfless person I'd ever met. It's one of the main reasons I married him. He was never the type of person to put himself first. He would always put you, Daph, and I first. Always–" her voice cracks "–always. He didn't do what they were suggesting."

CARTER

Thursday, June 9, 2022, Present.

A knock shakes me awake. I move my eyes toward the windows. I didn't even hear anyone pull into the driveway. But, how could I? I've been asleep on the couch for… I check my phone's clock… three hours. It's 3:00 in the afternoon. I meant to only sleep for a few minutes. Guess I've been tired.

On the front porch stands my grandpa and grandma Miller, moving up and down on their heels. I slide off my couch hesitantly.

When I open the main door, Grandpa opens the screen door, trying to manage a smile.

"Grandpa, Grandma, come in."

Linking arms, my grandparents come into my home, greeting me halfheartedly. Grandma Annie is dressed in jeans and a black dressy blouse. A silver necklace is placed around her neck, the pendant a silver heart. It's her usual outfit.

"Hi, honey," she smiles, taking a seat on one of the couches. Grandpa goes to the kitchen and grabs a glass from the cabinet. His plaid button-up sleeves are rolled up to his elbows. He slips the glass underneath the water dispenser on the fridge until it's full. He takes one sip and then comes to the couch. I sit on the opposite couch from my grandparents, the one facing the stairs.

"What is it?" I question, picking at the skin on my arms. I realize what I'm doing and steady my hands by sitting on them. It brings memories of Evie. "You guys know I love you, but why are you two here?"

Grandma and Grandpa hold hands as they sit next to each other. Grandpa gets to talking before Grandma can. "The sheriff called us and told us about the whole situation... About your dad."

I *expected that*. Grandpa basically trained Sheriff Reggie.

I wait for him to continue.

Grandpa looks at my grandma warily, his brown eyes full of an array of emotions. "I never wanted to worry your mother..." he starts.

What does he mean? What could that mean? That could mean anything.

I suddenly feel sick, yesterday's breakfast churning inside my acidic stomach.

"Just tell me," I cough, trying my best to keep myself in check.

I don't think I've ever seen Grandma and Grandpa look this worried to tell me something. Ever.

Grandpa goes on telling me how the day before Dad went missing he overheard a phone call he had. Dad was staying in the guest room at my grandparents. My grandma tells me that he sounded angry, which was especially odd. I have no recollection of my dad ever being angry, at least not in front of me.

"Naturally we eavesdropped from the kitchen," Grandma's ginger voice squeaks. Dad must have been sleeping in the guest room on the main floor. My grandparents' house has three guest rooms. Two of them are in the cool basement. The other three extra rooms were used for storage and things like that.

Grandpa coughs and squeezes Grandma's hand. "We couldn't hear much but we heard enough."

As Grandpa tells the story I feel as if I'm there. Grandpa has a way with stories: through them you can be transported places.

Dad's room door was cracked open a bit, just enough to where you could see him inside. He stood in front of the window, basking in the morning sun. I can imagine how the yellow light must have shined through his shaggy brown hair. Or how he stood, most of his weight on his right leg.

"No! I'm done, okay?" Dad had growled, his free hand clutching the back of his neck. "I can't do this anymore. I'm not this type of person."

The person on the other line did not agree with what my father had to say. My dad flinches at whatever the other person says.

"I want out," my dad says one last time, quieter. He isn't as confident as he was the first time. In fact he seems dejected. Put down. Stepped on.

He flinches again then hangs up. Grandpa reclaims that Dad took his right fist and punched the dresser in front of him. It clicks in my mind. My grandparents have had all the same furniture since my Dad was a kid. After dad disappeared we stayed at my grandparents' a lot, especially in the first few months. We didn't care how far away they were.

I knew the hole in the surface of the dresser wasn't there before he was gone. I knew it was new but I never once thought it could have been my gentle dad that made the gaping hole in the cedar.

Grandpa ends his story and I'm back in the living room, intently sitting forward. My fists are clasped together and hold up my head.

"That doesn't make sense..." I trail, eyeing the cedar planked floor.

It makes so much sense that it makes no sense. But, it proves the police's theory. It proves mine and Nix's theory more than it denies it.

"Carter..." Grandma chirps quietly.

I put my hand up. "This can't get out, Grandma, Grandpa. Never."

I look at them as they stand there, jaws dropped. Grandpa closes his jaw and looks to my Grandma Annie. Their eyes seem to say all the words they aren't able to say. Then, together they look at me and nod.

We've reached a mutual agreement.

My phone rings several times before Nixon actually answers. I can tell he isn't happy when his voice grumbles just by saying a simple "hello." It sends shivers down my spine. You don't often see or hear Nixon mad. When he is, the first thing to do is leave him be.

But this is more important.

"Hey, Nixon. How are you?"

Nixon mumbles underneath his breath, his voice deep and sharp around the edges. He doesn't answer me directly. In the background I can hear the machines beeping as usual.

I try again because I don't know what's good for me. "How's work?"

This time he answers in nothing but a barely audible mutter. "It's work."

"Look, I need you to press your dad for more details on this new body. It's important, okay?"

I think back on earlier and what my grandparents told me. I refrained myself from calling Nixon as soon as they left and it took a lot of restraint. Instead of calling him, I paced the length of my downstairs, thinking intently. But, I only lasted an hour. It's longer than I thought I'd get, to be honest.

Nixon grunts instead of speaking. My eyes wander to my arms as I pace the backroom's living room for the twentieth time. They are covered with crimson circles made by my fingers and their nails. With my pointer finger I poke one, causing me to wince. They are already tender.

"My grandparents just came over and told me some stuff and I just need to know anything and everything about that corpse. Okay? You would be doing me a solid." I take my free hand and run it through my greasy brown hair. My fingers get caught on some ratted pieces, pulling them out. I let the strands fall from my hand and onto the wood floor as I go back through the hallway and back into the kitchen.

I keep going. "Has the DNA come in yet? Wait, no. Don't answer that. It'll be another week or so. Do you know what color the hair is? Or are there any other marks on the bones other than the skull? Was there anything else in his pockets, or no? What weapon do you think the assailant used? Is there–"

It's like a bomb goes off, setting fire to everything in me. Nixon seems to be a completely different person as his voice surges. I am taken off balance and almost slip. My hand steadies me on my island.

"I. Don't. Know. I don't have all the answers, okay?" His voice rumbles with an unfamiliar throb. "I feel dirty sneaking around and getting these answers for you! I'm betraying my dad's trust and I could get arrested for disclosing classified information in an FBI investigation. I'm eighteen, Carter! I could get up to ten years! So, I can't help you!"

The line goes dead and I'm left in my unusually silent home. My heart pounds and my head runs a million miles per hour. Nixon has blown up on me before... but *never* like that. I mean he's my best friend.

Okay, Carter. Take this like a 'man.' You aren't a child anymore. Don't read into it.

I used to read into every little thing. Especially in middle school. Everyone was obsessed with drama. Luckily as I matured, I got better.

I fully understand Nix though. I mean what he said was all reasonable. The FBI was brought in and he could potentially be arrested. He's eighteen so it would go on his personal record. I'm seventeen. It most likely wouldn't go on mine. But, I have to be careful. My birthday, June 17th, is coming up quickly.

So is Evie's. It hurts my heart how close she made it to eighteen. All she wanted was to be eighteen so she could legally get away from her parents. June 14th can't come sooner. I don't know why but I feel as if I let her down in some way. I can already feel it in me that the 14th is going to be a rough day for me.

I hope I can celebrate her eighteenth birthday like she would. I know she's going to be looking down watching me as she stands next to her grandma. I'm sure she's been having a beautiful reunion with her grandma up there. Eve loved that woman more than anyone or anything. She loves her grandma like I love my mother.

I have no doubt she's up there. There is no doubt in me that she has been following me along, cheering me on as I got her killer behind bars. It's been the only helpful thing I've done for her since she passed, I'm sure of it. The thought of her happiness makes me forget Nixon's lack of.

CARTER

Thursday, June 9, 2021, Present.

I believe I've given Nixon enough time to cool off. So, I step out of my truck on the corner of Lincoln Street and Eighth, holding a bottled Dr. Pepper. My boot makes contact with the hot asphalt and I immediately feel it on the balls of my feet. I slam Big Red's creaky door and eye the beautifully orange sunset.

The night Evie died there was one of the prettiest sunsets I've probably ever seen in the valley. I wasn't aware of Evie's passing at the time so it didn't click. Until now. Seeing the oranges, pinks, and yellows in the sky today gives my heart a heavy mood of remembrance. The way the three colors blended and were assorted was perfectly stunning. I took a picture. It sits in my camera roll surrounded by pictures of Evie and I.

If I had known...

It makes me retch at the thought.

Why are the sunsets always the prettiest the day or night someone passes? I like to think they fabricated the sunset themselves, purposefully putting every color in a perfect place for those they love to admire.

It makes me wonder who designed tonight's sunset. Who died for tonight's picture-worthy sunset?

I tear my eyes off of the colorful fabrication and set them on Nixon's hunter green home. It's run down significantly and junk scatters the perimeter of the exterior. The yellow walled garage is filled to the brim with parts and clutter to the point where it overflows into the driveway. There's a rusty basketball hoop in the grass that makes a long shadow.

Making my way down the cracked and fragmented sidewalk, I notice the white curtain belonging to the large five foot window shivering, proving there's life inside. To the right of the window, the sun-bleached PVC front door stays shut tight.

The lengthening shadows crawl upon the lopsided front steps. Under my feet the steps are covered with some sort of ripping artificial grass, the type golfers use to putt on.

I've only been to Nixon's house a select few times to pick him up and stuff like that. In our year or so of friendship I have never been into his home. *Never*. He's been in mine countless times but he's never once invited me over. In fact he hated it when I had to pick him up.

My fist makes contact with the front door and I can hear inside the echo. The echo doesn't last long. The door knob turns, revealing Nixon on the other side. When he recognizes me, his face drops significantly, his facial creases deepening.

"Carter, why are you here?"

I give a half wave and feel stupid as soon as I do. In response I shove my free hand into my front pocket and roll back and forth on the balls of my feet. "On the phone it seemed like you were having a rough day." I hand him the chilled Dr. Pepper in my hand.

Nixon stares at it sluggishly with his weary gray eyes, seeming to not register it. His shoulders are dropped and his eyebrows are furrowed. The best way to describe him is defeated. Defeated and kicked to his knees.

He just seems hollow. I know exactly how he feels.

I urge the soda his way, waking him up. His fingers wrap around it and holds it to his side, letting it dangle there heavily. His eyes meet mine and he opens his door wide, letting me into his house for the first time.

I hide my smile as I step past him into the dark home. I step into a white carpeted living room separated from the front door entrance by only a criss-cross picket fence on top of a three foot tall white bricked wall. The heavy smell of animals, dust, and possibly animal pee hits me immediately, preventing me from breathing for a short amount of time.

Nix leads me to our left past the picket and brick wall and into a spacious living room. We don't go straight into what seems like a dining room that leads to a kitchen or right into a small, crowded hallway.

An old box television sits in a wooden TV stand in front of the white curtained window. In front of the TV, up against the wall is a tan couch with neutral colored flowers. To the left of the couch is a light brown recliner. That is where Nixon sits while I sit on the long couch.

“Thanks.” He tries to manage a smile. I can see how hard he tries.

I eye the elk mount above his head and nod a ‘you’re welcome.’ I then eye the white carpet. It’s stained in several places and is an assortment of suspicious colors.

“I’m sorry. My house is insanely messy. We don’t usually have time to clean,” Nixon explains, watching me look around the cream colored room. “We’ve been meaning to renovate and put in new carpet and stuff but we don’t really have the budget.”

I nod again and lean back more into the couch. It's shocking how much I sink. Sinking couches are my favorite couches.

“You don’t have to explain, Nix. I fully understand the no time aspect of life. Plus, I’ve always wanted to see your house from the inside. That mirror is pretty cool above the fireplace.”

It was a pretty cool mirror. It took up most of the wall above a brick fireplace and was barely dirty. In it I can see how gross my greasy brown hair is. I run a hand through it and it sticks up. I probably should have taken a shower.

It's too late now.

Nixon smiles slightly and shrugs, examining the mirror himself. "It’s always been there. Ever since I was little."

An awkward silence ensues as we stare at various parts of the room. Luckily, I've gotten used to the horrid smells so that doesn’t bother me as much. Not that I'd show it bothers me anyways. Nixon's feelings are too important to me. Especially since he clearly had one of the crappiest days in history.

"So..." I sigh, picking at the seams in my jeans. "Where's your parents?"

Nixon's chair squeaks as he gets up with his Dr. Pepper. I watch nervously as he makes his way into the kitchen, out of sight. I can hear the fridge open and close, followed closely by Nixon exhaling sharply. "Dad's at work while Ellie is out of town."

Ellie is Nix's step mom. She's an insanely nice lady actually. I met her once at the county fair during the summer in between junior and senior year. Nixon was eating with his dad and her one of those nights and invited me over. We basically just chatted about college and high school the entire time.

Nixon comes back into the living room, his soda replaced by two string cheeses. He throws me one and I catch it perfectly with one hand. Nix then collapses back into his recliner and clicks on the television. It automatically turns to some sort of western.

"You'll never believe what happened this morning," Nix growls, taking a *bite* out of his string cheese. I cringe and continue tearing off *strings* of the cheese and popping them into my mouth. You know, like a normal person.

"What happened?"

It takes Nixon a few solid minutes to actually get around to telling me what exactly happened, but I can tell by his darkening facial expression that he did not like it. His eye brows are creased significantly and his mouth is tightened into a straight line, causing his slim lips to disappear. I take one last look at him before finishing off my string cheese.

Nixon continues to stare at the television, seeming to watch the old western intently. A few gunshots sound as the cowboy is being chased by some bandits or something... I don't know.

"My mom showed up this morning," he simply states, his voice monotone.

At first I don't think I heard him exactly right. His mom left him while he was in elementary school. She didn't even say goodbye to Nixon. She didn't even say goodbye to Mr. Hodge. She just left and no one has heard of her since. No one has even seen her. So, there's *no way* she just showed up today. There is *no way.*

"What do you mean?" I question, sitting forward. Nix keeps his eyes on the TV. "She just *showed* up?"

Nixon nods and shrugs at the exact same time. "I mean I don't think she knew who I was. But, I knew who she was. I'm 100% sure it was her, Carter."

I feel my brows furrow. It doesn't make sense.

"Wait, so she showed up at Ace but didn't know who you were? I'm confused." I feel bad pressuring him for answers but I do it anyway.

"I was working at the cash register and she came up wanting to buy some paint. She told me that she had just recently moved in and that her new house was a horrid color. She talked to me like I was just any employee so I don't think she knew who she was talking to. Which also means she hasn't kept tabs on me over the years she's been gone. My dad posted pictures of me on Facebook all the time so if she really wanted to know what happened to me she would know what I looked like, no doubt."

My heart strings are pulled for my best friend.

I can't imagine...

No, I can. I can imagine.

When I was nine my dad abandoned me. I always thought it was never intentional and that someone had to have hurt him. He wouldn't have just disappeared on his own. But now all of that is beginning to dissipate.

There is a chance that he *chose* to disappear. It's possible that he killed a man and ran off to avoid being caught, even if there was a chance he wouldn't have been prosecuted for years to come.

He may not even know what Daph and I look like now. He wasn't here to watch us grow up. I'd bet he wouldn't even recognize me and Daphne... just like Nixon's mom didn't recognize him.

I have been trying so hard not to automatically assume he ended a human being's life and disappeared willingly. So *hard.* But, as the clues and evidence builds up it's becoming more likely. Much more likely.

But, unlike my dad, Miriam is back.

Nixon continues talking. "I mean I haven't seen this lady in ten years and she just suddenly shows up back. I wonder if she's going to make contact or something. Or come here. I mean Dad and I have lived in this house since I was a baby.

Him and Miriam bought this house when she was pregnant with me. What do I do, Carter, if she comes? Shut the door and tell her she should stay gone? She's clearly good at disappearing."

My first instinct is to tell him yes. He *should* tell her to stay away. It's too late now to reenter his life. But there's that tiny voice in my head that says the opposite. What would I want someone to tell me essentially?

"You let her in. You let her explain. Then you decide whether or not to kick her out."

Nix tears his eyes off the movie and finds my eyes. His gray eyes are full of frustration and his nose crinkles. "But what if I'm not ready to listen to her explain?"

I gulp sharply and relax all of my tightened muscles.

"If you wait until you are ready, you'll be waiting for the rest of your life. Every second is worth a limitless value and it only takes one second for everything to change while you are waiting."

NIXON

Thursday, June 9, 2022, Present.

I have never had a true friend until Carter Chase Miller, let alone a best friend like him. Heck I don't think I ever had a best friend until he came around. But I am glad he's come into my life. It sounds cheesy but I've been a better person since he came along... that is if you don't count the many years I can get in prison for giving him classified information regarding his dad and John Doe.

The sound of horse hooves and revolver gunshots echoes throughout the living room. Carter and I have been watching John Wayne classics for about an hour already. The sun is nonexistent outside and the only light comes from the TV and a floor lamp over by the window and the brick divider wall by the door.

I can tell Carter has probably never seen a John Wayne western in his life by the way his brown eyebrows are intensely furrowed. His caramel eyes are squinted and he leans forward, hugging a throw pillow to his lap. Yet, he still watches it with me, not criticizing it like most people would.

That's why I feel bad about the outburst I had this afternoon. It wasn't really about Carter anyways. It was just about my frustration with Miriam. After I saw Miriam, my day just continued to go downhill. Every tiny thing irritated me and brought me down. That's how it always goes.

Carter didn't deserve to have me take it out on him. Not after all he's been through. I mean all the things he has to worry about is insane. I can't imagine. He's grappling with the fact that his dad may have murdered someone and that he may be out there somewhere, choosing to stay away. His girlfriend was just *murdered*, most likely by her parents. Who knows what else is going on in his life at the moment.

Three solid pounds throughout my house, shaking me aware. I look at Carter and he looks at me as we realize someone's at the door.

Miriam is my first thought. It'd be an odd coincidence considering Carter and I were just talking about how much dread I felt about her possibly showing up at my house. That's exactly what I feel now: dread.

Carter must see how wide my eyes are because he gets up and goes to the door, no doubt purposefully not giving me enough time to get up. I lean forward, trying to see as my best friend opens the door up.

"Nixon?" a lady questions, out of view. I don't even need to see her to know that voice as the very one I heard this morning.

I watch as he shakes his head. "Nope, not me, ma'am."

She clears her throat. It's ragged but still very feminine. It almost sounds like a smoker's voice. All of the bubbliness that possessed it this morning is drained out of it.

"Do the Hodges still live here?"

Carter looks back at me quickly. When I nod in allowance he repeats the gesture to my deadbeat mother. I don't hear her say anything to the answer from Carter. Slowly–somehow–I start inching myself off of Dad's favorite recliner. Gradually I begin dragging my feet to the open door. toward what could be my demise. The woman on the other side of Carter is where I got my black locks. And my childhood trauma. It's traumatic to a kid when their mother suddenly abandons them. She was supposed to pick me up from school that day... and she never showed. I waited on the playground of A.J. Winters Elementary School for *three* hours. Dad had gotten home from work and found a note from Miriam stating that she had to leave. She couldn't explain clearly to him why though.

Dad found me sitting on a swing as the sun crept behind the West mountains of the valley.

When I catch the first glimpse of Miriam's raven hair, I urge myself to keep going and to not seize up.

Carter moves out of the way, permitting me to speak with the woman. She looks the exact same as she did earlier today. Her incredibly long raven hair is braided into two dutch braids and she wears mom jeans, sneakers, and a black, distressed AC/DC tee.

Her dark ocean blue eyes recognize me immediately. Her defined cheekbones seem to grow more hollow every second none of us say anything.

"Nixxy?"

"Don't call me that." *You lost the right to call me that the day you left me.*

Miriam flinches but nods slowly. "I deserve that."

Carter nudges me and I know what he's saying. His caramel eyes squint and he gestures toward the inside of my insufferable house. I want to tell him no but I owe him for today's visit even after my outburst.

"Come on in, Miriam."

The use of her first name causes her to flinch again. The worst part is I don't feel bad one bit.

I step aside and allow her in. She hesitantly slips past me, her eyes on her feet as they shuffle forward. Carter begins walking to the couch, showing Miriam to it. I inhale deeply, staring at the dark street. Shadows lurk at every corner and the summer moon is nonexistent.

I *can do this*, I repeat to myself about a million times.

What would Dad do if he comes home before Miriam's gone? What would he say?

I haven't even texted him or called him. He likely has no idea that Miriam is here and alive.

Pushing my hand forward, I close the front door smoothly.

"This place has changed," she nervously chuckles, watching me as I take my time getting back to Dad's recliner.

"That'll happen over the span of ten years," I whisper as I sit. I raise my voice to a normal volume. "What are you doing here after all this time?"

Miriam tries to manage a smile as she smoothes out the wrinkles in her baggy jeans. Her appearance has barely changed over the years. The only thing different is the nose ring she has now and her cheeks are hollower. Her cheekbones are the same, as are her eyes and the length of her hair. Her hair has always been one and a half feet past her shoulders.

"I could finally come back."

My brows furrow. "What is that supposed to mean?"

She shakes her head, looking at her lap. "Nothing. It's hard to explain. I can't explain it for a little while."

She leaves me for ten years and she can't even give me a good explanation. She owes me something better than 'It's hard to explain. I can't explain it for a little while.'

"*Why* are you here then?" I pressure, leaning forward. It's hard to make eye contact with her since she's to my direct left so I look at the ground.

Miriam clears her throat and shuffles in her seat. She coughs another time. "I'm not going to lie to you, Nixon. I'm here for a trial on Saturday."

That causes Carter to pipe up. I had forgotten he was even here.

"Trial? What trial?" Carter questions. He sits on the opposite side of the couch from my birth mom.

I have the same question. I've heard nothing about a trial. I look at Miriam. She fidgets significantly, not being able to sit still.

She doesn't look like she's going to explain but as soon as she finds me watching her she spills. "The Baker trial. I'm sure it's all the hot news here. It's not often a murder happens anywhere near here. Especially one of this magnitude."

Something that hasn't changed about Miriam is that she still overshares.

Carter shoots off the couch and stalks to the front door. He opens the front door and slams it. No warning. Miriam stiffens up as we listen to Big Red start up.

We sit in a loud silence, both of us still staring at the door.

"Did I say something wrong?" my mom asks, standing up. She moves to the window and peeks out into the gloomy outside.

I continue sitting. "Yes, Miriam. You did. Was that not clear?"

CARTER

Saturday, June 11, 2022, Present.

The sun rages outside as I drive smoothly on the highway toward Montpelier. My air conditioner barely puts a dent in the heat that swarms the truck's cab.

What'd I fix you for if you ain't going to work, I growl, rolling down both of my windows with the buttons on my door.

A hot wind runs through my messy hair, causing it to fly every which way. I smooth it back but it helps little against the seething breeze. I curse a little--I'm not proud of it, okay. Sometimes you've just got to let it out.

I'm usually a down to earth kind of person. But, something about today is rubbing me the wrong way. Not something... The trial. I'm sure Sheriff Reggie was trying his best to quiet it but nothing stays secret in a small community like ours. By now I'm sure all six thousand of our population is talking about it. Evie's tragedy is all anyone will actually talk about.

It pisses me off.

She's a person. A human being.

Not someone to gossip about. Eve deserves her privacy, even after death. It's all she ever wanted.

Evie Janiece Baker was not someone you could boast about and live after. She did *not* like it. I suppose she wasn't used to it though. She spent most of her life being criticized and hurt for stupid reasons. It's just proof of how sideways the world has gone.

First the abuse came because she was the one who survived in that car crash in third grade. And then her parents just racked up the reasons more and more as she grew up into the beautiful girl she was. Then, they killed her because she found out some insane—probably stupid—secret. She came across something she shouldn't have.

And that's all it took for Paul and Joanne Baker to *kill their daughter*. All in cold blood.

It's important to me that I go to that trial and make sure that they get prosecuted to the fullest of the law. Sheriff Reggie can't stop me. He can surely try but it's not going to happen.

The case is being held at the courthouse all the way out in Paris but I need to make a quick pit stop at the Baker house on Ninth Street. I swear I'm not going to do anything illegal, okay?

Montpelier is decently crowded today by several tourists. Bear Lake is a huge hot spot for tourists from all over the States and even from different countries. It's always weird for me because Bear Lake is an extremely small part of Idaho. A *very* small part. Like it's not the first county in Idaho your eye is drawn to when looking at a map. We are literally in the very bottom right corner of the state.

At the main intersection I turn right onto Main. It's a turn I've made more times than I could count. I've made it to go out toward the West side of the valley, the local diner named Dan's, the theater, and most importantly Evie's house. From Main Street you can almost go anywhere.

A strong sense of familiarity hits me as I turn left onto Ninth. The overwhelming feeling comes over me *every single time*. It's a sense of dread mixed with the feeling of sorrow for the past month's tragedies. If you told me two months ago what all was going to happen... I wouldn't have believed you. Even if I had believed you, I wouldn't have been able to prepare myself nearly enough in time.

Maybe one day I'll be able to look back and look at all of this differently. Evie taught me that the goal is to learn from absolutely everything we go through. Everytime she shrugged nonchalantly at every bruise that showed up on her, she taught me that. Everytime she went through misery, she taught me that. Her death taught me that.

Perhaps one day I *will* look back when I have my own kids, wife, and house and think *hey, now I know*. Now I know how to protect my future kids from the world's horrors. Because now I know what it feels like to go through that inhumane, barbaric terror.

I park in the driveway in front of the Bakers' garage and sit there for a moment. All of the Baker children are already at the trial so no one is home. Something's been bugging me so before the trial is the best time to give in. I've just had such a strong urge to look around. I'm not exactly sure why but I typically listen to my gut. Most of the time it ends up being wrong but this time it feels different.

I pull the key out of the ignition and step out of Big Red and into the searing sun. My hair sticks to my forehead and my underarms almost immediately begin to sweat. The lack of breeze causes my body to want to retreat into an air conditioned area. This summer has got to be the hottest yet.

The land is eerily quiet. There's no birds or trees rustling. There's not even a dog barking. The only sound is the trickling of water somewhere. Perhaps a sprinkler. Although this time of day is the worst time to water a lawn. I shrug it off and make my way to the front door. I try the knob but it only turns a little before jerking to a stop. *Locked.*

I cup my hands over my eyes and look through the big living room window through a crack in the curtain. It's dark and plain like the last time I was in there. It's clean and undisturbed. I put my ear to the glass and listen. The only sound is the washer jumping up and down dramatically.

Stepping away from the hot glass, I wipe my sweaty palms on my pants. My fingers run through my hair quickly, slicking it back off of my forehead.

The water stops trickling and suddenly sounds as if water's been pushed out of a pipe with a large powerful force. As quick as it happened, it stopped again and returned to trickling.

That's not normal, I think to myself. *That's not a sprinkler.*

Stealthily I round the corner of the house and walk between the white garage and home toward the noisy backyard. Each step is wet and getting wetter by the second.

I stop at the back of the corridor in between the buildings, surveying the flooding yard.

Water covers most of the ground, causing several areas to be muddy as it washes away layers of dirt. There's an old, rickety swing set to my left that stands alone. The sun has bleached it and it's surrounded by pools of browning water. To my right is a large muddy area next to the back of the two story home. Near the middle of it is a decent sized dog house, covered in red and white peeling paint.

My eyes wander to the leaky pipes causing the sudden flood. They sit next to the muddy dog area and spew water at different volumes. It trickles and then spurts and so on. But, as I stare, the water seems to be coming out slower and slower.

Cautiously I stomp through the wet grass, the stained water flooding into my sneakers. It's cold and comforting in the summer sun. I take my hands and run them through my brown hair once again as questions flood my own mind the closer I come to the pipes.

The pipes seemed to be underground once upon a time but now are out to the world due to their leaks. But, it's not two pipes that are spewing water... It's *four*. They are all spread apart a little bit—a few feet from each other.

"Four?" I hear myself repeating out loud. "That can't be natural."

There is no way *four* pipes all decided to leak at the same time. I might believe two but *not* four.

Chills grasp at my arm, sending me shivering. Each pipe seems broken with something angled like a fingernail...like maybe a shovel. There's nothing natural about how these pipes have been ruptured.

I kneel down before the first pipe, feeling the water hit my body in sprinkles. Each and every pipe's lacerated metal is the same shape and size. There's dents around the laceration where the shovel kept missing. The culprit wasn't strong enough to do one swift hit. They had to keep working on it and working on it.

I stand up, not caring that my knees are wet now. Water drips down my legs but it doesn't bother me. Not as much as the pipes do.

I stay where I am and survey the yard once more. But, this time my eye is caught by something glistening in the runny mud next to the dog house. Something metal unnaturally blinks in the pool of dirt.

Slowly, my feet take me closer and closer as curiosity takes over. The object blinds me in a way that restricts me from staring at it too long. The farther I get from the pipes, the shallower the water gets. Despite the dog house, there is no dog of any kind roaming around. Evie said she had a dog when she was little that stayed outside. But, one day it just disappeared. It was all another strange mystery. So, maybe I have found the collar of said dog.

I stop a good ten feet from it. Maybe the water uncovered the dog's body? It's a ridiculous notion since Evie said her dog likely ran away. But as I repeat constantly... *Anything* can happen in a small town. Plus, the thought of more bodies seems normal to me now, even if it's just a dog's.

I continue on with the thought in the back of my head that I may see bones the closer I get.

And bones are what I see.

My feet suddenly stop me two feet away from the discovery.

The body is almost completely under mud except for an arm and a hand. I can see some bones peaking through the mud but not enough to know what they are.

A silver watch has been washed free of dirt and wraps around an arm bone. It catches the light perfectly and immediately stirs up memories.

My legs give out underneath me, sending me to my knees. My knees sink into the soft mud slowly but surely. The mud coats my legs like it coats the body. All except for the skeletal arm, hand, and the glistening watch that have been washed by the flooding water.

When I was six years old I went to the mall with my mother. We strolled around for what seemed like hours in search of something perfect. We searched and searched every store.

Dad's birthday was the next day and I wanted to find him a gift he would keep forever and ever. I wanted to give him something that he could wear every single day and that when he was away, he could look at it and feel happy.

Mom and I entered the last store in the mall, our hopes dejected. As soon as I looked up, an item caught my eye, sparkling under a white display light. I let go of my mom's hand and I practically ran to the glass counter. We had wandered into a jewelry store with an abundance of necklaces, bracelets, earrings, and *watches*.

We ended up walking out of the store with a brand new, silver watch with words engraved on it "to the best dad ever."

Dad cried when I gave it to him the next day. He hugged me tight and refused to let go. He held me like he was proud of me and like he truly loved me. He held me like it was his last day on Earth. Then, after a few minutes went by, he let me go and said these words:

"Son, no matter what happens, who you and I become, or where we end up... I will always love you with all my heart. *Never* forget that."

Now, staring at his watch seems unreal.

The hands have been halted as if saying time has stopped. No hours have gone by. No minutes have passed. No seconds are ticking. The Earth has stopped spinning and the sun has stopped shining. I have stopped moving.

Vomit forces itself up my throat. I let it out to my right, missing my dad in time. Acid stings my throat as I continue, not being able to stop.

I sit in the water, not caring that my puke is surrounding me. I can't take my eyes off of the watch and what this means. The flood has washed away the dirt that has been covering my father for who knows how long. It was an intentional flood caused by someone. Someone had to have known about this. You don't flood a backyard for no reason.

I force my head's gears to stop working. Now isn't the time to be going over theories and what if's.

My father has been in Montpelier all this time. My father, Noah, has been in Evie's backyard this entire time. It's a backyard I've been in once before and I had no idea. I may have even walked on top of my Dad's skeleton without knowing.

My father was murdered by the same person who murdered my girlfriend. Paul Baker is a monster.

Behind me, footsteps echo as someone trudges through the water toward me. I tear my eyes off of the watch and turn my neck just enough to see the intruder. Her raven black hair is pulled up into a high ponytail and her cheeks are high and hollow. Her dark ocean blue irises look between me and my father's remains.

Miriam Page swallows sharply and keeps her eyes on my father's revealed bones.

"At least one of us got out."

SHERIFF REGGIE

Sunday, June 12, 2022, Present.

W*hat has happened to our safe little valley?*

I grew up here and nothing ever happened. Nothing interesting at all. The only crimes that were ever committed were small acts of robbery, drugs, and vandalism. Maybe some violent crimes but not much.

Nothing ever happened here.

Now I'm stuck with *three* murders. *Three.* And I have no idea what I'm doing.

Two out of three of those murders are linked directly to Paul and Joanne, my high school best friend and my high school crush. The weird thing about living in a small community is that everyone is linked with everybody in some kind of way.

Yesterday, an hour before the trial began I received a call from none other than Carter Miller. My favorite kid. He mumbled quietly and I could make out almost none of the words except "flooded," "Bakers," and "body." Then, the phone was taken from him and another voice took over. A woman's.

"Reggie, Noah Miller's skeleton is in the Bakers' backyard. It flooded this morning and must have washed away the layers of dirt. I ain't joking, Reggie. It's him."

I immediately knew it was not a prank. It couldn't have been. Plus, that woman's voice had a familiar ring to it... an eerie one. Carter was too shaken to have been playing a joke on me, and he wouldn't have joked about something like his dad's body showing up.

I did what any sheriff would do. I halted the court and told them we were on stand by and I headed directly to town. It was the most stressful fifteen minute drive you could imagine.

I grew up with Noah. We were on the same football team in fact. Me, Paul, and Noah. Noah was a year older than us but he took us in and didn't make us feel like the babies of the team like the others did. I'd say we were pretty decent friends. Then he graduated my junior year and went to the University Of Oregon and I rarely saw him again. He got married right out of college to some Oregon chick and they lived there. I only ever saw him again one time.

It just so happened to be the week he went missing too. It was at the local Maverik gas station at that one intersection of the highway and Main Street. I walked in as he was coming out of one of the aisles. He looked the same as he did back in high school and so did I. I recognized him immediately and greeted him.

His eyebrows were stiff and upturned and his facial wrinkles were as deep as the Grand Canyon. Noah's lips fit into a slim line as he pressed them together tightly, cradling two energy drinks in his arms. He nodded at me in greeting like you would to a stranger. I knew something was off. Noah Miller never forgot a face and more importantly, never forgot a friend.

I brushed it off and winded through the different aisles to the drink coolers. Noah paid and walked out the door. That was the last time I ever saw him.

It's because of this interaction eight years ago that I never *really* believed he had not disappeared.

Now, finally, it all may come into light what happened August 17th, 2013.

It makes me sick to think about the crimes that have happened in this county. Never in a million years would I have thought this would happen when I was sheriff.

Well, I suppose most of this happened while John Miller was sheriff, but I'm not going to blame him. No one could have predicted this. No one could have prevented this too. Or maybe someone could have. Who knows though. Can we really prevent things like this? Because it all seems out of our control at this point.

Or maybe it isn't. Like I said... who knows. Maybe I could somehow control all of this or at least make it less tragic. If that's possible. I don't even know how I would do it. Plus what if I fail?

And that's why I can't. I could be the laughing stock of Bear Lake County. Around here news and gossip gets around fast. One little mistake and everyone will know within an hour. I can't afford that kind of embarrassment.

Anyways, it turns out the body of Noah Miller was really in the Bakers' backyard. At least according to the fancy FBI crime scene unit from Pocatello–a city an hour and a half away. They say the bones positively match the identity of my old role model. The bone's age matched. The wilting hair matched. The watch on his arm matched. It was him. There can't be doubt.

The worst part was pulling up and finding Carter in the mud, surrounded by his vomit, staring at the one arm that was uncovered fully. A watch blinked in the blinding sun. He seemed to be staring specifically at it.

Later I would learn it was the watch he gifted his father so many years ago.

Carter Miller's hair stuck to his sweat-drenched forehead which glistened underneath the sun's rays. His chocolate brown eyes were glossed over and his body was tense. I'll never forget the helplessness I felt ricocheting off of him. It gave me a heavy heart that I could never express with words.

Now, standing outside the makeshift interrogation room, I can't forget any of it. Inside is Joanne, her blonde hair straight and laid upon her shoulders. She's in a tacky orange jumpsuit and does not seem happy about it. She's never been the type of woman to wear something that bright. It's sad I know that.

I open the door. Joanne looks up, her eyes wide with surprise. Then, seeing it's me, she settles.

"Reagan," she greets in a monotone voice. Her classic high pitched greeting is stripped away.

"Jo," I nod, taking a seat across from her into a wooden chair. I set the file in my hand down, making sure it causes a loud slapping noise. Joanne flinches and watches me carefully, her blue eyes oddly bright.

"What's that, Reagan?"

I ignore her, looking behind her at the wall. She doesn't try again but instead accepts it, waiting for me patiently.

I lean back with one hand resting on my gut and the other one on the tan case file. "What can you tell me about August 17th and 18th of 2013?"

Something flashes across her, causing her demeanor to change drastically. But, as soon as it comes it's gone. It's like a sheet was lifted on top of her, hiding any emotion she may let off accidentally.

She leans back as part of her facade. I haven't told her or Paul a word about Noah Miller's body in their backyard. "How do you expect me to remember something from nine years ago? That was so long ago, Reagan."

They never taught us how to interrogate a friend in training. They never taught us how to keep calm while interrogating a close and long time friend.

"Don't mess with me, Jo. We've been friends for too long."

Joanne furrows her brows and stares at the door. She remains silent and motionless for longer than I thought she could. She's always been talkative. I've never heard her silent before.

Without warning she turns back to me and leans forward. "You know what? I think I remember. Wasn't that around the time that guy we went to high school with went missing? Noah?"

I nod, refraining from scoffing. "Noah Miller. His son actually was dating your daughter, Evie."

Confusion flashes across Jo's face. She had no idea that Carter and Evie were dating. But also no one else in the valley did either. It's all news. But, now I completely understand why they hid it. Hearing the things Joanne and Paul did to Evie sums it all right up.

"Carter was not dating Evie. I would have known," Joanne growls, leaning forward again like clockwork. Her face darkens as she stares straight ahead, thinking. "It makes sense though that that wretched brat defied us. We told her she could date when she moved out and that it was forbidden before then. It doesn't surprise me that little *harlot* got a boyfriend."

No mother should speak of a daughter in that horrid way. It's not normal. It's not supported. It's never okay. A mother is supposed to love their child *unconditionally*. They are supposed to hug their kids and tell them they love them indefinitely. Not shame them. Not hit them. Not crush them. Not *kill* them.

I slam my hand on the table, shooting out of my seat like a rocket. I don't care that this is frowned upon. I don't care that they are recording this interrogation. I just care about avenging that beautiful Baker girl. She was supposed to have a happy, carefree childhood and a challenging but delightful adulthood. Both of those things I know she didn't get to experience.

No child deserves that. *None*.

My fingernails dig at the inside of my palms as I begin walking out the door. Joanne Baker is not worth me being fired for violence. I'm sure I could get away with it but I would never hit a woman or girl, even if they deserved it. I'm not Paul Baker. I have more worth than Paul. I have more self control.

I will get justice for Evie Baker the *right*, *legal* way.

The interrogation room door slams behind me and I storm forward toward my closet of an office. Swinging the door closed behind me, I march toward my desk full of trinkets. My hand takes one big swipe at the several items sitting on top of it. Papers and files fly off, dancing in the air around me, as do writing utensils, my name tag, and a notebook. The name tag crashes against the plain, cream-colored wall, creating an ear-splitting crack and putting a tiny dent into it. It clatters to the carpeted floor, landing with a surprisingly loud thud.

Sweat runs down my tan forehead as I lean against my partially cleared desk, my twitching palms on the wood.

Outside in the long hallway of the courthouse, county deputies stare at me... I'm sure of it. I would have if I were them.

Between strained breaths, I quit leaning on my desk and run my wet palms on my uniform's black pants. Hastily, I rip off the velcro on my bullet proof vest then unzip it. I tear it off and drop it on my desk, trying my hardest to catch my breath.

I curse for no weight has been lifted off my shoulders.

"Sheriff?" someone calls as my glass door creaks open.

Spinning around, I meet an FBI agent's gaze. My heart drops to my stomach. Agent Stevens watched that entire thing. I had forgotten he was watching the interrogation. To be honest, I forgot Pocatello's FBI agents were here. My memory has been nothing short of horrible lately.

"What?"

"It's okay to show emotion, Sheriff," The man coughs, shutting the door behind him. His blond hair is slicked to the side with gel and his white dress shirt is ironed. My eyes wander to my wrinkled, dark gray button up. "It shows that you care."

I clear my throat, leaning my backside against my desk. "How am I supposed to interrogate a woman I went to high school with and have history with, Stevens? I don't even know how to stay calm."

Agent Stevens nods carefully, sticking his hands into his suit pants pockets. He doesn't seem to eyeball the mess covering my floor. From what I've learned from Stevens, he's a pretty well rounded dude. Definitely FBI-y though: everything about him speaks 'official.'

"It's hard to live in a county with only six thousand people. Everybody is connected in some way. Everybody has history. It'll never be easy to interrogate or arrest friends, especially in this form," he says, his voice a quiet monotone. "Why did you go into law enforcement, Sheriff?"

Why did I go into law enforcement? That's a loaded but easy question–and generic. I wanted to change the world for the better. I wanted to be able to make a difference. I wanted to save people and interact with people. Now I'm not so sure I've been doing that. I feel more like a villain. So I tell him that.

Stevens nods again as the words roll off my tongue, as if expecting this answer. Like I said... generic answer. Every officer's answer is the same. They all want to create change.

"I know it was a classic case of abuse and that I couldn't have saved Evie Baker, Stevens. I know that. But I can't help but think we could have noticed the symptoms of abuse sooner. Someone at her school, someone in the community. Someone."

"Then do something about it."

I take a fist to my gut as I listen to those words. He's not wrong. But I don't know how to necessarily do that.

And there was someone who could have done something. Carter Miller.

"Look," Stevens starts, tightening his blue tie, "I'm going to interview Joanne Baker from now on, although I'd like you to be in the room. Okay?"

My head bobs up and down and I begin following Agent Stevens back to the interrogation room, not bothering to put my vest back on. The hall consists of only a few people but otherwise is deserted. A teenage boy and his mom stand at the DMV section of the courthouse, likely signing up for driver's education. The courthouse is basically just one big hallway with several different rooms. But, this newly built courthouse is a big deal bigger than the previous courthouse. They tore down the sagging building not too long ago and built this courthouse on the land.

Agent Stevens opens the brown door that leads into the interrogation rooms. It's much more modernized than the Montpelier PD—which is basically city hall—interrogation room. The mirrored window is actually clean and not cracked and the walls are the classic dark gray. The floors are spruce planked and in the middle is the classic metal table you see in all the movies. I think the decorators or whatever decorated it straight out of a movie. Although there isn't a singular light above the table; the room is fully lit with regular lights. Joanne still sits in her chair, her rounded face buried into her hands.

When we step in, she lifts her face up just enough to where only her dark blue eyes are exposed. She straightens her back as she focuses on me specifically. Her spray tanned hands fall to the table top, handcuffed to the table. On the floor is Noah's case file. I had forgotten about it.

Agent Stevens introduces himself to Joanne but her eyes are still set on me. Like I betrayed her. Her intense eyes are squinted and her age wrinkles are deepened. Even her blonde eyebrows angle down.

"Reagan, why did you have to storm out like that? It was uncalled for," she asks, sitting back into her chair. Her curled, blonde hair swings off her shoulders and runs down her back. "And you brought one of those big shot FBI gentlemen? That wasn't necessary and you know it."

I stand still at the door, not emitting any kind of emotion. The amount of control it takes is exhausting. My organs want to shut down and sweat trickles down my back. I rarely get clammy hands but today has been testing my limits. It seems every day brings some annoying, unknown challenge. I'm done with character development.

"Mrs. Baker, Sheriff Reagan will be sitting out and watching this interview, is that alright with you, ma'am?" Agent Stevens questions, picking the case folder off the table. Once it's firmly in his hand, he takes a seat across from Jo. She doesn't seem to affect him the way she affects me. He doesn't seem to show how disgusted he probably is with her. He treats her like a person even after seeing first hand what she and Paul are accused of.

"Don't have much of a choice do I?" she scoffs, smoothing her hair back over her shoulders. In high school her hair was always worn in its natural way: naturally curly. Now she straightens it and then curls it manually with a wand. The few days of jail have brought back those natural curls I fell in love with. I can still smell the essence of vanilla even from seven feet away.

Agent Stevens chuckles politely but presses on. "You and your husband Paul went to high school with Noah Baker, is that right, ma'am?"

She nods hesitantly. "He was a year older than us, but yes. How is this relevant to my daughter's case?"

Hey eyebrows knit together as if she could care less about her own daughter. My fists clench at my side, my dirty fingernails digging into my skin.

My FBI friend inhales extensively. I can hear the fresh oxygen entering into his lungs from his nose. He begins opening the manila folder, shielding the contents from her with one of the flaps of the folder.

"To be completely honest with you, ma'am, it doesn't have anything to do with your daughter's murder. It just so happened that something came up to lead us to investigate you for Noah Miller's disappearance."

My heart pounds against my ribcage as Stevens grabs the picture of the flooded yard by its corner and slips it in front of Jo. At first she looks at it with confusion, but her brain must begin to start up because her face starts twitching with dread and her skin goes pale. Underneath the table her leg begins to bounce, creating a consistently quick chain of *thumps*.

Her eyes begin to drain of their light and she immediately gains deep eye bags. She doesn't even seem to have the energy to ask if they cleaned up her yard or if anything was damaged.

Stevens grabs another photo, this time a closer shot of the decayed skeletal arm of Noah Miller, his watch blinking in the sunlight. It's blinding, even in the photo. It's almost like it's saying 'look at me, look at me.'

When Joanne makes contact with the photo she doesn't even have the ability to *act* surprised.

Agent Stevens leaves her a few more seconds to ingest the contents of the photo. I can't even look without being overwhelmed. Noah was a good friend of mine. He mentored me and took me in. Seeing the outcome of his life makes me sick to my stomach.

Stevens clears his throat once, breaking the deafening silence that has developed the room. "Can you tell me about this discovery of ours?"

Joanne stares at the photograph, studying it intensely. Continuously she widens her mouth then closes it again, as if not being able to put together the correct assortment of words. Based on the glistening sweat above her eyebrow, she knows she's in trouble. There is nowhere to run and nowhere to hide. She can't avoid this problem of hers. She can't exterminate this problem of hers.

"I took no part in it, Reagan," she quietly whispers, tearing her eyes off the picture to look at me.

"But you knew about it?" I sneer, my clammy fists getting tighter by the second. Stevens doesn't give me a disapproving look like I expect him to.

Joanne falls silent and I instantly know her role.

"Who killed Noah? Was it Paul then?" Agent Stevens presses, leaning forward onto his elbows. Slowly he begins spreading even more photos across the table, as if pressuring her or guilting her. It's smart.

Jo bows her head, conquered. "Yes. Paul."

I butt in again. I can't help it. A million thoughts and questions swarm my head at the same time, demanding to be heard and answered. "Why?"

Joanne looks back at the various photographs. A lot of them are just pictures of the bones laid out on a tarp and a specific one of the crushed pipes.

Her eyebrows shape into a confused state as her eyes stop on that certain photo of the pipes. It's just barely long enough to where you can't notice it if you aren't watching closely. But, she hastily moves her eyes away and looks back at me.

"Paul, Noah, Jason, and I were in some risky business—"

"—Jason?" I interrupt, stepping toward her and out of the shadows. "Who's Jason?"

A curse is concealed underneath her breath. But you can tell she doesn't want to fight me suddenly. Her eyes are downcasted and something pulls at her mouth's strings. She clears her throat and her shoulders sag deeper.

"The body found up Emigration," she coughs quietly, fiddling with the cuffs around her wrists. "Jason Pierce."

That name doesn't ring a bell in my mind and I don't think he went to school with us. I think I would have known. But, my questions don't go unanswered for long. It's as if Jo reads my mind.

"He was from California down on the coast somewhere. He was helping Paul run the business."

Now it's time for Agent Stevens to add questions that need to be answered. "Business? Were you guys into some black market business?"

Jo shakes her head from side to side, tapping her fingers on the table, creating an eerie echo. Her chin slowly drops down to her chest. "Illegal drugs," she murmurs.

I lower myself down just enough to where I can whisper in Steven's ear. With my mouth near his ear, my eyes are still set firmly on Joanne Baker. "The last sheriff, John Miller—Noah's dad—said that the drug presence had suddenly started increasing in 2011 and that I had to pay special attention to the drug cases because they were taking over the county. Although the presence has gone down these past year or two."

Most likely, the Bakers have been in the drug business since at least 2011, including this Jason guy and Noah. I always figured it was the addicts in the trailer park that were causing the sudden increase in the distribution of the drugs. This small community keeps throwing me surprise after surprise, that's for sure. Just when I thought it couldn't get more corrupted. Just when I thought my high school best friends couldn't get worse.

Noah definitely isn't the man I always thought he was. He was never the man I looked up to after all. He was a criminal committing federal drug offenses. Noah Miller isn't the selfless, giving man we all thought he was.

Over the course of the hour Joanne tells us tale after tale, giving us fact after fact. The shocking story goes that in 2010, Paul pressured Noah into bringing him drugs from Oregon or else he was going to hurt his growing family. Noah had no choice but to comply and soon the business rocketed. Paul was also able to employ a Californian by the name of Jason Pierce. He also got drugs to Paul and then all the drugs that were brought to Paul he gave to another 'employee.'

This girl I recognized as someone that went to school with us too. Miriam Page. The coroner's ex and mother to his teen. She was a druggie that sold the drugs to random teenagers and struggling addicts around the county and surrounding counties. Miriam was the first that wanted out but Paul did what he apparently did best: he threatened her saying he would harm her son, Nixon. Like Noah, she had to comply out of sheer love for her child. Paul gave her the 'important' job of running one of the branches in Las Vegas, Nevada and she left without a word to anyone.

This is where it got messy. Jason Pierce wanted out in 2013. He accidentally got his girlfriend pregnant and he thought 'hey, I should be responsible now.' He showed up to the Bakers' house and met with Paul in the separated garage. Supposedly, Paul was *not* happy. Jo could hear the yelling from the house. Then, it went quiet. It just stopped.

Paul came out of the garage, not followed by twenty-year-old Jason, and entered the home. Joanne immediately asked if he had hurt Jason. "He was just a kid," she constantly reminded him. By the way Jo explained it, I see it so clearly that for a moment, I become Joanne.

Paul storms to the kitchen, his forehead soaked with sweat, his eyebrows wettened. He stared straight ahead, not paying any mind to me. I follow closely behind him, asking question after question.

Paul? You killed that boy didn't you! I harshly whisper as he washes his steady hands in the kitchen sink. His clean, steady hands.

He ignored me, staring at his hands so casually as if he had just gotten done with the dishes. Paul steps away from the sink, his hands dripping tap water on the kitchen's carpet. I grab a dish towel laying on the kitchen table and throw it at him. He catches it effortlessly and dries his hands gingerly.

Paul, dear, what did he want?

Finally his deep voice splits the air. *Out. He wanted out.*

I hover a few feet away, acknowledging that Evie is upstairs playing in her room. I can hear the different toys hitting each other.

So you killed him? I whisper in a hushed voice.

Paul nods, keeping his voice loud, clearly not aware of our daughter upstairs. *Our business could have gotten out if I hadn't, Joanne.*

I hush him and point at the ceiling. My husband rolls his eyes. *She won't understand, she's only six.*

I scoff. *She's eight, Paul.*

Whatever, he growls, pushing past me and back into the foyer. He grabs his keys off of the hook hanging next to the door, then pulls his phone out of his front pocket. *Noah is still in town, he will help me.*

He begins typing away at his keypad, inserting Noah's number.

Joanne could be lying about her involvement in the whole Jason murder ordeal. We may never know. But, right now, she's our only witness. Likely Paul will just turn it around and say Joanne committed the whole thing, no matter how unrealistic it may be. Paul was able to get away with it this long, I'm sure he could somehow get away with it further.

The rest of the story goes that Noah was forced to help Paul get rid of Jason up Emigration Canyon in a secluded spot. But, Noah wanted out after that. Murder was apparently where he drew the line. As night appeared, Noah was dead. Late into the night he was buried in the backyard.

And that's how Paul Baker became a multi-murderer.

Joanne looks up at me and then at Agent Stevens. "Yes, Paul killed all of those people but he *never* killed Evie. Neither did I. We never killed Evie."

Oddly, I believe her.

CARTER

Sunday, June 12, 2022, Present.

I'd like to say I always saw Dad as his happy, selfless self but there was *one* time I had blocked away. It was something I had shoved down because it was just that one incident. I mean he never showed any negative emotions toward anything, not even politics. I probably wouldn't have remembered it if it wasn't for the new him that has been exposed to me.

To think that my dad bought and sold drugs to Evie's dad confuses me beyond belief. He likely didn't partake in doing drugs but he did aid Paul. It opened my eyes to a whole other version of my dad I didn't know was out there. I mean he was a completely different man when away from his family.

I can't imagine how difficult it could have been for him to lead two completely seperate lives. I should be mad but I'm more sympathetic and surprised than anything. It just makes me wonder what part of him was the facade and which was real. Was he a man involved heavily in drug deals or was he the selfless, happy guy I grew up with? Which of the two was the mask he wore?

Never in a million years did I think I would be questioning my dad and all the good deeds he committed over the years. I mean *come on*. I probably watched him help homeless people and pay forward in a drive-thru at least one hundred times. I guess I did always think he was kind of like some character in a fictional book. My father seemed too good to be true all of those years.

But, as I mentioned before, I saw him angry once and it wasn't even over something reasonable. He was just going through the mail and doing the bills. I don't remember what month it was or how old I was but I sat on the living room floor of our Oregon house, fiddling with a new Lego set. Through the kitchen door, he sat at our small, circular, wooden table, doubled over in stress. Briskly, I scanned that startling sight.

His chocolate eyebrows were knitted together in a way that was foreign and his smile lines were replaced with deep wrinkles. His reading glasses were placed on top of his scrunched nose, providing unwanted sight to his umber irises. Quietly, I set down my legos and leaned forward onto my palms.

Dad grunts quietly and begins pulling at the hairs on his newly formed beard. From here it still looks as prickly as it feels when he hugs you. Often when he hugged Mom and me he would start scratching us with that prickly beard, causing us to cry out and begin laughing. Little me could have never imagined missing that beard. But, here I am... missing that bristled beard...

A large *bang* echoes throughout our quiet home and my ears begin to ring. I shuffle backward away from the kitchen, trudging through my blocks. They penetrate me but my fear overwhelms me, not allowing me to cry out. I shuffle until I am basically secure against the arm of our red, tattered couch. I let my eye wander back to the kitchen where my dad sits, no longer visible. A creak splits the air as a chair moves back and my dad's footsteps can be heard as he nears the door separating the living room and kitchen. His large body slips in between the frame and he stands there nervously, fiddling with the hem of his shirt.

"Carter?" he questions quietly, making eye contact with the quivering boy behind the couch arm. "I'm sorry if I frightened you."

He remained where he was and so did I. I searched his eyes and he searched mine, both of similar color and shape. I wasn't fully sure why he had done what he did but all I knew was that it was sudden and he had never done it before. It was a new side of him. I wasn't used to big noises or anger, especially from my father. And my mother—who was at work.

My dad crouches down in the door frame and holds out his arms. "Come here, Carter. It's okay."

I immediately went to my dad. I stopped shaking behind the couch, watching him like he was some villain. I knew that wasn't my dad. I knew I trusted my dad no matter what. So, I went to his arms and embraced him. His arms wrapped around me tightly and I buried my face into his shoulder. And I forgot the moment.

My father then positioned his beard on my cheek and began shaking his head aggressively, laughing substantially, his laughter a joyous melody. As I always did, I cried out but soon began laughing, demanding between breaths that he let me go.

It was only once so how am I supposed to metabolize it? It was only one incident. How am I supposed to know what it all means or what it all meant?

CARTER

Monday, June 13, 2022, Present.

Even after everything that has happened, Montpelier Canyon is still my safe place. I still can go there to effectively clear my mind of the pounding thoughts protruding my brain. I grew up in Montpelier Canyon on several fishing, hunting, and camping trips with my father and no tragedy could steal the happiness I felt on those trips. Part of the reason why my dad and I were so close was because of those trips when we visited Grandma and Grandpa. I know what happened up here but it can't ever ruin those memories.

The green pines line the several hills and mountains that sit on both sides of US Route 89—which leads up the canyon. There's always one part that frightens me where a guardrail has been built. The hill dips way below the road, creating some sort of ravine or valley. At the bottom is the Montpelier Creek which runs over the creek's rocks and leads fish toward town with its current. It always scared me as a child because I thought we would somehow bust through the metal guard rail and plunge down the twenty-foot drop. We would surely be dead. But I realize now it was just silly childhood fears.

As I follow the road in Big Red, the split hill comes into view, towering over the Rearing Pond. Its sediment's peach tint is brighter than ever and the sagebrush on top is the greenest it's been in a while.

I slow at the turn-off for the Rearing Pond and turn right. Parking as far away from the shore as I can, I exhale deeply. An older man sits in his camp chair on the other side of the pond, holding his pole as his line is set in the murky water.

Since news spread to the town and to our family, there's been such a heavy hold on Mom, Daphne, and I's hearts. When walking around the house I felt like the walls were closing in and keeping me locked up. I had to get out of there before my brain exploded. And it was *going* to.

I tried to go over all the evidence in my head at home but all of it just bounced around endlessly, hurting more than helping. Sheriff Reggie informed Grandpa that he wholeheartedly believed that the Bakers *hadn't* killed Eve. Then, Grandpa told me. I don't know why but he did.

It's all a big pile of dog crap. Sheriff Reggie has no suspects now. NONE. Every time I think about it I can feel that one vein in my forehead pop out. I always begin to erratically sweat and shake with threatening anger. How could he believe those *murderers*!? They murdered my father *and* another man! It only makes sense that they could have hurt their daughter fatally. No one else makes sense for the crime either.

I'm just going to say it. They abused her. All those bruises that peppered her body were from *them*, more specifically *Paul*. If you could hurt your own child, you no doubt could *kill* them. I saw firsthand the abuse Evie received and how it affected her day-to-day life. I watched helplessly as she hid the bruises with jeans and hoodies. I was there when Evie showed up to school one day with a broken wrist.

I can't help but think I could have prevented her death if I had just told someone about the abuse.

Evie's cell phone—which she had the night she disappeared—showed back up at her home, underneath the couch and then in a cereal box. *Someone* took it off her chilling body after they shot her in *cold blood*. It was covered with the mud of the reservoir. She HAD it on her! Then they took it back and hid it. And then hid it again.

The 9mm semi-automatic pistol found in her parents' closet is a dead giveaway. It was purposely hidden behind a piece of cut-out wall in a botched attempt to cover their tracks. They never thought someone would look there, I'm sure. There is no other explanation for the obvious evidence against Paul and Joanne. There is too much against them for me to EVER believe they had no part in their child's death.

But the part that doesn't make sense is the way she was killed: Execution style, to the back of the head. It represents that the killer felt guilt toward the savage crime. They didn't want Evie to watch.

It rattles around, demanding to be rethought. It's killing me. I just want my questions answered. That's all I've ever wanted. Is that too much to ask?

My phone chimes once in my pocket and I'm pulled back to the buzzing reality around me. The man now battles a fish on his line, pulling his pole back and forth, and another car has pulled up, harboring a family of four. I pull out my cell phone and check it. It's a text from Kace explaining that he and his sisters are moving to Utah with his aunt by the 15th, a day after Evie's birthday.

Kace has always been helpful, even though he's been battling a new reality that doesn't have his older sister in it. His strength and courage empowers me. He has stayed together so nicely and perhaps I need to take some pointers from him. I can't seem to figure out how to not be an emotional wreck.

Or maybe I don't need to be strong. An unspeakable tragedy has happened to me, no one expects me to be okay. And that's okay because I'm not okay.

CARTER

Tuesday, June 14, 2022, Present.

Warm sun peeks through a slit in my blackout curtains, landing directly on my face, lighting up my darkened room like a flickering candle in a cave. I roll over, setting my back to the agitating sun. A grumble escapes my lips as my drowsiness slips away, leaving me unwantedly refreshed. My night's rest was filled with continuous tossing and turning and the sounds of my heavy breathing. Every tiny sound kept me awake and alert, even the pacing of my mother in her room downstairs.

My eyes slip open, being welcomed by the growing slit of golden light. It has been days since this room has seen the sunlight. Weeks even. Now I'm not quite sure if I welcome the summer's gleaming touch.

Sluggishly I slide out of my charcoal duvet and onto the floor beside my bed. The warm carpet welcomes me with open arms as I sit firmly, its comforting grasp tickling my mahogany sweats. Surrounding me are piles of socks, shirts, and jeans that scatter my carpet, purposely tossed in their spots by me over the days.

Using my bed as leverage, I pull myself back onto my feet, not being able to sit in the same place for long. I wander aimlessly toward the window, the slit of golden light causing my vision to haze. Taking a step, I move out of the way of the ray, my vision soon coming back.

My fingers grasp the blackened curtains and pull them aside, revealing a beautiful sunrise to my left. The yellows formulate with the oranges, dusting together in the clouds. As the sun begins its descent over the Eastern mountains the colors grow substantially, a bit of hot pink coming into play. The whimsical clouds absorb the array of colors, dotting the brightening sky.

"Happy Birthday, Evie Janiece."

I pause, dumbfoundedly hoping she'll thank me.

"A beautiful sunrise for a beautiful girl, huh, Evie?" I smile, my eyes moving around the sky in admiration. I look back, almost expecting her to be sitting on my bed, her legs crossed, or in the doorway. Unfortunately all that is on my bed is rustled sheets and a duvet and all that is in my doorway is a lingering silence.

I snap my eyes back to the beautiful fabrication but already it has begun to blend with a blue sky, the stunning colors draining. A knife saws at my heartstrings, its blade dull and unforgiving. I've always said that the day someone passes, the sunset is the most alluring thing you could experience as the arrangement of colors were fabricated by the dead. Purposefully they put every beautiful, vibrant color in its rightful place to make us stop and admire the creation. To appreciate.

Evie's sunset will always live on in my head, its oranges and pinks dancing as the night inched closer. It gives me a heavy mood of remembrance every time I imagine the artifact.

So, what do sunrises symbolize?

The morning before a child is born, do they mix the colors into the masterpiece before me, symbolizing life and creation? Or is it some higher power reminding us we are loved and that somewhere in this darkened world there is hope and light? I can't possibly pick a theory as there are too many. But I have always been sure that the dead color the sunsets. There is no doubt within me.

Behind me my nightstand vibrates with the turning on of my phone's alarm, the sound echoing unrelentlessly. I cross over to my bed and lean over it, stretching the farthest I can to reach my charging phone on my right bedside table. My fingers grasp it as my door creaks open.

"Sorry, Mom... Did I wake you?" I question, rushing to turn off my buzzing alarm. The bags underneath my mother's eyes are unmistakable.

She shakes her brunette head, an attempt of a smile forming on her chapstick-covered lips. Now my eyes focus on a small mug of brown, steaming liquid in her hands: coffee.

What kept Mom up all night?

Could it be the fact that during my parents' entire marriage, my father was involved in a drug ring with my girlfriend's parents? Or that my father was found after eight years, murdered and buried in my girlfriend's backyard? Or could it be the fact that my girlfriend was murdered a month ago as well? The amount of things that could be bothering my mom is endless.

"I was already up," she sighs, glancing around at my floor. She doesn't cringe or demand for me to pick up my mess. Instead, she looks to me with a comforting smile, as if *understanding*. "It's her eighteenth birthday today, isn't it?"

Briskly, I nod, my light brown mop of hair bouncing up and down with the movement. I pull my black hoodie around me tighter, embracing the warmth that comes from its soft fabric. "Evie almost made it to her desired freedom... This was the day she had looked forward to since the abuse began, Mom. And now she can't experience it. Now I can't experience it with her."

She was so close. The fact that if her birthday had even been 29 days earlier or if she hadn't figured out her parents' involvement in my father's disappearance and death 29 days earlier, she'd be alive. She'd be out of that toxic house and staying with me legally until she could find a place. She would have gone to college with me and she'd be laughing and happy.

"You okay, honey?"

Blinking, I look back to my mother. She holds her coffee still, the mug cupped in her palms. It's drained more since I last looked.

"Will be... You?"

She shrugs her dainty shoulders and takes her last sip, her eyebrows knitting together. The brown liquid runs down her throat, a smile uprising after it. "Want to watch movies today like we used to?"

The offer is tempting.

"I've got some important stuff to do today. Sorry, Mom."

My answer leaves her face solemn and her body posture dropped like a wilting lily. But, she quickly straightens and reveals her white, pedal smile. "That's okay. Another time, honey. Be safe."

And she steps out without another word, trying to take another sip of coffee but finding it empty already. My door shuts behind her, leaving me in a frighteningly quiet room. I don't stand for long before I'm walking to my dresser, the stale air hard to move through. My legs push my body through it, creating a burn in my shins. Rapidly, I pull off my sweatshirt and slip on a royal blue tee with 'Bear Lake Football' printed on it in bold, black lettering, a white border around the words. Our school's logo—the Bear Lake bear—sits underneath the words, its lines black and white.

I tear off my sweats and replace them with straight blue jeans. I never wear anything different. My 'style' hasn't changed since I was just a tiny child, especially not with the trends over the years.

With one hand I open my door and with the other I try to put on my socks, hopping dangerously toward the staircase. I successfully get one on and have to stop at the top of the stairs to put on the other. I slip it on and make my way down the staircase, being extra careful in my long, white socks.

At the kitchen table sits my mother, a full cup of coffee straight in front of her. She watches me carefully, analyzing my every odd move. When she catches me catching *her*, she shifts her eyes to the steam rising above her drink. I force my feet into my red sneakers and grab my keys off of the table.

My full hand lingers above the table as my eyes examine my struggling mother.

"I love you, Mom."

She looks up at me, startled. Her expression softens after a second and she repeats my words. "I love you too, honey."

And I'm out the door.

***

Police tape surrounds the creaking, pale house, settled in the stale heat: stapled to the front door, wrapped around the mailbox, restricting access to the backyard. A yellow piece lays limply in the trampled-on grass. Brown mud has been tracked through the front yard continuously, leaving behind a dried mess.

Only days ago it was a bustling hot attraction to the FBI, PD, and the Sheriff Department. Now all that is left is a deserted ghost house. I can already tell that for years to come it would be known as *that* house. Every town has one. The rickety old place where a tragedy struck, myths and campfire stories being told about it for decades. Evie would be known as the victim of the town's very own murderers, her beautiful face haunting the elementary and junior high students as they retold her story.

My own father would be known as the man who lived a completely different life who found himself stuck in an unforgiving drug business that led to his death.

This town's tragedy is my life and it would just be turned into ghost stories kids use to scare their friends and siblings.

The town's citizens will walk by this house hurriedly, watching carefully for the ghosts of its victims, not caring that what happened around and in this home single handedly ruined lives.

The Purple Sage was the town's ghost house before the Baker Murders and now it will be forgotten, even though it towers over Montpelier's very own elementary. Even as a kid that didn't live here and just visited, I knew about the Purple Sage and its theories and myths. No one seemed to know what really happened there but they know what happened at the white house on Ninth Street. That two story house with chipped paint surpassed the Purple Sage in popularity in minutes.

I step forward toward the house, a heavy hold of something on my heart as I move away from Big Red. My feet drag underneath me and my arms swing aimlessly at my sides. The sidewalk almost begins cracking every step I take, the concrete shattering away as the scene is disturbed. Looking behind me I find the sidewalk completely intact.

My breath-deprived lungs burn as I get closer to the blocked off front door. I try the scorching hot handle but it forbids me entry.

Next to the door is the red, barn mailbox, its paint as chipped as the house. It sits on a red wooden pole that is cemented into a rusted, vintage milk can. I open the door and peer inside. Nothing sits inside it but a lurking darkness.

I close it back up and step away off the sidewalk and into the grass.

Sheriff Reggie didn't believe me when I called him insisting on another search of the Bakers' house. He laughed and hung up. I thought maybe the FBI agent would hear me out but I couldn't get his number from anything. So, I might as well do the work myself. There has to be something they missed.

I truly believe that the PD and Sheriff Deputies did not search well enough. It's just a burning inkling I have that demands to be heard out. It haunted the little sleep I got last night, my nightmares full of screeching and the house's creaks—the windows to the house shattered with sticky red liquid pouring out of them, surrounding me. Then the door swung open and out came the entire Baker family, including my deceased Evie. First came out Paul, holding a shovel; then came out Joanne holding a knife; then came out Evie, a bullet hole in her forehead and covered in countless bruises all in different stages of healing. Next followed Riley and Allie, tears streaming down their small faces, their bodies shaking uncontrollably. And lastly Kace stepped out. They looked at me with their emotionless eyes, drilling into my soul as the blood filled the yard. I woke up as Paul and Joanne charged me, their weapons drawn, ready to take lives.

Now, standing and watching the home I am waiting hesitantly for the blood to begin and for the big, happy family to 'greet' me. Even though I know the parents are being held in jail thirty minutes away, the girls and Kace are staying at the local Super 8 hotel with their aunt, and Evie... well you know.

My eyes stay on the ghost house.

Trudging through the grass, I drift toward the backyard where I sat with my father's body only three days ago. The yellow tape is stapled to the white house and runs toward the white garage. It has been stapled to one wall of each building and shakes as I lift it up over me. I let it go and the tape bounces up and down, getting faster and faster as it gets closer to settling. I watch it as if it will create a sound that gives my location away, but the air is still clear and dull. My eyes scan the area, once again checking for prying neighbors or patrolling police. Now that I think of it I shouldn't have parked my truck next to the curb. I should have parked it a little down the street away from the house.

No one is watching, so I turn my body around and begin my descent toward the muddy mess of a backyard. The minute I'm in that backyard, my eyes are set on the two sheds that stay on the outskirts, both white in color and both out of the way. I do not look at the muddy scene before me. I do not try to remember how I broke down at the sight of my father's skeleton. I just keep my eyes on the shed ahead of me—the smallest one. It's only five feet wide and six feet long and has a slanted, blackish-brown roof that matches the house and garage's color. I try the sketchy door but find it secured with a padlock at the top. I give it one more good shake—it shakes my entire body—but it is no good. The rust around the padlock suggests the shed hasn't been opened in a while anyways.

Apart from the rest of the property sits a larger shed, its roof a dusty red. It sits between the next door neighbor's property and this one but technically it is the Bakers'. I walk to the shed, hope fueling my every step.

Turns out my surge of hope is helpful because the double doors come open with ease, swinging effortlessly. A shrill pierces the air as the hinges squeak, causing a headache to form almost immediately.

The sun barely illuminates the inside. I slide my phone out of my front pocket and turn on its flashlight. I enter the shed with no hesitation and no fight.

The mud is the first thing my eye is drawn to. The floor is disturbed with grimy boot treads, leading deeper into the pinched, airless shack. Perhaps the police officers did search this shed?

But what worries me is that the dirty boot prints enter but do not leave.

Boldly, I take another step into the darkness. Dim, white light shines over the different boxes, brightening their inconsequential items. There are dusty toys and antiques and glass, collectable dolls. Evie used to tell me that her grandma often collected porcelain dolls and had loads of them. She had one particular room where they were displayed on shelves and it so happened to be the guest room where she and her siblings would stay sometimes. Eve always said she was terrified of those dolls but wondered where they had all gone after her grandmother's passing. I suppose I've answered her question... but a bit too late.

A shudder runs through me as I maneuver past them. They seem to follow me each step I take, some reflecting feelings of abandonment, while others warnings. I shun away their beady eyes and motionless smiles.

The heated shed is hard to move through but whoever made the tracks set out a specific path that's easy to follow. The undisturbed mud is clear and urges me on silently—until it stops and merges into a big brown mess.

Either someone came into here with muddy boots and stayed or somebody came into here with muddy boots and ditched them and left barefoot. I *really* hope it's the second option because if I find one more dead body or if someone jumps out at me... we *will* have a problem.

Cautiously, I look through the boxes at the back of the shed that happen to surround the mud. I search one full of sewing supplies but find no boots. I search one with collectible Nascar cars but find no boots.

I come to a clothing box not far from the treads and begin lifting up different items of clothing. The clothing creates a layer of dust on my sweaty hands, the grime creating a sandy feel to them. I reach the bottom of the cardboard box and lift up the final winter coat. Apair of hunting boots are illuminated by my phone's flashlight. The black laces are untied and covered in the familiar mud, complimenting the camouflage fabric of the grimy boots. Three singular blood spots on the camo absorb my phone's white light.

Okay... Okay, Carter. Stop and think. Stop and think.

But without trying my heart's pace begins to quicken drastically.

Calm down!

My hands reach to examine the boots but I pull them back. I cannot have a single trace of my DNA on them. I have found so much evidence that I have to admit... I look pretty sketchy. I don't need any of that crap right now. I was already accused of killing Evie once, I'm not letting it happen again. Especially since they have no formal suspects right now.

I pad the pair of boots with the clothing just like I found them and begin to dial the sheriff's office secretary number. If I call Reggie, this will go nowhere.

My call goes through and I begin to explain what I have found, leaving out my name. Maybe if I leave out my name they will believe me and come. I'm sure everyone in the courthouse knows my name and knows who I am.

"What's your name, sir?" the lady asks, her customer voice soothing but straight to the point.

"Just get to the Baker house. Send the sheriff and send PD. Send the FBI. Send everyone," I demand, my voice shaking uncontrollably. I inhale, trying to stabilize it but it's unsuccessful. "I may have just found the evidence that will prove who killed Evie Baker for sure. So, get them here as fast as you can, ma'am."

And I hang up without another word and find my way out of the shed. I flick off my flashlight and sit with my back against the right door which has swung so far it's completely parallel to the wall of the shed.

All I need to do know is hope there is any trace of DNA on those boots. That's the solid evidence the police needs.

CARTER

Tuesday, June 14, 2022, Present.

A vain bulges out of Reggie's forehead as he leans forward on the table. I don't miss the dark circles that are still under his angry eyes. They match the color of the shadows in the room.

"How long has it been since you slept, Sheriff?" I taunt quietly. I may have single handedly helped solve the case and I want to shove it in his face.

Reggie scoffs, surveying me closely. "Shut up, Carter. Now is not the time to joke. To say you're in trouble would be an understatement."

I lean forward in my chair, the handcuffs rattling on my wrists. "I found the *killer's* boots, Sheriff. I found more evidence for you to use against the Bakers. You should be *thanking* me."

My body stiffens as Sheriff Reggie's hand collides with the table. The sound echoes in my head like a bell tower would in a deserted town. Reggie stares at me and I shudder. I've never been as good at hiding my feelings as Evie was. She was a master at it. I don't know how she was always able to compose herself so well.

"That's not the point, Carter! You *continued* to investigate even after everyone told you it was unsafe! You put yourself at risk *again*."

Who cares if I'm at risk, I want to snap. *Justice for Evie is what matters the most.*

The door to the interrogation room swings open, warm light pouring into the dim room. In its wake is the FBI agent that's been hanging around. Reggie stiffens up and smooths wrinkles from his gray button up. He immediately steps away from my table, his power slipping out of the room with the shadows.

"Sheriff, if you'd excuse yourself please," he demands quietly, rolling up the sleeves of his gray and white plaid button up.

With one side eye, the agent silences Reggie's churning disagreements. Reggie takes one last look at me before leaving the room and then shuts the door behind him, taking the warm light with him.

The agent pulls a chair out of the shadows and sets it on the side of the table directly opposite from me. He sits on it backward, the backrest up against the table. "I'm Agent Stevens, Carter. I'm here with the Pocatello chapter of the FBI. I am investigating your friend's murder and gathering evidence. I'm also assisting with your dad's murder as well. I'm sorry it took me this long to speak with you."

Agent Stevens watches me as I stammer to find words. "Nice to meet you." I lift my hands for the agent to see. "Can you take these handcuffs off now? I don't think I'm much of a threat."

The agent laughs, his gelled blond hair staying put as his head bobs backward. He stands up out of his seat and retrieves a key from the front pocket of his black dress pants. He unlocks the lock on each cuff, letting them fall onto the table.

The man then settles back into his seat, his arms crossed on top of the backrest of the metal unfolding chair. He watches me for a moment as I massage my wrists. I've never been handcuffed before.

"Carter, you probably have a lot of questions rushing through your mind right about now." I nod, waiting for him to continue. "After years of believing your dad was an honest, innocent man, you found out he was actually selling drugs on the side. Your girlfriend was just murdered by your dad's former business partners and you are currently in an interrogation room."

I nod again, not knowing what to say. What could I say? It's all true.

The agent presses on. "I have sympathy for you, Carter. This all can't be easy for you, huh?"

"Yeah..." I cough hesitantly. What's this guy's motive? He's young and has one of those baby faces, making him *seem* trustworthy. Yet I know he's not my friend. Recently I've learned that everyone has alternative motives and none include being my friend. Dave proved that the day he started ignoring me because I was hanging out with Evie. But, I've forgotten about him already. Why should I waste my breath on him anyways?

Agent Stevens looks at the two-way window to my left, eyeing it diligently. "The blood on those boots you found was AB-positive. According to Evie's medical records, so is she. We won't know if it's Evie's blood for sure for four weeks, but it's highly possible."

Relief doesn't come over me. It should, but I'm left with a hollowness that's so severe it breaks my heart. The confirmation won't come in for weeks, but I know that AB-positive is one of the most rare blood types. I don't know why I'm not relieved. Maybe it has to do with the fact that it means her parents may have actually killed her. It means that I officially live in a world where parents not only abuse their children, but are willing to kill them as well. In a few years I could possibly be helping bring my own children into this corrupted world. How can I protect them from the hard truths I have had to learn growing up? How can I stand around and just allow myself to even bring them into this world?

"Carter? Hello?" a voice beckons, pulling me out of my churning head.

I perk up and make eye contact with the agent, trying to manage a smile but failing. "Yes? Sorry." Stevens smiles and tilts his head as he watches me, worry lacing his face and upturned eyebrows.

"Sheriff Reggie has told you that investigating is dangerous and I agree. Yes, we have evidence that proves the Bakers as the most likely suspects, but there is a tiny chance that the murderer is out of custody and roaming free. By investigating, if that is the case, you are poking your nose into places you shouldn't and may uncover something the murderer doesn't want found. They killed your friend and they could easily kill you. Understand?"

I *know it's dangerous*, I want to scream. Reggie and my grandpa have told me so and I do understand that there are risks. But, how can the murderer be anyone but Evie's parents, and if it isn't and I find something proving someone else is and they come after me it wouldn't be so bad, would it? Even if I am killed, at least the killer will be caught and punished for taking away my best friend. At least I would be up with her, laughing with her and celebrating her unblemished, unpunished skin.

"I understand, but I feel..." I start, my voice trailing off. It grows quiet but Agent Stevens decides to finish my sentence.

He tilts his head again and then flips his chair back around to the normal way. He sits in the chair normally, his hands folding over his chest. "...Guilty?"

My body tenses as I sit up straight. "What? Guilty? Why would I feel guilty, Agent?"

It's like Steven's entire demeanor changes, shifting to an unfamiliar nature. His face no longer holds the same softness because it has been replaced by hard cliffs and ridges. He sits forward again, his arms resting on the table top as he stares into what's left of my soul.

The word I was thinking was helpless, not guilty.

"What do you have to be guilty about, Carter?" He presses again, trying to find a nerve to hit, and he is close to succeeding. I'm not sure how far he is going to go and it scares me.

"If you're suggesting–"

Stevens holds up his hands in mock defense. "–No, I'm not suggesting that."

The light around us flickers, diverting both of our gazes to the ceiling where the light snaps on and off. It chooses light and continues to dimly illuminate the room. The goosebumps that have risen on my forearms do not go away with the comforting light.

The agent coughs, flipping my attention back to him. "Why did you never tell anyone about the abuse, Carter? It could have been the difference between Evie surviving and dying. I mean, you could have prevented *all* of this. So, why didn't you?"

CARTER

Wednesday, June 15, 2022, Present.

Can't he guess that I beat myself about it every second I get? I know that I could have saved her. Trust me, I know, and I'll never forget it. It's my biggest regret and will forever be. But I also know that there was always that risk that it could get worse, that no one would believe her, that she could get separated from her siblings. I also understood that if I told someone–*anyone*–she could be free, alive, and finally safe and happy.

Did I take that away from her? Did I prevent that? I guess maybe I did.

Yes, I feel guilty.

Maybe I shouldn't have listened to her when they broke her wrist. I should have told someone.

Yes, I feel guilty.

"Carter?"

I snap back to reality to Mom's voice. I try to meet her eyes but they continue to stay on the black screen before me. My body feels stuck in cement on this couch, my mind drifting to random places. Places I do not want to go.

As my phone beeps Mom asks me a question.

What did she ask? I don't know.

My phone beeps again, setting me in motion. I know I need to immediately answer. I gave Nixon a specific ringtone. I pull my phone out of my front pocket, my limbs sore with exhaustion.

Mom's voice rings in my head again as I click on Nix's text. A link.

It brings me to an article by the East Idaho News. Evie stares back at me, her iceberg eyes watching as I get caught on her features. It's her senior cheerleader photo and the same one I have as my homescreen. Her dark blonde hair is pulled into a high pony, her natural curls curled more than usual. They are pulled up with a blue colored bow covered in rhinestones. Her first name is printed in white cursive on the left loop of the blue while 'senior' is printed in bold, white letters on the bows right tail.

Her smile is bright and happy, like the one she wore when she was with me.

On her left cheek is a temporary tattoo of the Bear Lake Bear mascot head and she wears her cheer uniform, the one with 'BEARS' in big white letters on the chest of her black shell. Her black pleated skirt collects around her thighs, one side of the inside of the pleats blue and the other white.

She stands on the track surrounding the field, her one white and one blue pom poms in her hands—which are in front of her. It looks as if she marching forward in her white, Nike cheer shoes, shaking her poms in a rally.

Everytime I open my phone, she takes my breath away. It's the same as I make eye contact with her portrait.

The headline above reads: New evidence in Baker Murder Case, parents confess to all charges but daughter's murder.

I read through the article, knowing everything already. It talks extensively about the blood found on the boots and how the evidence was 'anonymously' called in. It's weird knowing it was me and then reading about it in some article. It almost feel like I'm on the inside? I don't know. My mind is all jumbled right now. I haven't been able to think straight since the police station.

"*Carter Chase*," Mom snaps. I tear my eyes away from my phone, finally being able to focus on her voice, and find she's still standing beside the couch. She holds a basket of laundry in her arms and an unfamiliar impatience.

"Yeah?"

Mom narrows her eyes, not saying anything.

Maybe I should have been listening to her.

When my mother doesn't say anything else, I return to my article and continue reading. The journalist says an anonymous leak in the police department mentioned that Paul and Joanne haven't confessed to Evie's murder, in fact they completely deny they had a part in it. Paul confessed to the murder of my father and Jason Pierce, as well as the abuse of Evie. He also confessed to coercion, which is considered a class D misdemanor because the threats were to commit murder. Joanne confesses to being an accomplice, though I don't think she had much choice whether to keep the murders a secret or not—I'm not saying she's a victim.

They both confess to drug charges.

The worst part is that the police haven't even called us to tell us Paul confessed to Dad's murder.

My phone is snatched from my hands, leaving my hands bare.

"*Carter Chase Miller*, you look at me."

The basket of laundry is now beside me on the cushions. As she lingers over me, her eyes are churning with anger I've never seen before. But, I wasn't done with that article.

"*Mom*! I need that I wasn't done!"

I shoot off the couch, ignoring my aching legs and attempt to grab for my phone. Mom keeps it out of my reach behind her, her eyebrows upturned. I go for it again but she puts it into her scrubs pockets.

"Carter Chase, you will stop that right now. Reading that crap will drive you crazy, trust me. You are better off without this phone, at least for a day or two, okay?" Her face seems to try to relax but mine doesn't. The next few sentences had questions. The journalist was *questioning* the Bakers' involvement in Evie's *murder*. I can't let that happen. They are about to go down for taking her away from her future and that *journalist* was *questioning* how guilty they are.

"I don't need your opinion, okay? Leave me alone and let me do what I want. I don't need any more crap."

As I storm up the stairs, I feel a pit in my stomach. I've never yelled at Mom before. And I don't think it had to do with the phone at all.

***

I click with my computer's cursor, flipping through pictures of Evie and I. Some of them are only Evie. I stop on one of her standing with her front facing the window as she stands inbetween the bed and the window, right where I am sitting. The yellow sun pours through the window and around her, making her look angelic. I know I'm a pretty handsome guy, but she always blew me out of proportion with her looks. That's why I took it. I drag my hand on the carpet, almost feeling her presence.

Evie had pearly wings, though they were clipped and damaged from the years of negativity. She had a halo but it was rusty and discolored... dim. But, she had the face of an angel. She had the personality, the warmth, and the flawless looks. Though I don't think she ever felt like she had those things. I could see how insecure she really was, though she did hide it. Perhaps it was out of habit. She never had many friends and no family to confide in. In fact, it took her months before she could open up to me, but even then she continued to hide things. She would hide her bruises and her cracks. Sometimes she would cover her freckles—only on her bad days though. When her freckles were covered with a layer of foundation, I knew to hold her especially close because her parents had poked and made fun of them and her. I would help her wipe away the foundation with a wet tissue and then kiss her cheeks as she cried that she didn't deserve the love.

That she was a harlot, a mistake, a demon, a troll, and a stupid child.

Those days were bad.

And not once did she give up.

She wanted to but I didn't let her. I would tell her to take a deep breath and to spin around in a circle three times. After she would spin, wiping the memory and thoughts out of her head, I would take her into a hug and tell her the complete opposite of the names her mother and father told her.

I like to think that her wings are free and healthy now that she's with her grandma. That her halo is golden and giving off a dewy glow and her smile is ringing true.

I miss her.

I click to the next picture, admiring it for a few minutes before clicking again. And again, and again, and again, down the bottomless void of grief and memories. There are false memories too—scenarios—I have made while staring at photos that she isn't in. There's a picture of Mom, Daphne and me at Bloomington Lake up Bloomington canyon, a rope swing hanging beside us from a tree and the small lake stretching behind us. I imagine Evie next to us, her smile big and her bruises washed away in the melted glacier water. One of her perfect arms is behind my back with the other one in the air in triumph: like she won a fake contest on who could get the farthest out in the water on the rope swing or could jump off the cliff into the clear water first. Her fear was washed away with her purple impurities too.

I press my computer's touchpad again, landing on a real picture of us.

A knock at my door jerks me out of the void. I don't turn because I know it's Mom just by the softness of her fist against the door. Her footsteps are muffled as she makes her way around my bed to come to me. I do not look at her as she sinks beside me, her back against the bed like mine. I do not ignore her to be mean. In fact it's the shame that stirs inside me that keeps me quiet.

Mom is still in her scrubs as she stares at the selfie of Evie and I. We were in my truck, driving around the streets of Montpelier for absolutely no reason but to do it. I remember the music was low as we talked and talked. We talked about things ranging from favorite things to dreams. I told her the things I had never told anyone before.

I click again, finding a picture I took of Evie playing in Bear Lake on North Beach. Her hair is wild and let loose, but her arms are confined to a white long sleeve. She is looking back at me with a joyful expression. The still water is up to her shins as she wears the yellow athletic shorts she used for cheer practices.

"She was such a pretty girl," Mom says in a hushed voice, handing me my phone.

I nod, a smile spreading over my dim face as I look at how the sun compliments Evie. I do not take the phone, so instead she sets it above her on my bedspread. Maybe Mom is right about the phone.

"I'm sorry for snapping," I manage, shutting my computer and setting it next to me on the carpet.

Mom adjusts her posture, laying her legs in front of her. Her socks touch the wall my window is on. "You've been overwhelmed. We all have been. I know it's been hard these past few weeks—well, years, let's be honest." She pauses, setting her right hand on my knee. "We all are going to have to pull our weight though, Carter. Even though it's been hard, we are still a *family*."

A tear pricks my eye but I blink it away. *Family*. "I think it's impossible to return back to normal, Mom."

"I know, nothing will be the same. But, we can adjust and make a new normal."

I cover my mom's hand with my own, looking over at her. Her eyes watch me as carefully as I watch her. "What if I don't want this to be our new normal? I've never felt worse, Mom. I don't like how the grief feels. I feel... I feel like I'm getting nowhere, like I'm running in place and this big *monster* is lingering over me, judging my every move, my every decision, and affecting my every mood." I take a deep breath, losing Mom's gaze to look at the little of the sky I can see out my window. "This new normal doesn't have Dad *or* Evie in it."

"But, it has me and Daphne in it."

CARTER

Thursday, June 16, 2022, Present.

The afternoon sun pours through the window in our booth, causing the silverware to glint in it's light. I unfold the napkin the silverware is rolled into, letting the utensils clang against the tabletop.

"Bro, why'd you have to do that?" Nix questions, slowly sliding his rolled up fork, spoon, and knife towards himself as I reach to unroll them too.

I shrug and look out the window at the highway. "I don't know... Intrusive thought?"

Nix chokes, a laugh brewing in his lungs. "You had an intrusive thought about unrolling the napkin and letting the silverware clatter on the table?" He leans in. "People started to stare."

I wave him away and survey Ranch Hand. It's packed and loud for lunch, so I'm sure no one paid a second glance at us. Nix glares at me and sits back, his arms folded over his chest. He's been uptight since all of this stuff with Miriam, which is completely understandable. We are all sitting on the edge of our seats. The entire town is.

A waitress makes her way to our booth, slipping between tables full of people off of work for lunch and tourists taking a break in their uneventful sightseeing. She gives us a smile and pulls out her order pad out of her half apron. She glances at Nix but her eyes stay on me longer than they should. With the stare comes an uncomfortable feeling.

Nix catches her staring and clears his throat, bringing her attention to him. "I'll get a mickey mouse pancake and a glass of your hot chocolate please."

The waitress snaps out of her daze and nods, writing Nixon's order on her check. "And is this seperate or together?"

"Seperate," I reply, trying to manage a smile.

She nods and looks to me for my order. Her eyes watch me warrily, as if she's trying to survey me as much as she can. I readjust in my seat and look at the laminated menu for reassurance, taking a break from her gnawing eyes. "French toast combo with overeasy egg, bacon, and sausage links. And a Dr. Pepper, please."

After she leaves, Nixon shuffles forward, eyeing the waitress as she is putting our orders on some kind of spinning wheel that hangs in the paneless window. It looks into the bustling kitchen. "Okay, so she was being weird, am I right?"

I only shrug, watching her fill up a blue tinted cup with my soda. Nixon doesn't drop it though.

"What was her deal? She kept staring at you like you were some kind of freak."

Breaking my gaze, I lean my elbows onto the table, now facing Nix. "Nixon, I've been a suspect in Evie's case before and now everyone knows she was my girlfriend. That dude from East Idaho News keeps releasing leaked information, and a lot of it is about me. Plus, now there is all the stuff with my dad. I'm surprised more people aren't watching me." I close my eyes, taking in the darkness for a moment. "Look, I'm sure they all think some pretty nasty things about me."

Nixon looks out the window, his eyes watching as yet another car pulls off the highway and into the pothole-infested parking lot. "I don't particularly like journalists. They always pull stunts like that in cases like these, ruining lives whether they mean to or not."

The red-haired waitress brings me my Dr. Pepper and slides Nix's hot chocolate to him, silencing our conversation momentarily. A dollop of whipped cream floats on top of his hot chocolate, bouncing around at any movement. I try to smile at the woman but she doesn't return the favor. My stomach squeezes as she leaves.

"For a lot of journalists, that's what they have to do in order to eat and have a place to sleep. Everyone wants to hear the leaked information and so in order to get paid, a lot of them have to get that undisclosed information first before any other journalist gets it. I'm sure a lot of journalists don't mean to ruin lives." I take a long sip of my drink, ice hitting my lip. "Plus, they haven't ruined my life. If we are getting technical, Paul and Joanne Baker did. Now, can we please stop talking about murder and nosy people? I've had enough of it. That's all my life revolves around anymore."

Nixon pulls a forced grin and takes a sip of his hot chocolate. It leaves behind a cream mustache, earning a smile from me. "Nix, you do know that it is ninety degrees outside, right? Why'd you order the hottest drink they have?"

Nix only shrugs, setting his mug back down on the table. It's white with a black handle. On the front of it is the black silhouette of a rustic man's head, his beard wild and his hat brimmed. It's the logo for this trail stop diner. "Life's too short to not drink good hot chocolate, Carter." With that, he takes another sip, his smile broadening.

I motion towards his white mustache, a warm feeling stirring within me. "Is that why you ordered a breakfast from the *kids* menu?"

He slams his mug down and points at me aggressively. "Don't you *dare* disrespect my mickey mouse pancakes until you have had a taste of it's perfectness. Don't you *dare*."

"Fine, okay. I get it," I laugh, holding my hands up in mock surrender. I grab my unfolded napkin and wave it in front of his face, causing him to snap. He snatches the napkin and stuffs it into his front jean's pockets. He tries to hold back his smile, but fails miserably.

"You're a child."

"Says the one who ordered off the kids menu," I cough underneath my breath. The sun paints Nix's features as his smile falls dramatically into mock anger. But, he can't hold it long.

***

The waitress brings us our food twenty minutes later, catching us as we try to see how big of a tower we can make with little half and half creamer pods. We get to fifteen before she interrupts us.

She slides our food in front of us and then our checks, careful to avoid our fragile tower. We thank her and like clockwork, she goes off to care for other diners.

Slowly, I take down the tower, putting them back into their ceramic bowl. I'm afraid if it crashes, the cups will pop open and spill everywhere, earning me more stares.

Nix pokes me in the shoulder and points at his breakfast lunch. It's one big pancake as a head and two little ones for mickey ears. There is a piece of bacon acting as a smile and bunches of chocolate chips as the eyes. A big dollop of butter sits on the middle.

"That's..." I'm not sure how to finish that sentence.

Luckily, Nixon *tries* to finish it for me. "Majestic?"

I shake my head and spread my ball of butter around my six halves of french toast. I set down my fork and examine Nixon. He takes off his baseball cap and ruffles his black hair, waiting for me to praise his food. A groan escapes my throat and I throw my head back. "Fine, I guess it's pretty cool. But, you're still a literal child."

Nix cuts a chunk from his pancake with his fork and shoves it in his mouth, satisfaction plaguing his face.

Then my phone buzzes, a notification waiting for me. I pull it out and find it's yet another article. Rolling my eyes, I begin to put it away, but I read the name of the article and it intises me: New evidence is found in Baker case, will lead to a suspect.

I click on the notification and it opens up the full article. Immediately I'm reading through the article, scrolling past the headlining photo, which is a picture of 'M' hill. 'M' hill is the hill that towers over Montpelier, seen from multiple sides of the county. On it's side, facing the town, is a big, concrete, white 'M,' standing for Montpelier. It's a staple of the town and holds many houses at it's base and the water tower next to the letter.

Nixon says something but I keep reading. They found hair wound up in the shoelaces and fingerprints all over the boots I found. This article, though, does say that I found them though. It doesn't say my name because I'm a minor, but it does say that the boyfriend of Evie found the boots. In the other articles it just mentioned that an anyonomous individual found them. But, here in this article it is basically calling me out.

It scares me, but I know it shouldn't.

Although there is good news in the article.

In at least twenty four hours, the DNA found will be tested and matched to a profile.

But, I realize that profile won't be Paul's; he's bald.

CARTER

Friday, June 17, 2022, Present.

It has been over twenty four hours. Not a single word has came out about any results and no matter how hard I try not to think about it, I go over all the concerns. I've told myself over and over that they said it can take at *least* twenty four hours and as long as fourteen days. That's the timeline for DNA testing. All last night I tossed and turned, staring at various objects in the room until I got restless enough to sit up and research.

I didn't sleep, instead I researched on DNA testing and how it's done, how long it takes, what it tests for, and etc. Google wasn't easy to search surprisingly, and actually took a lot of will power. Perhaps that is why my head rages with a headache so severe I want to curl up in my dark room. But, I sit in the kitchen trying to force myself to eat. I don't remember the last time I ate and that scares me. Usually I over eat, but recently I have been *forgetting* to eat. Mom hasn't been home much to cook at all and Daph has been making food for herself—which I suppose is pretty worrying. Maybe

I'll cook a feast tonight. Then, we will be able to have leftovers for days. But that is even if we *have* food.

The fridge has things like eggs, sandwich ingredients, milk, and string cheese, while the cabinets hold various noodles and soups. Maybe instead of sitting here worrying, I should go grocery shopping for Mom. How has Daphne been able to fend for herself? There isn't even bread. Although, maybe it's because she ate all of the food. But, the bottom line is that I am a terrible brother. That is exactly what the lack of food is hinting at in my eyes.

Chev's bark rings outside, pulling me away from the cabinets. The door to the cabinet swings shut upon my absence, closing violently. I sneak to the window in the living room, in search of the car that must have passed that made him bark. But, what I find is *Dave* coming up the walk. Chev jumps around, noticing him, his bark full of puppy-like excitement. Dave pets my dogs head and begins toward my house—though he stops a few feet away from my porch and looks back at his truck hesitant. His smile falls as he must realize what he's doing.

What is he doing?

I haven't talked to Dave in what seems like months, and perhaps that's true. We used to be semi-close though ever since he was against me even remotely *looking* at the 'loner' of the class, I only talk to him when needed. I like it that way. I don't need to talk to people who aren't able to do a common decency and give people the benefit of the doubt. To be nice.

But, it seems I won't need to speak with Dave because he begins stepping away from my house. He doesn't even have the courage to come speak with me? He doesn't even have the courage to apologize? He chickens out and just *walks away*—and that makes my blood boil.

Shaking my head, I step away from the window, settling my eyes on anything other than the outside. I don't want to watch as he drives away. I don't care that I should give *him* the benefit of the doubt. Call me a hypocrite, I don't care. It makes me angry that after all this time he just *shows up* at my *home* and doesn't even follow through with his plan or whatever. Maybe he was here to apologize. Maybe he was here to cuss me out. Maybe he was here to make my life worse like that stupid reporter from the news. Whatever he was here to do, he didn't go through with it. That makes him a coward, and maybe someday I will be able to forgive him and whatnot.

The house echoes as knuckles collide with the door.

Perhaps he isn't a coward or chicken.

"What do you want, Dave?!" I snap, throwing the wooden door open.

"Last time I checked, my name was Jonah," a middle-aged man says on the other side of the screen door, his brow furrowed.

I take a step backward, losing grip of the door. It begins swinging closed but I catch it before it shuts me off from my visitor. Slowly, I open the main door back up and stare into the face of the man before me. He wears a white dress shirt and black slacks. Across his chest is the strap to his satchel bag. Another detective.

"What do *you* want then?" I ask, admiring his car that sits in my mom's parking spot. It's newer and freshly cleaned.

The man exhales in some sort of laugh and pokes at the screen door between us. "I'm from East Idaho News."

A reporter.

The reporter.

I step forward, the anger I only had a minute ago returning, although it is reserved for a completely different person now. *Jonah.* "Jonah Smith?"

Jonah smiles and attempts to extend his hand, though the screen stops him. "'Tis I."

"You're the man writing all those articles about me." It's not a question but more of a statement. To it Jonah only laughs. It's hesitant and fades out the longer I glare at him.

He clears his throat and looks behind him, then back at me. "Could I come in and speak with you for an article?"

I scoff before I'm able to hold back my reaction. *Who does this guy think he is? Why would* I ever *talk to him?* "Are you just going to make me look bad again?"

"Look, kid. My readers want the truth and nothing *but* the truth. That's important in a case like the Baker's. In order to give my audience the truth, I have to include all the evidence you have found. It isn't my fault it makes you look guilty again. Plus, I never *directly* used your name. I can't include your name because you are a minor." Jonah paints on a smile and holds the strap of his satchel tightly.

Upstairs, Daphne's bedroom door swings open and then closed. Her footsteps are faint as she walks around in the hall. Then, the bathroom door opens and closes and the house goes silent again. I turn back to the reporter.

"So, you found a loophole congragulations: 'Evie's boyfriend.' I understand that it's your job, but I have been the center of attention wherever I go and I am *not* loving it."

The reporter shakes his head and shrugs. "Kid, it isn't my fault people can figure things out. But, the real reason why I'm here is I want to get Evie's story." He fiddles with the marble buttons on his button up. "The happy parts. You know, the parts where she was inspirational and resilient. I figured you would have been around for those moments, yeah?"

I look behind me as the upstairs bathroom opens and closes again. Something flashes inside me, telling me Evie is on her way down the stairs now, but it's only Daphne, who is still in her pajamas. I smile at her and she looks at the man at the door warrily before sneaking off through the hall that leads to the back door and laundry room. I watch as she slips her work boots on and goes out of view as she goes into the laundry room further. The back door creaks as she must step out, on her way to feed the chickens.

Turning back to Jonah, I try to manage a smile. I think it fails but it's the thought that counts, right? He nods his head, waiting for me to send him away.

But, I step out of the way and let him come inside.

Not enough people knew the happy Evie—or Evie at all—and this is my chance to do something about it.

SHERIFF REGGIE

Friday, June 17, 2022, Present.

People are starting to stare, but why should I care? I'm used to it. The entire department probably thinks I'm crazy. Maybe the entire town.

"Sheriff, take a deep breath," Agent Stevens whispers in my ear as he surveys all the deputies and officers before us. A lot of the younger ones look like they are about to foil their pants, though the older ones look both unbothered and like they are on the verge of laughter.

Those older deputies and officers don't understand the pressure I am under, though. I have only been the sheriff for a little under three years and I have not one but *two* murders and a drug scandal on my hands. When I took over the position for John Miller, I thought it'd be easy. Bear Lake is a small county with little to none crime. I mean there's break in's occasionally, but nothing major like all of this. I'm freaked out. I'm not cut out for this job.

The DNA test still hasn't come in and it's been thirty seven hours. I know that it was unlikely to come in after the minimum time, but we have a dead teenage girl. You think the labs would be a little quicker. We have been on the edge of our seats since we sent in the hair and fingerprint.

I look around at the quiet people in front of me. One of them has made my job harder. "So, is no one going to tell me who leaked information to the press?"

The room stays painfully quiet and I only get blank stares. I try to ease my grip on my bulletproof vest to let some color into my knuckles, but I only seem to hold on tighter.

"Sheriff, let's go into the conference room," Stevens leans in and whispers. I nod and leave the officials in the main room of the Montpelier City Hall. Interrogating and yelling at my co-workers won't help the situation.

Agent Stevens closes the door behind us and turns to face me, his back to the door. He crosses his arms and I focus on relaxing. "It could be a good thing someone leaked some of that information," he sighs, peeking through the blinds out into the lobby.

"How could it possibly be a good thing?"

Stevens lets his hands fall to his side. "Hypothetically, if Paul Baker didn't kill that girl and the real killer is out there, the real killer might feel pressured to come forward." He shrugs. "From my experience with working with the FBI, a lot of the time the evidence may clearly point to someone but if you look harder it isn't that black and white."

I step forward towards the agent. "Are you saying that you're hesitant that Paul Baker killed his daughter? I'd love to believe that, trust me, but there is no evidence shifting away from him. So, that leak did nothing but betray the trust of the county officers and deputies. I'm sure you know just as much as I do that trust is a crucial thing to have in the police force. Without it, someone could be seriously hurt—or killed. How am I supposed to trust them with information anymore?"

Stevens nods in understandment, surveying me in the way that I *hate*. He looks at me like I'm a kid even though I'm clearly *years* older than him. He looks at me gently and just quietly listens. I hate it. I'm not some kid in a tantrum. We are dealing with murder cases.

"We've just got to be sure, and that DNA test will make it so we know for sure. You don't want to put someone behind bars if you aren't completely sure. Plus, Paul Baker is *bald* and there was hair on those boots. We are talking about life behind bars at this point. In the crime world, you've got to be sure, that's all, Sheriff."

Stop looking at me like that. Stop talking to me like that.

Someone knocks on the conference room door, snapping me from my inner rant. Stevens turns around and opens the door to find a PD officer. Some small kid. He is one of those uneasy ones that seem scared half to death to be around me and the FBI agent.

"Sheriff, someone is here to see you. It's the girl's little brother."

Past him stands a teenage boy, shifting nervously from foot to foot as he stands surrounded by at least ten cops. When he makes eye contact with me, he settles.

"Yeah, okay," I sigh, waving him over with my hand. He starts toward the conference room quickly, his hands stuck in his pockets. Maybe he has more information about the night before Evie Baker was killed. The poor kid has barely given us much, just that there was an abusive argument and broken items. I can't imagine how scared he has been. I can tell he has held in a lot. The bad thing about bottling it all up is that you soon explode. When that does happen I just hope there is someone in his corner to be there for him.

He gets to the door and looks between me and Stevens. "Can I talk to you guys?"

"Is this about Evie?" Stevens asks, ushering him into the room. He closes the door, shutting out the noise of the bustling people out in the lobby.

Kace swallows and nods, his eyes calm.

I no longer grip my vest tightly, I realize. He's got evidence that will help. He's finally ready to speak against his father to put him away indefinitely. I have been waiting for him or his little sisters to come forward.

"Take a seat," I smile. "Would you like a hot chocolate?" I motion towards the Keurig in the corner on a table. I probably shouldn't offer this kid coffee.

"Do you have coffee?"

Stevens seems unbothered by his request. I didn't think kids that young drank coffee though. "Yeah... sure."

I make my way to the table and stick a coffee pod into the top. I turn on the machine as Kace takes a seat at the head of the table. I grab a paper cup and place it underneath the spout and push the start button. It takes a second too long to heat up and relief spreads through me as the brown liquid starts pouring into the cup.

Behind me, Stevens is asking Kace about how his junior year of high school went. Kace replies calmly, saying it could have gone better, probably hinting towards the death of his sister.

I quietly remind myself not to try and bring up those painful memories as much as I am able.

I set the steaming cup of coffee in front of the sixteen-year-old and he thanks me with a half smile. From the fridge, I hand him creamer, which he graciously pours into the drink.

Stevens and I make eye contact. I wonder if he is as anxious as I am to hear what new evidence there is.

The boy takes a sip of his coffee, leaving the creamer in the middle of the round table. He sets it down and looks into the now caramel-colored coffee. "There's an article saying you sent DNA from those boots you found in the shed to a lab to get tested. It said that you would get results in twenty four hours, is that true?"

I take a seat to his left while Stevens takes one to his right. "Yeah, it's true, son."

"It's been more than twenty four hours so you must have results by now, right?" He takes another sip, cringes, and then takes another. I'm guessing coffee isn't his preferred drink, but based on his eye's dark circles, it's what he needs to stay awake.

"We don't have the results yet, no. Twenty four hours was just the minimum time. It could take up to 14 days. Truth is we don't know how long it will take," Stevens tells him, leaning forward onto his elbows. "Sooner or later we will get a match though, don't you worry."

Kace nods and looks out the window, which looks over the alleyway and the drug store's parking lot. The squad cars are parked there with some officers out there starting a few of them as a call comes over the radio: some kind of parking problem where someone parked in front of someones driveway, blocking them in.

I bring my attention back to the boy and watch as he takes a longer sip. He rapidly gulps down half of the cup and sets it infront of him. He then slides it away from him to the middle of the table, like a child refusing to eat their dinner or something.

He takes a deep breath and looks at me.

"You won't need to wait for that DNA to match," he says, biting his lip. "It's mine."

Stevens talks before I can. Which is probably a good thing because I'm still trying to decide if I heard the kid right.

"What do you mean, Kace?"

"It was me, Agent."

"What was you, son?" I feel my gut clench and my heart drop.

With the calmest eyes I have ever seen, Kace Baker looks straight at me again and clasps his hands in front of himself.

"We do terrible things for the people we love, Sheriff."

Oh, please no.

EVIE

Monday, May 16, 2022, Past.

The reservoir is deserted with not a soul in sight. My guess would be because it's a weekday and everybody's out at work. But still I expected to see some retired folk attempting to catch a fish or two… but nothing.

So, I sit on a pretty good sized boulder on the shore all alone.

This reservoir holds some pretty good memories from before my grandma died. We used to come and fish here a lot actually. Probably about fifteen times during the summers. I always looked forward to it. And then the accident happened and all those memories were just… well… *memories*.

This boulder I'm on has been here all of my life and more. I remember it from when I was just a child. I would sit on it as we fished, eating a ham and cheese sandwich usually.

I haven't been back here since then. But now as I sit here all of those memories have begun to rush back. The blue water holds so many different kinds of fish that my happy family caught.

I don't even know why I'm sitting here doing this to myself. Those memories are just making me mournful. But, I guess I just wanted to visit this place before heading to wherever walking and hitchhiking take me. Kind of like a final goodbye, you know?

The blue water stretches for a mile and is undisturbed in the sudden heat. Today's weather is a complete one-eighty from yesterday. The rain clouds have disappeared, leaving behind a cerulean sky the color of my eyes. As the sun rises it avoids the clouds, continuously shining on the valley. A bird chirps in the distance, quickly followed by a familiar rumble.

Dad.

My arms launch me off the boulder, my feet landing firmly on the loose rocks. Above the reservoir, on the dirt road that runs parallel to the body of water, tires spit rocks around the homely road.

I duck behind the large boulder just in time to watch a maroon Ford Ranger speed down the road toward the North side of the water. It doesn't resemble my father's white F-150 like I believed it would. My heart calms as I convince my galloping mind that my dad doesn't know I'm here. No one knows I'm here. Not even Carter.

I place my hand on my chest, feeling my rushing heartbeat as it drifts back to normal. Sweat bursts through my forehead and the back of my neck. *Oh, gosh.*

Soothing my abrupt anxiety, I take the hair tie off of my wrist. I gather up my hair and tangle it into a low ponytail. It gives memories of school and home so I rip it out, letting my awkward hair fall to my shoulders. The strands tickle my neck and cheeks but I don't mind. The sensation—as small as it is—is a gentle reminder that I am here and alive.

A sudden splash causes me to jump out of my skin. I hide behind the boulder once again. My father deliberately gave away his position by throwing a rock into the water, knowing I'd be scared half to death.

But when I look up, an airborne rainbow trout glimmers in the morning sun's rays. It slips back into the water, making an identical sound to the one I've just analyzed. A rush of relief drowns me and I get back up onto my feet, presenting myself to the excited environment.

"I'm not scared of your tricks," I quietly inform, crossing my arms around my chest. I feel silly as I survey the land, my fear hidden deep within me. Nothing but a facade of strength shows.

Until I hear another truck coming and my fears rush back. This one sounds even more familiar and I will not take my chances. For whatever reason I feel it could be possible for my parents to find me, no matter how many times I tell myself. And so I duck behind the boulder once again, my hair going completely airborne for a split second. As I settle, so does my mud-caked dirty blonde hair. The natural curls lay heavily around my shoulders, weighing me down lower.

I slide the tip of my head over the boulder just enough to deny or confirm my father's presence. And my heart stops as the answer becomes clear.

A white F-150 creaks into view, coming to a raspy stop on the small shoulder of the dirt road. The majority of the truck sits on the road but it is clear it meant to park there and only there. My swarming head plunges below out of sight and my eyes squeeze shut. A popular myth I believed as I kid was that if you don't see them, they don't see you. Why am I following that now?

Maybe it's because I am simply *just* a kid. I may have grown up faster than the kids in my grade but that doesn't mean I don't hold childish fears. I never had much of a childhood and whenever my mind or body goes into panic mode I suppose I go back to those unexplored childish natures. It could be a coping mechanism or plain mental illness. Maybe a mix of both.

"Evie?" a contradicting voice calls, breaking the suffocating silence. The warmth of it almost makes me want to lift my head back up and then myself and then head toward it. But I stay put. Call it the trust issues I've developed over the years.

"Evie, come on I know you are here somewhere, I saw you. It's Kace, come on, it's okay," my brother's voice calms. I can hear distinctly as he makes his way down the metal staircase leading from the road to the rocky shore.

It takes a minute for me to trust it's really him but with a small peek over the rock, I find his comforting, tinted blond hair and soft face. His appearance brings a smile to my face and I shoot up out of my hiding spot.

He seems shocked at first but his features soften rapidly. My lovely brother begins walking toward me, his arms outstretched. A lump begins growing in my weak throat as I stumble over the rocks toward my emotional rock. Each step I take brings me closer to the love and comfort I will receive from my wise brother. He's always been the one in the family that couldn't be shaped or manipulated by my parents. Their actions never affected him and I hope will never in the future.

I reach him and collapse into his arms. He holds me partly up with no assistance from me, keeping me safely off of the sharp rocks below me—even though those are the least of my problems. Sultry tears run down my cheeks, no doubt creating ugly, defined streaks in my dirt covered face. But I do not care. I didn't even have time to say goodbye to Kace.

"You shouldn't be here," I sob into his chest. "Dad or Mom could have followed you, Kace."

Kace lifts me off my knees and back up fully onto my feet by my bruised shoulders. He continues stabilizing me with his sturdy hands and shakes his head in defiance.

"They didn't follow me. Both of them have been passed out drunk on the couch since four in the morning. They don't know you're here, Evie."

I feel my brow furrow. "That's out of character for Mom and Dad, Kace. Trust me, they would have come after me as soon as they saw I wasn't in my room. Not with what I know. Tell me the truth."

Kace groans, rolling his eyes. He glances behind him and then back at me in defiance. "*Fine*. They were driving around all night looking for you. I didn't want to freak you out, okay? But they didn't follow me. Don't you trust me?"

I trust my brother with my whole life.

I take the backs of my hands and streak them across my face, wiping away my degrading frailty. Looking up at my younger brother I swallow sharply, attempting to get rid of my uncomfortable lump. "How'd you find me? How'd you know I was here?"

My brother shrugs and ushers me to follow him as he begins to walk around the shore–he knows walks calm me down. He remembered. He quickly runs his fingers through his ill-kept hair, and stares at the terrain before us. Slowly the rocks begin to become scarce and we are surrounded by mud and browning grass.

"I'm glad you found me though, Kace. I felt sick to my stomach that I couldn't say my goodbyes to you."

Kace solemnly shakes his head. "What are you doing out here, Evie?" His head slowly turns and he examines me as we walk, his bright blue eyes compassionate. He was blessed with the brightest eyes of the family. They are the same color as mine and Dad's but hold something different... something promising in their depths.

"I can't stay in that house, you know that. I'm going to hitchhike and walk my way into Wyoming," I quietly explain, my eyes on my feet as we trudge through the mud at a calming pace.

Kace laughs to himself and shakes his head for what seems like the hundredth time. "And you thought that was the most rational option?"

I nod... then I shrug... and my head finds itself shaking like Kace's. I don't know why I thought this was a smart idea. Of all of the things I could have done I chose the most irrational. This is why Kace was always the favorite. He has the brains while I have the scar above my eyebrow demonstrating what I am to my unforgiving parents.

Kace stops moving abruptly and turns to me quietly. "If you are going, I'm going with you. I'm not leaving you ever."

This time it's my turn to laugh and I do. It's a sad, hollow sound that shakes my bones deeply. I stop walking and turn to my ambitious brother. "You are going to leave me. It's what is best. Someone needs to be there with Allie and Riley."

He shakes his head firmly, planting his feet.

"*You can and you will, Kace.* You hear me?"

He steps back, his mouth hanging half open. His eyebrows deepen toward his eye sockets, creating an unfamiliar shadow of rebellion over his chiseled face. Kace snaps his mouth back closed, his teeth smashing together. His eyes darken in a way I've always hoped they wouldn't. This version of Kace is completely and utterly a surprise to me.

"What makes you think that suddenly Mom and Dad will not look for you, Evie?!" he inhales sharply, stepping toward me. "You can't hide from those two forever. They have people *everywhere* that are involved in their 'business.' They will always find you. Especially with the valuable information you hold."

Something about his demeanor shoves me back a step. But, I fret this alternate Kace is right. I'm kidding myself if I think I can get away from their corruption and abuse. That's almost as stupid as thinking if I close my eyes tight everything will be okay and everything will work out on its own. If I can't see it, it's not happening.

My brother unhinges his jaw and shoves his hands into his blue and gray windbreaker's pockets. "You know that Dad killed Noah Miller. That information alone will get *you* killed."

It breaks my heart but it is extremely correct. I'm just hoping the piece of notebook paper with my boyfriend's dad's name will be of use if anything should happen to me. If Mom or Dad happen to show up I will ditch the bag in a place where the police will find it and I will run until I'm caught.

He takes another step toward me, his expression becoming more serious with each step. "They won't stop looking for you until they have silenced you for good, Evie."

I know what he's implying.

Somehow I've always known that death hasn't been far behind me. I saw first hand how quick it came for Grandma. I know how fast it can come for me.

I face the water, shunning my arising tears from my strong brother. He's the strongest between us and that's always been a fact. The water ripples quietly, hiding fish underneath its static surface. Under my nose is all those fish and I wouldn't even know it until I'm swimming along with them.

The fresh water seems to be calling for me, tempting me. I want to go into it but I have information to share with the Wyoming police. I have a duty to finish. I could have stayed in that house and let myself get beat into silence but I chose to escape and share my story. Never in my life have I been more terrified... but *strong*. It's a riveting feeling.

Kace shuffles directly behind me, set back a good ten feet, his movements almost undetectable.

"I have to do this, Kace. I'm sorry and I love you but I have no choice but to run. If I don't make it, then at least I died trying, right?"

He says nothing as I stare ahead of me, taking in the good memories I once had here. Once Mom, Dad, and I took a canoe out on this reservoir to fish as Grandma watched from the shore, her hands on her large hips and a smile on her pink lips.

His strong, defiant voice shatters the silence that has settled upon us, setting unwanted chills up my spine. I shake dramatically as electricity pulses through my body: "You're my sister. You need me, Evie. Everything I do, I do for you... and what I'm going to do is going to be for *you.*"

My mind takes seconds to process what is being said to me. Seconds have always been the difference between succeeding and failing in my life and it's no different now.

I'm shook by a cold voice as Kace rummages around in his jacket's pocket.

I turn my neck to meet his eyes, not bothering to turn the rest of my body. He pulls out a small black object.

It's barrel rapidly comes into focus, only ten feet away from my head.

His iceberg eyes stare calmly at me as he raises the pistol directly in front of his body, pointed straight at me. He holds it with two level hands, his muddy boots planted in the wet soil.

"Mom and Dad can't hurt you anymore...You've been hurt for the last time."

I turn my head back toward the reservoir's gleaming surface because I don't have time to react as a deafening sound splits the air.

Fear doesn't paralyze me as I always thought it would.

Everything goes black,

and I don't know if I welcome the instant peace.

CARTER

Saturday, June 18, 2022, Present.

When I imagined the moment Evie's killer was being moved past me, I never imagined *this* moment. To begin with, I always imagined it to be Paul or Joanne... not quiet, innocent Kace. I mean the kid rarely talked and when he did he was a ray of sunshine like his sister. I would have never guessed he could commit a cold-blooded crime against his older sister whom he loved and cherished and protected.

As he tells his story on the stand he leaves no detail unturned or told. He looks down at his clasped hands and softly states every step, his voice unwavering as he retells the frigid elements of Evie's death.

He tells us how he simply *guessed* Evie would first go to the reservoir. But, before that he came and checked *my* house for any signs of her. He was probably right outside my home as my family slept, watching. A murderer stood outside my home. But, when he found no sign of his distressed sister, he headed to one of the only places that still held good memories from her happier past... and he sat at the rearing pond, watching for her, waiting for her to emerge from the creek's brush and large bushes. Kace watched without detection as she walked herself up the dirt road and to the reservoir.

She probably never even knew she was being watched.

What seems like hours later, *sixteen-year-old* Kace's sentence is given. No one gasps. No one flinches. Kace sits at the defendant table, his back completely to me and he doesn't move an inch. His head stays drooped, his chin resting on his chest.

Twenty-five years Kace will be in incarnation. He will be forty one years old at the time of his release.

Is it bad that I'm glad he wasn't tried as an adult? If Kace Baker was tried as an adult he would be confined to prison for all of his life. Stuck behind bars, stuck with the revolting men and women placed deliberately in there for horrendous crimes. I'm glad he will have a chance to live a life... even if it's too late by the time he is forty. Essentially because he protected his sister, he no longer gets a life to live. He no longer has privacy.

Kace Baker protected his sister, my girlfriend, and is being punished. He should have let Paul and Joanne take the fall for Evie's murder, no matter how dishonest that may be. Kace doesn't deserve any of this.

He swore to protect his older sister from harm and that's what he did. The normal human would think that's repulsive but no one has lived his life. In Kace's mind, it's completely justified. In his mind, nothing was wrong with what he executed.

Don't get me wrong, I am *furious* at Kace fro doing what he did. Evie could be recovering in Wyoming somewhere, far from her parents. She would be safe and she would have the opportunity to live her life. Her life was taken way to early and it was taken by someone she loved dearly. I won't be able to smile and laugh with her anymore. Kace took that away and nothign will change that. I can change my attitude towards everything, but it will never change what he did. He took away our Evie when she was so close to freedom.

Two sheriff's deputies gather at Kace's side and lift him up hesitantly, quietly telling him it's time to go. Kace only nods and begins walking alongside them from the defendant table, his posture solemn and regretful. You wouldn't be able to tell by his voice that he was deeply saddened by what transpired with his sister, but you can by the way it looks like the world's heavy boots are shoving him down. He fights it but you can easily notice the toll it's taking on him. His eye bags are darkened and his youthful face has been replaced by a wrinkled, pensive, somber one.

I squeeze Mom's hand in remembrance of Mom's hollow face. In some ways my mother and Kace are much alike.

Kace's eyes scan me as he shuffles past my pew. For a boy so accomplished at killing, they are remarkably soft and benign. His handcuffed hands lay still in front of his ill-fitted, bright orange jumpsuit and begin to twitch as he nods his head gently at me. My body temperature drops as I watch the boy continue past me. Just sixteen. That hasn't fully hit me until now. It knocks me bleak, squeezing the air out of my wheezing lungs.

My air does not return to me as he stops in front of his cuffed parents who sit accompanied by deputies, the sound of his rattling handcuffs splitting the muted air. Their shattering sounds take me back to nails on chalkboard or the merciless sound of metal on rusted metal, its sound causing any and every ear to bleed immediately. Not only does the song of the cuffs represent the ghastly sounds of bondage but also the dreadful loss of innocence and safety in the world. If a sixteen-year-old could do this to their own sister... What is to become of our doomed world?

Paul's sly smile fills my nightmares. Mom squeezes my hand back as she recognizes the rising emotions in me, setting me back in my place. Everybody is already talking about our family, we can't give them more to gossip about to their neighbors, co-workers, friends, and family. In a small community with no privacy, we have to be careful. Especially now.

Paul does not break eye contact with his only son. "I knew what you were from the beginning. You're just like me. You were born to spill blood, my son."

It has always frightened me how a boy of Kace's age is able to hold their anger inside themselves quietly, keeping it from the public eye effortlessly. You would never know what is going on in his head by his face. That's what makes him so dangerous.

His eyes glint in the court room's fluorescent lights.

"I will never be me again, and it's all because of you."

And with that he walks from the room, being tailed by his own personal guards, perhaps knowing he will never see his father again. Perhaps being completely content with his father having been given the life sentence only hours before he received his own.

There's no telling what caused his warped mindset and what caused him to be able to even *kill* Evie. Perhaps it was family genetics or some kind of personality disorder. Maybe he wasn't his self and he had no control that May morning. There are so many answers to that question that seem liable, though we may never know what made Kace snap. It's a question people will be asking for decades: what made little, 16-year-old Kace Baker kill his sister?

But, I do know he isn't the first child that has been capable, and I know it isn't his fault he was raised in the company of two liars, two abusers, and one murderer.

And as he walks through the doors, you could never even begin to guess what is happening underneath that gentle face.

That face of an angel hiding that mind of a killer.

CARTER

Sunday, June 19, 2022, Present.

This is a heck of a way to spend my birthday. The mournful sniffles that protrude the air bring a heaviness into the church. I pass quietly chatting elders as they sit in the hall, the brochure with Evie's face on it covering their mouths. They stall as I slip past and stare at me with solemn eyes. I nod my head at them and carry on through the church, ignoring their immediate whispers.

But, focusing on their whispers also keeps my ears away from the occasional sobs that echo throughout the hallways. I wonder how many of Evie's family members are here. She never mentioned any aunts or uncles, not even the aunt who Allie and Riley will be staying with over in Utah. I don't even know if she has any grandparents left. Or cousins. The Bakers were an isolated family.

The beige walls close in on me the farther away from the whispers I get, shoving the sounds of sniffling into my head. Off in the distance I can hear somber music playing out of a speaker or television, the artist's voice laced with tearful melody. No doubt hooked up to the music is a slideshow of Evie's face. I wonder how many pictures there will be. I get the sense that they would need to scrape the bottom of the barrel to find pictures of Evie.

I wore my nice clothes today. I reserve these clothes especially for funerals and weddings. I've used them more for funerals than weddings. The soles of my leather Oxford dress shoes fill the church with squeaks each step I take closer to the chapel. I learn to ignore it but I hope others will as well.

"Carter," a voice bellows, awakening me from my mindless walking.

I turn to find Dave following me. His hand is in front of him with his palm outstretched as if he's reaching towards me. His hand drops to his side as he makes eye contact with me, his fingers playing with the fabric of his dress slack's.

I say his name quietly under my breath and try to manage a smile. I fail. I haven't spoken with Dave for what seems like weeks. Last time we spoke, he was criticizing me.

Dave stands awkwardly in his place, his face turning somber. We stand like this for what seems like hours. He looks down at his white dress shirt and then at the ground. "I'm sorry, Carter. About Evie. About everything and especially how I acted."

Part of me is mad he won't even meet my gaze. The other part of me understands that shame he must bear within.

He slowly looks up from the solitude of the ground, water welling in his eyes. He opens his mouth but I raise my palm, stopping him. "It's okay, Dave. I understand."

With that I turn on my heel and continue through the echoey hall. Ahead of me the chapel's open doors come into view. A select few individuals in black stand next to some pews, exchanging polite conversation. I tear my eyes off the folks as I enter a bit of a lobby, leaving Dave in my dust. I want to be nice, but I'm afraid if I stay in front of him any longer, I may lose my temper. Plus, Evie's funeral is not the place to fight. And maybe now is the time to start forgiving.

The seering sunlight pours through the double glass doors, basking the carpeted area in heat. On an old floral couch sitting between the chapel doors and the church's main doors, are three cheerleaders dressed in cold, gray dresses. They watch a television to my right with wet eyes. When they meet mine I shudder. Madison Porter lifts herself off the couch and crosses the lobby to join me. She stands a foot in front of me but doesn't say a word. Madison's a grade below me and we used to be friends at one point last year. We shared three classes together, although we haven't talked at all this year, not even in the halls when we pass each other.

Her lips curl into a sober form of a smile and to my surprise she wraps her tan arms around me. My body tenses momentarily but as I inhale her vanilla scent, I calm. My shoulders relax and I wrap my own arms around her comfortably. It feels so nice to feel the warmth a hug gives. The tighter she hugs, the more tears dare to threaten my eyes. Normally I would keep them bottled up but they slowly seep out as her long, curled brown hair tickles my cheeks.

I don't want the feeling to diminish but she breaks from the hug, tears running down her own tan cheeks. "You and Evie were dating, right?"

It doesn't surprise me that Madison would know. Nothing stays a secret in Bear Lake. The majority of the residents have police scanners where they can probably hear all kinds of things. It doesn't shock me that the word got out. So, I nod.

Madison gives me a half smile. "I kind of assumed… I mean you didn't make it public so I figured you didn't want anyone to know and I thought that was weird cause y'all were cute and now… and now I see why. I'm so sorry, Carter."

When I say nothing she gestures toward the television where a slide show does in fact play, a song about angels playing over the haunting images. My saturated eyes drift to the picture that flashes on the screen. It's a picture of a little girl holding hands with an older woman. Her bright blue eyes are illuminated with happiness as they stand in front of her grandmother's garden, sunflowers surrounding them. Golden light shines upon their smiling faces, highlighting their love for one another.

Evie's freckles are generous and her dimples deeper than I ever saw them.

The screen flashes to another photo. This time she's younger—a cheerful toddler playing in a bed of flowers, dirt smudged across her cheek. Her iceberg blue eyes are open and filled with a glistening glee that I always thought was so incredibly unique. Evie was so unique.

"She's gorgeous, isn't she?" Madison sighs, watching the screen as intently as I. "I have been sitting here for twenty minutes already and I can't stop watching. I've probably watched the entire slideshow ten times already. It's jarring, isn't it? Scary?"

I nod slowly because that's exactly it. I've always thought it was so haunting the way her life changed so quickly. The way her family drifted and transformed. Evie Janiece Baker never had a chance, even from the start when her grandmother was with her. No doubt Joanne and Paul would have snapped sooner or later, even if the accident hadn't happened. I just wonder what went through their minds and what led them to break to that huge extent. Paul and Joanne are and were sick.

"I never got to see the real Evie," Madison coughs as a picture I submitted flashes on the screen. It was a simple selfie taken in my truck. I remember it clearly. It was Christmas and it was taken as I dropped her back home, around fifteen minutes after we had our first kiss. "I'm sure you saw the real Evie though, right?"

"I like to think so…"

Madi doesn't seem to notice I don't want to speak.

"That's a cute picture of you two," she smiles at the Christmas selfie. "When was it taken?"

The picture flashes off the screen and next comes a baby photo. Evie lays asleep in a basket of sunflowers.

I retell Christmas's events to Madison who listens earnestly, her brown eyes wide. I don't know why I suddenly begin talking to her about Evie. Maybe it has something to do with not being able to share any of our special moments over the course of the past seven months. To be completely honest, I haven't really noticed how much of a toll it has taken on me to keep so many secrets: from my mom, from Nixon, from Daph, and from myself even. But, it doesn't matter because I did it for her. I did it for Evie.

"Have you gone to see her?" Madison abruptly says as I finish. I stare at her, my eyebrows furrowed.

"What?"

"It's her viewing right now. Down there," her steady finger points down another hall as someone comes out of the relief society room. Their eyes are downcasted and watch their feet as they leave the room.

I've never been a fan of funerals but I hate viewings even more. A body sits in a casket for everyone to look at and watch. A specialized individual dresses and preps the body to make it appear less dead and sticks it in a room of crying people. It's unjust, it's scarring, and it's terrifying... especially with what has happened to Eve.

"It's a closed casket viewing," Madison chimes in. "With her wounds and what not they voted against it."

Relief does spread over me but not much. Madison means the bullet hole embedded in the back of her head. She means the bruises her father gave her. She means the black eye given to her the night before her death.

I don't know what causes me to do it but I begin walking away from Madison Porter, my eyes set on the relief society room. I stop in front of it at one of the doorways, peering inside as sweat builds on my forehead and neck. The insides are deserted except for a polished, walnut casket and several green padded chairs, each used for Sunday school services. Fluorescent light pours through the white curtained window, somehow bathing the room with a cold, plain gleam. My toes tickle to move but my head keeps me firmly planted in the doorway of the medium-sized room.

I haven't seen Evie since May fourteenth, which was the day I took her to the North Beach shops out at Bear Lake. I can still hear her dove-like laugh when I received my *huge* pineapple ice cream monstrosity. I can still hear the seagulls chirp as they flew on the beach of the lake, scouting for any dropped sandwiches.

After all this time how am I supposed to walk into this door and accept she's gone forever? How am I supposed to accept that our story has ended? I had all these dreams and goals with her and now *none* of them will come true or be completed. The moment I step through this doorway is the moment it all ends. I've never liked the endings in books or movies, especially when they are this bitter. I don't want to be another character that doesn't get their ideal ending.

Abruptly, my heart pulls me through the door. I never got to say goodbye. All I remember is hugging her on May fourteenth. I know everyone thinks teenagers can't be in love with someone but I was... and I never told her; with her fifteen or ten feet away I have that final chance to tell her everything I didn't get to say in time.

Tears prick my eyes as I hover toward the closed casket, feeling drawn toward the funeral spray of sunflowers that sit on top of a lace cloth on the coffin. My hand leaves my dress pants pockets and slowly lifts up away from my body. The tips of my fingers lightly touch the cold wood. Gradually my fingers slide and my palm rests delicately on the polished surface.

That signature lump begins to grow in my throat, restricting my breath.

"I thought we'd have more time," I cough quietly, trying to diminish the wedge. Then, I restate my promise I made to her so many days ago after her parents were arrested. My fingers tickle with a warm sensation. "I *will* find you again. Either in another life or in another world but for *sure* another body and time. I swear I *will* see you in another life. We *will* meet again, I promise."

On the other side of this wood is the girl that has been my sole focus since November. Gone but not gone. A lingering spirit but forever absent. How does one even change their focus? What do I do with my life now? Do I move on, go to college, and just forget? Do I find someone else I'll be able to cherish and protect in ways I couldn't with Evie?

I lift my hand and return it back to my pocket, leaving a sweaty handprint on the wood. I wipe it with my other arm's sleeve and return that one to its pocket as well.

"Eve... I guess our story ends here..."

***

The funeral ceremony takes place in the chapel, an immense amount of the heaven's light pouring through two frosted glass windows that sit near the front of the room. They are small and hidden but disperse a surprising amount of light. A member of the church plays the organ in between talks and hymns.

Allie and Riley now slink down the stairs off of the platformed lectern, their eyes watching the crowd nervously as they walk back to the middle section of the pews, returning to their family. They gave a talk together about how inspirational Evie was to them.

They settle back into their seats next to their aunt Jeanne, who gave a talk only twenty minutes ago. To be honest I don't remember much of Jeanne's talk but I think it had to do with the love Evie and her grandmother–Jeanne's mother–shared. She seemed to improv most of the things she said. Jeanne really shouldn't have given a talk because Evie always told me that her aunt was never around as she was growing up. Especially after Evie's grandma passed.

I rise from my chair as the bishop of the Bloomington Ward announces my name, identifying that it's now my turn. I have never been the type to get nervous in front of a crowd but as I make my way hurriedly toward the chapel's podium, my heart quickens. Sweat builds on my neck and the chapel's freezing air turns charred.

My legs shake dramatically as I climb the minimum carpeted steps up the platform which is surrounded by an oak pony wall, a wall that only comes up part way. My hands tremble as I pass the green padded seats where people often sit when they are waiting to give talks in church. The only people that sit in them are the organist, pianist, and the bishop.

The balding bishop encourages me with a nod as the hushed room watches my every anxious movement.

I settle in front of the lectern and clear my throat, avoiding to look across the fifty plus people in the green padded pews. I never expected this turn out for Evie. I thought there would be fifteen people at most but the community has pleasantly surprised me.

"Hello," I blare into the microphone, causing an uproar of electrical ringing. Several of the people before me jump as I do, exclaiming lightly as their ears are pierced. My feet take me a little away from the microphone and I quietly apologize to the church-dressed folks.

"As I'm sure all of you know... I'm Carter Miller. I've recently become quite well known."

It was meant as a shallow attempt as a joke but everyone stares blankly back at me, their eyes black and beady.

I pull out my phone and open it, revealing my short speech I wrote only yesterday. I lay my phone on the lectern's oak surface and clear my throat again, silently praying for comfort.

"I was probably one of Evie's only friends for the past seven months," I begin to read into the microphone. "I'm sure you all know I was even dating her. Because of this I got to see Evie at her happiest, as rare as it was. But, I also got to see that twisted, broken part of her that she tried so hard to keep away.

"I met Evie Janiece officially at Paris's Halloween Carnival. I had classes with her our junior year *and* senior year but I never really spoke with her. But something intrigued me about her. Call it an instinct that someone needed my friendship. On Halloween I made the decision to take a risk and speak with her. I didn't realize how big of an outcome that decision would make on my life for the upcoming months.

"I recently spoke with my little sister about this moment that changed my entire life and she asked me one simple question: if you knew what would come from that decision, would you have walked over and talked to her at that cotton candy booth? I didn't hesitate. I *immediately* said yes."

The sitting crowd watches me curiously. In the middle, in roped off pews, sits Evie's remaining family members. The amount is low and solemn. I count only five.

"I like to think that I helped Evie and lifted a great deal of her burdens. Although I will always be apologetic that I never told anyone about the abuse. I knew it was happening. I knew what they did to her and I never told. I used to think that if I hadn't made that mistake, she'd be alive with me and we wouldn't have gathered as a sorrowful community in the Church of Jesus Christ of Latter-day Saints. I used to think I could have avoided this entire ordeal but the truth is that I couldn't."

I shift my eyesight to Allie and Riley as they eagerly watch me. Riley's cheeks flush momentarily upon contact. "Evie told me to never tell anyone because she knew if her parents got in trouble in some kind of way, she could get separated from her siblings—especially Allie and Riley. They could get separated and never see each other again. Evie was strong in that way and loving. She loved her siblings till the end and protected them until the day she died. I just pray that you all will remember her courage.

"I know that I will remember Evie's dedication and love as she battled her monsters and demons. She kept the courage and scars of a war hero. And she never once complained to me. Even in her darkest moments she remained a bright, yellow light that gleamed of endurance and devotion. Everyday she taught me something new, and everyday she was an example to her siblings and to me.

“The things she went through taught me that life is short. We all know that. But anything can happen in a second.”

Over fifty eyes stare at me and I no longer feel that approaching doom or fear. In front of me are members of our small community, ready to learn the lessons Evie taught me. They are ready to perhaps change the world and make it a better place.

“And so I leave you with this...” I sigh, forcing my shoulders up from their demoted position and squaring them. “It only took 1 second to pull that trigger and it only took 1 second to ruin Evie’s life. So why waste another second of yours?”

Epilogue

Every family has secrets. Now, if you met my family you would understand. My dad is a murderer. My brother is a murderer... *my* murderer. Mom is an accomplice. Allie and Riley were the 'normal' ones in the family... Well, the most normal you can get in a broken family. Oh, and I am the *murdered*.

Before Grandma died, my family was more normal than you'd think. We were a happy family. In fact, we were a typical Idahoan, American family. Yes, us. We weren't always crazy and broken.

As the oldest, Mom and Dad supported me in everything. They came to all my plays, programs, promotions, and award ceremonies. They loved me and they loved my siblings. They weren't drunks back then. My mom didn't do drugs. My dad didn't sell drugs. We were a normal family—as I said earlier.

Back then, Mom and Grandma were inseparable. They had a beautiful Mother-Daughter bond and were so close. Even as a child, I recognized that. Grandma made my mom an amazing mother and kept her in check.

Then she died—as you know—and I hadn't. Something in our family changed after that. Mom became cold toward me.

She refused to talk to me or go near me. As an eight-year-old, I really didn't understand why Mom suddenly acted like she didn't love me. I mean, it's not like she was the one that watched Grandma die beside her. *I DID*. So why was she that way?

I still don't know the answer, honestly. And I never will find out.

After the accident, *everything* went wrong. Mom began drinking and so did Dad. It was like he was finally showing his true colors or something. He seemed so comfortable with being drunk. With being mean. Them being intoxicated was a common occurrence in the house. But, what I noticed is that she was only cold to me and Dad was only mean to *me*. Not Kace. Not Allie. Not Riley. Just *me*. What was an eight-year-old supposed to do with that information?

I met evil when I was only a child. I mean, daily my parents mocked me and told me I was ungrateful, stupid, wicked, sinful—the list goes on and on. They told me I was the villain, not them. The older I got the more I realized that Mom blamed me for Grandma's death. She blamed me for living. I 'took away her life.' I took away her '*purpose*.' What was that even supposed to mean to a child?

And then they began to hit me. It was more Dad then Mom but she instigated it. Dear old Dad was careful though. He made sure to not leave bruises anywhere visible. It was usually my arms, legs, and torso that were attacked. Because of this I was never allowed to wear dresses, shorts, short-sleeved shirts, and tank tops.

I used to cry when they punished me. When they hit me. But, as time went on, and the more they did it, I became numb to the pain. But, only to the pain. I wasn't insensible to the mental and emotional torture.

My parents were very careful and were never caught. No one suspected anything. That is until I met him. *Carter Chase Miller.*

Before him I had no reason to live or laugh or smile. In fact I doubt I truly did those things before I met him. Do you know how *suffocating* it feels to not be able to laugh and smile for almost ten *years*?

Oh, Carter was a miracle. No doubt about it. I didn't deserve his friendship... or so I was told daily by my parents. Watching him from the afterlife was agony. I had to watch as he looked for a dead girl, not knowing I had been murdered. I had to watch as he mourned me when my body was found. I had to watch as he was suspected for the crime. It was infuriating.

Of course, I didn't want my real murderer to get caught though. It would ruin Kace's life. He was set on a path of success, he was. He didn't murder me out of spite or hate... he took me away from this before my parents could. We knew I would be dead before I turned eighteen. I—in a way—accepted that fate. I just wished my last breath was a sigh of relief... and I think it was. I *know* it was.

Kace is still my brother... until the end of times. Even after everything he is still my brother and I still love him. He's sick, I know, but he'll get help. Plus, I know it wasn't his fault. He's not the villain even if everyone says he is. Mom an Dad raised us. We had no chance in this world.

Now the real plot twist was that Dad was a murderer too. I found that out the night before I was taken away. Mom and

Dad were in the kitchen, having a hushed fight. They mentioned Carter and so my ears perked out in the living room. My mother had told my dad that she had ran into Brinley Miller just that day. Brinley had recognized my mother and father from Noah's old yearbooks. Somehow Noah's disappearance came into it.

As I stood rock solid in the living room in front of the woodburning stove, I didn't know why that shook my mom up so much. I didn't understand why my mother was frightened that the police would begin to look back into Carter's dad's absence.

And then it came to me.

My father told my mother to calm down and that no one would ever find out what really happened to Noah Miller in 2013.

Shock rushed over me and I stepped back without thinking, running into the metal stove. My phone sat in my back pocket and as I came into contact with the stove, it caused a rippling echo.

My parents went hushed and my father came into the living room, finding me frozen in place with my body trembling. Next thing I knew he grabbed my arm and dragged me into the kitchen for my mother to see. He yelled at me. I don't even remember what he said. It was all a blur. Then my parents began fighting about what to do with me. I watched helplessly as they decided my fate... all with the help of a few fragile, glass dishes and wooden chairs. I shrank into the corner and... well you know the rest.

I watched as Carter sneaked into our backyard as it was flooding from the ruptured sprinkler system—a sprinkler system ruptured at the hands of my brother Kace. I suppose my brother wanted that skeleton to be found, although I bet he never thought it would be Carter who did.

I watched as he found that lifted skeleton hand connected to a body still under the mud. His father's watch was still hanging on it. I wanted to puke. I never knew where Noah's body was, but seeing that... I knew what that meant. We both knew that we didn't need confirmation. We both knew that was Noah Miller.

Oh, it was family business and I dragged Carter in. When I see him again I will continuously apologize, I swear. No one should experience finding their dead father's body. *No one.*

Now me... I wouldn't mind finding my dad dead. In fact, I looked forward to it some days, as horrible as that sounds. But can you blame me? Just because my dad didn't pull the trigger, doesn't mean he didn't contribute to my death. Kace mercifully killed me because he knew eventually my dad would. He was saving me that pain. I'm not saying it's probable thinking because it isn't. Kace is sick and will get help but he wholeheartedly thought he was doing what was right. To him, he was saving me from pain. It may not sound logical to you but it sounded logical to him. That's all that matters.

That's all that ever mattered.

But what matters the most is that my dad and my mom are behind bars. They can't hurt anyone. They can't sell any more drugs. Allie and Riley are no longer at risk. Although I'm not sure how I feel about them with Aunt Jeanne. Aunt Jeanne was never around when I was growing up. She stayed away from my family and perhaps that's because she knew what was happening behind closed doors. But if she did know, she id nothing to stop it or prevent it. I could be alive right now someone had prevented my death. But I'm not blaming nyone. That's the last thing I'd want to do. It is only my arents' fault.

When I came through the doors of the afterlife, my randma was there to greet me. I remember the peace I felt s I stepped through that veil, shedding away the suffocating ain and guilt. My grandma warmed me and comforted me as collapsed to the ground. It had been so long since I had seen er beautiful face.

I will never forget that moment as she hugged me and rushed her fingers through my hair like she did when I was oung. I just wish she could have met Carter. She would have oved him.

When I told her about him she smiled and nodded understandably, somehow already knowing everything about the boyfriend I left behind. As we walked through the white city she told me that she believes the whole reason why her and John Miller never got too serious was because God encouraged her that he wasn't right for her. In one strong sentence. As she watched over me as the years passed, she began to realize the true extent to why her Heavenly Father told her that. If she had married John Miller I would have never had Carter. And she wouldn't have had me. She told me directly that because she listened to Him the saddest but most beautiful "love" story was created and formed.

And now I know we may not have gotten our happy ending but maybe it isn't about the happy ending... but instead about the story.

Evie Baker:

a story now told

Article written by Jonah Smith,

posted June 18, 2022

Evie Janiece Baker was born a ray of sunshine on June 1 2004 in the Bear Lake Memorial Hospital. She spent much her childhood at her grandmother Lena Marlowe's sid gardening, crafting, and cooking. Her grandma Lena was th light of her life and was always there to make Evie smile, eve after she passed in 2012. According to her boyfriend, Evi often spent her nights talking with her grandmother, tellin her about her day.

When Evie was in 7th grade, she discovered cheerleadin and fell in love with it. She loved it so much that she cheere for six years and was always the happiest cheerleader on th field, mat, and court. She lifted the crowd in ways you couldn' even imagine. Cheer kept her going, for it gave her somethin to do and something to focus on.

Evie always excelled in academics and maintained a 4.0 cumulative G.P.A. all throughout middle school and herfreshman, sophomore, and junior years of high school. She prided herself in always having A's and studying even when it wasn't the easiest.

Evie and her boyfriend Carter officially met on Halloween of 2022 at the Paris Elementary Halloween Carnival. She was working the cotton candy booth when he figured he should say hi to the girl he had in so many his classes. Their friendship blossomed from there, granted with a shaky start.

Carter and Evie spent their free time hanging out and going on adventures. They often went to the lake to explore the shore and went on picnics at camping spots. No matter where they were, they were always able to make the best out of every situation. Carter recalls one specific time when his truck got a flat tire while on a drive up Green Canyon (above St. Charles, Idaho).

"We were stuck there for hours while I waited for a friend to come bring us a spare because I had recently taken mine out. It was a good thing we had service. While we waited, we made the most out of it and we picked wildflowers. It was then when Evie handed me a small bouget of yellow, white, and blue flowers that I knew she was a keeper. We laid on a blanket I had underneath my seat and just listened to the animals. I was actually sad when my friend finally showed up. I could have stayed there for hours!" says Carter Miller.

But, Carter didn't ask Evie to be his girlfriend for months. He finally asked Christmas Day in 2022 and it was a yes!

"Evie was really strong and I'll always remember how brave she always was," Carter told us. "I knew about the abuse and I could see how much it took a toll on her. But, she kept going on. I was there for her on the bad days and on the good. I will never forget how bright her smiles were even after the rough start she got to life."

According to Carter, Evie Baker could light up any room she walked in. Especially when he was in the room. He says she always made him feel special in a way no one had. He was sad that there wasn't many people willing to be her friend. She would have lit up their lives as well.

Evie had big dreams and goals for the rest of her life. She was going to go to college and rent an apartment with Carter or live in a dorm. She was planning on getting her Master's in social work and Bachelors in psychology. Evie wasn't completely set on what she was going to do after college, but she knew she wanted to work with children in similar situations as she did growing up.

Evie Janiece was a light and will never be forgotten for her bravery and resilience. Though she didn't techncially survive, she is still a reminder that we *can* survive. We can make it through anything and she shows us that.

She reminds us that we never know what is going on in someone's life, so we have to treat everyone with kindness.

Smile at that random stranger in the grocery store. Maybe they could be in dark place and that small gesture could make them feel less invisible.

Have a conversation the cashier at the convenience store. It could mean more to them then you could ever imagine.

Wave at a passerby. It might make them smile after they were convinced smiling wasn't possible for them anymore.

Any small thing can brighten a day. Any small thing might save a life.

Acknowledgements

I can't proceed with the acknowledgments without thanking the pile of hashbrowns I just had for dinner. That's all I wanted for dinner and so that's what I had. Best craving ever. But anyways, holy moly I wrote a book?! To begin, I want to first thank my friends, those in my personal life, and those all across writer's Instagram—especially my beta readers: Lara, Jewell, Stella, Sera, Daphne, Lorelei, Ry, Asteria, Breeze, Kathryn, Cate, Trinity, Star, Abby, Harry, Ryn, Halsten, Britta, Scarlett Li, Artemis, H.R. Phoenix, Mia, Lynn, Mira, Henry, Clay, Annabel, Karoline, and Lynnie. (my gosh why are there so many of you?) This book would be crap without their amazing feedback. I also want to thank my family—mainly my dad and mom—for just walking past me and not engaging when I'm mumbling to myself scatteredly (is that a word? If not, it is now). You could have put me in a mental hospital but you didn't. You also helped so so much on the cost of everything, which was kind of essential. Oh, and my sisters Kynlie, Teya, Taylor, and Layni for not making fun of me for talking to myself. Thanks guys. You're true buds.

The person I want to thank most of all, though, is me. I know that sounds a bit self-centered, believe me. But honestly, I could not have written a book if it wasn't for mini Miya. She was the one that decided that our dream was to write a book and get it out into the world. Mini Miya *and* present Miya decided that we wanted to change the world.

...me do it through teaching, and some do it through taking ...adership positions. But, we are choosing pen and paper as ...ur passage because in an unsure and crazy world, sometimes ...ll we need to calm the storms are those two things. That and Jesus Christ and Heavenly Father. They are the ultimate homies and I am so grateful for them and the blessings God gives me each day, seen and unseen.

And lastly, I want to thank you, my amazing reader. Your support means so very much to me and I am eternally grateful! I mean, you are reading the *acknowledgements* so, you, my reader, are simply astounding. I would LOVE if you could leave a review by the way ;) (I hate asking but it helps more than you know). Reviews can be the difference between this book being successful or not!

Thank you all for coming with me on this crazy, dark, melancholy adventure shared between Evie and Carter.

See you next time, losers.

Love you <3